W9-AUK-739

The well-bred but penniless Bright sisters must each go their separate ways—following their destinies to undreamed-of new lives ... and loves.

And strong-willed Anthea is the first to strike out on her own.

A BAD MAN'S DESIRE

At first glance, the lovely Easterner Anthea Bright seems woefully unsuited for her position as the new schoolmarm in Haven, Kansas. But behind that fine finishing school polish is a fiery spirit and a determination to succeed. Gabriel Jackson, however, is a different kind of challenge. The intensely passionate, devasatingly sexy man is Haven's most disreputable citizen—and he's put Anthea's level head and her heart in a furious spin. How can the prim, pretty newcomer hope to stand firm to her principles when she feels breathless whenever Gabriel's near? And though a small voice inside tells her the "bad man's" not nearly as bad as his reputation would suggest, does she dare surrender to this dangerous stranger who is bound and determined to make Anthea his bride?

"Fans of Jill Marie Landis and LaVyrle Spencer will find Law their cup of tea."
Publishers Weekly

Other Avon Romantic Treasures by
Susan Kay Law

THE LAST MAN IN TOWN
THE MOST WANTED BACHELOR

*If You've Enjoyed This Book,
Be Sure to Read These Other*
AVON ROMANTIC TREASURES

A BREATH OF SCANDAL *by Connie Mason*
THE MARRIAGE LESSON *by Victoria Alexander*
NEVER MARRY A COWBOY *by Lorraine Heath*
ONE MAN'S LOVE: BOOK ONE OF
THE HIGHLAND LORDS *by Karen Ranney*
THE PRICE OF PASSION *by Susan Sizemore*

Coming Soon

ONCE TEMPTED *by Elizabeth Boyle*

Susan Kay Law

Marrying Miss Bright

The Bad Man's Bride

AVON BOOKS

An Imprint of HarperCollins*Publishers*

This is a work of fiction. Names, characters, places, and incidents are products of the author's imagination or are used fictitiously and are not to be construed as real. Any resemblance to actual events, locales, organizations, or persons, living or dead, is entirely coincidental.

AVON BOOKS
An Imprint of HarperCollins*Publishers*
10 East 53rd Street
New York, New York 10022-5299

Copyright © 2001 by Susan Kay Law
ISBN: 0-7394-1754-1

All rights reserved. No part of this book may be used or reproduced in any manner whatsoever without written permission, except in the case of brief quotations embodied in critical articles and reviews. For information address Avon Books, an Imprint of HarperCollins Publishers.

Avon Trademark Reg. U.S. Pat. Off. and in Other Countries, Marca Registrada, Hecho en U.S.A.
HarperCollins® is a trademark of HarperCollins Publishers Inc.

Printed in the U.S.A.

To my grandmother,
Hildegard Carlson.
I only hope that someday I can be
as great a grandmother as you.

Chapter 1

October 1885

Much to her heartfelt dismay, Anthea Bright really was in Kansas now.

And to think that it had not been long ago at all that she'd not only anticipated her residence in that state, but had deliberately *chosen* it. Her miscalculations weren't usually so, well, *huge*.

My dearest sisters:

I am delighted to be able to report to you that my first week on the job has vastly exceeded my dreams.

Anthea stared at the words she'd just neatly penned in her precise hand—her fourth attempt at beginning this necessary letter—and decided they weren't *entirely* a lie. After all, nightmares counted as dreams, didn't they? And even in her worst ones, her imagination had proved too limited to envision the true disaster of her first week as schoolmistress of the Haven Township School.

I have eighteen students, ranging in age from five to sixteen, each of them bright and hardworking and imaginative.

Now, that was even closer to the truth. Though the handful of blotched, misspelled, and downright inaccurate compositions stacked at one end of the rickety table that served as her desk attested otherwise, she'd collected ample evidence during the past week of her pupils' fiendishly bright and imaginative tendencies . . . as long as their activities were bent toward making life as difficult as possible for their brand-new teacher.

As to the schoolhouse itself, there are three large windows on each opposite wall, and in the morning when I arrive, the room is flooded with cheerful sunshine.

Not through the windows, however. Thin boards covered four of them, and the other panes were so grimy, streaked with soot from within and mud from without, that no mere sunlight could burn through the coating.

However, plenty of light gained admittance through the wide gaps between the laths in the wall, striping the old puncheon floor like a Hudson Bay blanket. She'd have to do something about those openings soon or her ink would freeze in its well once the weather turned cold.

Perhaps she should have tried penning fiction instead of teaching to generate income, Anthea thought with wry amusement. She hadn't suspected she had such a gift for enhancing the truth.

The resounding crash of the schoolhouse door against the wall made her jump. Her pen shot across the page in a streaking line.

The school building faced west, and bright spears of late afternoon sunlight burst through the door, squeezing around a broad figure that seemed to take up the entire entrance. She squinted against the light, unable to make out any features except the outline of wide shoulders and great height haloed in dazzling gold.

"I—" Anthea swallowed hard, forcing formality and assurance into her voice. If she'd learned one useful thing in her first week of teaching, it was that a good illusion of confidence was nearly as effective as the real thing. "May I help you?" she asked in tones well learned at Miss Addington's Select School for Young Ladies. A very useful skill, that particular tone.

The low growl she received in answer might have been intended as a greeting or a threat. Her heart thudding hard, she mentally cast about for an available weapon and found none. She'd been assured upon her arrival that tales of the Wild West notwithstanding, Haven was ever so much safer than her hometown of Philadelphia.

The figure stepped into the room and the door slammed shut behind him. Her eyes adjusted slowly, the hazy outline sharpening.

She would have guessed that since her arrival six days ago, she'd met nearly every resident of the small town. But not this one. She might have forgotten half the names and faces who'd dropped by the schoolhouse to pay their formal respects—and satisfy their ill-concealed curiosity—before abandoning their children to her inexperienced care, but she never would have forgotten *him*.

Even without the corona of sunlight, he was impressive. She wondered vaguely how he'd even managed to fit through the door. His old, copper-toed boots were as scarred as the floor upon which he'd planted them. A healthy coating of good Kansas dirt covered denim trousers faded to near white. His pale blue shirt looked as if it had been washed by someone who didn't know how, the sleeves rolled up over forearms sturdy as fence posts.

A black hat that looked older than he did rode low on his forehead, obscuring his eyes. A full day's growth of dark beard shadowed a jaw that was probably uncompromising under the best of circumstances and right now was set at a downright threatening angle.

She reminded herself—and once again, even more firmly, before she was able to get her voice to work— that a miscreant was unlikely to accost a small-town schoolteacher on a placid, sunny Friday in a schoolhouse that half the county passed on their way in and out of town. "May I be of assistance?"

He jammed those forearms over a chest that seemed hewn from granite. "What the hell do you think you're doing?"

The new schoolmarm looked *exactly* as Gabriel Jackson had pictured her.

Damn it.

A small, prim woman, as plain and ruthlessly

proper as ordinary cotton gloves, with a neat little nose angled high and proud. A nose just like all the others that fine, upstanding ladies had been looking at him down all his life. She must have boiled her shirt-waist for hours to get it that blinding white, the collar lace so stiffly starched it had to be cutting a dent beneath that precise chin.

At his outburst, she pokered up immediately. Predictably. "Pardon me?" she asked with what he figured was deliberately exaggerated politeness, emphasizing his bad manners by contrasting them with her good ones.

"I asked what the—"

"Oh, I *heard* you perfectly well." Her chair scraped back as she stood, her back ramrod-straight. Probably from the stick that ran all the way up her ass to her neck, he thought uncharitably. "I just didn't understand you. Though the obvious answer to what I was doing was writing a letter, happily undisturbed until *you* interrupted, I somehow doubt that is precisely the question you posed."

She bent to riffle through a stack of papers at her desk, as if dismissing his presence. The bow of her black sateen teacher's apron bobbed at the hollow of her back, right above the sharp protrusion of her bustle. Who had invented those things? Someone determined to make sure that a man didn't get even the slightest hint of the shape underneath? Somebody as humorless as this woman, without a doubt.

"You the teacher?"

"Hmm?" She tugged out a paper, pondered it with a small frown of concentration. "What a clever deduction. Since I'm the only one here."

He sputtered. Something he couldn't recall doing in

his entire adult life, but he supposed it was better than biting her head off. Though not nearly as satisfying, to his way of thinking.

She arched an eyebrow, coolly superior, and he had a vivid memory of that same look on another teacher's face, in this exact same schoolhouse, nearly twenty-five years before. He'd attended school for an entire week before deciding it wasn't worth either the trouble or the bruises he'd earned from the other students. Bruises that the teacher clearly had had no intention of attempting to stop and which she no doubt had considered well earned. For he was Gabriel Jackson, wasn't he?

He dropped his arms, hands fisting against his sides. He wouldn't let the same thing happen to Lily. He might have had no one to rescue him, but Lily had him. It would make all the difference.

The woman's gaze flicked briefly to his clenched fists before she focused them firmly back on the crumpled paper she clutched. Her skin drew tight around her mouth, across her smooth forehead, and he wondered if maybe she wasn't quite as unruffled and confident as she appeared after all. The thought pleased him immensely. Deliberately he stepped farther into the room, knowing the bulk he'd gained since he'd last set foot here proved conveniently intimidating on occasion. Lord knew he could have used it then.

She took a furtive hop backward, just a little one, before she caught herself. She drew herself up—maybe she'd be chest-high on him now, but Gabriel wouldn't bet on it—and stuck that delicate nose in the air. So she'd a bit of courage after all . . . or she'd simply been too sheltered, too protected, her whole life to recognize trouble when she met it.

"Is there something specific you wanted?" she asked. "Or did you come by simply to snarl at me?"

"It's not what I want," he said. "It's what I don't want. I don't want *this*—" He shot a glance behind him, found nothing. He stared for a long moment, blew out a heavy sigh, and stomped back to the door, bootheels worn down to a thin slice of leather clomping hard on floorboards warped into waves a river would envy.

Heavens, Anthea thought, hoping—in vain, she suspected—that he wouldn't return. She'd been in town scarcely a week. What could she have done to offend that man so much? While it hadn't been an entirely successful week, still . . .

Though perhaps it didn't take much to offend him. He looked to be a permanently ill-tempered sort under the best of circumstances.

The door flew open again, as hard as the first time. Anthea winced, uncertain that the deteriorating structure could withstand such abuse.

He charged back in, towing a small girl. Her head dipped down. Tangled hanks of hair hid her face, and her arms wrapped tightly around her thin middle.

"This is what's the problem!" he snapped.

Anthea slowly made her way toward the pair, giving herself time to consider. The child was one of her students, of course, the one who'd claimed a place in the farthest corner of the classroom, deep in the shadow cast by a boarded-up window, as far away as she could manage from the rest of the students.

She hadn't whispered a word the entire week. Anthea had tried a few times without success to pry a few words out of her, until her attention was inevitably drawn back to more immediate matters. Like the fact that Charlie Skinner had managed to spark a fire—*outside* the confines of the old coal stove. Or that Olivia Cox had burst into bloodcurdling screams yet again.

I should have tried harder, Anthea thought now, studying the skinny, quiet girl standing three feet from the man, her shoulders hunched, eyes fixed on the battered toes of her boots. A wide band of sharp-boned, pale shin showed between her sagging, grayed socks and the hem, a good four inches too short, of the threadbare, soiled dress she'd worn all week.

Oh yes, she should have tried harder, Anthea thought with a guilty pang. But at the time, she'd been unsure whether the girl was even capable of a response.

Oh, the poor child! How could he *let her go around like this?* Anthea resolved right then to do better in the future, giving the girl as much help as she could. Since in Anthea's admittedly brief experience in Haven, few men had bothered to involve themselves in their children's schooling, except to complain endlessly about the cost of the already sparse budget, this awful man was likely all she had. The girl needed all the help she could get.

She leaned down, trying to peer beneath the lank, greasy blond curtain. "Hello," she said softly. "Is there something I can help you with?"

He snorted. Snorted! If she couldn't manage to instill a good grasp of geography and orthography in her young male charges, she vowed, she would at least make certain they owned better manners than this cretin.

Though it assuredly wouldn't take much.

"You *should* be helping," he said. "But you're not. That's why I'm here."

"I'm sure this would be much simpler if you could be a bit more precise about what exactly you are objecting to."

"Show her, Lily."

"Lily? Oh, so *that's* her name," Anthea said without thinking.

"You didn't even know her *name*?" he asked, with a look that clearly indicated his opinion of a teacher who didn't even know the name of a student who'd occupied her classroom for an entire week.

"She wouldn't tell me," Anthea murmured. "I asked some of the other children, and they . . . well, Lily is not what they told me."

"I can imagine." He jammed that aggressive jaw even farther forward. Anthea could only be grateful that those particular students were not in the schoolroom at the moment, for she doubted she could have prevented him from ensuring in a robustly physical manner that they never called Lily an unflattering name again.

"It's a lovely name, Lily," she said, watching carefully for some sign of response from the silent girl. "A pretty little flower, just like you." Lily's head lifted a fraction—not enough for Anthea to glimpse her face, but enough so that she decided Lily could hear and understand her after all. She'd wondered.

"Show her what you learned in school this week, Lily." His tone turned gentle and soft, the likes of which Anthea would never have expected to come out of that abrupt, scowling man.

Lily plucked at the hank of hair shielding her right eye, pulled it aside, and peered uncertainly at Anthea.

"It's all right," Anthea said encouragingly. "Go ahead."

Lily shuffled over to the makeshift bookcase Anthea had fashioned out of two crates she'd found in the otherwise empty coal shed and a couple of boards that she suspected were supposed to reside on the north wall of the schoolhouse. It held only five books—four that Anthea had managed to salvage when everything was sold and tucked into her suitcase before leaving home, and a spineless copy of *Michel's Geography* she'd unearthed from beneath the teacher's "desk."

With one more tentative glance at her father, Lily carefully pulled out Anthea's copy of *Pilgrim's Progress*. She straightened visibly, squaring her fragile shoulders, and balanced the book gingerly on her head. One grimy hand held aloft, ready to catch the book if it tipped, she inched one foot forward, then the other, making her way across the floor with an awkward, vigilant grace that somehow suited her.

She shot Anthea a hopeful look, pride mixed with disbelief, which nearly broke Anthea's heart.

"Oh, Lily, that's wonderful! Perfect. Even Miss Addington would have to approve your posture. It took me a month to learn to walk across the floor without the book sliding off, and I had the crushed toes to prove it."

"Miss Addington?" His scowl said he wasn't at all sure he wanted to know.

"Of Miss Addington's Select School for Young Ladies," she informed him. "I was tutored in deportment and posture by Miss Addington herself."

He made a sound of distinct disgust. Anthea was so accustomed to hearing Miss Addington spoken of in tones of unequivocal respect and downright reverence that she found herself gaping.

It was yet one more example that nothing was the same in Kansas.

"She needs to learn to read." His frown brought his hat even lower on his brow, shielding his eyes completely. It was most unfair that he could see her expression so easily while he effectively hid his from her view. "She needs to learn to add, to write. Useful things. And *you*—" perhaps she should be glad she couldn't see his eyes after all, Anthea decided, for she had no doubt that at the moment they held an accusatory glare—"you're teaching her to balance a book on her head! Of all the useless, stupid, *worthless*—"

"Stop it. Please."

To Anthea's surprise, it worked. The man snapped his mouth shut, cutting off words that likely would have blistered what remained of the paint off the old walls. She tried to recall exactly how she'd achieved such an effect—if it worked on *him*, surely it would work just as well on Theron Matheson on Monday.

"Lily, would you do me a favor? There's a jar of gingersnaps one of the students brought me on the table in my soddy." Anthea suppressed a shudder at the mention of her soddy. Originally delighted to discover that she'd have the original schoolhouse as her home, instead of having to board with local families, she'd been completely unprepared for the reality of a house built entirely of dirt—dirt floor, dirt walls, dirt ceiling held back only by a strip of dirty muslin. Perhaps it would be as warm as advertised come winter, but Anthea remained unconvinced that the entire structure wouldn't come washing down upon her head in the first healthy rainstorm. "I don't want to waste them, but if I eat them all myself, I'll have to alter my clothes by week's end. Could you rid me of some, do you think?"

Lily looked to the man for permission, and at his curt nod, she fled for the door as if she couldn't wait to escape. Anthea didn't blame her one bit.

"Does she talk?"

"Sometimes. Not often."

Gabriel cursed himself for not having had the sense to send Lily out himself. Of course she shouldn't be standing there, with her big ears and bruised heart, while he and her new teacher argued about her future education.

It only served to underscore the truth he'd always known: he was simply not fit to raise a child. He'd no experience. Nor any inclination, if it came to that. If there'd been anyone else . . . but there wasn't, and it was no use wishing it. If there was one thing his life had taught him, a single lesson hammered home mallet stroke after mallet stroke until it was finally pounded into even his thick head, it was that there was absolutely no use in *wishing*.

"Now. If you'll remove your hat." She linked her hands over her apron, pearl white skin against sheeny black fabric, proper as a nun.

"My hat?" What the hell did she care about his hat? Something about her, cool control layered over quick pride, kept him off balance, halfway between anger and unwilling fascination. Lord knew he'd never met her like before.

"Yes. I don't allow them to be worn in my classroom."

"Oh?" The fascination won out. "In case you hadn't noticed, ma'am, I'm a few years past the schoolroom."

"It's of no matter. I can hardly expect the boys to be

held to standards of deportment the men of Haven can't manage, can I?"

Where *was* this female from? Boston? New York? Philadelphia? Someplace where men minced around in spats and expensive tweeds, hands soft as a woman's, more manners than muscle.

Well, she wasn't there anymore, was she?

He watched her mouth curve up, verging on a smile, as he lifted his hand toward his hat. But when he merely jabbed the brim with his thumb, tipping it back a few inches, that promised smile veered down into a disapproving frown.

It was an expression he figured that the children in her classroom were already very familiar with.

Shifting his weight to one side, he hooked his hands in his pockets and commenced to stare her down. He didn't expect it would take long.

"So? You gonna make me stand in the corner now?"

Chapter 2

She surprised him. That stick he'd imagined supporting her posture might just be made of pure steel. Oh, her eyes flickered once or twice, but mostly they remained firmly on his. Pretty eyes, he noted, big and blue as cornflowers, full of life. When he looked in them, he decided that she wasn't nearly as plain as she first appeared. Not quite a small, brown wren of a woman after all, not with those lively eyes.

"Oh, for heaven's sake!" she said at last. Rising to her tiptoes, she reached up and snatched his hat right off his head. And then she stared, appalled, at the limp black hat in her hand as if she'd just grabbed his drawers instead of his hat.

Now, *there* was an interesting thought.

He chuckled, a rusty sound that surprised them both.

"That was not very well done of me," she admitted, gesturing lamely with the hat so that the brim flapped like a crow's wings.

"It was almost . . . *impolite*, you might say."

"You might. If one weren't gentlemanly enough to overlook a lady's lapse." Oh, the impulse, born of a week's frustration, that had spurred Anthea to grab his hat was such a terrible mistake! She realized it the instant she surrendered to it. And not only because she'd just handed him clear evidence that her self-containment was not nearly as complete as she preferred others to believe.

But because this man, without his hat, was far more dangerous than she'd imagined. He was *handsome*, startlingly so, his thick, dark waves of hair barely tamped down by the ring his hat had caused. Badly cut, it curled low and raggedly around his collar, and was anything but unappealing for all that it should have been so. His bones were sharp and uncompromising, the angles as harshly beautiful and explicitly defined as a canyon's walls. His eyes seemed formed of midnight, a color between blue and black and sin.

If only he hadn't laughed! Anger was easier to deal with; it got her back up. Firm words sprang out before she thought to bite them back. But that brief instant of shared amusement made him seem approachable, *possible*, to the point that she wondered if she'd get her tongue to function properly again.

"About Lily," he began.

She gave herself a mental shake. This was a purely professional discussion—an important one, no less—and as such, it deserved her most assiduously professional attention.

"Mr. . . ." She tilted her head, wondered if this

would be yet another admission that marked her as an amateur. "I suppose it's obvious that, since I didn't know Lily's *first* name, I don't know your last either."

"It's Jackson. Gabriel Jackson." He nodded toward the door. "She goes by Ross."

Gabriel's shoulders tightened as he waited for her to ask why his last name wasn't the same as Lily's. But she just tilted her head, studied him as if lost in thought. Likely she'd heard the story around town already. He'd always provided the town's grapevine with half its conversational fodder anyway, so much so he figured they should be grateful to him for coming back to Haven, just to give them something to talk about. Though he sure hadn't seen any sign of gratitude so far. Perhaps the teacher was just now putting him together with whatever wicked tale they'd filled her tender ears with.

"I'm Anthea Bright."

But there must have been no tales as yet. For if she'd heard about him already, she sure wouldn't have stuck out her hand for him to shake. It was small and pale, her fingers long and elegant. And ungloved.

He couldn't remember the last time a hand was extended to him in Haven in such a common gesture of courtesy. Never, probably. Certainly he'd never been offered a *female's* hand.

Not in public, anyway.

He realized he was staring and grabbed her hand quick, in case she might belatedly realize what she'd offered and snatch it away. He'd expected her to be fragile, her bones small and breakable as a bird's. Instead, she'd a surprisingly firm grip, an energetic shake. But her skin was soft and clean, as finely textured as new satin, and he held on while she seemed to forget that she wasn't supposed to stand there with her hand in his. He released her the instant she made a move to pull away.

"Now that we've observed the niceties, shall we get down to business?" Anthea said, firmly reminding him, not to mention herself, of the matter at hand.

It had been a small breach of etiquette, shaking a man's hand. Especially so when his, and her own, were bare. But in this case she'd considered her professional responsibilities paramount. She'd felt it imperative to begin as she meant to go on, meeting him as an equal.

A tactical error, surely. For the sensation of his hand, rough-textured, big enough to swallow both of hers in his one, touching her naked skin was anything but professional.

It was a mistake of the sort she could not allow herself to make again. She slid back a step. Hardly even noticeable, she thought, but it made her more comfortable.

"Now then, Mr. Jackson—"

"Gabriel'll do."

"Not for me, Mr. Jackson."

"I suppose it wouldn't." He matched her step, and then some, because his legs were longer, and ended up closer to her than where they'd started. "Can't promise I'll answer to it, though. Don't have a lot of practice in answering to *mister*."

"I'm sure you'll manage somehow." She refused to back up again; it would seem too much like surrender. "But I assume it's Lily's managing that concerns you now. How old is she?"

He thought about it for an oddly long moment. "Nine."

"She's small for her age." Anthea frowned, pondering. The girl's arms were fragile as dried reeds, her skin the color of chalk. "Has she seen a doctor? Perhaps there are other reasons for her—"

"She's fine. She just needs to learn to read, and it's your job to teach her."

"It is, but—"

"There's no buts." Any warmth she'd imagined in him was completely absent now. His expression was set, closed. She'd been warned about this at the institute; few parents welcomed a teacher prying into a family's life. Her responsibilities began and ended with the schoolroom. But Anthea had wondered even then about the practicality of that particular policy; surely a child's home life had some effect on both behavior and learning?

"Constant interruption is not conducive to productive discussion, Mr. Jackson."

"So don't interrupt, then."

"I didn't!"

"She's got to learn," he continued without inflection, "and not how to swish across a floor with a book on her head."

Anthea sighed. She supposed that, from his perspective, it seemed a frivolous thing upon which to expend class time and energy. But on Thursday afternoon, in the middle of a routine recitation of the thirteen original colonies, even her brief experience had told her it would be impossible to keep Billy Pruitt in his seat much longer without using straps. And she'd gotten heartily tired of seeing pretty Olivia Cox slumped over as if she claimed eighty years instead of twelve.

"I am charged with teaching many things," she said

reasonably. "Including matters of health and hygiene, of which excellent posture is an essential part. Not to mention that good manners and deportment will be tremendously valuable to their future, should any of these children have high ambitions for their lives. It is my hope that I will help to ensure that they are comfortable in whatever situation they might find themselves in someday."

"She's gonna need to know how to cipher a helluva lot more than she's gonna need manners."

"Why can't she have both?" Anthea asked, trying very hard to hold to the "reasonably." She'd been warned against allowing parents to interfere in her curriculum; while she, of course, was to be sensitive to local needs, *she* was the expert, and if she allowed parents to dictate their individual desires for their children, the class as a whole would never accomplish anything. At the time she'd wondered at her so-called expertise; six weeks at the teacher's institute scarcely qualified her, but she and her sisters had been unable to spare any more time or money for her training. The six weeks had been a stretch at that, and God bless Miss Addington's instruction for allowing her to pass the certification examinations with flying colors.

If Mr. Jackson was an example, however, she could be quite confident that her own inexperienced judgment on such matters was a good deal more accurate than his.

"It is hardly my place to interfere in your home life, Mr. Jackson, but don't you think—"

"Let me tell you how it works, *Anthea*. I send her to school. You teach her how to read and write, and you send her home. That's it. I'll do my job and get her here. I expect you to do yours."

She chose to ignore his outrageous breach of etiquette in using her given name, because she suspected her objection might turn out as well as the hat debacle.

"Oh, I'll do my job, all right. And it is my job to educate my students not only to the best of *my* abilities, but *theirs* as well. I fully intend to prepare them for whatever future they choose, in all ways. What if Lily chooses to marry someone from outside Haven? Or she evidences exceptional gifts and wants to attend college? Don't you want her to be well prepared for whatever path she follows?"

Gabriel had to stop that train before it left the station. If her teacher persisted in filling Lily's head with frilly, impossible dreams, the only one who was going to be hurt was Lily. "Whoever marries Lily is going to marry her because she knows how to work. She needs to know how to make sure the grocer isn't cheating her, and how to stretch a dollar until harvest. Ain't nobody going to marry her because she can pour tea with her pinky up or dance without tripping on her flounces." Life was going to be tough for Lily. He knew only too well how tough. There was nothing Gabe could do to change Lily's birth, or the years that had followed. All he could do was make sure that she was up to the challenge that awaited her. And he wasn't letting any bit of classy fluff who'd come west to civilize the natives interfere with that.

"How can you say that?" Her color was up, a flush that bloomed from that stiff lace choke collar and turned her cheeks the color of roses. "Put boundaries on her life before she even has a chance to explore them? Don't you want more for her?"

"I don't want anything but for you to do the job this town hired you to do."

"But—"

"No. You'll do what I say, or I'll be sitting in the back of that room every day making *sure* you do."

The schoolteacher was steaming. He could practically see the smoke curling out of her pretty ears. Trying to hold back words she was too ladylike to scald him with, she'd pressed her lips together so tightly they'd practically disappeared. He almost hoped she'd lose control and let fly. He was sure it'd be downright entertaining.

She had her hands folded tight against her waist. Her hair was scraped back just as sternly, a gleam moving across the smooth surface whenever she tipped her head. But one strand had let go, falling loose to curl against her shoulder. He wondered how it had dared disobey.

"Your hair's falling down."

"What?" She blinked at him.

"There." He pointed at it and, because he'd never been good at resisting temptation, nudged it with just the tip of his finger. It was as warm as if she'd been sitting in the sun, and she jumped a good three inches when he touched her.

If he kissed her, he thought with amusement and a surprising amount of temptation, she'd spring right through the roof.

"Oh." She reached up, the wash of color on her cheeks deepening into a riot, and fumbled to tuck it back into place, obviously trying—and failing miserably—to pretend that his blatantly forward gesture hadn't occurred. Or hadn't mattered if it had. "Thank you. I . . ."

She was so delightfully easy to fluster that he was sorry he hadn't tried it earlier. Perhaps there were some advantages to sheltered, prissy eastern school-teachers after all.

And he was not above taking advantage of them. "Don't go filling Lily's head with nonsense. Teach her what you're supposed to and stay out of the rest."

He turned and disappeared before Anthea had a chance to gather her thoughts.

One of the faults Anthea admitted to was that she really hated not having the last word. And so, as she gathered her papers to return to her rabbit hole of a new home, she listed all the things she *should* have said to him.

And nurtured a growing suspicion that coming to Haven was an even bigger mistake than she'd already suspected.

Her aborted letter to her sisters rested on top. Thoughtfully she gazed at the empty doorway that Mr. Jackson had so thoroughly filled. Just how, she wondered, was she supposed to explain *him*?

Excuse my delay in completing this letter and sending it off. I was interrupted by a concerned parent. It warms my heart to see the passion they hold for their children's education . . .

On Saturday afternoons, Stoddard's Emporium occupied much the same place in Haven society as the First Community Church would the following mornings. It provided a perfect opportunity for the town's residents to chew over bits of news from both near and far, all the while giving every appearance of attending to necessary business.

On the east side of the large room, Calvin Stoddard held court, a clean white apron wrapped over his substantial belly, big hands planted firmly on the top of a glass-fronted case. Dried codfish swung from their tails behind him, bumping several hefty hams.

Adonijah Matheson had his skinny butt plopped precariously on top of a pickle barrel, the stem of an unlit pipe clamped in his teeth while he expounded on the apparently many flaws of Kansas's Republican senators. Knute Sontesby bent half an ear in Adonijah's direction while he dug through a box of nails and kept an eye on his wife, Johanna, who was spending a disconcertingly long time lingering over the bolts of calico while she chatted with Arozina Culbertson, who had all the juicy details about the Gellhorn girl's *very* hasty wedding.

Thisba Stoddard pumped up the sales of the new shipment of dried peaches they'd just received by scribbling down her personal recipe for cobbler— which was, she assured Esther Mott, the best she'd ever tasted. And by the way, had she heard that Albert Lacey had taken himself off to Saint Louis again? Amazing how many *business* trips the man seemed required to go on.

Anthea stood in front of a display of stationery supplies and dithered.

She was not often given to dithering. In fact, Kate would no doubt maintain she leaned toward being the decisive type, although Anthea believed she'd some way to go before matching her older sister in that regard.

However, she hadn't much experience in pinching pennies before, either. She'd taken her position for only one reason, which was to send as much of her salary home as possible, providing the bulk of support for Kate and little Emily.

But oh, she could make such good use of those beautiful pads of paper in the classroom! Penmanship would no doubt improve immensely with one of those newfangled Waterman pens. She needed books and cleaning supplies. And wouldn't those lemon drops serve as wonderful rewards for the winner of next Friday's spell-down?

She sighed and moved on. The fact that her school was woefully undersupplied was not her fault. Her family had to come first.

"What can I do for you today?" Thisba asked, energetic and unrelentingly cheerful, the perfect shopkeeper's wife. "We've some new fabrics in. Not the choices you're accustomed to back east, I suppose, but you might be surprised. They're quite lovely."

"I'm sure they're beautiful," Anthea replied, all the while racking her brain for the names of the two women who'd been chattering with Thisba and were now smiling at her with bright expectation. It was most unfair; they had only one new person to remember, while she was expected to recognize dozens and dozens. "I don't believe I'll have much time for sewing anytime soon."

"Oh?" Frowning, Thisba put down the pen she'd been using to add a long column of numbers. "The children giving you trouble?"

"Nothing unusual," Anthea said quickly. "It's always a bit of an adjustment to settle down after a summer's vacation, of course. For all of us. No, I simply meant that, as this is my first position, I intend, at least initially, to devote *all* of my energies to doing the job you engaged me for."

"Hmm." The woman to her right, who was carefully sorting through a bowl of walnuts, plucking out the plumpest specimens, drew her brows together. "I know my Theron is no trouble, of course, but some of those boys . . ." She *tsk*ed, shaking her head.

Ah. Anthea's memory clicked blessedly into place. Letty Matheson, who'd hovered over her twelve-year-old son, Theron, the first day of school until his ears were as red as a tomato. He'd clearly felt it necessary, after she'd finally fluttered out of the school, to prove that, despite being half a head taller than Anthea, he was not his mama's "little boy."

No, *trouble* was not what she would have termed Theron, either. He was far more devious and persistent than mere trouble.

"I *told* that Phillip Cox we should have hired another man this winter," the tall, narrow-shouldered woman flipping through a pattern book on the counter murmured, "but God forbid he should listen to what a *woman* says—"

"Hush, Esther," Thisba said with a warning glance.

"Phillip Cox?" Mr. Cox was the town banker, head of the school board, and the man who'd telegraphed Anthea of the school's job offer in the first place. "Have you always had a male teacher?"

Thisba studied her consideringly for a moment, then sighed. "Might as well know what you're getting into," she said. "Usually we do. Especially in the winter, when the bigger boys are in school. You don't even have the Krotochvill boys yet, do you?"

"The Krotochvills? No, I don't believe so."

"You'd know it if you did." Thisba nodded. "Heard their harvest was a bit behind. They'll be there this week. Next at the latest. The size of a barn, both of 'em, and they got nothing in their lofts but moldy old straw, either."

"Something to look forward to, undoubtedly." And to steel herself against, Anthea thought. "Why didn't they hire a man this term, then?"

Thisba shot a quick glance at her husband, who was sawing thick slices from a fat sausage and handing samples out to the men who crowded his side of the room, before she bent toward Anthea and spoke in a lowered voice. "Because they're too *cheap*, that's why. Been trying to get those men to spend somethin' on that school for years, but they all say it was good enough for them, it's good enough for their sons. Gonna stay just like it is till it falls right down around their ears."

"I see." Anthea stared at a thin cardboard box on the counter, holding dozens of spools of threads, their rainbow colors brilliant against the dull gray cardboard. It was somewhat lowering, she decided, to discover yourself hired because you were the cheapest labor available. "I—"

The steady buzz of conversation that had hummed like a running flywheel since the time she'd entered the store had abruptly stopped, she realized. Thisba had her gaze focused firmly over Anthea's shoulder, her welcoming storekeeper's smile compressed into a diapproving line.

Curious as to who could have spurred that expression on Thisba's face, Anthea turned. Ducking his head to fit under the low doorjamb, Gabriel Jackson stepped into the room. He paused for a moment just inside, letting the door slam shut behind him. He scanned the room, briefly meeting the eyes of everyone there, but there were no polite nods or welcoming smiles, the common courtesies of greeting conspicuously absent.

Until he saw Anthea. She held her breath—why, she couldn't have said; surely he wouldn't do anything untoward *here*—until his attention settled on her. "Ma'am," was all he said, unsmiling, his eyes unreadably dark. She nodded numbly in response.

And then he ignored them all, stalking over to a crate stuffed with tools and selecting a heavy hammer, weighing it briefly in his hand while he stood in the square of sunlight cast by one of the broad front windows.

He was half a head taller than any man in the room, and outweighed everyone but Calvin Stoddard. And those substantial pounds were arranged *very* differently on him than on Mr. Stoddard. Miss Addington would have been thoroughly appalled to know that Anthea was noticing the arrangement of any man's . . . *pounds*, but Anthea had always been much in favor of appreciating the wonders of nature, wherever they might be found.

Anything else would be ungrateful, in her opinion.

Gabriel dug a coin from his pocket and tossed it in the storekeeper's direction. Stoddard caught it by reflex, then his mouth pinched sourly, as if he longed to hurl it back. But Gabriel had already headed out the door.

Ever since they'd left the schoolhouse yesterday, Anthea had been unable to get Lily's narrow, sad face, her big, wary eyes, out of her mind. She could not imagine why Mr. Jackson allowed the child to go around in such an unkempt state. His neglect seemed clear. And yet, she remembered the gentleness in his voice when he spoke to Lily, so different than his typical tone that Anthea thought perhaps she'd imagined it. And he'd made the effort to come and speak to

Anthea about his concerns. Even if Anthea vehemently disagreed with his opinion on the matter, it was still more than any other man in town had bothered to do.

She didn't know where her responsibilities lay in this matter. Didn't even know what she *could* do, much less what she should. But she knew full well she wouldn't rest until she did something.

"Excuse me for a moment," Anthea said to the women beside her.

But by the time she gained the front stoop of the store, Gabriel was already riding away at a clip that appeared downright dangerous for a busy street, as if anxious to put the place behind him.

Shading her eyes, she decided he was beyond calling distance. He moved easily on the back of the horse, a big, beautiful, red specimen, their rhythm and strength perfectly matched.

Just beyond the edge of town, he rounded a bend where the road curved around a giant old oak, taking him out of view. She dropped her hand and turned to go back inside. She caught sight of two women across the street standing in front of the bank, watching her with undisguised interest—the town's unrestrained curiosity about its newest resident was difficult to accustom herself to—and she waved politely. Their answering nods were distinctly cool, and with a flip of their skirts, they turned and disappeared through the broad, copper-toned double doors.

Shrugging, she reentered Stoddard's, mentally running through her shopping list for items she could delete. Calvin Stoddard had generously offered her credit the moment she'd arrived, but the last thing she wanted to do was end up owing most of her first month's pay to the store.

"I believe a quarter pound of coffee will do," she told Thisba when she reached the back of the store, "Green Rio, please. Plus a half pound of white sugar and . . ." Her words trailed off as she realized the women hadn't budged from where she'd left them, but instead stared at her with wide eyes and open mouths. "What is it?"

"He—he *spoke* to you," Thisba said in a scandalized voice.

"Well, yes, I—"

"Do you know who that is?" Letty's round, still pretty face grew pink just at the thought. "That's *Gabriel Jackson*."

"Yes, I know. He came by the school yesterday after class was dismissed, and—"

"You were *alone* with him?" Esther Mott crowded in to make sure she didn't miss anything good.

"I suppose I was, briefly. He had a question about—" All three women sucked in a shocked breath, stopping Anthea's explanation in its tracks. One would think she'd shown up at the store in her petticoats, given the expression on their faces. "What exactly is wrong with Gabriel Jackson?"

"He's a bad man." Thisba gave a shudder that could as easily have been titillation as revulsion. "He's a very *bad man*."

Chapter 3

"A bad man?" Anthea repeated. Had she actually been in serious jeopardy yesterday afternoon? While the thought had initially occurred to her when Mr. Jackson burst into the schoolhouse glowering, she'd discounted it pretty quickly. While he might be bad-tempered, stubborn, and thoroughly misguided, at no time had she truly felt as if her person were in danger. "How . . . bad?"

"Well, I'm not one to gossip, of course, but . . ." Thisba cleared off the clutter on the counter with one sweep of her hand and leaned on her forearms. "There's more than one of us who took to locking our doors for the first time in years when he showed up again, I can tell you that much."

"He's a *thief*?" Anthea found it hard to credit. For

one thing, he was simply too large to sneak around effectively. And her experience with his personality indicated he'd be far more inclined to barge boldly in during full daylight, simply lay claim to whatever he wanted, and dare you to stop him.

Letty snickered. "You might say that. Though most of what he stole . . . well, locking doors isn't going to solve *that*."

Esther's expression was pinched. "Now, Letty, nobody's ever known for sure."

"Hah! They know one thing for sure, at least. He up and took that child home with him after that Ross woman died, didn't he? Why'd he do that if she wasn't his?"

"It's bad blood, that's what it is. Knew it the instant Helen Jackson showed up with him in her belly and no husband."

"But he must be closing in on thirty." Anthea tried to sort through the bits and pieces of a story the rest of them clearly knew by rote. "You couldn't have been more than a child yourself back then. How could you know what happened?"

"*Everybody* knows," Letty said, clearly torn between being unwilling to disabuse Anthea's flattering determination of her age and telling the story with the authority of a true witness. But then, she'd never been the sort to let logic interfere with a good gossip. "My mother caught my brother playing mumblety-peg with him once. Whipped Davey till he couldn't sit down for a week."

"But I know good Christian women such as yourselves wouldn't hold Mr. Jackson accountable for his mother's sins," Anthea ventured carefully. She could hardly afford to antagonize her students' parents, the very people who'd engaged her for her position and paid her salary. But there was something in the unmitigated glee they took in relating Gabriel Jackson's notorious past that didn't settle well.

"Oh, he's committed plenty of his own, don't you worry. I myself stumbled across him dead drunk, propped up against the back wall of Phifer's Livery on my way to church one morning. Nearly got fuzzy myself just on the fumes, and he couldn't have been more than fifteen," Esther informed her.

By now Johanna Sontesby had wandered over to join the fun. "Broke my Knute's nose, he did," she chimed in. "And for no good reason at all, Knute told me. Caught him by surprise so Knute didn't even have a chance to defend himself. Of course, it's still a right handsome nose," she added loyally.

Thisba's voice dropped to a fierce whisper. "My sister Agnes would be married to that fine Herbert Babcock by now if not for him. But Jackson distracted her with those devil's looks—whee, I remember when my father found out, like to think he was going to explode, he turned so red—and by the time she come to her senses, Herbert had already hooked up with Kitturah Sinclair. Agnes had to marry that worthless Rollin Skinner instead. Who else would have her after?"

Anthea had heard enough. "Mr. Jackson has a student in my class, however, and as such, it's my duty to—"

"He sent her to *school*!" A recitation that had been mostly entertaining turned seriously worrisome, if Lily Ross occupied the same schoolroom as Letty's precious Theron. "Why, I didn't think that even Gabriel Jackson would have the nerve!"

"Well, of course she's in school. She's of an age," Anthea said.

"Since when has anything been beyond him? I wouldn't be surprised if he was the one who brought Clarinda Ross here in the first place. *Convenient* for him," Johanna said with heavy emphasis.

"And now he's flaunting that whelp in front of decent children?" Deeply offended, Thisba shook her head. "The bastard's bastard."

Anthea's patience snapped abruptly. It was one thing to gossip about a grown man who no doubt had earned much of it, and who, she was certain, was fully capable of defending himself quite adequately if he so chose.

But Lily was *hers*.

"Nevertheless," Anthea said stiffly, "she is one of my students—one who causes no trouble, at that—and she has every right to attend classes. It is not my place to deny her. Quite the opposite, it is my responsibility to encourage her as much as possible."

"Hmm." Anthea did not like the way Letty's round eyes had narrowed. "Isn't there something in your contract about sending home children with offensive uncleanliness?"

To Anthea's dismay, there was, right between the clause about expulsion for unchaste language and the requirement that Anthea practice "firm and vigilant but prudent discipline."

"That child does not belong in the same classroom as properly raised children. And what good is an education going to do her, anyway?" Esther gave her opinion with all the firmness of one convinced of its accuracy. "No doubt she'll end up exactly the same as her mother."

Anthea managed to mumble only the briefest of excuses before she, thankfully, made it out the door without all the words boiling up in her chest exploding out of her mouth. She needed her job too much to allow a quick and ill-considered response to get her fired. Not to mention, she would hardly be of any use to Lily if she were shipped back to Philadelphia. It was essential to deliberate carefully before choosing a wise and responsible course.

She was halfway home before she realized she'd forgotten all about her groceries.

No matter. By then she'd figured out exactly what she had to do.

Gabriel positioned a nail against the fence rail, gave it a tap to set the point, and drove it home with two quick strikes of his new hammer. He stepped back, eyeing his work critically, and decided it would hold.

For longer than the rest of the place, anyway.

It was a dump. It had been a dump when he was a kid, and twenty years hadn't helped matters. He'd tried—ineptly when he was young, infrequently once he'd left Haven—to fix it up, but it had always fallen apart faster than he could patch it back together.

He scanned the small compound without a trace of nostalgia. He couldn't believe the tiny shack he'd been born in was still standing; he'd figured on a gust of wind blowing it to Missouri years ago. The stables were in even worse shape; it had taken him a solid two weeks of work before he'd dared lodge Old Bill there.

Lily crouched in the shadow of the house itself, trailing a piece of twine for the scrawny, moth-eaten feline that was the only thing she'd brought from her mother's house save the clothes on her back. He waved enthusiastically at her when she glanced up, pasted what he hoped was a friendly, reassuring smile on his face. It wasn't an expression he'd had much reason to practice, and he guessed he was really bad at it, too, because Lily whipped her attention back to her cat and quickly led it around the side of the house and out of his view.

Sighing, he reached down and scooped up a handful of nails. He wondered, not for the first time, if it'd be better for Lily if he just packed up and got her out of Haven as quickly as possible. But he'd barely managed to lure her out of the house where her mother had died; only the promise of a bowl of stew and a handful of peppermint sticks had budged her. Often he woke up in the morning expecting to find her gone. Insisting she ride off with a man she barely knew would send her fleeing for sure. And he figured she'd balk at leaving her mother's grave behind. She slipped off to visit it at least twice a week; he always followed her, just to make sure she got there and back safely.

Not to mention that running out of town with his tail between his legs, abandoning his mother's land, would just make Phillip Cox too damn happy. There'd been a time when pissing off Cox had been the only source of entertainment in his life, and old habits died hard.

He poked through the nails, attempting to find one that wasn't coated with rust. He should have picked up some more while he was in Stoddard's, but another old habit interfered. He never spent more time in town than was absolutely necessary.

Though it almost would have been worth it. He'd bet those biddies had lit into Miss Bright the instant he'd left, just because he'd acknowledged her presence. Might have been fun to watch. He wondered if the teacher could hold her own against the combined forces of the morally upright, not to mention thoroughly self-righteous, ladies of Haven.

He had the oddest notion that she just might.

He felt a tug on his shirtsleeve. Lily had snuck up without his notice. She had the old cat tucked in the crook of her arm, their narrow, suspicious faces a matched set, and it was all he could do not to scoop her up and hold her as closely as she held her pet.

It was the first time she'd come to *him*, the first time she'd dared touch him, and it left him in the uncomfortable grip of feelings he'd no experience with and had never particularly wanted. "Yes?" he said softly, afraid of startling her away; the girl was as wary as a skittish doe.

"She's coming."

"Who?"

"*She.*" Lily pointed toward the road. "The lady."

"Well, what do you know about that." Anthea was marching down the dust road, her head high, a silly black ostrich feather at least a foot high bobbing along on top of a hat that Gabriel figured was the height of fashion—he'd bet Anthea Bright would wear nothing less—but looked pretty darn ridiculous to him. Her posture was perfect, her gloves impeccable, and she had the hat she'd snatched off his head pinched between two fingers, held away from her body as if she were carrying a dead mouse she'd found on her bedroom floor.

"What do you suppose she wants with us, Lily?"

Lily screwed up her face in concentration, then shrugged.

"I don't know, either," he admitted, earning him a startled look. "Let's go find out, shall we?"

Anthea's determined pace didn't falter until they met her a dozen feet in front of the house, in the dubious shade of a struggling cottonwood tree that should have been put out of its misery years ago. Then she stopped abruptly and just stood there, her face serious.

"Well?" he finally asked. "I don't know about you, but I don't have all day to stand around in the road."

She thrust the hat at him. "You forgot this."

"Figured you might want to keep it. Since you seemed so fond of it and all."

"No." Color tinged her cheekbones. "Not that it's not a perfectly lovely hat, of course, it's just that—"

"Not exactly your style, hmm?"

"No." She waggled the hat, as if that motion would encourage him to relieve her of her burden; clearly she was in a hurry to discharge her duty. For some reason, he wasn't in the mood to let her off so easily.

Finally, when he could tell she was mightily fighting the temptation to jam it on his head herself, he took the hat and plopped it in place. He deliberately tugged it low, shielding his eyes, knowing it allowed him to look to his heart's content while giving nothing of his own expression away.

Her task completed, he expected her to turn on her pointy heels and trot away. But she still stood there, flexing her elegant fingers as if she didn't know what to do with them now that they no longer had his hat to crush.

"Well?" he asked again.

Anthea had practiced what she planned to say all the way to the farm, weighing the exact phrases so that they sounded firm but not judgmental. Now, however, she found her carefully constructed speeches no match for Gabriel Jackson.

"I would like to speak to you," she ventured. "If you have a moment."

"Seems like what you're doing already. Speakin' to me."

"I suppose I am at that." She flicked a glance at Lily. Anthea had hoped that, in her home environment, Lily would be more relaxed and secure than she was in the alien surroundings of the schoolroom. But she seemed just as wary, just as wrapped in on herself.

And every bit as dirty as Letty Matheson had complained of.

"Alone. If Lily doesn't mind giving us a moment."

But apparently Lily did. She scowled, sidled a little closer to Gabriel.

"Lily, why don't you go on in and start setting things out. It's almost suppertime."

Lily's lower lip popped out like a prairie dog from its hole, and for an instant Anthea expected a mutiny. But Mr. Jackson was not the sort of man one argued with, and Lily took herself off, dragging her toes in the dirt as she went into a house that looked every bit as unkempt and neglected as Lily herself did.

Gabriel hadn't looked away from Anthea, not once. She felt his steady regard, solemn, indecipherable. She was not accustomed to men spending so much time simply *looking* at her. It might have been flattering if it weren't so unsettling.

"How'd you find us?"

"I asked." And the women in Stoddard's had been simply delighted to tell her, smugly sure that Anthea would follow instructions and ensure that Lily Ross would be kept far, far away from more legitimately born children.

"You're not terribly interested in keeping your job, are you?"

"Oh yes, I am," she said with a fervency that surprised Gabriel. He'd pegged her as a favored daughter, raised in comfort, who thought it a grand adventure to come teach on the frontier. Never mind that Haven hadn't been the frontier for almost thirty years; it surely seemed the height of uncivilized wildness to her.

"We're not exactly properly chaperoned." He tossed off the line for no other reason than to see her reaction. He'd never expected it to spark a reaction in *him*. But still . . . there was something about a woman being all properly fastened and covered and buttoned that made a man's hands itch to undo them all. He wondered if, while Miss Bright was getting herself all gussied up in the morning, it had ever occurred to her that all those layers just made a man want to start *un*-layering. And whether she'd be shocked if she suspected—or if that was exactly *why* women did it in the first place.

"You're the father of one of my students," she went on. "It's not only perfectly proper for me to make a home visit, it's a requirement of my job. The school board understands that."

"Who said I was her father?"

"What?" she asked, startled. "But . . . I just assumed. *Aren't* you her father?"

He contemplated her while he considered. She knew Lily was illegitimate, and obviously considered that *his* doing. Why should it matter to him if Anthea Bright had jumped to the conclusion that he wasn't the kind of man who'd *be* a man? That he'd abandon his daughter until forced to take responsibility?

He shouldn't care what she thought. He *didn't* care. He'd willingly accepted Lily as his responsibility, and therefore he was bound to make her welfare his first priority. Having his blood in her veins was hardly a recommendation, in most people's minds. Was he a worse father than *no* father?

But more than likely it made no difference anyway. The good folks of Haven were bound to think what they wanted about him and Lily no matter what he said about it.

They always had.

So he remained silent, watching the thoughts spin behind those expressive eyes, and let her wonder for a while.

"If it's gonna take some time for you to work up to saying whatever it is you've got to say, can I get back to fixing the fence while you do it? Some of us don't have time to waste."

"Of course," she agreed quickly. It'd be easier to broach the subject, Anthea decided, if his hands were busy. If he was occupied with something besides staring at her.

She accompanied him to where a neat stack of salvaged lumber lay beside a broken fence. He picked up a pry bar and bent over the fence, putting his weight into levering off a piece of rotting wood.

"This isn't too *rude* for you? My working while I've got a visitor?"

Anthea supposed she deserved that. And the sneer that underlaid the smoothly spoken words. "Not when the visitor is uninvited."

"That's true, ain't it? Showing up without an invitation has to be almost as bad as, oh, say, wearing a hat inside." He pried off the remaining splinters and straightened. Miss Bright wore a neat, gray coat, the large, black buttons glossy as gems, and the walk out to his place had brought a flush to her cheeks. She had lovely skin, the kind carefully nurtured by creams and potions and parasols.

He was used to women who'd earned their lines, by work and sun and life. He liked those lines, the character and fortitude they revealed. So it surprised him to find that her skin . . . interested him. That he wondered how her cheek would feel to the touch, if it hinted at the softness to be found in more protected parts. He'd spent more time than he liked trying to remember what she'd felt like, in that brief instant when he'd nudged back her hair.

And she looked as tense as a drawn bowstring. "You don't seem too happy to be here," he said. "Why don't you just say it and get it over with?"

She sighed, as if resigned to forcing herself through something she dreaded. "Lily, she . . . I can't allow her in the classroom like—"

"Damn it!" He hurled the pry bar at his pile of tools, where it landed with a violent clang, and planted his hands on his hips, viciously pleased to see her flinch. How could she? How could *she*, with her pretty, clean gloves and her pretty, clean life, deny even this simple advantage to Lily? "She might not be the easiest student you have, and she might not look nice in the program on parents' night, but she's a child, she lives in this township, and she's got a right to an education, just like all those other kids."

"But she's—"

He was in no mood to listen to her excuses. The injustice of it burned him. "What happened? You find out that she was a bastard? Those sanctimonious old harpies make it clear that they didn't want their precious darlings contaminated by her?" He jabbed his forefinger at her. "And you, Miss Propriety Is Everything, you'll always do what the good, upstanding citizens want, won't you—"

"Now, wait just a minute!" Unconsciously she mimicked his combative stance, one fist jammed on her hip, one finger stabbing the air a few inches from his chest. "This isn't about me. And it isn't even about Lily's parentage. If you want her treated just like everyone else, the least you can do is give her a *bath*."

"A bath? What's that got to do with anything?"

She threw up her hands in exasperation. What did men know about anything? "It has everything to do with it! If Mrs. Matheson and her cronies are looking for a reason to get Lily out of school, it's our job to make sure that they can't find one!" How *dare* he? How dare he assume she'd meekly allow anyone to run one of *her* students out of her school? "How do you expect the other children to treat her when she comes to school looking like—like—" Even with Lily out of earshot, she couldn't bring herself to say it.

"You don't know much about anything if you think that how Lily looks is going to make any difference in how those little brats treat her," he said, more mildly this time.

"You don't have to make it so *easy* for them to single her out!"

"So go ahead," he said. *Our* job, she'd called it, he

thought in wonder. As in *hers* and *his*. Well, what do you know about that?

His suggestion stopped her in midtirade. He was almost sorry. He rather liked the look of her in battle mode.

"Go ahead what?"

"So go ahead and give her a bath."

She blinked at him. Big fat eyelashes, she had, a sensual lushness at odds with her appearance. "But—"

"She's been with me all of six weeks," he said. "Her mother was the county whore."

She jerked as if she'd been struck. "Surely, now, that was uncalled-for."

He'd long ago given up trying to pretty things up for people too pure for reality. The truth was the truth. His mother might have given birth out of wedlock, earning her the condemnation of the town, but Lily's mother had been a whore in truth, choosing to settle where there was no competition for the service she sold.

"I tried. Heated up a few tubs for her, made sure she knew I was going to be gone for a while. But I guess she didn't feel good about stripping down in the house of a man she'd just met, least as far as she could recall." He sighed. "Can't say that I blame her. No way in hell I was going to put her through me forcing her into it. God only knows what she'd think I was trying to do if I started ripping her clothes off."

Oh, dammit, the woman was going to cry. He could see it coming, sympathy and moisture welling up in her eyes, and panic rose just as quick. If she was going to bawl, she could go drip all over Lily, not him. After all, Lily was the one who needed a bath.

"So if you want her to come to school clean enough

not to offend your tender sensibilities, you're welcome to give it a shot," he finished in a rush.

He bent, grabbed a hefty piece of lumber, and balanced it over a boulder. Bracing it with his knee, he reached for a saw. "If you're gonna do it, you'd better get started. I'm done talking. You've got half an hour before I'm coming in for supper."

If Lily's grooming wasn't good enough for Miss Anthea Bright and her new friends, then *she* could damn well do something about it.

Lily huddled in the galvanized tin basin set smack in the middle of the shack. She shivered; the water had been warm when they'd started, but it had gone cold before Teacher had gotten all Lily's clothes off. A few inches were left in the washtub. Some of the rest of the water had turned the dirt floor for two feet around the tub into a sloppy mess. A lot was on Teacher, whose hair was every bit as wet as Lily's.

When Teacher and the man—Gabriel, he'd told her his name was the first day he'd brought her here, but she knew she wasn't supposed to say a man's name— had sent her into the house, she'd known what it meant. What it always meant when a man and a woman wanted to be alone.

But she'd peeked. She wasn't supposed to peek. *Stay out of sight, shut up, and don't look.* She could still hear her mother saying those words, even though she was in that grave out by the bend in the river, because she'd said them so many times.

But today Lily had looked anyway, peering over the edge of the window while her heart pounded like the man's hammer, and all she'd seen was Teacher and the man yelling at each other.

And then the man had gone back to work, and Teacher had stomped into the house and started heating water.

Lily didn't want to take a bath. Bad things happened when you took off your clothes.

But Teacher was a lot stronger than she looked, and now she was scrubbing at Lily's head like she was trying to rub all the hair right off it.

Teacher scooped up a pitcher of water and dumped it right over Lily. She sputtered and swiped at her eyes, to find Teacher smiling at her like she had when Lily had walked all the way across the room with the book on her head, just like Teacher had shown her.

"There you go," Teacher said. Lily liked her voice. It sounded all chirpy and springy, like the birds. "Isn't that much better? What a pretty child you are under all that grime. Mr. Jackson is going to be so surprised when he sees you!"

Lily didn't think she wanted the man to think she was pretty. But she liked it when Teacher said it.

The teacher, Lily knew, was a lady.

Lily wasn't a lady. She wasn't a lady because her mother wasn't a lady. That was why, when they'd gone to town, nobody ever talked to them. Why other ladies crossed the road when they saw them coming. And why the other kids called her a bastard.

Maybe, Lily thought, if she tried really hard, if she did everything Teacher said, she wouldn't be a bastard anymore.

Chapter 4

"It is exceedingly kind and considerate of you, and I do appreciate it most sincerely, but it really is not at all necessary for you to escort me home. Not *at all*," Anthea insisted. For the sixth time, but who was counting?

Gabriel, apparently. "I heard you the first time," he said, "and hearing it a full half dozen times doesn't make me inclined to agree with you any more than hearing it once did. No matter how pretty you say it."

They were in his front yard again, though now the sun had gone soft and rosy-colored, skidding low in the sky, and the temperature had dropped a good ten degrees. Which made it all the sillier that they were merely standing there, risking a chill, instead of hurrying off to their respective, very much warmer, homes.

Except Anthea had no intention of taking one step down the road with Mr. Jackson at her side, and he appeared equally as determined she wasn't budging an inch without his escort.

"I walked all the way out here without any incident whatsoever," Anthea pointed out with what she considered irrefutable logic. "In fact, I quite enjoyed the stroll. I am certain my return trip will go just as smoothly."

"Nope." Gabriel settled into a comfortable stance, his weight on one hip and thumb hooked into his pockets, as if preparing to stand there as long as it took. "It's wild out here on the frontier, you know. Danger lurking all over the place for a pretty lady."

A pretty lady. He meant nothing by the words, Anthea told herself; they were an automatic courtesy—not that he'd shown much tendency to courtesy—and further evidence that he'd spout just about anything to get his own way. It was with some pride that she managed to ignore them completely. Although certainly the air did not seem to hold the same chill it had only moments before.

"Haven has been settled for decades," she reproved him. "The road is well traveled, as I'm sure you're aware. Not to mention that several of my students reside along the way, so that in the *extremely* unlikely event that I should require assistance, it is only a few yards away at most."

Of course, the fact that several of her students lived along that road was the precise reason she didn't want Gabriel strolling along beside her, and they both knew it.

"Oh, but it would be terribly impolite of me to let you go trotting off unescorted."

He was far too amused by this, Anthea thought. And if he threw his good *manners* back in her face one more time—especially with that amused, taunting gleam in his eye—she was going to forget every single nicety that Miss Addington ever taught her and shove those words back down his stubborn throat.

"But—"

"My mama taught me better than that," he informed her.

She pursed her lips and contemplated another tactic. If even a tenth of what she'd heard in Haven was true, he'd hardly been raised to genteel etiquette. Still, she shuddered to think what he might do were she foolish enough to point out that little detail.

And then she shivered again, because her good woolen cloak was not enough armor against the evening wind when the clothes beneath were damp, for Lily's resistance had ensured that Anthea had received nearly as much of a dousing as Lily.

Gabriel frowned. "You're cold," he said. "Wait here." He sprinted into the house. Anthea barely had time to appreciate his easy, strong lope before he returned, holding a crumpled wad of thick, gray blanket.

"I half expected to find you a quarter mile down the road and moving fast by the time I got back."

"It would have been simpler, wouldn't it?" The idea had never occurred to her, Anthea realized with some dismay. For while she'd like to believe that she'd stayed put because she refused to take the easy way out, she had to admit it was far closer to the truth that she simply liked the challenge presented by Gabriel Jackson. If nothing else, he distracted her from her loneliness and worries most effectively. "However, *my* mother would turn over in her grave if she knew I ran off without saying a proper leave to my host."

Their appearances were reversed from when she'd first arrived. For she'd primped before setting out—only because she felt it important to present a neat and competent appearance, and for no other reason—while he'd been disheveled and sweating from his work. Although it had hardly distracted from his essential attractiveness, and she had to agree with Letty that, if he'd taken a few things from the young ladies of Haven before he'd left town, it wasn't because he'd snatched them by force. More likely they'd been handed over to him with eager enthusiasm.

But now Anthea herself was the one unkempt, her clothes drying into unattractive wrinkles, her hair hanging heavy and rumpled around her shoulders. But he'd washed up at the pump before coming in from his work, and changed his shirt, and now his hair lay in damp, thick waves against his brown neck. It had seemed remarkably intimate to her, to see a man rough and messy as he came in from his work, and the transformation in his appearance as he cleaned up seemed the sort of thing a wife should witness and no one else.

He looked at her, and then at the blanket clutched in his big hands, and a half smile lifted the corner of his mouth. His movements slow and gentle, so careful she could easily have moved away—which, she realized dimly, she would if her senses hadn't apparently abandoned her—he laid the blanket around her head and shoulders, softness and warmth settling over her.

He didn't touch her, not once in all that tender movement. It didn't matter. Her skin warmed and flushed and tingled as if he had laid his palms right upon her. Her eyes were level with his throat, with the wedge of skin exposed by his open collar. She'd no idea that small bare space could be so . . . interesting. Thank heavens gentlemen didn't generally go around with their collars unfastened. She'd never get anything done.

Though it wasn't really *gentlemen* who were the problem, was it? Just this most ungentlemanly man.

"There," he said, giving the blanket one final tug around her. "Are you warm now?"

"Very," she murmured without thinking. And then her usually reliable good sense came flooding back to her, along with a hefty dose of mortification. Oh, what could he possibly think of her? Though she supposed he was not entirely unaccustomed to women staring at him in a daze, it was quite unlike her usual demeanor.

She jumped away, safely out of reach. But when his smile widened in wicked satisfaction, she realized that if, by some blessing, he *hadn't* noticed her foolish reaction to him before, she'd just made it impossible for him to overlook.

"Are you ready to go?" he asked.

"Not if you're still planning to accompany me," she returned.

His eyes gleamed, daring her to state it outright. That she was afraid to have him escort her. Afraid of what the town might think, afraid to be alone with him . . . afraid. But she wouldn't say it, and they both knew it, because he'd enjoy hearing it just too darn much.

"Besides which, I am quite confident," she added quickly, "that you would never leave Lily unattended for so long. And I couldn't ask you to."

"Lily will be fine."

"Oh, no, she's much too young to be left by herself." Why hadn't she raised this issue before? Finally, an argument she could win.

His expression shut down, becoming as forbidding as slab granite. "I don't know what it's like where you come from, *ma'am,* but out here we don't cotton to coddling children."

There'd been too much emphasis on that sneering "ma'am," and more heat than called for in his answer. As if, in questioning his care of Lily, she'd cut a shade too close to the bone. Anthea filed that information away for further reference. Though she had an uncomfortable suspicion that she shouldn't be quite so interested in collecting a bulging mental file of tidbits about Gabriel Jackson.

"But surely she'll be frightened? Left alone at her age? I—"

"Miss Bright." There was an edge to his voice now, honed of impatience and something darker. Something that made her all the more determined to convince him to allow her to return home alone. "I'm sure you had servants to watch over you your whole life, making sure so much as a sliver didn't stick in those perfect white hands. But half the kids in the state who are Lily's age have full charge of their younger siblings, much less themselves. She learned long ago to stay out of trouble, I promise you. Not to mention that she manages to walk all the way to school by herself every day."

"Yes, but . . ." Anthea had to concede that point. "If *she* can do it by herself, whyever can't I?"

"That's in daylight." His smile flashed, quick, knowing. "And surely even you realize there are more dangers for big girls out here in the night."

Anthea blessed the thickening darkness, clinging to the fervent hope that it might camouflage cheeks that she knew full well were burning red. "It's not night yet," she managed.

"Close enough."

"Oh, I'll be home long before it's fully dark," she assured him. "I'm quite fast, you know."

"It's only gonna get darker, the longer we stand around here *discussing*."

"I really do not feel comfortable leaving Lily alone."

"She's working on getting supper ready. Besides, she was alone in the house for three days after her mother died before anybody found her, and she managed."

He tossed off the fact so easily it was a full half minute before the impact struck home. But it took only a second after that for tears to lodge in her throat and spring to her eyes. "But she . . . Oh, Lily."

"Oh, shit." He grabbed her arm around the wrist and started off down the road, towing her behind him exactly as he'd towed Lily into the schoolroom the day they'd met. "You're not gonna do that. You are *not*."

Anthea tried to dig in her heels, but quickly discovered she wasn't going to stop moving forward unless her arm suddenly separated from her shoulder. "I'm not going to do what?" she managed.

"Cry. Whimper. Weep. Wail. Drip all over. Whatever it is you're fixin' to do."

He sounded so panicked it lightened her mood. She'd bet her last dollar—if she *had* any dollars—that he didn't sound like that very often.

She'd think about Lily later. When she could weep to her heart's content.

"I'm not going to cry on your shoulder."

"That's right, you're not. Because I'm gonna get you back home before you have the chance."

By now they'd made it almost all the way down the rutted path that passed for the drive to his home, nearly to the main road. Where it was not out of the realm of possibility that someone might ride by, and how exactly would she explain Mr. Jackson, with his hand clamped around her arm, dragging her down the road like he was a Kiowa warrior claiming his captive? It'd take a better twist on the truth than even the ones she'd written to her sisters to keep her from losing her job.

She gave a yank, hoping to slow him down enough to get his attention. "You can't pull me all the way back into town like this!"

He stopped but kept her wrist in his hand. "I can't?"

"You can't," she said firmly, hoping against hope that he wouldn't demand a reason. His thumb and his finger linked around her wrist with plenty of room to spare. Great big hands, work-roughened, strong. She swallowed hard.

"Would you rather I carried you over my shoulder like a grain sack?" He eyed her up and down. "You're not that big. Bet it wouldn't be much trouble."

She gaped in horror until she caught the gleam in his eye. "It occurs to me that I have a bit of a problem here, don't I? If I start home, all you need to do is simply trot along beside me. Whereas, short of tying you down, I cannot *force* you to stay behind."

"You're welcome to try." The gleam sparked stronger, flickered deep.

"I believe I'll forgo the pleasure. For now." And then she wondered at what she'd said, for his wild grin was all out of proportion to her words.

"Good that you finally figured this out. I was beginning to wonder. Smart woman like you, the logic
should have been obvious a long time ago."

"It certainly should." Anthea feared she was devel-
oping a worrisome talent for overlooking the obvious
where Mr. Jackson was concerned.

The fact that Anthea couldn't sleep that night was
entirely his fault. And the fact that her insomnia could
be attributed to *nothing* that he'd done, rather than
something, only laid the blame more squarely on his
head . . . somehow. She hadn't quite figured that out
yet, but she knew that it just had to be his fault.

He'd been the perfect gentleman the entire way
home. It made her crazy.

Because she'd been prepared for everything *but*
nothing. What, exactly, she thought he might do, she
didn't really know. But not *that*. So she'd been skittish
as a new foal, jumping every time a step took him a
hairsbreadth closer to her, stumbling over her answer
every time he opened his mouth. All because she was
sure there was some hidden trap there, laid for her embarrassment and his amusement.

They'd passed two families she knew, the entire Bickersdyke clan, packed into their buggy and on their way
into town, and then Esther and Abe Mott on their
way home. None of them had bothered to hide their
amazement at seeing the schoolteacher in the company of the notorious Gabriel Jackson. She'd greeted
them with all the stiff politeness she could muster.

Mr. Jackson had appeared a lot more comfortable
with the situation. His bright, jovial "Howdy" just
made her want to kick him, because he was clearly enjoying the moment at her expense.

She wondered if Mrs. Matheson and Mrs. Stoddard would even wait until the sun came up before turning up at her door. She was pretty sure Mrs. Mott wouldn't wait till sunrise to tell them.

But beyond that, he'd walked properly at her side, steps matched so closely to hers she didn't have to hurry a bit. Considering the relative lengths of their legs—although she knew perfectly well the last thing she should be pondering was his *legs*—he had to have been attending to her pace, though he gave no sign of it. Once or twice he touched her elbow, briefly and with complete circumspection, to assist her over a deeper rut in the road, but he dropped his hand the instant she was safely on flat ground again.

But then there'd been that moment at her door. He hadn't entered her house. Surely even *he* wouldn't flout the proprieties so blatantly as to do that, but he'd poked his head in and taken a good look while she fluttered—she was very much afraid she'd fluttered—at his side. When she protested, he simply said he'd been making sure she hadn't entertained any uninvited visitors during her absence.

Frowning deeply, he'd shaken his head as if disappointed in her soddy. But she'd seen his house, and so she doubted that the condition of her place was what disturbed him. And then he'd looked at her, just looked at her, while all the air rushed out of her lungs.

When he'd brushed the lock of hair over her shoulder that first day they'd met, one knuckle had skimmed her neck. She would have sworn she hadn't noted it then; she'd been made too breathless by the abrupt impropriety of the gesture. But now that exact spot burned, as if his fingers had been hot as pokers and had somehow marked the place permanently.

Twilight suited him. All those angles in his face, all that darkness in his coloring, his eyes. All that mystery, picked out in shadows and the last rays of sunlight. He could have done anything—*anything*—at the moment and she wouldn't have been surprised.

What else should one anticipate from the most notorious man in town? He was clearly not bound by the rules and expectations that the rest of them were.

For a heavy instant, she'd been certain he was going to kiss her. There was something in the angle of his head, the absolute focus of his gaze, that warned her of his intent. And it was only after he touched his hand to his brow as if saluting her and turned to saunter away that she realized to her dismay that she hadn't been prepared to stop him.

It was that weakness, more than anything else, that kept her staring at her ceiling all night long. She knew the rules that well brought up women must follow. She *knew* them. Even Gerald hadn't kissed her until they'd been properly betrothed. And really, hadn't that entire episode, painful as it had been, proved conclusively all the reasons she shouldn't so much as inch a little toe from the straight and narrow?

She flopped over and kicked the quilt away. Her nightgown was wool flannel, old but sturdy, covering her from chin to toe. It had been one of the first things she'd packed, sure she'd appreciate its warmth in the depths of a plains winter. However, the soddy lived up to its billing in at least one regard. Its thick walls provided excellent insulation, more than she wanted right now.

Not one shred of moonlight lightened the blackness. Her toes had learned through brutal experience not to go stumbling around in the soddy at night, so she reached over and lit the candle she kept beside the bed. She jumped to her feet and headed over to the single window just to the side of the front door. Surely she'd sleep perfectly well once the proper temperature was achieved. She refused to lose sleep over that man.

There were no panes in the tiny window. To shield herself from prying eyes—and whatever creatures one of her charges might decide it was amusing to introduce to his teacher—she kept a rectangle of toweling securely tacked over the opening. But now she thought she wouldn't be able to breathe if she didn't get at least a bit of fresh air.

The tacks refused to give way, for she'd had the Pietzke twins, who'd spent most of recess the first week of the term crouched over a gopher hole, in mind when she'd fastened them. Tendrils of hair stuck to her forehead, and she rummaged in a nearby crate, unearthing a bent tin fork. She wiggled the tines beneath the edge of the tack, putting her weight behind it. The tines twisted like thin wire as the tack finally gave way, and she peeled back the toweling, sighing in relief as the breeze wafted through, its crisp, fresh bite welcome in the stuffy space.

There was a sharp crack, the crunch of a heavy footstep on the acorns that littered the ground beneath the big oak guarding her door. She dropped the flap immediately as her heart kicked up a frantic beat.

Who, or what, lurked in the shadows outside her home? She tried to tell herself that, whatever it was, it was likely harmless. The great black dog that lived at the Sontesbys, no more than a half mile away. Or even one of her students, sneaking out from his bed to play yet another trick on the teacher.

But those comforting theories were no armor

against images spawned by one too many dime novels splashed with vivid descriptions of rampaging Indian warriors and vicious outlaws. And hadn't Mrs. Mott told her just yesterday about how that terrible Jesse James had ridden through here not five years ago? The papers *said* he was dead, but one never knew about the papers these days.

Diving back to her bed and pulling the covers over her head held a definite appeal. But that would hardly protect her, would it? Better to know what she faced.

She reached over and plucked at the flame of the candle, snuffing it out. Nudging the corner of the toweling back with her forefinger, she placed her eye to the small opening.

The moon was bright, picking out the outlines of the well, showing light on the packed, bare patches of the school yard. She studied the deep shadows beneath the great oak while a breeze shivered the branches and made shifting patterns of silver and black dance on the ground.

And caught a transient flash out of the corner of her eye, a liquid gleam of pearly light on polished metal.

Moonlight on the barrel of a gun.

Chapter 5

She gasped and whirled, plastering her back flat against the stacked sod wall. Dried stalks of grass pricked her through her nightclothes. It was a good two feet thick at least, that wall. Surely impermeable to a bullet, one would think.

The knock on the door, no more than a foot from her ear, nearly sent her through the ceiling.

Oh, Lordy. She tried to compel her brain to work, forced herself to listen over the thunder of her heart.

She groped her way to the corner that served as her kitchen. Her knee whacked the edge of a crate she'd yet to unpack and she swallowed a shout of pain. The stove, where was the stove? Thank goodness, there it was.

She groped for the heavy iron skillet that she'd left on the top, as it seemed the simplest place to store it, and lifted it in both fists, weighing its worth as a weapon. Not bad . . . There couldn't be a whole lot of heads in the world hard enough to stand up to good cast iron. If she wasn't shot dead away before she got close enough to use it, that was.

She flew back to the window and was reaching to nudge up the toweling with her fist when the knock came again.

"Miss Bright? It's me, Gabriel. Open up and let me in."

The moonlight wouldn't have been too helpful if he'd really been interested in sneaking up unseen. But skulking around wasn't his aim tonight, and he noted how easy the big autumn moon made it for him to see a ripple of motion in the stuff she used to cover her window. God! It was perfectly obvious she was standing right there. Someone could pop off a shot and have a fair chance of hitting her. He could reach through the empty panes and grab her. Hell, he could have knocked out what was left of the flimsy wood framing and crawled right through the hole before she'd even woken up.

She was one sitting pigeon, the pretty schoolteacher.

Which was exactly why he was here.

"Come on, let me in."

"Hush! Someone might hear you." Her voice hissed from behind that ridiculous curtain. As if that could protect her. "Is there something wrong with Lily?"

A "yes" would get that door open faster than he could get the word out of his mouth. But he didn't have the heart to use Lily against her.

"She's fine. But I'm getting cold. Let me in."

There was a long moment of hesitation. "You've got a gun."

"You didn't think I was going to run around in the middle of the night without one, did you?" He shifted, the rifle tucked comfortably in the crook of his elbow. He could have it in shooting position in moments. "We've got coyotes. Wolves, too."

"What do you want?" She sounded more curious than suspicious.

"I need to talk to you."

"So talk."

"What, out here? Someone might wander by. Or hear and come to investigate."

"Who's going to wander by at this time of night?"

"You never know. You willing to chance it?"

The silence hummed with her indecision. "Put your gun down and step away."

"Oh, for Christ's sake. It's not loaded." He waggled his free hand in his pocket, brass clinking together. "Got my bullets right here."

"Nevertheless, I'm not undoing this latch until you place your gun down right before the door and take three steps away. Either that, or I'm going to scream louder than you've ever heard any woman in your life, I promise you. Every man from here to Centervale will come running, and what happens then will be your problem."

"You got good lungs, huh?"

"Superb."

I'll just bet you do.

He bent slowly, so she wouldn't take fright and start hollering after all. Though any woman of sense would have started screeching the moment she saw a man with a gun lurking outside her house.

He set the gun gingerly on its side—the piece had served him well, and deserved the proper respect. He backed up the requisite three steps and lifted his hands, palms out, to show he was harmless. "Good enough?"

"We'll see." She eased the door open, angling her body through, obviously ready to spring back inside if he so much as twitched.

The moonlight hit her in increments. An arm first, the pale flash of her hand followed by a froth of lace around her wrist. Then the gleam of her hair, loose and heavy and glossy. Finally a glimpse of her face, all moon white and shadows, no shades in between. That seemed appropriate to him; he didn't figure there were a whole lot of areas of gray in her.

She kept a wary eye on him, scooping up the rifle with a careless hand. It swung around as she straightened, inscribing an arc that took in most of his lower regions.

"Holy hell!"

He closed the distance between them and grabbed the rifle from her hands before she could utter a peep of protest. "What do you think you're doing? The thing's loaded, for chrissakes. I rather favor some of those parts you're aiming it at."

"Loaded?" Her mouth thinned. "You said it wasn't loaded."

"Of course it's loaded." He stamped by her, ducking his head to get under the low frame of her door. "What good would it be if it wasn't loaded?"

"But . . ."

She wavered in the doorway, backlit by moonlight, hands linked before her waist. She seemed a creature spun from the night, a sprite or wraith or something else from the kind of stories he knew about only vaguely but figured her mother had probably read to her before tucking her in to her nice clean bed every night. She sure didn't look like a sturdy woman with her feet planted firmly in the plains.

"That was a damfool thing to do. Why the hell'd you open the door?"

A bit of temper flashed through her confusion. "You *told* me to open it!"

"And you're going to just yank open the door to a man you barely know just because he *asks* you to? I didn't even say 'please.' " He shook his head in disgust. "Where *are* you from?"

Her brows drew together. "Philadelphia."

He snorted. "Figures."

She frowned at that. "What's wrong with Philadelphia?"

"It ain't Kansas."

That particular tone always made her snap to attention, her back straightening like it was braced with a board, chin lifting to a regal angle. He knew that much about her already. "Well, *that* is certainly true." She fixed her eyes on him. "What *do* you want?"

Oh, now, there was a question, all right. He'd had a reason for coming here, a good and sound one. But now he could admit that curiosity prodded him as well, a hint of intrigue at how she'd look dressed for bed.

He could have predicted the nightgown, yards and yards of sturdy fabric the moonlight couldn't penetrate even a bit. A pity, that. But her hair was unexpectedly rich, a thick fall of shiny brown turned pale in the silvery light, rumpled in waves over her shoulders where she'd crushed it against her pillow as she lay.

The darkness suited her features as well, softening the precise lines, playing up eyes that were lovely by day but damn near mesmerizing by night. A man could happily spend every hour from sunrise to sunset looking into those eyes, testing every way to make the expression in them shift and change. Not to mention a few more hours by candlelight.

"You should come on in," he told her. "You'll catch your chill. There's a bit of winter in the air tonight."

"Oh." As if she felt the temperature for the first time when he mentioned it, she hugged her arms around her and shivered. "There is, isn't there? But you do seem a bit overly concerned with my temperature."

"You've still got my blanket."

"Oh, of course. I should have realized." She smacked the heel of her hand on her forehead. "You couldn't sleep without it, could you, and tramped all the way here just to fetch it back?"

"Sure thing. I don't have much to spare, you know."

"Hmmm." he kept his face impassive while she studied him and then shrugged, apparently making up her mind at last. "Let me get a light."

She moved quickly, touching a match to two lamps nailed high on the far wall, adding three tallow candles for good measure, chasing all the shadows in the room into forgotten corners.

The blanket he'd draped over her shoulders now lay across her bed, tangled in a wild jumble with a quilt and linen sheet. She'd slept beneath it, and the thought started a low humming deep in his belly.

It'd been a long time since he'd been alone with a woman, alone in a room with a bed. Since before he'd come back to Haven. And even longer than that, for he'd been too busy on his ranch to run around sniffing after skirts. He'd done more than his share of that in his youth, and thought he'd moved beyond it. But he must have left it alone too long, to feel this hot kick of desire at such simple provocation.

"Well." She ducked her head, hair falling across her face so he couldn't see her clearly, and hurried to the bed, snatching off the blanket and shaking it out with a snap like a maid.

"You're a messy sleeper." He wouldn't have expected it of her. He would have thought she'd be as disciplined asleep as she was awake, lying still and rigid under carefully placed blankets. But relaxed in slumber, apparently Miss Bright was a wild woman.

Perhaps that was her true nature, he mused. Who knew what the right man could lure out of her?

"Yes." She folded the blanket into a precise square, smoothed it over her forearm. "My sisters battled heartily over having to share with me."

"Sisters?" Why did he care enough to ask? he wondered. He knew he should leave, but it seemed immensely more interesting to stay here and watch her fidget while she tried to figure out a way to eject him, and wonder how long she'd dare to continue to answer his just-this-side-of-forward questions, her eyes dark and wary of what he might do next.

"Yes. Two. One older, one younger." Her hand kept stroking the blanket. "You?"

"No. There's no one."

A small smile. "Except Lily."

"Except Lily," he agreed.

She lifted her head, pushing the heavy fall of hair behind her ears, and met his gaze directly. "Why did you come here, Mr. Jackson?"

"Brought you this." He extended the rifle.

"What?" Of all the things he'd said or done, that one might have surprised her the most. Her mouth opened; candle flames were reflected in her wide eyes.

"You can't stay here alone, Anthea." He used her given name deliberately, anticipating a protest, finding none. "Not completely unprotected."

"I'm sure it's perfectly safe."

"There are wolves. And coyotes, and rattlesnakes. And a few other things as well."

"I've heard the coyotes." She swallowed hard. "They won't come into town, will they?"

"Not usually. But wouldn't it be smarter just to be prepared?"

Her uncertain gaze leveled on the rifle, then skittered away as if the sight of it disturbed her. "I don't know how to use one."

"I'll teach you." He crossed the room, pulled out her hand, and laid the gun across her palm so she grabbed it by reflex. "Come out to the farm anytime, I'll show you. Until then, it's fairly simple. Point it and pull the trigger."

"That much I knew." Her smile was wan. "Whether I can hit anything or not is another matter entirely." She held it awkwardly away from her, as if she knew that, once she grasped it fully, there'd be no giving it back.

"I don't guess you'll be hunting jackrabbits. I figure something'll have to be pretty darn close to you before you get desperate enough to use it, anyway, so hitting it shouldn't be too tough."

"That makes a certain amount of sense," she admitted reluctantly.

He should step away right now. This was too important to scare her off by his up and kissing her. But she smelled good, of violet water and store-bought soap, and so he guessed he'd stay. For a little while longer.

He inhaled sharply, held the scent in his nose for a moment before continuing. "A blast'll likely scare off most any animal, anyway, even if all you hit is that tree in the front. And as for the rest . . . a loaded rifle pointed in their direction by a nervous woman'll do a lot to dissuade 'em. Nobody but me knows you can't shoot."

She nodded. "But there's the rub, isn't it? For near as I can tell, the only human in Haven who needs to be dissuaded by the business end of a rifle is you."

"That's true enough, isn't it?" He grinned. "Don't you forget it, either." The shared joke should have broken the tension that simmered between them. Instead, it only thickened it, as her gaze swung to his and stayed, her mouth soft and open in welcome.

"Oh," she murmured, "I don't imagine I will."

"Will you come? So I can teach you?"

"I . . ." She stepped back with a little shake as if swimming up from a dream. "I don't think . . . I can't keep this gun here. What about the children?"

"There is probably not a single house in this entire county that doesn't have a loaded gun under its roof right now. And I'll bet at least half your students have already bagged their first meal. I had by the time I was seven."

"I suppose you're right."

She sighed, looked down at the rifle.

And so he played his trump. "And if the situation ever comes up where you might need to protect the *children*, you'll be prepared."

At that, she wrapped her fingers around the gun. "Thank you. I think."

"You'll get used to it," he reassured her.

"I certainly hope not." The decision made, she stood easier now. Her face sober, she gazed at him steadily. "Why, Mr. Jackson?"

Ah, jeez, he thought. Didn't the woman even know not to look at a man like that, not when the night was deep and quiet, when the candlelight fluttered on her skin, and the smell and look of her only made a man wonder about the taste of her?

He should have brought her very much more than a gun. He should have built her a moat and a fence, hired a fleet of guards, locked her away to protect her from everyone. Protect her from him.

His throat thickened, words coming hard. "Why did I give you the gun?"

"Yes."

Because when you talked of Lily, you said "we." Because you've got no clue what you're getting into, and I'd be sorry if you got hurt. Because you heard all the bad things about me and still opened the door to me in the middle of the night just because I asked you to.

Which were the very reasons he was going to get himself out of there before he did something they'd both regret.

"Lily's under your care for several hours a day. I needed to know you could protect her, if you had to."

"Lily." Her smile faded, and he was tempted to tell her the truth. That he couldn't sleep, thinking of her there alone and unprotected. "Of course."

He'd worried about her. Imagine that, *him*, worrying about the prissy schoolteacher. Except right now she didn't seem at all prissy. Not even in that night-

gown that covered almost as much as a nun's habit—
he could see a bit of her ear, showing where the hair
looped behind it. And, of course, her hair itself, wanton, lush hair that would have made a courtesan's career. Many a man would have paid a fortune to spend
a night wrapped in it. No wonder she kept it tightly
scraped away during the day. It was very unteacherly.

But she hadn't seemed shocked to be alone with
him. Hadn't hurried to cover up in a wrapper; he very
much doubted that she'd even given a passing
thought to the fact that she stood before him in nothing but her nightgown.

"Please greet Lily for me," she murmured.

Lily. Ah yes, Lily. The very reason he would leave
right now and do his best to forget what she looked
like by candlelight. Because Lily needed her more . . .
well, certainly not *more* than Gabriel wanted her, but
Lily's need was far more worthy than his.

"I'll do that."

He dove for the door and slammed it emphatically
shut behind him. And then he remained for a long moment, pondering what was on the other side.

He reached for the latch. Instead, he brushed his fingers over the rough wood of the door before he turned
and headed home.

Phillip Cox sprawled in the big, oxblood leather
chair in his study, a decanter of whiskey on the small
mahogany table at his elbow, a half-empty glass of it in
his hand. He only allowed himself the informality of
sprawling here, in the sanctuary of his study, long after
midnight. And even then he did it with a twinge of
guilty pleasure and defiance, knowing that his father
was frowning fiercely down—or up—from wherever

he was, for he'd been as resolutely rigid of posture as he was in all other things.

Phillip was a fortunate man and he never forgot it. Of course he was. He'd inherited his father's bank, but had an instinct for business that was all his own, and his hard work had expanded that small bank into a wide-ranging enterprise that had taken him from solidly comfortable to moderately rich. He held a respected and important position in the community.

His home was lovely. More than lovely, and expressly designed to suit his taste. His health was excellent. His looks were—not to be immodest, but Phillip strongly believed in being honest with himself—still more attractive than most. He'd lost only a little hair, gained but a few inches around his waist.

And he had his daughter, his beautiful, brilliant, marvelous Olivia, the light of his life. Oh, certainly he would very much enjoy having more children. He still had hopes; Cleo was not yet thirty. But even if they were not so blessed, there was still his cherished Olivia, and who could be greedy for another child when they were already blessed with such a wondrous one as she?

Of course, they could hardly have another child if he didn't have marital relations with his wife.

Phillip took a final sip of his whiskey, set the glass carefully aside, and rose. The fire had been small to begin with—autumn had been mild thus far—and now only a thin layer of glowing ashes remained.

He made his way slowly through his sleeping house, taking pride in the great, shining windows and the thick rugs spread over gleaming wood floors. The staircase wound upward, wide and high, to an entire floor of bedrooms, a house designed to serve a family for years.

Their bedroom was at the far end of the hall, behind a door both solid and beautiful. He eased it open, the well-oiled hinges silent.

She'd left the drapes open, and moonlight bathed the bed, throwing shadows against the far wall. He made no effort to muffle his footsteps, but here, too, the rugs were deep. In any case, she didn't move when he came to stand beside the bed and stare down at her while he stripped silently in the dark, laying his clothes neatly over a nearby chair.

Oh, Cleo.

Every man on earth would have called him lucky. He had everything he'd ever wanted, including Cleo for his wife. And the one thing he'd wanted beyond all else, always, with every breath, he couldn't have.

He'd never been able to make his wife love him.

She was an angel in the moonlight. His angel, preternaturally beautiful. Her skin was even lovelier than the finely woven linen of the bedsheets, her hair pale and shining against the pillow. The edge of the sheet was high over her shoulders, so he could see only the smooth curve of her neck where it disappeared into the snowy froth of lace at the neckline of her gown. But even that tiny bit of skin was more arousing than any other woman brazen and naked, for it was Cleo's skin.

Her breathing was so quiet he couldn't hear it, even in the deep silence of the room, though his ears strained for the sound. He'd spent a great deal of time watching her sleep, for, at some time over the years, their habits had diverged. On evenings when he was tired, when the comfort of his bed called him early, she'd had to stay up with Olivia, or to finish her day's duties. On nights like tonight, when his work had kept him up long past sunset, she was fast asleep—at least by all appearances—by the time he found his way to their room.

She was the most exemplary of wives. Charming to his colleagues, obedient to his wishes, attentive to her duties. Entirely due to her efforts, the house ran smoothly, his life thoroughly comfortable. She would never deny him outright.

But he knew her better than she knew herself, and he knew full well that he never reached for her in the night but that she wished he were another man.

He brushed his fingers over the edge of the bed, where fine lace drifted over thick quilts. He couldn't remember a time he hadn't loved her. Since he was old enough to know that girls were different from boys for a reason, a wonderful one. And maybe even before that. Certainly as soon as he'd been old enough to understand the concept of love, she'd already been irrevocably lodged in his heart.

Gently he lifted the edge of the bedclothes and slid in beside her. She'd suggested shortly after Olivia's birth that they keep separate bedrooms, as befitted a proper couple of their station. And so, she'd said then, that she would not disturb him when she had to get up in the night with their infant daughter. So he had his own room, through the dressing door on the far side. He'd never spent a full night there; he could never sleep the night through without her next to him.

Except it was becoming increasingly difficult to sleep with her beside him, as well.

He laid his hand on her shoulder. He knew exactly

how it felt under his palm, the way the smooth ball of bone and muscle and silken skin filled his hand. And yet his breath quickened, as it did each time he touched her.

Just as it had the very first time, on their wedding night, all those years ago that sometimes seemed as near as yesterday. He'd been a thrilled and nervous and overwhelmed virgin, and she'd been none of those things.

The tension in her body now was perceptible, a twitch of muscle, a slight hitch in her breathing. And then she relaxed just as quickly, so that no one else would have suspected she wasn't fast asleep. But he had no doubt she'd been awake since the moment he entered the room.

He'd known, too, all those years ago when she'd given herself to him. To Jackson, he mentally added, forcing himself to think the man's name, accepting the bitter bite that came with it. He'd been fully prepared to forgive her . . . She was so young then, with the natural rebelliousness of a beautiful, spirited sixteen-year-old. It had hurt—oh, it had hurt, as if they'd reached in and taken a slice right out of his heart.

But he'd been willing to look past it, beyond it. It was obvious Jackson's feet were already pointed on the road out of town, and a solitary road it would be. Anyone could see that—even if Cleo was too momentarily dazzled to recognize it. And she would, he'd believed, eventually give in to her parents' wishes, his devotion, and the simple good sense of marrying Phillip Cox, for she was in truth an intelligent and dutiful girl in all ways but that one.

He'd been right about her marrying him. But there was one thing that he'd been completely wrong about, the one thing that mattered. He'd always assumed that someday, somehow, through his patience and the satisfaction and companionship of building a life, a family and home together, she would grow to love him, too. Not with the giddy, immature infatuation she'd felt for Jackson, but a truer, deeper, richer love that would be his alone. He smoothed her hair aside, exposing the soft skin of her ear, and bent down to kiss her. The cloak of her hair had held in her warmth and scent, and they enveloped him as he came closer, leaving his head a little dizzy with her.

Their wedding night had been such a disaster. Not so much the physical act itself—that was awkward and fast and messy, of course, but they were hardly the first couple to have that particular experience on their wedding night. They would overcome it, he'd hoped, learn together what pleased each other. But there'd been those weeks of weeping afterward, which gradually faded into her silent, stoic, ice-edged tolerance. And so he'd never, despite his best efforts, been able to overcome the specter of Gabriel Jackson.

And now he was back. And Phillip knew he would have no chance if Jackson decided he wanted his wife after all. Which he would do, of course. She was Cleo. Certainly the bastard would never have forgotten her, had just been waiting for his opportunity to return and claim her.

His hand slid down, cupped her breast through a thin layer of fine cotton, molding it gently, and he heard her quick inhalation. There were delicate little flowers embroidered on her bodice, and he felt the bumps of thread, tiny petals that shielded her flesh from him.

He'd learned a few things since their wedding

night. More than a few, if it came to that, and he swallowed down the thick surge of guilt that always accompanied the remembrance of where he'd learned those skills. Tonight he couldn't allow the regret and remorse to stop him, as he had so many times before.

He fingered her through the embellished fabric, found the tiny peak of her nipple, and squeezed it lightly between his finger and thumb. It beaded up, a small nub so nearly the size and texture of the heart of one of the flowers that he nearly didn't recognize it at first. His heart gave a heavy, hopeful thump.

"Cleo." He nudged her onto her back and looked down at her in a rectangle of moonlight. Her eyes were wide, her face expressionless. She reached down, lifted her nightgown to her waist, and spread her legs. Always the dutiful wife, making it simple, submitting to her husband. Ensuring he got his husbandly rights over with as quickly as possible.

But not tonight.

In business he was a careful and persistent man, undeterred by difficulties. He used that perseverance now, in something that was ever so much more important to him. When he lowered his head to kiss her and she turned slightly to face the window, he kissed her cheek instead, her temple, her ear, the corner of her mouth. He did nothing to shock her, nothing she could arm herself against. His hands insinuated themselves over her skin, the contact so light she would not be tempted to avoid it.

The moon dropped lower in the sky, slanted light in a glowing rectangle across the bed as he explored his wife. Would it have been different between them, all these years, had he had the knowledge and the control to do this on their wedding night?

She was as lovely now as she had been then. Her breasts were fuller, hips wider . . . The fact that it was his child that caused those womanly changes enchanted him. He loved the curve to her belly, the soft cushion of her thighs.

And, slowly, he found barely perceptible evidence of what he sought. Cleo's chest rose and fell on a deeper breath. Her lips parted, just a shade. When he drew a line down her center with the tip of his finger, there was the slightest of quivers.

Oh, at last! He could barely contain his own excitement, one that was only in its least part sexual.

He sucked in a breath, held it as he slid his hand down farther, over her stomach, and deeper still. He fluttered his fingers lightly, and when she lifted her hips toward his touch he almost shouted for the joy of it. He heard a sob of pleasure, the sweetest sound he'd heard since his daughter's first cry.

Then she knocked his hand away, a sharp whack of her fist across his wrist that sent pain shooting straight up his arm and into his chest. Confused, he looked up to discover he'd misinterpreted her sob completely. Wetness glistened over her cheek, reflecting moonlight like diamonds strewn over satin.

And then he knew. No matter what he did, no matter what he'd learned, Cleo would never respond to him. She would never *allow* herself to.

He hurled the covers aside and vaulted from the bed in one violent motion.

"Phillip?" she asked quietly.

He didn't look at her. He couldn't.

Naked, he strode through his house, the mansion he'd built for her, for their family, and returned to the sanctuary of his study. He picked up the glass he'd abandoned, noting how the moonlight sparkled on cut crystal as brilliantly as the tears had glistened on her cheek.

He hurled the glass into the hearth, shattering it into a million pieces.

Chapter 6

"Thank you, Olivia, that was lovely." With a nod of approval, Anthea dismissed Olivia Cox after her recitation. The girl was as quick as they came, hungry to learn, and so despite her unfortunate tendency to shriek loud enough to be heard in Kansas City whenever one of the boys teased her—which, of course, only encouraged them to exploit that tendency at every opportunity—she was still one of Anthea's favorite students.

With a sigh Anthea surveyed her classroom, alert for hints of budding trouble. Billy Pruitt was half off of his bench, aiming for the temptation of Mina Culbertson's copper-bright braids. Mina did not suffer such torment meekly, as evidenced by the wheel-sized splotch on the far wall where Mina's inkpot had hit and splattered when she'd pitched it at Billy's head last week.

It was not to their teacher's credit that she secretly wished that Mina had better aim.

"Billy!" she said sharply with her best warning scowl, and he slunk back to his spot.

Her second week on the job had gone scarcely better than the first, though Anthea was at least getting better at anticipating trouble and heading it off at the pass rather than merely responding to crises.

Lily sat far in the back of the room in her preferred spot near the door, and Anthea felt her heart soften every time she looked in that direction. Anthea was afraid she'd made little progress on the academic front with Lily thus far, but once, when she'd bent over the girl to show her how to form the letters of her name, she'd surprised such a pure, bright smile out of her that Anthea realized right then and there why teachers took on this miserable job after all. She could continue on a long time, just on the promise of receiving a smile such as that from one of her pupils.

The Pietzke boys were wiggling in place as if their pants contained an entire colony of biting ants. In the back, Charlie Skinner shifted from hip to hip, finally tipping the book he was reading entirely off his lap. It fell to the floor with a thud that caused the entire room to glance up for a moment. A giggle burst from Olivia, which she quickly squelched by the effective technique of clapping a hand over her mouth.

The Krotochvill boys were seated back to back, using each other for support, while they scratched a slate pen across the slates they balanced on their knees. And little Jennie Bickersdyke, her youngest student, had her tongue tucked between her brand-new front teeth as she tried valiantly to trace the alphabet on a torn piece of paper smoothed across one bony knee.

If Phillip Cox had been there at the moment, she would have whacked him over the head with her measuring stick then and there. How could he, and the two other skinflints who comprised the school board, believe the school to be adequately supplied? She'd like to see them spend an entire day with *their* butts planted on the rough, warped boards that passed as benches and not waste all *their* energy wiggling instead of learning. And just how was she supposed to teach appropriate penmanship when her students had no solid surfaces upon which to write?

Anthea admitted to herself that her patience was worn a bit thin around the edges. She was verging on exhaustion, both from long days in the schoolroom and, she had to admit, a few short nights' sleep. For each time she crawled into bed, she found herself listening for the crunch of a heavy boot outside her window.

But she hadn't seen Mr. Jackson once.

It disturbed her that, despite her best efforts, she kept anticipating his arrival. But he'd promised to teach her to shoot. Although reliability was probably not among Mr. Jackson's most prominent qualities. And she'd half expected to have him come charging in, temper blazing, to complain on Tuesday evening, since she'd spent a full half hour that day teaching the niceties of formal introduction.

Not that she wasn't perfectly *relieved* that he seemed to have decided to leave her alone after all.

Still and all, however, she'd had enough.

"Get up," she said, more sharply than she'd intended.

Sixteen pairs of eyes lifted in surprise.

"You, there." She pointed at several of the largest boys. "I want all these benches moved up against the outside walls." They were quick to comply.

"From now on—until I can convince the school board we are in severe need of proper desks—you may sit on the floor and write on the planks themselves," she said when all the planks were rearranged to her satisfaction.

"Sit on the *floor*?" Olivia Cox's striking dark blue eyes went wide. "But . . . that wouldn't be proper, would it?" Olivia had embraced Anthea's lessons in deportment as if she'd been born to them. Anthea suspected that, even at her young age, Olivia's sights were set far beyond the borders of Haven. And Kansas itself, for that matter.

"There are instances when practicality must be paramount, and one must use prudent judgment to recognize them," Anthea told her. "It is certainly not beneficial to have one's back permanently bent from the strain, and one's penmanship illegible, from being required to work under grossly inadequate conditions."

Yes, this was much better, Anthea decided. There were obvious advantages to having the boys' side of the room separated from the girls' by such a broad expanse. Just let Billy try to sneak across unnoticed now.

Anthea glanced at her lifeline, her precious copy of Welche's Teachers Classification Register, frowning when she saw that geography was scheduled next. While it was undoubtedly an important topic, she'd yet to find a way to engage her students' interest in it. Luxembourg didn't seem vitally important, she supposed, when one had never ventured more than thirty miles from Haven.

She forced an enthusiastic smile. "Now then, for our geography lesson." It took all her discretion not to echo her charges' groans of protest. "Let's try something other than a recitation today, shall we?"

"Yes, *ma'am.*" While Theron Matheson's words were always scrupulously polite, the expression on his face was far from it—at best skeptical, frequently downright snide. "A geography *bee,* I suppose."

Theron was not enthusiastic about the various competitions she'd instigated to encourage and inspire the students. She might have understood his distaste if he'd been a poor student, but he was naturally clever, if somewhat lazy. She'd finally concluded that Theron would dislike anything his teacher suggested. One of these days, she speculated, Theron would protest *lunch.*

"Actually, I was wondering if any of you had ever been taught how to dance."

"Dance?" the Krotochvill boys chorused in unison, their tones equally appalled.

"Yes, dance," she said firmly. It was hardly approved curriculum. But as far as she could tell, approved curriculum wasn't nearly as effective as it was supposed to be.

"I can polka," Jennie Bickersdyke piped up.

"You can not!" her brother protested.

"I can too—"

"I was thinking more of a cotillion," Anthea put in quickly, having already had ample experience with sibling disagreement.

The students stared at her, wide-eyed, mouths open in shock.

Olivia was the first to recover, prettily pink-cheeked with excitement. "Could you really teach us to dance, Miss Bright?"

"Well, I don't see why not."

"We can't dance," little Anna Culbertson said soberly. "Papa's a Presbyterian."

"Oh." Now, there was a bit of a dilemma. She could hardly ask her students to go against their parents' beliefs, even if she herself considered dancing to pose slight danger to their moral development. They would hardly be waltzing cheek to cheek, after all.

But if the boys looked relieved, the girls appeared on the verge of mutiny at the prospect of having their plans spoiled.

"It's not as if there'd be any music . . ." Anthea mused.

Mina, who'd commenced pouting the moment her sister had spoken, now smiled slyly. "Besides, *Mama's* a Methodist."

"Well, that's all right then, isn't it?" She couldn't see the harm in it. She truly intended for it to be a geography lesson, and there'd be no music at all. Not even vocal, for to her everlasting dismay, Anthea's singing was little better than no music. And the children would scarcely touch each other. In fact, the "dancing" she proposed was hardly different from organizing a game of red rover at recess, wasn't it?

"Come here, Olivia." She indicated a spot near the boys' side of the room. "You'll be France."

Her attention then focused on the boys, who were all trying to shrink into the wall to avoid being the first one forced to brave the dance floor.

"Charlie, if Olivia's France, and I'm standing in the middle of England, where's Austria?"

Anthea's spirits rose as she arranged the children around the room in the guise of all the European nations she could dredge out of her memory. She'd always loved dancing. Though she couldn't sing on key if her life depended on it, she possessed an unerring sense of rhythm. "Now, for the first steps."

More moans from the boys, a bit louder this time. But by now Anthea was inspired. "Theron, during the German unification, where did Prussia attack during the seminal battle?"

While Theron might be thoroughly suspicious of both dancing and his teacher, war was an activity much dearer to his heart.

"Denmark."

"Very good. So you, as von Bismarck, shall walk over to 'attack' Michael. No, no, you can't charge!" She hurried to intervene as Theron drew an imaginary sword and prepared to hurl himself into battle. "On my count. Walk *slowly*, one step with each beat. One . . . two . . ."

"I'd be bleeding dead on the field if I attacked that slowly."

Anthea smiled. "I suppose you would. Still, for our purposes—"

"This sure ain't like anythin' *I* ever learned in school," Gabriel Jackson drawled.

Thankfully, Anthea had her back to the door. While it had left her unprepared for his interruption, it also shielded her expression from Mr. Jackson. She took a moment to compose herself before she turned to face him.

"That is undoubtedly true, Mr. Jackson. What is unclear is exactly what you *did* learn there."

The low buzzing from the female side of the room reminded Anthea so much of the women in Stoddard's store that she figured the daughters of Haven must have been listening to their mothers far more than the elder ones would have appreciated.

"Is there something I can do for you?" she asked with stiff formality.

He looked even more disreputable than usual. His denims were worn across the knees, and looked like they were bought before he grew to his current proportions, they clung so tightly to his powerful frame. His shirt was open at the neck, of course—she wondered if he ever buttoned up properly—and a tear in the left sleeve exposed a hefty slice of solidly muscled biceps. He still hadn't trimmed his hair, and it curled long and shaggy against his threadbare collar.

"Nope. Just figured I should see what you're doing in school."

Completely at ease, he dropped to the floor and propped himself against the wall.

"Ain't you gonna make *him* take his hat off?" Theron said, a jeer streaking beneath his words.

Mr. Jackson arched one brow, a look that said he'd more than welcome her attempts to rid him of his hat this time. And that he wouldn't be caught by surprise again.

"He's not one of my students, Theron. And I am certain that even Mr. Jackson would be willing to admit that he is hardly an appropriate person upon whom to model one's manners." She hoped her smile was far more serene than she felt. "Besides which, he won't be staying long."

"Oh, I think I'll be staying awhile."

"While your concentrated interest in Lily's education is quite commendable, I really can't encourage interruptions during the hours that school is in session. We have too much work to do to countenance visitors during that time, but I'd be pleased to discuss . . . whatever it is you wish to discuss this time . . . with you after the children are released for the day."

He bent one knee and rested his wrist on it, looking by all accounts like he was settling in for the duration. "Don't mind me." He waved his hand at her. "Carry on."

"I really must ask you to leave."

"Quiet as a mouse, that's me. You'll never know I'm here."

As if *that* could ever happen. His compelling presence flooded whichever room he entered, lodging irrevocably in her consciousness.

The buzzing from the girls notched up to a recognizable twitter. Mr. Jackson appeared to have a gift for sparking that sound among clusters of women wherever he went.

The boys, on the other hand, were absolutely delighted by his appearance. The Pietzke twins were visibly relieved to have Anthea's dance lesson interrupted, and Theron was obviously gleeful at the prospect of his teacher being taken down a peg.

She could not afford, she decided, to have Jackson's presence interrupt her stated lesson plan. There'd be no hope of her ever regaining her tenuous control of the classroom if she didn't stand her ground now.

"If you insist upon remaining, I suppose I can hardly throw you out."

"Well, now, isn't that the most gracious invitation you ever heard?"

Determined to ignore his presence, Anthea threw herself into choreographing her dancers. Though she had to acknowledge that her monotonous, if emphatic, "one, two, three" made a poor substitute for the lively strains of a string trio. Not to mention that demonstrating European history made for some uniquely interesting steps. But the children's delight at being released from yet another recitation was infectious. She assigned Lily Switzerland and even lured her into attempting a few halting steps.

So Anthea was smiling happily, warm and flushed with the exertion of demonstrating an exceptionally energetic maneuver, when she nearly tripped over Mr. Jackson's great big feet and had to do a quick sidestep, arms wheeling, to regain her balance.

"Oh, excuse me, Mr. Jackson. I hadn't realized . . . well, I should have been more careful."

"Yes, you should." His mouth angled down, a handsome scowl he'd worn all afternoon growing deeper as the session progressed. It took little intuition to discern what he thought of her innovative lesson plan. His forbidding expression didn't intimidate her as it once had, however.

At least, she didn't think it did. Never mind the shaky tremor in her chest when he lifted his strong chin and fixed his blue dark eyes directly on her.

"I'm afraid I tend to get carried away in my enthusiasm."

"I noticed that about you right off."

Now, why would such a simple statement, and an obviously polite one at that, have her cheeks heating? Maybe just the fact that he wasn't the type of man to mouth automatic pleasantries, and so she kept looking for hidden meanings in everything he said.

It was a habit she simply *must* break.

"You should dance with her, Mr. Jackson." At Anthea's startled glance, Olivia dimpled prettily. Innocently, one might even have thought. If one hadn't had as many years of experience with scheming sisters as Anthea had.

"I really don't think that's appropriate."

"Oh, yes, please!" The rest of the girls chimed.

"We'd get *ever* so much better an idea of what the steps are supposed to look like!"

That was quickly followed by a chorus of the ever-popular *"Please,"* delivered with the wheedling whine that had pried many a concession from reluctant men since females had first discovered the efficacy of that particular entreaty.

"He can be Russia," Lily ventured.

It was the largest collection of words anyone in the room except Gabriel had ever heard her string together, and it was enough to silence them all.

She clearly regretted her speech immediately. She dropped her gaze to her toes and picked at her thumbnail as soon as she realized everyone's attention had swung to her.

Anthea dropped to her knees in front of Lily. Gently she smoothed back a hank of hair—it was still thin and dull, but now at least it was scrupulously clean—allowing her to look into her face.

"Lily?" she asked softly.

"That's the biggest one, ain't it? Russia?"

Anthea caught her breath on a bubble of exultation. "Yes," she said carefully, trying to keep from startling her. "That's perfect."

Her eyes met Jackson's. While the last thing in the world she wanted to do was dance with him, there was no longer any choice. Lily must be rewarded for the risk she'd just taken in speaking out in front of the other children. Surely he understood that.

Holding her gaze the entire time, he unfolded from the floor, so her head had to tip back as he stood all the way up. *Way* up, more than a foot taller than she, and even more with that infernal hat. He was as intriguingly forbidding as a deep, dangerous, dark mine that held the promise of fabulous gems within.

Perhaps she could recall a dance in which he would not actually have to *touch* her, she thought frantically. Or invent one; how would he know the difference? For to put her hand into his, even in such innocent circumstances, seemed somehow irrevocable. How would she ever be able to continue to keep him at the appropriate distance, the very *necessary* distance, if she finally knew what her hand felt like in his?

She couldn't remember what *any* man's hand felt like. It seemed a perilous thing, to retain only the feel of Gabriel's hand and no others'.

He took a step toward her, and her foolish, misbehaving heart fluttered.

"I don't dance."

Anthea shoved a damp rag across the battered floorboards of the schoolhouse and cursed Gabriel Jackson with each swipe.

Swoosh.

Infuriating.

Scrub.

Arrogant.

Swab.

Overbearing.

Swish.

Male!

Anthea sat back on her heels and shoved a damp hank of hair off her forehead with the back of her wrist, surveying her work with satisfaction. Working off her frustrations rather than stewing in them was a new habit she was dutifully attempting to cultivate. If it didn't exhaust her enough to allow her to finally fall asleep tonight before her spinning thoughts got so twisted up she'd never drop off, at the very least she'd have something productive to show for it.

After he'd refused to dance with her in front of the entire class—not that she wanted to dance with *him*, but it was the principle of the thing—he'd snagged Lily and left the schoolhouse without so much as a cursory excuse. Twenty minutes before the end of the school day! What kind of example was that for his daughter? Not to mention the rest of Anthea's less-dedicated students.

Yellow-bellied, that was what he was, she thought with vengeful glee, and wished she had the opportunity to call him that to his face. Outright scared, and of something so simple as a dance.

The floor of the schoolhouse would never again gleam; it had taken too many years of abuse for that. However, she'd managed to scour off at least the first layer of grime.

Nice to know that *he* was good for something, if only incentive.

She dunked the cloth in the pail of gray, soapy water by her side, sloshing with abandon, and put her back into ridding the floorboards of a dark splotch that she was afraid even to speculate upon the origin of.

With the worst of her fury burned off, there was room for the worry to seep in. Better that Mr. Jackson returned to renew her anger; anger, she could deal with.

Worry . . . worry, she didn't like at all.

Finally surrendering to the obvious truth—the stain had defeated her—she dropped the disintegrating rag into the pail and sat up. The paper in her pocket crinkled as she straightened. She'd received the letter from her sisters earlier that day, scanned it quickly because she couldn't wait, and tucked it away for meticulous examination later. Her shoulders and legs protested the unaccustomed exertion, so she decided to stay where she was on the floor and pulled out the letter.

It was a breezy and cheerful missive, pure Kate. Anthea frowned over it, trying to decipher the truth behind the clutter of a sprightly recitation of daily activities. While Anthea felt restricted to a close, if somewhat rosy-colored, approximation of the truth, Kate wasn't generally hampered by such compunctions. Kate would lie without a blink if it would protect either of her younger sisters.

Her frown deepened when she reached the paragraph where Kate related the progress of Emily's lessons.

I've pulled Emily out of that school. The teacher is woefully ineffectual, spending more time in trying to control her wayward students than in actually teaching.

Anthea winced, Kate's assertion skimming a bit too close to home.

I will not have Emily's education hindered. So I've determined to instruct her at home until I can find a more appropriate and congenial situation for her, one

*where her gifts will be appropriately nurtured. She is
still sunshine itself, of course (I do not know how she
managed to escape inheriting both my temper and
your penchant for worry!), and she maintains that
whatever arrangements are best for me are naturally
so for her. But I'm finding it quite enjoyable—perhaps
you are not the only one destined to teach!—and with
my focused attention and without the varied distractions of the schoolroom, she is making wonderfully
rapid progress.*

*Besides which, it keeps me occupied. Wouldn't do
for me to be lured into indolence, or even worse, when
she's in school all day, would it?*

That made Anthea smile. Kate was as congenitally
incapable of indolence as she was unwilling to suffer
fools.

The explanation *sounded* perfectly reasonable. However, Anthea couldn't help but wonder if Kate had actually withdrawn Emily from her school to save the
expense of tuition.

Sighing, Anthea refolded the letter and tucked it
safely back into her pocket. There was nothing she
could do about that immediately. She would send
every penny of her pay to them as soon as she received
her first month's wages and pray that it was enough.

As long as she didn't lose her job before the month
was up, that was.

And that seemed a likelier possibility than she'd
ever expected. She couldn't help but mentally count
down the trouble she'd managed to get into in a few
short weeks. First the conflict over allowing Lily Ross
in the school. Then being seen in Mr. Jackson's com-

pany . . . more than once. And, of course, her deviations from the typical curriculum.

All in all, she was hardly looking forward to her first official school board meeting next week with glowing anticipation.

Of course, nearly all of it was Gabriel Jackson's fault. Goodness knew it *had* to be his fault. She generally didn't put much stake in gossip. And she really didn't see how the weather could be laid at his door. But, since apparently a good half of the things that had occurred in Haven the last two and a half decades were his responsibility, why not her current difficulties, too?

Pursing her lips, she studied the length of the stovepipe that made its way across the cracked ceiling before turning abruptly to thrust through the roof, its exit marked with a wavering, black, cloud-shaped smear of soot spreading over a good six-foot area. She doubted anyone had tried to clean or repair the stove since the day it had been installed.

Since scrubbing the floor had proved grossly inadequate to the task of evicting *him* from her mind, perhaps the challenge of cleaning the stovepipe would do the trick.

Chapter 7

Gabriel worked in his fields, rooting out the blasted, stubborn stands of wild mustard and sunflowers that insisted on sprouting right in the middle of his wheat, and cursed Anthea Bright with each whack of his hoe.

Stubborn, opinionated *woman*.

He heaved the tool in a giant arc, sliced it down hard. The tangle of weeds gave way easier than he'd expected, and he nearly whacked off his toes in the process.

Women and working never did mix well, he thought sourly.

He leaned on the handle of the hoe, yanked a crumpled kerchief out of his back pocket, and mopped the sweat off his forehead. The unusually warm autumn seemed determined to hang on as long as it could, causing his winter wheat to sprout faster than he'd anticipated. If this kept up, it'd be too big, he guessed, to survive the winter. But then, what the hell did he know about it?

Damn, but he hated farming. Always had. Farming was too much in the grip of things a man had no control over, luck and the weather and whatever some rich guy somewhere decided to pay for a wagonload of grain. He much preferred to work at something in which his own effort and brains had more to do with the final result.

He'd never intended to plant this land, any more than he'd ever wanted to own it. When he'd come back to Haven last March on one of his infrequent visits to his mother, he'd intended to stay for only a week or two. But he'd found her failing faster than he'd realized, and decided to stay. To wait for her to die, if the truth be told. She might not have been everyone's idea of a good mother, but she'd loved him, and deserved better than to die alone.

But she'd lingered, and he'd found himself at loose ends. Almost on a whim, he'd planted a few fields of sorghum and oats. It'd brought in a few dollars and kept him from going stir-crazy from sitting by his mother's bedside all day. Better to grub in the fields, he'd figured, than to run into town and take his frustrations out on a few hard heads.

Not that those heads didn't damn well deserve it.

After harvest, when it looked like his mother would hang on for who knew how much longer, chaining him there, he'd taken his small profits and plowed them back into the land. What the hell, he'd figured. Maybe he'd have enough before he returned to Colorado to buy that pretty little mare he had his eye on.

But then there'd been Lily. And then his mother had just up and died one night, only a few days after he'd begun to believe maybe she was going to recover after all. By then it'd been too late, the seed already in the ground, Lily to deal with, and he'd been stuck in Haven for at least a few months longer.

He'd've rather been stuck in hell than in Haven.

Which brought him back, of course, to that infernal schoolteacher.

Troubled, he gazed back across the width of the fields, the bright green of the new wheat seedlings at odds with the autumn gold of the rest of the landscape, to where Lily played in the shadow of the house. She pulled a string for the old gray mouser that was never more than a few inches from her side except when she went to school.

He wished there were someone—anyone—to tell him what was the right thing to do. He thought longingly of the wise advice of Sam Conner, his partner in the ranch. Sam had raised three of his own, two fine young sons and a lovely daughter—not to mention Gabriel, who'd been a wild and hot-tempered seventeen when they'd met—and would certainly know better than Gabriel the right thing to do.

He'd watched Lily as she'd danced—though even Gabriel had to admit what the children had done could scarcely be called dancing—under Miss Bright's careful encouragement. Lily had bloomed and brightened, her usually grave expression lightening to something that, while it wasn't quite happiness, at least allowed for the possibility of it.

She needed that so much. Miss Bright's feminine attention clearly had an effect on Lily that Gabriel didn't. Couldn't.

And yet . . . he was so afraid that the teacher's blind and sheltered optimism would break Lily's heart. Give her hopes and dreams that had nothing to do with the real world, with Lily's world.

He grabbed his hoe and strode across the fields. He propped it against the side of the house and squatted down next to Lily, which sent the suspicious cat slinking off around the corner. Lily's withdrawal was less obvious but no less complete. Her shoulders hunched and she turned to the side, so all he saw was the fall of her hair as she scratched a design in the dirt with a pointed stick.

Gabriel longed to just scoop her up and hold her tight until her wariness of him vanished. But since he figured that was more likely to terrify her, he remained where he was, careful to keep his gestures small, the distance between them consistent.

"Look's like it's gonna rain."

Lily sneaked a quick glance at the low, gunmetal clouds gathering in the west. She shrugged and nodded, then drew her brows together in concentration as she etched another line in the dust.

"What are you doing?"

She tucked her tongue in her cheek. *"L."*

"L?" With a little imagination—though Gabe had never been blessed with much imagination—the dirt scratches could possibly have been an *L*. "For Lily?"

She bobbed her head again.

She seemed so fragile, her hold on the earth no deeper than the shallow letters scraped into the bare ground, as easily wiped away. He hated to think of what kinds of things the other children, the children who had proper parents and proper homes, said to her. His hands flexed in anger. Why couldn't they, who had everything given to them, be kind to Lily, who'd lost what little she'd ever had?

Anthea would blunt their cruelty as much as she could. He trusted her inherent fairness that much, at least. But maybe he should just take Lily from Haven as fast as possible, and the hell with the wheat. It wouldn't be the first money he'd ever wasted in his life. He could make more.

Despite what her fancy teacher thought, Lily would never be welcomed in elegant ballrooms and shiny drawing rooms. But Gabe didn't figure that mattered so much—neither would he. And there were plenty of people in the world, ordinary, decent people, people who hadn't grown up on tales of wicked Clarinda Ross and the bad blood she'd passed on to her daughter, who'd at least give Lily a fair chance.

"Lily?" he asked gently. "Are you ready to leave?"

She looked up at him in surprise. "Go to school?"

"No, not to school." He swallowed hard. Maybe he shouldn't give her a choice. Maybe he should just make it for her.

But no one had ever given *him* a choice, not until he'd been old enough to take it. He couldn't bear to do the same to her. "No, away from here." He paused, trying to find the words that would appeal to a little girl. "This isn't my home, Lily. I have a place, far away. You would like it, I think. I have a friend, Sam. He'd love to be your friend, too."

She tilted her head to the side like a little bird. He couldn't read her expression. Not acceptance, but not rejection, either. At least she was listening. "And horses—you could have your own horse. I could teach you to ride."

Lily turned her attention to the west again. Not to

the freshening storm, but to the cluster of cottonwoods that hugged a bend in the creek. To the shady little oasis where he'd buried both her mother and his himself because Reverend Shute had declined to have such sinners contaminate the sacred ground of his church's cemetery, Gabriel recalled with a fresh surge of anger. Even though they both knew full well there were worse sinners buried there. His mother, and Lily's, had hardly sinned alone, had they?

And if what he'd sometimes suspected was true, his sire occupied an honored spot in the churchyard, just as Lily's would likely claim one when the time came.

"Well, Lily, what do you think?"

Through the thin hanks of her hair, he caught the gleam of moisture in her eyes. She looked back down at the ground and scratched a long, wavering line in the dirt.

Well then, Gabriel thought. *That's that, at least for now.*

"Do you know what comes after *L* in Lily?"

She shook her head, drew the lower leg of the letter.

"Would you like me to show you?"

After a long moment, she solemnly handed him her writing stick. He swallowed hard and took it.

"It's an *I*. First you draw another line, like this . . ."

Anthea went to sleep with her sheets over her head. The sky opened up just before she retired for the night, and she quickly decided she'd rather suffocate than risk having dirt, and heaven only knew what things she'd rather not think about, rain down on her from the ceiling. For surely the dirty strip of muslin tacked to the underside of the sod ceiling would not long withstand such a downpour.

She awoke slowly, without any sense of the time,

and gingerly poked her nose above the edge of the sheet. A trailing end of unraveling thread tickled her nose, and she brushed it away.

Her home—her *room*—was dark under the best of circumstances, making it difficult to judge the time accurately. Still, a graying rectangle lightened the far wall, about where the window should be, so she guessed it must be daylight.

She rolled the sheet toward the foot of the bed, the blankets inside, hoping to fold . . . whatever . . . inside. If snakes or worms had dropped there during the night, it was not a discovery she was prepared to deal with before coffee.

Mud squished between her bare toes as she climbed out of bed and she grimaced, adding washing her feet to the list of chores to be accomplished before school began.

But the mud outside her door was not nearly so malleable, she discovered when she tiptoed outside to head for the necessary. For sometime during the night, the temperature had plunged abruptly, freezing the rain-softened ground into hard ruts.

Might as well look on the bright side. The sod walls insulated as well as advertised. And if winter had truly arrived, there'd be no more rainstorms to endure until at least March.

It was later than she'd realized, and she rushed through dressing, grabbing a handful of crackers and a thin slice of cheese before hurrying across the distance to the schoolhouse, munching as she went.

Huge, dark splotches marred the sides of the schoolhouse as she approached. She squinted, trying to make them out. The sides of the structure hadn't been white for a long time, but the weathered gray they sported now wasn't nearly as black as this.

Mud balls, she realized when she neared. Great, sloppy handfuls of mud plastered the entire building. They spattered over the windows, smeared down the sides, clumped heavily under the eaves like wasps' nests.

And they'd all frozen as hard as the ground, she discovered when she experimentally prodded one with her finger. It would take a chisel to pry them all off, she thought, and set to work.

By the time the first student arrived, a corncob fire sputtered merrily in the stove, two big tin buckets of water wisping out their first steam on top.

Theron showed up, his eyes eager and bright as he poked his head in the door. Theron, who usually dragged in at the absolute last moment, delaying his entrance as if every second of freedom was precious.

"Gee, Miss Bright, what happened outside? I know it rained last night, but I never heard of it coming down like that."

"A fascinating phenomenon, isn't it?" she replied cheerfully. "So much so that I've decided to put aside our scheduled lesson plan for the day in favor of studying physical properties. Specifically, the effect of temperature changes on water as well as on an emulsion of Kansas dirt and water."

"Huh?"

She got up from her desk, crossed to the stove, snagged one of the steaming buckets by its handle, and handed it to him with a large rag torn from an old sheet well sacrificed to the cause. "We're going to clean the schoolhouse," she told him serenely. "And while we're at it, perhaps you'd care to theorize on just how all that mud managed to attach itself to the walls."

Not bad, Anthea thought, eyeing the cluster of students scrubbing down the front side of the schoolhouse. All the other walls were, if not sparkling, certainly cleaner than before they'd begun.

It had been . . . She would not go so far as to say the day had been *fun,* but it had been satisfying. They'd reversed their usual routine, spending their recess and lunch hour inside, where she'd fortified them with hot cider spiked with cinnamon and the warm oatmeal-nut cake she'd stirred up before school, which even she had to admit turned out nicely. She thought most of the children considered themselves well compensated for their efforts.

She'd assigned the girls the task of toting warm water to the cleaning crew and hunting sharp, sturdy sticks to scrape at the mud spots where water and cloth proved inadequate. She'd originally set the younger boys to the same task, but they soon campaigned successfully to be allowed to do "men's" work as well.

In the midst of—mostly—industrious activity Anthea managed to squeeze in a surprising amount of instruction. They poked at the heavy crust of ice glazing a deep puddle and speculated on why the ice would float when most solids sank, and discussed the implications of that fact. They theorized how long it would be before the ice in the nearby stream froze solid enough for skating. And they conducted a rousingly competitive spell-down at the same time they scrubbed at the walls.

"Jon?" The oldest Krotochvill towered over her, perhaps taller even than Mr. Jackson, and then she pushed him determinedly from her mind. She simply must stop having stray thoughts about that man. "There's one last clump, over there above the door. Do you think you can reach it?"

He grinned at her, happy that he'd gotten to spend the day out-of-doors rather than cooped up in the schoolhouse. "Sure thing, Miss Bright."

"Excellent." Hands on hips, she stood back, searching for any missed spots. "You've been a wonderful help today, Jon. Thank you."

Unaccustomed to praise, he flushed and bobbed his head in acknowledgment, then turned his attention to the last frozen mud ball with renewed energy.

Giggling burst around the corner of the building, followed by a chorus of "shush!" and then a dead silence that every teacher in the world, even such an inexperienced one as she, knew better than to ignore.

She'd left several of the students on that side, charging them with collecting the various pails and used rags left behind in their chores. She hurried around the corner now to find Lily's small, fragile figure in the middle of a tight circle of students.

"What's going on here?" she said, voice sharp with concern.

The children murmured low, incoherent, automatic demurrals. They moved back in a tight huddle, leaving Anthea a clear path to Lily.

"Lily?" Anthea bent down and smoothed Lily's hair back so she could look into her face. Her features were tight, eyes dull and controlled, the expression of one who'd learned well to give nothing of her inner self away to those who would find too much entertainment in it.

She didn't move.

"Aw, she's okay," Charlie said. "We was only funnin'."

Anthea shot him a look that shut him up immediately and returned her attention to Lily. Small chunks of mud studded her hair. Someone might have pitched handfuls at her, but it also could have happened innocently in the course of their day's efforts.

Dirty water had wicked up her skirt, darkening it to the knee. Beneath the short hem, mud splattered her shins and the gray of her sagging socks. But many of the other children looked every bit as disreputable; Lily *had* been clean when she'd arrived that morning.

And Anthea *would* do something about those outgrown skirts at the first opportunity, she resolved. No matter if Mr. Jackson objected or not.

She turned Lily around. And there . . . Now, *that* was not innocent at all.

Across Lily's back, the letters dark and smeared against her almost white shirt: BAS TURD.

Anthea had to swallow hard before she could force the words out of her tight throat. "Who did this?"

Silence. Anthea straightened and, hands on hips, marked them one by one. A few—Jennie, Olivia, Billy Pruitt—shifted uncomfortably under her scalding regard. Anna refused to meet her eyes entirely. Theron returned her glare with one of his own. Charlie sullenly dropped his gaze to the ground, scraping his toe in a wide arc.

Well, it couldn't be as easy as that, could it?

"I have a few questions for you, children," she said in a tone so pleasant several of the girls glanced up in surprise.

"Suppose—just suppose—one of your parents did a terrible thing. It was a mistake certainly, but say that, just for the purposes of our example, they were worried about you and had to steal a horse to get you to the doctor. They get caught. Should *you* be hanged for horse-stealing?"

"But we didn't do anything!" Ham Pietzke burst out.

Anthea merely looked at him impassively until what she'd just said registered. "Oh," Ham mumbled, and shoved his hands deep into his pockets.

"It's not the same," Charlie insisted.

"No, not precisely," Anthea admitted. "But while I would have preferred to avoid this topic entirely, as I deem it is *none*"—here she paused to glare at each student in turn, willing her words to sink in and take hold—"of our business what goes on in another family, I think the principle holds true that no one person should be held accountable for anyone's actions but their own."

Olivia Cox, cheeks bright, moved over to stand beside Lily. "Especially when they weren't even *born* yet when something happened. Isn't that right, Miss Bright?" she said, and Anthea could have hugged her.

"That's right." So here was one more topic the school board likely would take her to task for next week, Anthea thought glumly. Still, she couldn't let it pass unnoticed, as she was sure most of her students' parents would have preferred. "How many of your fathers voted for President Cleveland?"

The students exchanged puzzled glances, trying to find the trick in her question. Then Mina shrugged and lifted her hand. One by one, several followed suit.

With the exception of Theron, who kept his arms stiffly by his sides through sheer stubbornness, for Adonijah Matheson was the most devoted Democrat in town.

"There, you see?" She smiled with as much brightness as she could summon while her more cautious side screamed, *Anthea, what are you doing?* "He has a son, you know, that was born . . ." Oh, dear. "And you know that President Cleveland is a bachelor. If your fathers can forgive his . . . mistake . . . enough to elect him *president*, surely a *child* born, through no fault of his or her own, into such—" she paused delicately, prayed for the future of her job "—circumstances must be treated with all due respect and the Christian charity afforded to any other person."

A few of the boys nodded glumly, unhappy to have their fun spoiled. Softhearted Olivia looked as if she was about to burst into tears of guilt and sympathy at any second.

"Now that we're all agreed on that point." Anthea smoothed her expression, endeavoring to look as unthreatening as possible. "Who did this?"

She marked each student in turn; with the lone exception of Theron, who glowered back at her with clear defiance, all refused to meet her eyes. Guilt, apparently, was not enough to prod any student into breaking their code of complicity.

Briefly she pondered asking Lily directly. Lily, she suspected, would do anything her teacher asked, including reveal the culprit. But would that simply leave Lily open to even more distress? It seemed too likely to invite retribution to risk it.

"Since no one seems in the mood to confess for the sake of the others, I'll simply have to punish you all.

Tomorrow you shall spend the entire morning copying several long sections of the Bible, which I shall assign to you then."

Resigned grumbling rumbled through the group.

"And then, since people who choose to fling filth must also clean it up, you shall all spend the afternoon cleaning the necessaries from roof to floor. To *beneath* the floor, in fact." The structures desperately needed it, especially the boys', as thus far the smell had effectively deterred her from scrubbing the place herself.

The murmurs of protest burst into a chorus of pained yelps. Anthea held up her hand for silence. "Nevertheless, you shall do so. Unless you would all prefer I speak to your parents about your disobedience and unkindness."

They quieted abruptly. While Anthea suspected several parents might not have approved of all her actions, the children didn't know that. In many households, a bad report from the teacher meant an automatic trip behind the shed.

In the back of the group, Theron smiled slyly. "And by the way," Anthea went on, "anyone who is absent tomorrow—although I am certain you would be truly ill, and not trying to shirk your duties—will have the opportunity to perform their service *next* week. All by themselves."

Theron's smile vanished and Anthea bit back her own grin. If the students knew that someone *else* would be cleaning the necessaries next week, their usual lack of care was likely to become far, far worse.

"You're dismissed. Lily, would you stay for a moment? There's something you could assist me with, if you would be so kind."

Lily nodded solemnly.

As Theron brushed by Anthea, she tapped him on the shoulder. "Oh, and, Theron?"

He swung around, belligerence written large on his smooth young face. "Yeah?"

"Your penmanship is improving. However, your spelling still needs a fair amount of work."

Chapter 8

From a considerably less than stable perch on the high point of his roof, Gabriel scanned the sky, low, flat, and gray as tin, and wondered if it would snow before it got much colder. The seedlings needed insulation before the temperature really plunged and settled in for the duration. At least, so he'd been told when he purchased the seed.

He was probably the only man in Haven who actually *hoped* for snow. But then, he'd never thought the same as the other men about much of anything.

He inched over a fraction and slapped another shingle over a thin spot in the roof, grabbed a nail from the pouch he'd slung at his hip, and started securing the patch over one of a dozen leaks last night's rain revealed. Sometimes it felt like he'd spent half his life trying to keep this place together, when all he really wanted was to grab a sledgehammer and start tearing the place down—and not stop at the edge of his property, either.

But at least now he could afford real shingles. That was something.

"Hello!" a hearty male voice called from down below.

So who the hell could that be? Nobody had called on him since he'd been back. Nobody but Miss Bright, a nagging voice at the back of his head reminded him. He tried to convince himself that he wished she hadn't visited him either, but even he wasn't that good at lying to himself.

Gabriel skidded down the steep pitch of the roof on his butt, bracing his heels on the edge, and peered over.

Damn. How'd he not recognized that voice? It seemed odd that he hadn't; he would have thought he'd immediately have identified that voice in hell. Which was pretty much the only place he'd ever expected to hear it again.

Gabriel eased his way, crablike, back up to the top of the roof and dug out another nail, securing the shingle more firmly with a couple of whacks that were harder than the job required. Hard enough that he risked knocking a hole clear through the entire thing, and then where would he be?

Then he'd just have to pack up and take Lily out of town after all, he thought in sudden inspiration. It wouldn't be his fault at all; it would be fate.

"Can't you come down?"

"No," Gabriel said flatly, and punctuated it with a smack of the hammer against an already flattened nailhead.

"I need to speak with you."

This time Gabriel didn't even bother to answer.

The wooden ladder chattered against the side of the house where he'd left it. He resisted the urge to plant his boot on the top rung and shove.

He kept his grip on the hammer but let it fall to his side while he waited.

Phillip Cox hadn't changed much, Gabriel noted when the man popped his head over the edge of the roof. Which only went to prove, once again, that life wasn't fair. At the very least Phillip should have lost his hair or his teeth. Preferably both.

Phillip's eyes were cool and bright as he met Gabriel's, but there were lines arrowing from them, and deep scores bracketed his frown. Hard to tell if they were tension, or just the marks of age and having been a stiff-necked bastard for all of those years.

Phillip stayed where he was, manicured hands resting on the top rung of the ladder, waiting for Gabriel to speak first. Gabriel set his jaw and refused to give him the satisfaction.

"I came to inform you that your mortgage is in default. You have until tomorrow to vacate before the bank takes possession of this property."

Whatever reaction Phillip had expected, it wasn't Jackson bursting into laughter.

"Nice try, Cox. But I've a copy of the mortgage papers too, you know. And I know the next payment's not due until May."

"Oh?" Phillip raised one eyebrow while inside it was just *damn, damn, damn*. "When did you learn to read?"

Jackson's eyes blazed for just a second before his expression shut down. The man had ever been easy to needle. Phillip hadn't been more than nine or ten when he'd learned that the best way to deal with Jackson was to let his own temper hang him.

"Over the years I've learned *lots* of things you might be surprised at," Jackson said with a suggestive sneer.

For an instant Phillip saw red, pure, brutal red like sunset over a battlefield. His hands clenched around the top rung and squeezed as if they held the bastard's neck instead.

"I don't imagine most of them are things to be proud of," he managed with admirable smoothness.

"Learned enough not to be hornswoggled by lying bankers," Gabriel said, remembering that there'd been a time, very long ago—even before Cleo, and in truth Cleo was probably *because* of what Phillip had done to him—that Gabe had believed Phillip's smooth friendship and innocuous face. It had left him with his pants around his ankles, his ass on the crap hole, and the outhouse door wide for all the world to see.

Yeah, he'd learned a lot since then. Started learning right then, come to think of it. And began wondering just why Cox took such delight in his misery.

Cox's smile was as genial as it was artificial. "You can't blame a man for trying."

Gabriel met his eyes levelly. *Oh, yes you can.*

Finally Phillip looked away, his calculating gaze sliding over the roof, as worn and patched as an old quilt.

"This place is held together by spit and twine, and just barely at that," he commented.

Gabriel lifted one brow. "So?"

"It's not worth much," Phillip said, looking up at him. He wasn't used to looking up at anyone; he *hated* looking up at Jackson. He'd climb on up there himself, but Jackson had always been an unpredictable sort. If Phillip angered him, Jackson might take it in his head to shove Phillip right off the roof. And Phillip fully intended to anger him.

"You might as well turn it over now. You know you won't be able to pay the mortgage come spring, so why not forfeit it before the taxes are due? Save yourself the money, not to mention the trouble."

Jackson shrugged, unperturbed. "Got the wheat in already."

Phillip fought back a flutter of panic. He'd make this work. He always made things work. "I inspected those fields as I came in."

Gabriel scowled at him. "Don't go poking your nose in *my* fields."

"Technically speaking, the fields are as much mine as yours," he said. "They look a bit . . . straggly, don't they?"

The Turkey Red was worrying Gabriel a mite, too, but there was no way in hell he would admit that to Phillip Cox. "The Mennonites have had good luck with winter wheat west of here."

"Yes, I'd heard that." His lip curled. "But it's an odd concept, isn't it, planting in the fall? Around here, we generally stick to the tried and true. A most reasonable approach."

"Yeah, well, some people are drawn to . . . adventure." It was unfair, putting such heavy significance on the last word, and he knew it. He should have long outgrown needling that pompous ass about his wife. But apparently he hadn't, he thought as he watched Phillip's face flood with color.

"In fact," Gabriel went on, "I'm finding I rather like it here. A lot more than I used to. Maybe I'll stay this time."

The world wheeled around Phillip. He looked up at Gabriel, perched on that damn roof like the king of the world, and nearly lost his grip on the ladder.

When Gabe, three years younger than he, had been a kid, Phillip had beaten the stuffing out of him regularly. He hadn't known then why the poor little bastard annoyed him so, but he surely had. When Gabe was eleven, he started fighting back. When he was fourteen, he started winning. And when he was nearly sixteen, he . . .

Phillip's mind jerked back from the image as if it burned. It *did* burn, the picture of his beautiful Cleo, gasping and flushed in a way he could never make her, in Jackson's dark, unworthy arms.

He had to get Jackson out of town once and for all, he thought now, struggling for air. *He had to.*

It took everything in him to make himself speak normally. "I have a customer interested in this property," he lied smoothly. "He asked me to inform him as soon as the bank foreclosed this spring. However, all things considered, perhaps you'd be interested in cutting your losses and selling now?"

Afraid he'd give himself away, Phillip scarcely dared breathe.

Jackson seemed to consider the notion. "Why wouldn't I just sell it to him myself, then?"

Phillip strove to look regretful. "I'm afraid the man's not interested in dealing with you personally."

"That's too bad." Jackson shrugged and reached for a shingle, giving every indication of dismissing the matter. Phillip felt his panic rise again, pushing up against the base of his throat.

"I'm prepared to make you an excellent and generous offer on his behalf."

Clearly interested now, Jackson paused in midmotion. "How generous we talking about?"

Phillip gulped air and named a price fully twice as much as he knew the property was worth. But if it got Jackson out of town, it was worth every penny of that and then some.

Jackson rubbed his chin as if considering the offer. "I don't know, I—"

"Yoo-hoo!" a woman's voice sang out brightly, and Phillip bit back an uncharacteristic curse. He'd been so *close* to getting Jackson to agree; and he'd always made it a policy to close a deal fast, before the other party had enough time to think.

He glanced down to find that schoolteacher he'd hired. Gads, but he'd gotten her cheaply. He sure hoped he didn't have to fire her for consorting with undesirable elements.

Clutching her hand, so thin and small she looked as if she might blow away if she didn't cling so tightly, was the girl.

His heart twisted, a sharp, surprised stab before he could ward it off as he usually did. Deliberately he turned his attention back to Miss Bright, ignoring the child.

"You're home late today, Lily," Jackson said, and he slid down the roof with confident speed, digging in his heels and halting himself only a few feet from Phillip. Damn. For a second Phillip thought he might slide right off, saving Phillip no end of trouble.

"We had a few things to attend to, Lily and I." She lifted her face up to them, squinting into the brightness, and the late afternoon sunlight struck her face full force.

Why, the little teacher was actually vaguely attractive. Funny that he'd never noticed that about her before. But then, he wasn't given to noticing any woman but his wife.

"Oh, hello, Mr. Cox," she said politely. And then her gaze slid past him to Jackson, and her smile kicked up another notch. What *was* it about Jackson that intrigued women?

Maybe he'd fire her after all, the budget be damned.

"I'd like to speak to you, Mr. Jackson, if you've got the time."

"Sure." How *did* he do it? Miss Bright was gazing up at Jackson, her eyes dazzled, her cheeks pink. The merest possibility of that same expression on Cleo's face made him ill.

"Cox, if you'd move your butt down the ladder, I can do as the lady requests."

"Oh. My apologies. I was wool-gathering for a moment."

Unaccustomed to ladders, he cautiously made his way to the ground. After tipping his hat to the ladies, he stepped aside while Jackson slid down the ladder as if it were greased.

"I wasn't expecting you," Jackson said. His words were flat and unwelcoming, but a hint of a smile lifted the corners of his mouth, and his eyes gleamed. And not with wicked speculation, either—well, there was certainly a fair amount of that, but warmth simmered beneath it, too.

Well now, wasn't this interesting? While the expression on the teacher's face was hardly new, Cox would have bet a fair chunk of his fortune that Jackson wore that look only rarely, if ever.

Hmmm. Phillip's mind spun, sifting through possibilities. Perhaps he'd best keep Miss Bright around after all. Surely it would cast a pall on Cleo's precious memories if she saw Jackson besotted with another woman. He wondered if he could encourage the relationship.

Of course, he'd prefer to simply get Jackson safely out of town. Permanently this time. It was a more dependable strategy than hoping for Jackson's fickle attention to settle on such an ordinary woman.

Still, it was always preferable to have alternate plans. He felt better having at least one.

"I apologize," she said, her hand resting, light and reassuring, on the little girl's back. "I did not mean to worry you by keeping her so late. Lily was kind enough to stay after for a bit and assist me."

"She's an excellent worker," he said with a touch of pride.

"That she is." Miss Bright broke into a beaming smile, and Jackson looked about as happy as he ever got. Which wasn't exactly overjoyed, but was more than Phillip had ever seen.

"I'd like to speak to you, if you don't—" She broke off, her gaze sliding toward Phillip.

"You still here?"

"I was just leaving," Phillip said. Only a short time ago he would have objected forcefully to his daughter's teacher being alone in the company of the likes of Gabriel Jackson. Now he considered it a fine idea.

First things first, however. "I'll be by first thing in the morning, to work out the details of the sale—"

"I decided not to sell."

"But . . ." Phillip paused for a moment, allowing himself time to regroup. And his head to stop buzzing. "It's an excellent offer. You'll not get a better one."

"Not interested."

Striving for a bland countenance, Phillip attempted to strengthen his case. "Farming's a chancy business, as I'm sure you're aware, and your mother's land has never produced much. And, of course, there's always the possibility of natural disaster. Fires are common, as well you know, and—"

Jackson's eyes narrowed to glittering slits. "If one single spark catches anywhere on my land, you'll be answering to me. And that's a threat, just in case you didn't notice it."

Phillip drew himself up stiffly. "I was merely pointing out the vagaries of nature, not intimating a threat. And I certainly do not appreciate your implication otherwise."

"And I would not *appreciate* someone burning down my place."

"I see we have nothing further to discuss, until your mortgage is due, or you discover you can't pay your taxes after all. Or you decide you have enough sense to accept an offer that is far better than you had any right to expect."

He turned to Anthea, studying her so long and speculatively that she shifted uneasily. "My daughter speaks highly of you."

"She is a delightful child," Anthea returned. "As bright as she is lovely. You have every reason to be proud of her."

He beamed immediately, his smile broad and sunny and completely alien to his austere features.

He was a truly attractive man after all, Anthea realized. She'd never noticed it before beneath the frown that he always wore.

He sketched a courteous bow in her direction and took his leave.

"What was that about?" Anthea asked after he was out of earshot, tightening her hand around Lily's. "Are you leaving town?"

He contemplated her for a long moment. "Would it matter?"

"I . . ." For the life of her, Anthea couldn't come up with the proper answer to that question. "No" would imply a lack of interest and concern on her part. And would be a lie, she thought with a sinking feeling.

But "yes"—oh, there were dangers in yes, ones she knew and a dozen more she barely even suspected.

His quick, brief grin, as if he'd planned precisely the spot he'd put her in and delighted in it, let her off the hook.

"Not right this minute," he told her. "Mostly I was just pulling Cox along for the fun of it. But I will soon."

"But where will you go?" Better not to examine too closely why the notion disturbed her. But while it would have been easy to chalk it up to worrying over one of her favorite pupils, Anthea prided herself on facing herself honestly.

He shrugged, clearly unconcerned. "Got a ranch in the eastern part of Colorado. Raise horses and cattle and sheep—at least until we figure out which one is the most profitable. We're doing pretty good with all of them so far."

So much for her image of him as a struggling farmer, holding on to this meager piece of land by stubbornness and not much else.

"But if you've got someplace else to go, why didn't you sell this place?"

" 'Spose I will, eventually. But right now, hanging on to it annoys Cox enough to make it worth the trouble."

"Oh." She struggled to resist the temptation to ask more questions, probe deeper, learn something more of this surprisingly complicated and unpredictable man. But what would be the point? To become even more intrigued with him than she already was?

"So what is it that brings you out here this afternoon?" he asked, tugging a cloth from his back pocket and starting to work the dark streaks of grease and dirt from his long, lean fingers.

"I'd like to speak to you." She raised her eyebrows meaningfully and tilted her head in Lily's direction, hoping he'd take the hint.

Nevertheless, she was surprised when he picked up on it. He didn't really seem the type to notice subtleties.

"Lily? I've been up on that roof all day. I'm getting hungry. Would you mind going in and starting supper so we can eat early?"

Lily glanced suspiciously from Gabriel to Anthea. "Are you staying to eat?" she asked.

Oh, now, *there* was a right fine idea. Dinner in Gabriel Jackson's home. She could just imagine what Mr. Cox would have to say about that. Come to think of it, however, he hadn't seemed particularly concerned to see her here. Nor overly worried about leaving them alone together. "I won't leave without speaking to you first," Anthea told her.

Lily frowned, recognizing the kind of answer adults gave when they didn't want to say a real yes or no.

"You should stay," Lily said.

Anthea looked to Gabriel for help. He merely lifted one brow and waited, a faint smile curving his mouth.

"We'll see," Anthea temporized.

Lily had disappeared into the house before Gabriel rounded on the teacher. "So what did you do this time?"

Chapter 9

"**I** ...." She couldn't hold his gaze. Pink colored the curve of her cheek—anger, embarrassment, the crisp chill in the air? Maybe all three. Gabriel didn't know her well enough to be sure. It stunned him to discover how much he wanted to. Her slight shoulders shuddered beneath the fuzzy red shawl she wore over her charcoal-colored cloak, and he had a quick, potent flash of her shivering from something entirely different from the cold.

"Would you rather talk in the stables? It's warmer."

"If you don't mind. Yes, I'd like that." Anything for a five-minute reprieve, she thought.

From the outside, the structure looked as if it might fall down any moment, and so the inside surprised her. It was well kept, the marks of a twig broom on the scraped earth floor, a neat pile of striped blankets stacked on a chest in the corner. Well-oiled tack hung neatly from nails on the far wall, and the wood enclosing a box stall looked brand-new. The air, degrees warmer than outside, smelled of horses and hay, leather and sawdust.

"Tell me," he demanded.

The close quarters made them seem uncomfortably alone, him even larger than usual. She had to swallow hard before she could speak. "There was an incident at school today," she finally said. "Someone wrote on the back of her dress in mud. We washed it off after school, but . . . I'm not sure Lily even realized what it said. She didn't seem overly disturbed by the episode, but I thought you should know. In case she brings it up later."

As far as Gabriel could tell, Lily hadn't appeared particularly upset when she got home. But Anthea certainly was. The color in her cheeks became hectic, her eyes deeply blue with worry. A frown marked twin lines between her brows.

"What did they write?" he asked, words stripped of all inflection.

"Does it matter?"

"Yes."

Lily debated for an instant. He looked calm—too calm; his face was never that expressionless unless he was trying to hide everything behind it. Still, she didn't see how she could keep it from him.

She searched for a way to soften the word, found none. "Bastard."

He nodded as if he'd expected as much. "Who?"

"I don't know."

A muscle ticked in his jaw. "You really don't know, or you just won't tell me?"

Caught, she chose a careful line through the truth. "I suspect, yes. I have no evidence."

"I want to know."

"Why?"

He just stared at her, eyes fierce, arms rigid at his sides.

"That's what I thought," she said. "While I admire your wish to protect Lily, I can't have a hand in your running around assaulting children."

"I wouldn't beat them up," he said grudgingly.

"Oh?"

"I'd just put the fear of God in them."

"Fear of God and Gabriel Jackson, you mean."

"That too."

"It'll only make it worse for her, if they think she went running to tell. They'll just get sneakier about it."

He didn't answer, refusing to admit that she was right. For he'd told the teacher, all those years ago, and look what *that* had gotten him. Jumped by a full half dozen boys on the way home from school, that's what, both his face and pride badly bloodied. But *God*, he wanted it to be different for Lily. He wanted to *make* it be different for her.

"Unless you plan to keep her out of school permanently," Anthea said.

"What?"

"It's an option I've been considering." In the warmth of the stables, she slipped the shawl from her head, and her hair shone softly in the dim light, a healthy gleam. "She is definitely behind in her studies. I don't think I'm telling you anything you didn't already know in pointing that out. I could tutor her after school; with such concentrated attention, I believe she could make rapid progress. And she would not be subjected to the unkindness of the other children."

Gabriel pressed his thumb and forefinger to his eyes and blew out a concerned breath. "Do they *all* treat her badly?"

"No, not all of them. But none of them are likely to take her side in it, either. It would require a child of unique character and courage to be able to stand against all the rest."

He considered the teacher carefully, trying to decide if perhaps she was suggesting the easy way out, solving a difficult problem by the simplest solution: eliminating Lily from her classroom. And then he discarded that idea; whatever else she was—and he was certain she was wrong about very many things—he was convinced she had Lily's best interests at heart, even if her ideas on the subject differed greatly from his own.

"I don't know what's right," he said. "I didn't stick it out, and sometimes I wish I had."

"You didn't go to school?" she asked, clearly taken aback.

"Sure I did." He grinned ruefully. "For almost an entire week."

"A week? But—" She broke off, shot him a worried glance.

"Yup, an entire week. Bet you figured me for completely uneducated, didn't you?"

She rushed to reassure him. "Oh, no, of course not, I . . ." And then Anthea caught sight of the expression on his face. "Oh," she said, embarrassment washing through her. He'd been putting her on, very much as he had Phillip Cox. She devoutly hoped he held a better impression of her than he did of Mr. Cox.

But his eyes were warm with amusement, his smile without the hard, bitter edge of the one he'd given Mr. Cox.

"I'm not touchy about my lack of formal education," he told her. "If there was one thing I learned when I left Haven, it was that there are lots of ways to learn things, and I was good at most of them."

"It's perfectly obvious that you are."

She sounded sincere, Gabe thought. Miss Fancy Finishing School herself. Imagine that.

"The kids weren't any kinder to the town bastard in my day, Miss Bright. And I wasn't much interested in taking their abuse. So how can I ask Lily to bear up under the same thing when I didn't? But she's gonna need every advantage in life she can come up with. Not just book learning, but learning how to deal with people who are stupid enough to hate her just because of who her mama was."

"It's unfair, I know." Her voice was soft, her eyes kind and pretty. If *she'd* been his teacher, they'd have had to drag him out of school with a team of oxen. "I'll do my very best to protect her, keep as close a watch as I possibly can, but I can't absolutely promise there will be no further incidents. They are . . . inventive, and far more experienced at evading a teacher's supervision than I am at providing it."

"And you think it'd be best for me to keep her home?"

I think it would have been best if you had married her mother and avoided this entire situation, Anthea thought with a sudden surge of anger. She must not forget that, while the other children's actions were unconscionable, *he* had created this situation in the first place by not fully accepting his responsibility.

She'd been near to forgetting his culpability, drawn in by his rough but potent charm, and by how hard he seemed to be trying to make it up to Lily. But that did not change the truth.

Was this how he'd seduced Lily's poor mother in the first place? Good sense was an ineffective shield against his very male attractiveness. Anthea stepped back and drew her shawl more tightly around her shoulders.

"This is not a decision that I have the right to make for your family," she told him. "I will do my best for Lily's welfare, whatever you decide."

He scrubbed a palm roughly over his scalp, leaving his hair even more disheveled, dark waves ragged and rich against his neck. "Why don't we ask Lily, then?"

They found Lily, stretched to her tiptoes, standing by the stove in the corner of the shack allocated as the kitchen, banging on the bottom of an opened can with the heel of her hand. A large blob of cold beans shot out and plopped unappetizingly into the bottom of a blackened pan.

"Almost ready," she said without turning around.

"Lily, Miss Bright and I were wondering, would you rather stop going to school in town?"

Her hand stopped in midwhack and she shot a startled glance in their direction. "No school?"

"Not *no* school, exactly," Anthea put in quickly. "A special school, just for you, here at the farm. I'd come over each day, after my other duties are completed. I promise."

Carefully Lily set the half-emptied can aside and turned, wiping her hands on her skirt. "You . . . don't want me there?"

"Oh, no, of course not!" Anthea flew to Lily and dropped to her knees in front of her. "I will miss you terribly during the day. I just thought that perhaps you would prefer to have your own private lessons."

"Why?"

She exchanged glances with Gabriel. He shrugged, turning the explanation completely over to her. *Thanks a lot,* she thought.

"The other children . . ." Her movements slow, her touch gentle as a new mother's, she brushed a strand of hair off Lily's forehead. "I do not want them to hurt you, Lily. I could not bear it."

Her lower lip popping out in protest, Lily jammed her arms across her narrow chest. "I'm not a scaredy-cat," she declared.

"I never thought you were."

"Want to be with you."

"Lily." Gabriel rubbed beneath his breastbone, where a strange, hollow spot opened up the moment Anthea touched Lily, touched her with the kind of reverence that every child should feel at some point but he doubted Lily ever had. The fact that his mother, for all her other flaws, had loved him like that was probably the one thing that had saved him.

Lily hovered on the verge of falling completely in thrall with her teacher. He wanted that for her, that sense of importance, the warmth of knowing someone cared for you most of all. And yet there was so much at risk there. He didn't think Lily could stand to have her heart broken again. And one way or another, her teacher would never hold a position of permanence in her life. How would Lily feel when it was time to leave for Colorado? Or when Miss Bright left for another position when this term was over?

Lily would be left behind, even more alone than be-fore. And filled with dreams for a kind of life, Miss Bright's kind of life, that she could never have.

"Maybe it's just as well," he ventured. "You can stay home with me during the day, and I can tutor you some, too. Now that winter's coming, there'll be less work for me during the day. My mother taught me, so I guess I could figure it out. Miss Bright can come over every once in a while . . ."

Anthea didn't take kindly to his suggestion. Lily liked it even less, and the two of them, faces side by side, glowered at him in tandem.

"Want to go to school," Lily repeated with convic-tion.

"We wouldn't want to impose on Miss Bright," he said lamely, "asking her to come out here every day."

"It's no imposition," she said, eyes as frosty as her clipped tone. "Lily can come to school, just as she does now, and I'll walk home with her as I did today." *I'll keep her safe.* Gabriel understood the implied promise every bit as clearly as if she'd voiced it aloud. "We'll have a little extra lesson then, and Lily will be caught up in no time. Why, I bet she'll be shooting past the rest of the children before we even know it!"

Every day. She was going to come here every day. Panic and anticipation flooded him in equal measures. How was he supposed to get anything done if he knew she was here, bending over Lily's lesson, her warm eyes shining and a few strands of hair clinging along the fine curve of her cheek?

But before he got his mouth open to object, Anthea continued briskly on. "Now, about that supper. You don't really plan to have just beans, do you?"

Lily shook her head. "Crackers, too."

"Crackers." Anthea planted her fists on her hips. Nice hips, he noticed vaguely, trim and shapely. And right now, attached to a woman who appeared to be none too pleased with him. "No vegetables? Fruit? Anything *green* whatsoever?"

"Hey, don't look at me." He spread his hands wide. "I never claimed to be able to cook."

She sniffed. "It's certainly not a proper diet for a growing child."

"I haven't starved yet."

Her gaze swept him from head to toe, ready to judge his statement and find it wanting. Except halfway down, right about where his chest narrowed into his waist, something changed. Her perusal slowed down, lingering along the way, and her expression warmed to something that was a far sight from disapproval.

His muscles contracted immediately, going taut with his effort to seem unaffected, as if having his physique thoroughly and conspicuously inspected by a woman were an ordinary thing. Blatant sexual interest flared to life, low and hot in his belly.

Her scrutiny made its way back to his face, and he grinned lazily. Poppy red color burst on her cheeks, and her gaze flew away.

"Come on," she said hastily, wrapping her hand around Lily's, "let's see what we can do about supper."

The two females shooed him outside, which suited Gabriel well enough. It was better, he figured, to be out of there while Miss Bright swished around doing patently female things, cooking and smiling encouragement at a young one. He'd been too long without a woman in his life on a regular basis, which surely accounted for his odd, persistent susceptibility to this one.

And so he went to care for his horse, giving him a good rubdown and currying, which had Old Bill nudging his shoulder and nickering in gratitude. Giving all his attention to the familiar task, he could pretend that his life was the same comfortable, hardworking, simple one he'd owned a mere six months ago, before it got complicated by a lost little girl and her concerned and surprisingly attractive teacher.

She sent Lily to fetch him—he'd bet it would be a while before Anthea would allow herself to be alone with him again, for she'd softened toward him for a moment, let her defenses down. And Miss Bright seemed very devoted to her defenses. When he would have headed straight for the house, Lily pointed to the well.

"That her idea?" he asked, and Lily bobbed her head yes.

Half-amused, half-insulted, he quickly splashed water on his face while Lily waited impatiently, hopping back and forth from foot to foot.

"Good enough, do you think?"

She took his question seriously, and inspected him as conscientiously as any officer reviewed his troops. Finally she deemed him acceptable. His shirtsleeves damp and his hair dripping, he entered his decrepit old house and walked into a home.

The air simmered with rich smells, bread and frying bacon, cinnamon and some other spices he couldn't identify, scents so strong and delicious that when he sniffed deeply his stomach growled in anticipation. On the table, beautifully brown biscuits peeked out from a basket covered with a snowy white cloth. A half-dozen crockery bowls, glazed deep blue, stood on a table set with pretty flowered plates that they'd dug from God only knew what corner of the house; the last time he'd seen them was Christmas when he was maybe ten or so.

Anthea hovered beside the table, looking both uncertain and proud, her chin lifted as if to dare him to object.

"You've been busy."

"Lily showed me where everything was." Flour dusted her narrow dark skirt like sugar sifted over chocolate cake. "I didn't mean to overstep by rummaging through your private things, but the supplies within plain sight wouldn't have made much of a meal."

"It's fine." For the first time, he began to get an inkling of why men married. There was a certain undeniable appeal in returning to a clean home after a long day, to a table full of good food and a woman to look at over that table, knowing she'd come to your bed in a few hours and you'd fall into her, all softness, smelling of baking and woman.

Appalled, he mentally slammed the brakes on that train of thought. It was immensely easier, he reminded himself, and in the long run both mentally and financially cheaper, simply to hire a housekeeper. She'd be perfectly adequate to fulfill all those functions except warming his bed. And there were more than enough women willing to fill that need without getting shackled for life to one of them.

She'd fried apples in butter and sugar, and her biscuits seemed to have been created by angels, as light as clouds. Diced potatoes glistened brown in bacon grease.

They ate in silence. It wasn't companionable but tentative, as if they were uncertain how this all fit into their lives. And they were hungry, because it was late, so that they had to light a lantern halfway through. They were both too aware that if a stranger wandered by, he would have taken them for a family: a mother, a father, a child.

It scared them almost as much as it tempted them.

Lily drooped before she was halfway through her wedge of the marble cake they'd baked in an iron skillet. Gabriel sent her up to bed in the loft with his repeated assurances that yes, he'd wake her in plenty of time for school.

"Why don't you leave the dishes," he told Anthea. "I'll take you home now and clean up later."

"No, we'll do it together," Anthea said without thinking. *Together*. There could be nothing *together* about the two of them. "Thank you for allowing me to stay for supper."

He shoved back his rough wooden chair, stacked his own plate with Lily's, and carried them over to pile by the dry sink. "Hey, it was such a sacrifice. I'm sure I'd much rather have eaten plain beans and dry crackers."

"It's the hardest thing for me, eating alone every night," she admitted, clearing her own dishes. "I'm used to being with my sisters. Some of my students' parents invite me now and then, but I don't want to impose too often. It gets lonely. And it's not much fun to cook for one."

Anthea set her jaw before she could say anything else. She was giving too much of herself away, and she doubted it interested him in any case.

Gabriel scooped up the bucket of water that had

been warming through dinner on the stove. "Wash or dry?"

"I'll wash," she decided. "Drying doesn't take as much skill."

"For all you know, I'm an *excellent* dishwasher."

"You don't strike me as the domestic type." He was about as domesticated as a mountain lion, she thought. Even less likely to be tamed. But that unwilling fascination existed all the same, even knowing the danger he represented. "I have to say I'm surprised you even offered. My father would have hired half the city before he would have washed a plate."

She plunged her hands into the hot, soapy water. He stood by her side, a little too near, the length of clean white linen looking out of place in his big, work-darkened hands.

"Then I'll confess to being surprised, too." He took the plate she handed him, and he swept the cloth over the surface, his elbow nudging hers gently. She swallowed hard, and even though she *knew* it was a bad idea, she swung her arms a little wider as she washed, so that her forearm, her shoulder, brushed his now and then. Innocent on the surface, not innocent at all underneath, and her heart stuttered and skipped.

"I wouldn't have figured you for knowing how to cook," he said. "Not that well, anyway. Thought you'd have someone who did that for you all along."

"We did, at first."

He reached for the next dish, and his fingers skated over the back of her hand, wet and soapy and warm with dishwater, a quick, lovely glide.

"My mother died when I was nearly fifteen," she said matter-of-factly. "Only a few weeks after my younger sister's birth. I missed her terribly, and took to lurking around in the kitchen. Spending time with the only other motherly person in the household, I suppose. Mrs. Hargreaves decided that, if I was going to be there anyway, she might as well put me to work. Turned out I had a talent for it."

She was not at all the way he'd first believed her to be. A stiff and proper woman whose life had held nothing but balls and luxuries and formality, who'd gotten bored with her easy life and come to Kansas on a whim.

It had been safer to hold to that first impression. Now she seemed more approachable, more . . . possible. Not a pampered princess on a throne her daddy built, but a real living, breathing, tantalizing woman.

"And then, after my father died," she was going on, "when we found out that—" She stopped, as if realizing she was revealing too much.

"You found out . . . ?" he encouraged her, even while he scolded himself for asking. It would have been a far sight smarter to let her remain the untouchable princess. He hadn't liked the princess; the woman, he liked far too well.

She gave a little shrug that was meant to be careless but didn't quite achieve it. "Let's just say that Mrs. Hargreaves had more lucrative opportunities than staying with us," she said lightly.

The steam drifting up from the hot water misted her face, and her skin glistened in the lamplight. It loosened her hair from its pins and rich brown strands curled near her chin.

"Is that why you came here?" he asked. "Because you needed a job?"

"Mostly." She kept her head down, her attention, too resolutely unwavering to be natural, on the water that frothed around her arms. She'd rolled up her sleeves to her elbows, and he could see inches of her forearms, from elbow to wrist, white and firm and sleek. "I could have taken a position at Miss Addington's. They offered me one. But I couldn't imagine how it would be in a few years, instructing the daughters of the girls I attended school with, seeing their kind pity mixed with gratitude that it was I and not they who were brought to that."

She handed him the last plate and dropped a pot in the water with a thunk and a splash that dampened her blouse. "I decided that, since my life was changing whether I liked it or not, I might as well *really* change it. Kansas seemed like a good long way from Philadelphia." She laughed then, a bright sound. "Oh, was I right about that!"

Carefully he set the still wet plate on top of the stack of dried ones. "Promise me you won't hold this against Lily."

She glanced up from her work at last. "I won't hold wha—"

Her mouth was still open on the word when he snagged her wrist with his hand and gave a yank, pulling her hard up against his body and bringing his mouth down on hers.

Chapter 10

She was dazed for an instant, too stunned to react. She stood still against him, neither responding nor pulling away. And then she flew into sudden, riotous motion, throwing her arms around him, clutching great fistfuls of his shirt, her wet hands making damp spots on his back, and hanging on as if their lives depended upon it. And it almost felt as if they might.

Her heart thundered against her breastbone; he could feel it hammering against his own, their rhythm wild and uneven, nearly painful. Her mouth remained open, and he could taste her, cinnamon-sweet. He nudged her mouth wider with his tongue, licked deep inside; she shuddered against him.

He slid his hands up the narrow slope of her back. He felt the boning of her corset, felt the edge where it ended and all that was between him and skin was the thin layers of her shift and her blouse. She fairly burned with life, the heat of her skin scalding his palm even through the fabric, her body lean and strong and vibrating with energy.

She pushed herself closer, nearly knocking him off his feet. He wrapped his arms around her, lifting her up to her toes so her full weight, delicious and arousing, rested against him. Her mouth was his completely; she gifted him with full access, let him explore where he would, met his every foray with fierce and unexpected enthusiasm.

How could desire rise so fast, hit so hard? It burst open in full bloom, as if it had been there all along, waiting, growing, and he couldn't imagine how he'd resisted it so long. Resisted *her*, all furious passion and pure sweetness at once.

A sudden burst of wind rattled the old shack to its bones, bringing him momentarily to his senses. He wanted to ignore it, to sink back down into the carnal pleasures of her mouth, her body.

But he couldn't. Because Lily, sweet, wounded Lily, slept above them, and he couldn't risk her heart to salve his own needs.

He grasped Anthea by the upper arms and held her away from him. She looked exactly like what she was, a well-kissed woman. Her color was high, her eyes hazy, her mouth glazed with moisture from his kiss. His arms shook, fighting the powerful need to pull her back, knowing he musn't. For her sake, and for Lily's sake.

"Damn," he said. "That wasn't supposed to happen."

Her lovely daze shattered immediately. Her back snapped straight, her expression pinched with disapproval. "No, it most certainly never should have happened," she said stiffly. "I can't imagine but that it wasn't one of the worst mistakes that you ever—"

He couldn't help but smile, and gave her a little shake in lieu of kissing her to shut her up, which was what he really longed to do.

"Not 'damn, I didn't want to kiss you'," he told her, "but 'damn, you weren't supposed to be *good* at it, and I was supposed to get it out of my system once and for all.' "

"Although I'm certain it would have been *far* better if I hadn't been caught unprepared. It took me a moment to—" Halfway through her justifications, his words finally sunk in. "What did you say?"

"I said you might have just ruined me for all other women."

She blinked up at him, for once completely at a loss for an appropriate response. Miss Addington had never addressed *this*. "Oh."

He tipped her chin up with his knuckle, touched the corner of her mouth with his thumb, and wished it could be more. "Oh? Just oh?" he teased.

"And I thought you surprised me when you kissed me," she said. "But what you just said topped it." And then she peeked up at him through her lush eyelashes, a flirtatious look that he would have sworn she didn't possess. Perhaps all women were born with it, just one of their many instinctive mannerisms designed to drive men crazy.

"If that was what you can do when you're caught unawares," he said, "I hate to think what you'd be like when you give it your full attention. Did the last man who experienced it live?"

Her smile was delighted. And completely delightful. "Depends upon your definition of *living*."

Oh, who would have thought she was such a wickedly dangerous woman? She was supposed to be stiff and offended and awkward in the aftermath, easy to put away from him, easier to forget. Instead, she made no move to pull away. Her steam-loosened hair drifted down around her shoulders. The skin of her cheek against his palm was as fine as silk, and she rubbed lightly into his touch when he thought to move it. His other hand flexed on her upper arm, a gentle squeeze he couldn't stop because he wanted so badly to test her flesh, somehow, somewhere, and that seemed like the safest place. But even there wasn't safe at all. She was firm, surprisingly strong, and he remembered how she'd clutched him when he kissed her, and knew she could dig her fingers hard enough into his flanks as he entered her that a man would know he was welcomed.

He yanked back his hands because he knew, if he left them on her any longer, they'd not be content with innocuous areas such as chin and arms.

Not that you could call him *content*, anyway. But the fact that she kissed with a courtesan's skill and a bride's eagerness only made it all the worse. It did not change the fact that she was emphatically not a temporary kind of woman and he was a very temporary kind of man. Every word she said, every conversation that passed between them, only proved their essential unsuitability all the more.

"Come on, I'll take you home," he said quickly, before his good sense could assert otherwise. Of course, he should send her off alone; any dangers for her along the way were far less hazardous than the ones he posed.

But he was going to see her home anyway.

"I—" She gave herself a shake, as if she must throw off the remnants of clouding passion before she could think clearly. "That's not necessary," she said crisply.

"We're not going through that again."

"No, we're not."

"That's good. Because I'll only follow you home anyway to make certain you get there safe and sound, and so I might as well escort you."

She pursed her lips as she studied him. He tried a glower to spur her agreement. Instead she smiled, a smile brilliant and heady enough to send him reeling.

"All right."

He took her down the back trail to town, on a narrow path that wound through fields of drying corn, stark and twisted in the moonlight. They walked past the black, empty squares of harvested ground until the trail twisted on itself to follow a small stream bordered by bare cottonwoods and willows.

"Is this the same stream that runs by the school?" she asked him.

He nodded.

"Why didn't you take me this way the last time, then?"

He didn't answer, his smile flashing white as moonlight in the darkness, satisfied and a bit mischievous.

Because that time *had* been a test, Anthea thought. A challenge to see if she would allow herself to go in

public in his company, if she'd let the rumors she'd
heard and the proprieties she followed overrule what
was right.

She struggled to muster up the suitable anger at
him for putting her in an untenable position. Instead,
she couldn't help but feel a tinge of pride that she'd
passed. Not an appropriate reaction, she chastised
herself. Not at all. But then, she'd hardly been experi-
encing appropriate reactions ever since she'd met him,
had she?

Certainly her response to his kiss had been anything but proper. For every bit of passion she'd buried
deep within her, every emotion and sensation, had
come pouring right out, filling her up and taking her
over until she'd kissed him back so hard he'd all but
had to peel her off him.

She should be ashamed of that, she supposed. Except the gleam in his eyes, the dusky flush on his
cheekbones, the heavy bellowing of his breath in and
out of his chest, had indicated beyond any doubt that
he'd been nearly as staggered by the experience as she.

You might have just ruined me for all other women. It
was gallant foolishness. And clearly untrue. And still
her heart lifted at the memory, and her cheeks heated,
and it was all she could do not to stop in her tracks
right there, grab him by the shirtfront, and plant another one on him.

And oh, wouldn't *that* be foolishness? Taken by surprise was one thing. Initiating . . . contact . . . between
herself and the most notorious man in the entire town
would be senseless indeed. Especially when it was
perfectly obvious to her that he was far, far beyond not
only her experience but her ability to manage.

Small animals rustled in the long grasses along the

path. The air was cold, the moonlight sharp. Their footsteps crunched on thin sheets of ice that crusted over puddles formed by the snow the sun had melted that afternoon. They strolled side by side in a silence that was both companionable and thick with intoxicating expectation.

Suddenly he draped his arm over her shoulders, his action so unexpected she startled. His arm was heavy, warm, so very much more efficient than her shawl.

"It's cold," he said, answering her unspoken question.

That was when she knew she'd lost all sense. It was one thing to allow him to kiss her—all right, and to kiss him *back*—when she was taken completely by surprise, when she'd no time to think and armor herself against the delicious sensation of his skilled mouth hard on hers.

This was something else. She could think now—barely, for his torso was rock-solid against her side, the warmth of his breath stirring the free hairs at her temple, but she managed to hold on to a few shreds of clear judgment. And so to allow his arm to remain was now a *decision*, her *responsibility*, a deliberate choice instead of merely a response.

And yet . . . oh, he felt wonderful. It had been so long, and she had so loved the feel of a man's strong arms around her. There was really nothing to compare. And it was all the more delicious now that she was a woman grown instead of the sheltered child she'd been then, even if it was only a few bare months ago.

And, she admitted to herself, because it was Gabriel, and the likes of him had never been in her life before, nor would ever be again.

For the likes of Gabriel Jackson were rare indeed.

So rare that she was immensely sorry when they rounded a bend in the stream and the moonlight revealed the small, shabby entrance to her soddy, the dried grass on its roof gleaming silver.

He escorted her to the door and took his arm from her shoulders with no reluctance that she could detect. Her shoulders felt naked and cold, uncomfortably so, without him. How could she become accustomed to the feel of him so quickly?

"So," she said lamely, torn between her better sense, which warned her to shoo him on his way as quickly as possible, and the humming, vibrant insistence of the rest of her, which wanted anything but. She should be clinging to her virtue—what remained of it, at least—but couldn't summon the will.

"So," he repeated, giving her no help at all.

He merely looked at her, his arms at his sides, his face impassive and brutally handsome, his eyes dark and hot and fiercely intense. And the decision came from deep within her, nothing conscious or controlled, as impossible to hold back as the nightfall.

"Aren't you going to kiss me good night?"

He didn't move, only stared at her so long and hard that she felt herself grow flushed and hot.

"No," he said at last, shoving his hands deep into his pockets as if to keep them away from temptation. "No, I'm not going to kiss you."

"I—"

"And if you ask me if it's because I don't *want* to kiss you," he went on without stopping, an undercurrent of savagery beneath his softly spoken words, "I'm going to turn you over my knee. Because you know damn well I *want* to."

Oh yes, she knew. It showed in every tense line of

his body, the urgent heat of his eyes, the rigid set of his jaw.

"I'm not going to kiss you because, if I so much as brush your mouth with mine, I'm not leaving here tonight."

She tried to form the word "Oh," but it lodged high in her dry throat. A part of her longed for him to take the decision out of her hands. It would be so simple to abdicate responsibility to him. Easy to sink into a blur of passion and not think.

But he wasn't going to do it. Wasn't going to let her get away with being swept up in passion and blaming it all on him the next morning. If she wanted him to come in, she was going to have to ask. For he made no move, just loomed tall and dark and too near over her. She had to bend her neck back to look up at him, his features lost in shadow, the moon streaming silver over his broad shoulders.

"I didn't think so," he said, a wry, pained smile lifting his mouth. "Go inside and bar the door behind you. I'll leave when I know you're safely inside."

She couldn't force her feet to move. Didn't want to be alone on the other side of the door, leaving him here on the doorstep, unsure whether she'd ever see him there again.

A muscle ticked in his jaw. *"For God's sake, Anthea, go inside!"*

A part of her, the wild, deep part that kept her from sleep at night, his face and body filling her wide-awake dreams, called her a coward. Her other half, her wiser half, named her prudent.

She whirled, pushed blindly at the door, and fell inside. She kicked the door shut and shot the bolt in one violent move, then spun and fell back against it, her shoulders against the rough wood, her hands flat on the splintery plane of the door.

Her breath came hard, the sound harsh to her own ears. Her head fell back against the door with a thunk.

And she didn't know if she'd just made the smartest move of her entire life . . . or done something she'd regret forever.

Anthea did not tutor Lily after school on Monday. Instead, she accompanied her home without incident, waved good-bye at the front door, and hurried back to the school without setting eyes on Gabriel.

It was not, she told herself—and nearly believed it—because she was *afraid* to see him. She simply had much to do to prepare for that night's school board meeting, her first since the term began. It was important to the continuation of her career, and thus vital to her family. And she was not at all confident that it would go smoothly.

She spent the hours before the meeting in a fair fever of preparation. She dragged the benches back into their original positions—it would not do, she concluded, to have the parents ringing the walls of the room with her in the middle like a gladiator in a ring awaiting her fate.

She pored over her list of requirements at least three dozen times, assuring she hadn't forgotten any supplies or repairs that were truly necessary to the school's efficient and effective function. Then she added three more that weren't, reasoning that it was wise to show her flexibility by compromising on those items early on. She practiced her well-reasoned and logical arguments several times as to why all the other purchases were absolutely crucial to the success of the school year, just to be certain, but she couldn't imagine that there would be any trouble. These were their *children*, after all. Surely they were as dedicated to the success of their children's education as she was, regardless of the current poor condition of the school. Surely they must simply have overlooked its inadequacies up until now. Perhaps the previous teacher had not *cared* enough to campaign for better.

Well, now they had a teacher who cared. She surprised herself by how deeply she did so.

By six-thirty, a full half hour before the appointed meeting time, Anthea was dressed, pressed, and shined, hovering at the door of the schoolhouse, ready to welcome the first arrival.

At the last minute, she scurried over to tamp down the fire in the stove, which she'd built that morning out of a few old corncobs scrounged from the coal shed. Her petitions for better insulation and a good delivery of fuel would take on somewhat more urgency if their noses were in danger of freezing off. She was fully confident in their eventual agreement to her requests, but a little extra incentive couldn't hurt.

At 7:02 Anthea perched on a rickety stool at the front of her classroom—the same stool so well acquainted with Theron's hindquarters that she was tempted to paint his name on the top—and surveyed the collection of people who'd gathered. If there was one thing that could be said for the inhabitants of Haven, she thought wryly, they were prompt.

However, she was beginning to suspect that *forward thinking* could not be counted among their most prominent qualities. One of the reasons she had chosen Kansas, of all the places she could have gone— never mind that Haven was the first school besides

Miss Addington's that had offered her a position and she didn't dare refuse—was that it was the first state to give women the right to vote in school board elections. It seemed so progressive, so far beyond the careful boundaries of women's work in Philadelphia.

But apparently the progressiveness of the state legislature did not apply to the men of Haven. In the front of the room, the three members of the school board held positions of honor behind her makeshift desk. Phillip Cox, impeccably dressed and even more impeccably self-assured, claimed the center position, his hands folded before him, silvering brown hair gleaming with oil. The two other members of the school board flanked him: Calvin Stoddard, his bulk dwarfing his chair, and Knute Sontesby, a silent man whose genially handsome features were marred only by his once-broken nose.

She scanned the rest of the room, finding two—*two*—women. Cordelia Pruitt, a widow, balanced precariously on the far edge of one of the benches, as if to ensure she took up no more space than necessary. Esther Mott occupied the spot next to her, clutching a paper on which Abe, who'd been called away to Kansas City on urgent business, had written down precise instructions on how she should represent him this evening. Anthea knew this for a fact because Esther had scurried up to her first thing to assure her of it. The last item on the list instructed Esther, when in doubt, to defer to Phillip Cox.

Oh, there'd been other women there that night. They'd delivered the platefuls of cookies, cakes, and other delectables that weighed down the plank laid over two upended crates that had been pressed into duty as a table. They'd informed Anthea they'd see her after the menfolk had concluded their business, and then headed off to the Sontesbys' house, leaving the important work of the evening to wiser heads. Which apparently meant *male* heads.

Anthea half expected them to ask her to leave as well.

Mr. Cox nodded at Calvin, who promptly rapped his broad, blunt knuckles on the table, calling the meeting to attention. Sitting a few feet away, Anthea smoothed her hands over her stomach, fluttering with nerves, and tried not to wish that Gabriel had come. What support did she think she would find from him, anyway? He made no secret of the fact that he disapproved of many of her teaching techniques.

And just when had she begun thinking of him simply as Gabriel?

"First, I'm sure I speak for all here in formally welcoming you to Haven." Anthea suspected that the smile Mr. Cox bent in her direction was the exact same one he used whether greeting his best customer or foreclosing on a mortgage.

"I am very pleased to be here." She swallowed hard. As challenging as she had found her first day of teaching, this evening was every bit as challenging—and as important to the success of the rest of the year. And while she'd taken this position as a means to support her family, she'd also discovered an unexpected and powerful pride in the job. "I've given you a comprehensive list of what I believe are the most crucial needs of this school. I realize it is quite extensive, but—"

"Yes." Again the "trust me" smile. "I'm sure we're all properly impressed with your . . . enthusiasm. Our regular agenda for these meetings, however, is to address the concerns of the attendees before receiving petitions from the teacher."

Anthea frowned. They were going to hear *complaints* before considering her requests? Oh, she was sure they were going to be hurrying to support her after hearing a list of everything she was doing wrong.

"I gotta concern." Marshall Pietzke, a dour farmer with the mark of long days in the sun on his copper-tinged face, creaked to his feet. "It's about all these manners you been hammerin' at—"

Behind him the door creaked open, and Mr. Pietzke automatically glanced behind him. When Gabriel entered, the shock of it must have made Mr. Pietzke's statement flee his head, because he shut his mouth abruptly and plopped back down to the bench.

"Mr. Jackson," Phillip Cox said smoothly, "how unexpected of you to join us this evening."

"Wouldn't miss it," Gabriel said cheerfully.

"We do begin promptly at seven o'clock, however. Just for future reference."

"Heard that." Unconcerned, Gabriel took the nearest empty seat, two feet from Adonijah Matheson at the end of a bench. His gaze met Anthea's briefly—so fleeting, and yet it rocked her, a connection arcing through the air between them so powerfully that she couldn't believe it didn't take visible form.

She realized she was smiling at him and forcibly wiped the expression from her face.

Mr. Matheson's mouth pinched sourly. He stood, hustled conspicuously down the aisle, and wedged into a small space between two other men on the far side of the room.

Gabriel's expression didn't flicker. Anthea didn't

know if he'd become inured to such behavior years ago or if he was simply very, very good at hiding it. She, however, could feel anger bubbling up inside her, demanding to erupt. Whatever Gabriel had done in his past, there was simply no excuse for the actions of the residents of Haven now.

"About those manners you mentioned, Mr. Pietzke," she began hotly. Gabriel caught her eye and shook his head. For an instant she considered ignoring his cue; he deserved defending in this particular instance whether he wanted it or not. But clearly he did not, if the determined frown that followed was any clue. He appeared ready to clamber over the benches and the crowd, and clap his hand over her mouth if he must in order to shut her up.

"I got a complaint too." Fred Skinner stood and hitched up his pants over his broad belly. "I think we'd all agree that one of a teacher's most important responsibilities is to set a fine, upstanding moral example for our kids."

The low murmur that rumbled around the room sounded distinctly like trouble to Anthea.

Fred sniffed and rubbed his chin in the serious contemplation the topic deserved. "It's right there in the contract, ain't it, Phillip?"

"It most certainly is," Mr. Cox agreed.

"Well, then, hanging around with what you might call an undesirable element seems to me to be in violation of that clause, don'tcha think?"

Gabriel looked thunderous, eyes dark and blazing under brows drawn into a slashing line, his jaw aggressively set. Anthea wasn't sure if the panic that sent her heart into a gallop was mostly because she was about to lose her job or because her school board meeting seemed about to degenerate into a barroom brawl at any second.

"Fred, you are aware that I personally selected Miss Bright to fill our vacancy, are you not?" Mr. Cox asked.

"Well, yeah." Skinner nodded placidly, obviously confident that, considering Cox and Jackson's legendary feud, Cox would come down firmly on his side in this matter. "We know you're kinda busy down at the bank, Mr. Cox, so it'd be perfectly understandable if maybe you didn't notice that—"

"When have you ever known me *not* to notice something of importance?"

Skinner began to look confused. Clearly the conversation wasn't going quite how he expected, but he wasn't quite sure where it had gone wrong.

"And you are also aware that I have entrusted my Olivia to Miss Bright's care as well?"

"We *all* are entrusting our children to her, Phillip," Calvin Stoddard put in carefully, his mouth puckered in consternation. "Which is why we all want to be careful of the example she sets."

"Yeah, and *this*"—Adonijah leaped to his feet and jabbed a finger in Gabriel's direction—"is not appropriate company for a schoolteacher to be keepin'."

Gabriel got lazily to his feet, an action that Anthea figured didn't fool a single person in the room. Danger seethed around him, and for the first time since she'd met him she began to understand just why exactly the people of Haven were so convinced he was a bad man. When he looked like this, any person with a brain would turn and run in the opposite direction rather than confront him.

Apparently, however, the men of Haven weren't

well blessed in that department, for they buzzed with tension, coming to their feet and clustering behind Adonijah.

"Oh, for heaven's sake." Phillip Cox's tones clipped through the tension in the room. "This might have been acceptable when we were twelve, but surely we've outgrown such posturing since then."

"But, Mr. Cox . . ." Matheson looked distinctly disgruntled at the thought of having to give up fighting Gabriel with the advantage of a full dozen men on his side.

"Sit *down*, Adonijah."

Unhappily Matheson dropped back into his seat.

"Now then." Cox's sharp gaze searched the room, pausing to mark each man in turn before continuing. "Is there anyone here who's witnessed any . . . misbehavior on the part of our new schoolteacher?"

Anthea shot a guilty glance at Gabriel, still standing at the back of the room glowering, arms battle-ready at his sides. Certainly that kiss would fall under the heading of misbehavior, if not downright sinful transgression.

"But, Phillip, we all saw her going out to that farm and—"

"I saw her going to your farm, too, Marshall. Are you telling me there was something less than proper in that?"

Mr. Pietzke shifted in his seat, red creeping up his thin neck. "Of course not, I—"

"All right then." Cox nodded as if that settled the matter. "It is clearly part of a teacher's duties to visit the families of her students. And as long as Lily Ross is a student in this school, I will hear no more about the matter."

"Now see here." Adonijah was not about to give up yet. "About that very thing—"

"The subject is closed," Cox said with as much heat as Anthea figured he ever displayed.

Phillip Cox was the last person she'd ever expected to come to her rescue. From the expressions on the faces of other attendees, it shocked them even more than it surprised her. Including Gabriel, who shrugged in answer to her questioning glance as if to say, *Who'd have thought it?* before he reclaimed his seat.

Anthea let out the first easy breath she'd taken since the meeting started. With the firm support of the president of the school board, her position seemed secure. For as long as she could keep her relationship—no, it wasn't a *relationship*, it was merely a circumstantial affiliation—with Gabriel on a strictly professional basis.

Mentally she increased her estimates of what school repairs and supplies she might gain tonight. If Phillip Cox was willing to give her his support on this particular point, surely she could talk him into a few more books.

Chapter 11

Anthea whipped across the distance between the schoolhouse and the Sontesbys', vaguely wondering why the frozen puddles weren't melting in her wake, for surely steam surged from every pore.

They'd kicked her out of her own school board meeting. *Kicked her out.*

For all Phillip Cox's support on the issue of her connection with Lily and Gabriel, his assistance evaporated abruptly the instant money was mentioned. She'd detailed her carefully prepared requests and all the valid, painstakingly constructed reasons that they were absolutely necessary. Mr. Cox, and all the other men attending, listened with an impatience they had not bothered to conceal. Then they'd refused them all with a vague excuse about the difficult economy, maintaining they'd all managed to learn just fine without such luxuries.

Luxuries! She made a sound of disgust. As if enough coal to keep their fingers from freezing while trying to copy their penmanship lessons could be called a luxury!

And then they'd shoved her on her way, claiming they had further matters to discuss but they just knew she'd enjoy herself more with the other women than being bothered with the details of their meeting.

They'd all but patted her on her head.

Anthea slapped the Sontesbys' front door with the flat of her hand and winced—but with a certain vengeful satisfaction—when it flew open and rebounded against an interior wall.

A circle of a dozen startled women looked up at her, teacups halfway to their mouths, plates of delicate cookies balanced on their knees.

The furious outburst roiling inside her would do her no good at all, should she surrender to it. She sucked in a deep breath, willing herself to remember the higher goal rather than indulge in temporary satisfaction.

"Had a lovely first meeting, did you?" Thisba Stoddard asked wryly.

"It did not go precisely as I imagined, no," she admitted. "However, it was very . . . interesting. And informative."

Mrs. Sontesby snorted. "I'll bet it was."

"Now, now." Cleo Cox, elegant in blue watered silk, gestured to the tea tray that rested on a small table beside her. "I'm sure Miss Bright could use some fortification before we bend our efforts to prying every little detail from her."

Once Anthea was settled on a needlepoint chair

with a cup of very hot tea and prettily sugared white cookies, she looked around the group of women. Bright, interested mothers who, to a woman, had evidenced far more effort and concern for their children's instruction than their husbands had. "Let me ask you a question," she ventured carefully, aware she might be treading on sensitive ground but both genuinely curious and deeply alarmed for the future of her students' education. "Don't any of *you* ever attend the school board meetings?"

"What would be the point?" Ella Bickersdyke sampled a slice of Thisba's famous custard pie.

"That's easy for *you* to say," Esther Mott put in. "George does whatever you tell him to do anyway."

There was general laughter, while Ella protested— but not too hard—before she smiled knowingly.

Anthea set her teacup aside and thought hard. Expending effort trying to convince the school board and the others who'd attended the meeting that all the supplies and repairs were truly necessary didn't appear to be the most expedient approach.

Knowing the topic must be broached delicately, she considered her words carefully, "You know that your children's education is my absolute first priority."

"Oh, dearie, you don't have to tell us. You've already got the job," Thisba said.

"I do believe, however, that I could do my job far better with certain essential supplies. And the children can hardly be expected to concentrate properly when they are physically uncomfortable during the day."

Letty shook her head. "If you're thinking to pry some funds out of those misers, I can tell you right now not to bother. Every teacher for the last ten terms has tried, and all of 'em—even the men—have been turned down flat. There's no chance they'll shake out more than a few dimes for you, no matter how pretty you ask."

If she could get Phillip Cox to agree, Anthea decided, the others would fall in line. It had not taken a long residence in Haven to discern to whom all the others deferred.

And Mr. Cox was exceedingly fond of his wife. "Mrs. Cox, your husband is such a doting, proud father. Surely for the sake of his daughter's education he might be willing to reconsider improvements."

Thisba's mouth thinned. "He'd buy the entire state for Olivia. Unfortunately, he's not nearly so interested in *public* works."

If Anthea expected Cleo to defend her husband, she was quickly disabused of that notion. Cleo's expression remained serenely uninterested. "I never interfere with Phillip on business matters."

"Nobody does." Esther brushed crumbs from her severe black skirt.

"My husband doesn't consider fancying up the school a provably sound investment. And he believes that individual families and students must be responsible for their own educations. They'll appreciate it more if it's not handed to them."

Thisba applauded. "Oh, you repeat what he's told you so very well. And it's ever so easy for you to say, isn't it?"

Disquiet flickered over Cleo's lovely features. "I—"

"Have you ever," Anthea put in quickly, afraid they were on the way to veering far from the matter that concerned her, not to mention veering toward a skirmish she emphatically did not wish to get drawn into, "considered raising money for the schools in another way? Beyond subscription or taxation?"

"Hmm." Ella Bickersdyke's brow furrowed in thought. "If the money were raised independently— say, by the Haven School Women's Committee—it wouldn't fall to the school board as to how to spend it, either. Would it?"

"The Haven School Women's Committee?" Letty Matheson asked. "Who's on the Women's Committee?"

Thisba rolled her eyes. "You are, of course. And all the rest of us, too."

Out of the corner of her eye, Anthea saw Cleo Cox drift to her feet and slip out of the room. Had the turn the conversation had taken upset her? Anthea could hardly afford to offend such a powerful family. But when Esther called her name, she put Cleo out of her mind.

"Did you have any particular endeavor in mind, Miss Bright? We could have a box social, I suppose. Or a bake sale."

"Why not both?" Or a party, she thought, and her spirits lifted. There'd been a time when she'd lived for parties. And while that life had shattered abruptly upon her father's death, something of that gay, carefree girl still remained in her. "Maybe a dance? A dollar or two a ticket won't raise everything we need, of course, but it would certainly be a healthy start." Enough to convince the women to continue after she left, she hoped.

"A dance?" Leola Skinner whispered the word, scandalized.

"A dance," Ella repeated, her eyes dreamy. "George hasn't danced with me since the Babcock wedding."

"I'm not sure I remember how," Letty admitted.

"It'll come back to you quickly. I'd be happy to give a few lessons," Anthea assured them, liking the idea better all the time. How could the women object to her teaching their children to dance in the name of geography if she was teaching *them*, as well? "Waltzing, certainly, and perhaps a cotillion as well. They're not difficult."

"All I ever knew how to do is polka," Johanna said.

"You'll like these," Anthea said. "And Mr. Sontesby looks as if he'd be quite sturdy to hold on to while one is spun around."

"Miss Bright!" Johanna tittered behind her hand, then smiled. "He certainly is," she agreed.

This just might work, Anthea thought. If she could get the women committed enough to the idea, they'd talk their men into it. "Perhaps Saint Valentine's Day."

"Oooh." There was a collective sigh.

Perfect. She'd read them correctly, these sturdy, hardworking, long-married women who'd put aside the frivolities of youth for real life long ago. The romance of it captured their imaginations. And while it was going to be a bit tricky to struggle through until February without additional funds, holding it on Valentine's Day promised the best chance at getting the women to nag their husbands into the event.

"Now then," she said, addressing the practicalities, "you are all far more conversant with the resources of Haven than I am. What shall we do for music?"

Cleo stood just outside the Sontesbys' house, trying to decide what to do next. She could go over to the schoolhouse and ask Phillip to take her home. He'd do it—whatever she asked of him, he almost always gave her immediately.

But then she'd be alone with him, and he'd have that eager and wounded look on his face, and she'd be reminded again that she was a far poorer wife than he was a husband.

She'd left the other women because she never knew what to say to them. She supposed she should have been miffed at the things they'd said about Phillip, but most of them were true. He was immensely careful with money, which was why he'd provided such a comfortable life for her and their daughter. And why the bank and all his various businesses were so profitable, which was every bit as good for the town as it was for them.

But that was Phillip. And there was no denying the truth of what Thisba said: Cleo had never fought for education or anything in her life. Not once. And she had spent all of it deeply regretting that she had allowed the one thing, the one *man*, who really mattered to slip away without a fight.

The distinct chill in the late evening air didn't bother Cleo at all. Her cloak was the warmest that money, and her husband, could buy. And the truth of the matter was, Cleo simply did not feel things as deeply as other people. It was as if she lived her life in a bubble that separated her from the real world, a bubble that thinned only rarely. For she was comfortable in her familiar bubble, would not allow it to weaken if she could help it.

She stepped away from the house and slid silently through the night toward the schoolhouse. She'd wait outside until it appeared that the men were ready to go home. It shouldn't be long; they were farmers, most of them, and even the congenial company of their companions could hold them only so long when their workday started very early the next morning.

Buggies, no doubt driven here by those men whose wives were even now plotting rebellion in Johanna's front parlor, studded the school yard. The horses' heads hung low, as though they were half-asleep, patiently waiting until they were needed. A couple of riding horses were tied to a post. They likely belonged to men whose wives had to stay home with children too young to be left in charge of the household, she speculated idly.

Cleo wandered closer, and one of the horses snorted, its exhalation smoking the air. A big, handsome chestnut, that one, remarkably similar to Gabriel's horse.

Her heart picked up speed, as it always did at the slightest thought of him. The merest memory could send her senses spinning. *Gabriel.* Now, there was the one person who could shatter her bubble, bursting her free into a world of color and light and *feeling*. And she would let him do it. Longed for him to do it.

It wasn't his horse, of course. Whyever would he attend a school board meeting, for all that he'd enrolled that daughter of his? He'd always stayed as far away from the townsfolk as possible.

It was painful to think of the daughter, as vivid an emotion as she'd allowed herself to experience in many a year. The image of his strong hands on another woman sliced fresh hurt deep through her. But it was also undeniably exciting.

She always knew when he returned to Haven. It didn't take long; the town grapevine buzzed with the news within hours of his arrival. And each time she'd waited for him to come to her, for he must be as powerfully drawn to her as she was to him. The kind of love they'd shared could yield nothing less. And why else would he return to Haven? Certainly not just to visit that mother of his, who'd been no kind of mother at all to Cleo's way of thinking.

No, he'd come back to breathe the same air as she did, to catch precious glimpses of her on the street. But Gabriel had done the honorable thing and stayed away from her every time, leaving town, she suspected, when the ache of being near her but not with her became too much to bear.

But this time he'd remained in town longer than ever before. And she recognized now that all those other times she'd given him no encouragement to come to her. Though he could not doubt her love; she'd shown him, all those years ago, with all the fervency in her young heart and body. But he'd been so strong in his resolve to do the right thing, far stronger than she was.

For she knew that such love was rare. And that it could not be denied forever.

Gabriel stepped out of the schoolhouse. He'd attended the meeting just long enough to make sure everyone knew they hadn't run him off, and then left them to their cigars and their conversations about crops and politics that he figured would pick up considerably the instant he'd relieved them of his presence.

The air was crystalline and cold, stars glittering like ice chips, strewn thickly against the blue-black sky. He blew out a breath, watched it curl up like smoke in the yellow light leaching out of the few remaining win-dowpanes. He looked toward Anthea's soddy, won-dering if she'd run home after they'd chased her out of the meeting, and if he dared wander over there to check on her.

It had practically killed him to keep his mouth shut while they'd brushed aside her every suggestion as if her opinion mattered no more than that of a transient bummer passing through town.

Not that he was in favor of throwing a whole lot of money into improving the school, either. It didn't take a bunch of fancy equipment and silly books to teach reading and writing, which were, in his opinion, all anybody needed to learn in school. Hell, he'd learned everything that really mattered in other ways. He fig-ured folks who had enough brains to learn something would find a way to do so if they had an ounce of am-bition in them.

But that didn't give them the right to treat Anthea as if she didn't matter. He would have jumped in and made *sure* they listened to her, by God, or they'd have him to deal with, except he knew darn well that *his* support was far worse than none at all.

No lights glowed through the fabric covering her windows. Either she'd gone over to the Sontesbys' with the rest of the women or she'd dropped right into bed to sob her disappointment into her pillow. And while just the thought of her in her bed was enough to send warmth spiraling low in his gut, he didn't figure the kind of comforting he'd be likely to give her was what she needed right now.

Not to mention that, for all he liked to prick her about being seen in his company, he didn't want her to have to deal with the aftermath of his being seen entering her home alone. For all Cox's puzzling approval—he wondered what the crafty bastard was up to this time—he didn't imagine they'd tolerate Anthea consorting with him in a way that clearly had nothing to do with Lily's education. They'd run her out of town on a rail. And whatever else he felt, or didn't feel, for her, he knew one thing clearly and surely: he didn't want her to leave. Not yet.

"Gabriel."

The light from the schoolhouse windows was behind him, and he squinted into the darkness until she moved into a small square coming over his left shoulder. He blew out a disappointed breath when he realized that it was not Anthea, but Cleo Cox.

"Cleo." He nodded politely, reflecting upon the fact that those were the first words that had passed between them in damn near fifteen years. Not that there had been all that many words back then, either. "Or would you prefer Mrs. Cox?"

"Cleo's fine," she said softly, moving closer to him. The years had been kind to her. Even in the unflattering window light, she was still a beautiful woman, her face smooth, her thick hair upswept. "It would be a bit ridiculous to insist on formality at this point, don't you think?"

"I guess it would," he said, shifting uncomfortably. For one of very few times in his life, he'd prefer formality. "Would you like me to fetch your husband for you? I think they're pretty much done with the business part of the meeting."

"Oh, that's not necessary." Somehow she'd drifted closer yet, though he hadn't noticed the motion. But he knew damn well *he* hadn't moved; his feet were still firmly planted on the bottom step. It made her, always small, seem tinier yet, her nose level with his belly. If he moved forward, he'd come smack up against her. But if he moved back, up a step, well . . . even *he* wasn't comfortable with the thought of what she'd be eye level with then. "He'll be out soon enough," she went on. "I'm not in any hurry. Are you?"

"I should go."

"Oh, don't go!"

Her face was taut in the light, fine features pale and drawn with strain, and he rocked back on his heels, wondering what she wanted from him. An apology, perhaps? He supposed he could give her one, if it would make her feel better. He *had* taken her virginity and left without a second glance. Never mind that he'd always understood very well that she'd been using him every bit as much as he'd used her. Women still liked to pretty up such things.

And she'd hardly wasted any time in marrying Cox afterward, had she? It had concerned him only long enough to ascertain that she hadn't carried his child to her marriage. Once that was clearly not the case, he'd put the entire episode out of his mind. Hell, he could hardly remember it. He was sure it was the same for her.

But perhaps not.

"Is there something I can do for you, Cleo?"

She flicked a furtive glance at the closed door behind him. "Couldn't we . . . We were friends, once, before anything else. It seems like we should have been able to hold on to that, shouldn't we? After everything we meant to each other?"

Friends? He couldn't recall them ever being *friends*. They'd certainly never conversed about aspirations or values or even the future, much less any of the hundreds of other things that women insisted on talking to death. As he remembered it, they hadn't exactly done a lot of talking at all.

Her eyes gleamed, as if they harbored a bit of moisture. Just what *did* the woman want? He had known her well enough once to know that she wasn't exactly straightforward and up-front about her plans.

Had Cox sicced her on him? Was he supposed to be so dazzled by her charms that he'd hand over his land after all? He wouldn't put it past either of them. Though if that was the case, he sure didn't appreciate their estimate of either his intelligence or his perception.

"Something tells me your husband wouldn't approve of that," he said. "Our being *friends,* I mean."

"He wouldn't have to know." Her voice dropped as she said it, to almost a whisper, as if she knew even as she formed the words that they were wrong.

So it was supposed to be their little secret, was it? Now, *that* was something he remembered well; she'd always been terrified that someone would find out he'd spoken one word to her, much less done a whole lot more.

Perhaps she didn't have ulterior motives at all. Maybe the upstanding Mrs. Cox was bored with her perfect, and perfectly dull, little life. How much time could you spend shopping, anyway?

For a second the idea of what Phillip Cox would do if he found out that his wife had once again turned to Gabriel for entertainment made him grin. He wouldn't touch her, of course—he was no longer fifteen, thank God, and prone to such absurdities—but the notion was worth a moment's amusement. But then he realized Cleo was smiling back at him, the corners of her pretty mouth upturned and trembling, and he wiped the expression from his face.

Her smile faded slowly, as if it had been a long time coming and was now reluctant to disappear again. "Gabriel."

He didn't think he cared anymore whether she was out here to please her husband or to spite him. All he knew was that whatever she sought was something messier than he wanted in a life that was already too messy for his liking.

"I really do need to get home to Lily," he told her as the light in her eyes dimmed. "If you'll excuse me."

She stared at him for a moment, lifted her rounded chin into the air. "So go," she said, blocking the small space at the bottom of the stairs.

He couldn't get around her without brushing hard up against her. Not without vaulting over the handrail, and he was afraid she'd read too much into his unwillingness to touch her.

Oh well, he decided. What could possibly happen if his body brushed hers in passing? She'd jump him on the front stairs of the schoolhouse?

He reached out and grabbed her by the shoulders, intending to move her bodily out of the way. Just then the door behind him slammed open, emitting light and hearty male laughter and Calvin Stoddard, and Cleo gasped.

Calvin froze on the top step, letting the door swing slowly shut behind him, his heavy regard shifting from Gabriel to Cleo and back again. "Well, well," he said evenly, "what do we have here?"

Gabriel dropped his hands and tried to look as if he had nothing to be guilty about. He *had* nothing to be guilty about, damn it.

"What we have here," he said flatly, "is Mrs. Cox coming to inquire if her husband is ready to go, and me heading home."

"Seems to me that you stepped out here some time ago, Jackson."

"You have nothing better to do than keep track of my movements, do you, Calvin? Since you're so interested, I was enjoying the air for a moment. It's a little close in there."

While they talked, Cleo edged away, giving him a clear path. Gabriel bounded down the steps and headed for his horse.

"I'll just bet it was," Calvin called after him. "Close, I mean. So much so that I don't figure you'll be comfortable coming to the next one, huh?"

"Oh, I wouldn't count on that." Gabriel paused in the process of untying Old Bill to give Calvin a hard glare. "I expect you'll all be seeing a lot more of me. Given I have Lily to watch out for now and all."

Cleo was firmly facing the door, as if she couldn't risk turning around to bid him good-bye, and shadow and light sliced her figure in half. Calvin loomed over her shoulder, arms jammed over his chest, as if she were pampered royalty and he a tower guard, ready to die to protect his king's bride.

It was stupid, entirely spurred by pride, and Gabriel knew it, but he still couldn't resist. After mounting, he paused to run his hand companionably down Old Bill's warm neck, and spoke clearly into the cold night and Calvin's equally cold glare. "Good-bye, Cleo. Imagine I'll be seeing you soon."

Chapter 12

❧

In November, Kansas decided to take pity on foolish easterners. Indian summer burst into town, the benign sun banishing all reminders of that early snow as if nature designed the weather specifically to keep silly mortals from presuming to predict her. Anthea was grateful that it prevented her from having to dip into the tiny—ridiculously tiny—allotment of fuel she'd pried out of Phillip Cox.

Somehow, though Anthea had not been able to settle in her mind quite how it had happened, she'd fallen into taking supper with Gabriel and Lily each weekday. She told herself that it was only sensible. She was there until nearly suppertime anyway, drilling Lily on her lessons, and didn't relish the thought of trudging home to a cold and lonely meal.

On the practical side, it saved her money to eat Gabriel's food instead, allowing her to send more to her family than she otherwise might have. Still less than she'd planned, she thought guiltily, for she had vastly underestimated the necessary expenses that her stipend did not cover. And it was not a matter of her just sponging off Gabriel, she told herself with staunch rationalization. Gabriel and Lily ate far better with her assistance than they would have if left to their own devices.

She considered it a useful part of Lily's education. She still spoke so rarely Anthea considered it a victory to pry a full sentence out of her. But Lily stuck so close to Anthea's side, she might as well have been fastened there, becoming a fair little cook in the process, a skill that would serve her in good stead whether she chose to marry someday or she needed to earn a living.

Anthea had yet to decide whether Lily stayed so near because the child had taken a liking to her or because she was determined that Gabriel and Anthea would not be left alone; she looked distinctly unhappy each night when Gabriel insisted upon escorting Anthea back to her house.

Always he chose the back road so they would remain unnoticed, while Anthea was acutely aware they were alone every step of the way. Only the consoling thought that it was far too late in the season for him to attempt to seduce her somewhere along the path kept her from jumping half out of her skin each time he brushed near.

And there, Anthea thought as she carried a platter of fried ham and sliced potatoes to the table and sat down, was the crux of her dilemma. For Gabriel kept *touching* her. Frequently, easily, as if it were both his right and his pleasure.

Just like that, she thought, shivering with the slight contact. He came in from the stables, and before he took his own seat, he passed behind her and put his hand, ever so briefly, on the back of her neck. His fingers were cool, a little damp from a fresh scrubbing, long enough that they spanned her neck easily. His little finger dipped down beneath her collar into forbidden territory, a casual touch that felt anything but casual.

He slid into his chair and nodded his approval at Lily, who carefully balanced a plate piled with golden biscuits that still steamed from the oven. To all appearances it seemed as if he hadn't even noted he'd touched her, while Anthea sat there frozen, every nerve she possessed vibrantly alert, her skin tingling in anticipation of feeling his hands on her again.

She could recall perfectly the first several times he had touched her. A nudge of his hands against hers as they walked together through a narrow portion of the trail. His chest hard against her back as he reached over her shoulder to grab a fresh coffee cup while she stacked dishes in the cupboard. Once, his knee fell wide under the table, bumping firmly against hers and staying a full ten seconds longer than it should.

But now there'd been so many brief touches, she could no longer keep track of individual instances. She knew only that she wandered through each evening lost in the warm haze of sensation he'd spun.

It was not that any one was remarkable, in and of itself. Or even obviously improper. It was that they were nearly constant, too frequent to be as accidental as they seemed, carrying a meaning much deeper than they should have. As if each were a promise, a whisper, even a portent of all touches to come that would not be nearly so easily contained.

She couldn't even protest them. They seemed too unplanned, on the surface too ordinary. Mentioning them would reveal how deeply they affected her, keeping her balanced on a keen edge between antici-pation and dread, her normally tidy, clean-edged world misty and disordered by the sensations he called forth in her when they had no visible effect on him at all.

Except now and then, like right now, his controlled facade cracked. When he'd look at her over a threshold or a table or something else equally ordinary, and his expression would be anything but. His eyes would be hot, his nostrils flared and he looked every bit as bad as the gossips claimed he was, a man clinging to control by a very thin thread, one that threatened to snap at any moment. And the worst of it all was that rather than warning her off as it should, it excited her so much that she was very, very tempted to try to snap it so com-pletely it could never be spliced back together again.

Except she absolutely must not do that. Her life was not entirely her own. She had responsibilities not only to her sisters but to all the children entrusted to her. To Lily most of all, not because the girl was her charge but because there was no one else who would do for her what Anthea was determined to do. She could not ig-nore all those obligations simply because she'd met a man, a completely inappropriate man, who made her insides quiver.

Unable to hold his heated gaze, she dropped her own to her empty plate. For if she looked at him any longer, she was likely to do something completely shocking. Like dive across the table and plant her mouth on his, just to discover if his kiss was as wildly exciting as she remembered, for she must have built it up in her imagination to more than it was. Surely no man could kiss like that. And wouldn't *that* be a good example for Lily?

She fumbled for an innocuous topic. "Lily made the biscuits almost entirely on her own tonight. Don't they smell delicious?"

"Sure do." He grabbed for the plate.

Anthea cleared her throat meaningfully, bowed her head, folded her hands, and waited.

Dutifully Lily mimicked Anthea's position. A beat later Gabriel set the plate back down and laid his hands flat on the table, waiting with barely concealed impatience while Anthea murmured a quick prayer. She considered it simply another part of her duties to ensure that Lily received a modicum of spiritual training. Certainly she was not going to get it from Gabriel. And while he was nowhere near giving thanks along with them, at least he no longer growled when she delayed his dinner with such things.

They ate in silence, the food tasteless in her mouth. For she longed for darker, richer flavors than food, ones that fed far deeper, more elemental hungers.

Utensils clinked against plates, scraped over the surfaces of platters. Evening surrendered to night outside the small dwelling while tension simmered inside it. Both Lily and Gabriel rarely spoke during meals, something to which Anthea found it hard to accustom herself. While she couldn't help but be flattered by their intense concentration on the food she prepared, she considered congenial conversation as important to meals as good fare. But in this aspect of their education she'd failed miserably; any overtures she made were greeted with one-syllable answers and blank stares until she'd given up.

She pushed her barely touched food aside when Gabriel and Lily cleaned their plates for the second time. As she rose to clear the table, Lily joined her, their teamwork as natural as if they'd been doing this for years, while Gabriel pushed his chair back and stretched in satisfaction. He linked his hands over his flat belly, long legs stretched before him, and watched her in a way that Anthea decided was either disturbing or flattering—she didn't know which—but had her cheeks heating regardless.

If things had worked out differently, Anthea thought suddenly, this could have been her life in a few years. A man, a child, a *family*. Warmth washed through her, quickly followed by dismay at the thread of her musings, and she frowned. She'd been quite pleased with how little energy she'd wasted on Gerald and what might have been, though it had taken enormous effort to rise above her grief. But she'd been grieving more than just her canceled engagement then, and she refused to waste a broken heart on a man who'd proved unworthy of it. She was not about to begin now. But sometimes . . . sometimes the regret sneaked in and caught her unawares, as if she'd only delayed the mourning rather than escaped it.

"What's the matter?" Gabriel barked out, the outburst so abrupt Anthea jumped and juggled the stacked plates she carried.

"Excuse me?"

"I asked you what was the matter now."

"But I . . . What makes you think there's something the matter?"

"You frowned." His own frown slashed down, severe and forbidding. "A lot."

"I . . ." As far as Anthea could recall, he'd never initiated a conversation with her unless it was to lodge a complaint about her teaching techniques. He had certainly never inquired about her well-being. "Why do you ask?"

"And why do you look so suspicious? God knows some of that politeness you're always yammering about had to sink in sooner or later," he grumbled. "Sorry I asked."

"If you've suddenly decided to experiment with the 'catch more flies with honey' school of thought, you might do well to sound a *bit* more gracious about it. If you don't mind a suggestion, that is."

His expression clearly said he *did* mind a suggestion, and a few other things as well.

"I'm going to feed Broom," Lily said abruptly.

"The cat?" Gabriel repeated. "You just fed it an hour ago."

"Oh, no," she assured him. "I'm sure she's very hungry. I just know it." And she marched out without a second glance, Gabriel staring after her, befuddled.

"What do you suppose that was about?"

"Do you think she was disturbed by our arguing?" Anthea asked.

"That wasn't arguing. That was downright congenial, unless you've got a lot less backbone than I gave you credit for."

"I know that. But she's just a child. Perhaps she took it more seriously."

Gabriel shrugged. "I've given up trying to figure

out the female of the species. Don't know why I thought it'd be any different if she was nine."

"Oh, I suspect you've figured out plenty of things."

He grinned, wicked and knowing. "Maybe one or two."

Anthea decided that pointing out that she hadn't intended her comment as he had obviously taken it would only get her in deeper. Instead, she retreated to the much safer action of clearing the table.

"How about some coffee?" Gabe asked.

"Oh, of course. Sit down." She reached for the mugs on the high shelf over the stove. "It'll be just a moment."

"That's not what I meant." His hand came down upon hers, stopping its motion, and everything inside her went equally still. His hand was big and hard and rough from work, a thousand miles from the last male hand to touch her, a thousand times better than she remembered it being. She closed her eyes, breathed in the smell of supper and man, breathed in the moment, creating a memory because she had too few like this, when she realized exactly why God had created skin that could *feel*.

"I wasn't asking you to wait on me." His voice was low and intimate, inches from her ear, and still he didn't move away. Now, this *was* improper, she thought in a vague corner of her mind. And she didn't give a darn.

"I was asking if you wanted to sit a moment before we finished cleaning up and have a cup with me."

"Have a cup with *you*?" He could not have missed the breathlessness in her voice. It only remained to be seen whether he would now take advantage of it. And whether she would allow it before her good sense returned.

"Yes. And talk to me."

"Talk?" She knew she sounded slow, but the connection between her brain and her tongue seemed to have been compromised when his hand touched hers. "Why?"

"Just because, that's why," he growled, and yanked his hand away. She sighed before she could stop it.

"If you don't want to—" he began.

"Oh, no, of course not!"

If he had half a brain in his head, Gabriel thought, he would have taken the escape route Anthea had offered and dropped the subject. When had he ever been the slightest bit interested in *talking* with a woman? Not that he wouldn't much rather be doing something other than talking with Anthea, too. Unfortunately he didn't expect that to be happening any time soon.

But he couldn't sit across from her for one more meal and not ask what was on her mind. It would have been immensely safer to leave things as they were. What good could come of getting to *know* her? Far simpler for both of them if he continued to regard her as a prissy, rigid eastern schoolteacher with big ideas, too naive and rosy-eyed to see that those fine ideals would never survive here in the real world.

Except that he'd already discovered there was more to her than that. And when she'd risen from the table and that frown had flickered across her face, dismay and hurt and a wistful sadness, his curiosity had finally gotten the better of him. He was going to find out what made Anthea Bright so sad.

And if it was *someone,* he thought, flexing his hands, that someone would be talking to *him*.

And so, while she stared warily at him, he poured them both coffee and handed her one. She gingerly dropped back into her chair, hands wrapped around her cup, darting uncertain glances at him as if she expected him to pounce. And while that idea undoubtedly held a fair amount of merit, it was not what he had planned.

Not yet, anyway.

He waited with what he considered admirable patience for her to start spilling her secrets. In his experience, the second a man gave the faintest appearance of being willing to listen, a woman started babbling. But she just gulped down coffee and fidgeted in her chair.

Well, when had she ever made it easy on him? What made him think she would start now?

"Heard from your sisters lately?" he barked out.

"My sisters?"

Jesus. Was a simple, polite question from him so strange that she couldn't register it? Her mouth screwed up in consternation—a very kissable position, he noted—and he could almost see her thoughts spin. *What is he up to now?*

"Yeah. Thought maybe you had bad news from home, that's why you looked so unhappy."

"I didn't look unhappy," she said, looking distinctly so.

"You did," he said. He would have rather walked on coals than continue with this conversation. He charged on, determined to have it anyway. "I know it wasn't something I said, 'cause I hadn't *said* anything yet. So is that damned Cox giving you trouble again?"

"I wasn't un—" She stopped, sighed. "Okay, maybe I looked a bit unhappy. It was just a stray memory, and I'd prefer to keep it safely buried. It's really not worth the trouble of discussing, and I'm more than a little annoyed that I thought of it now. Satisfied?"

"*Satisfied* isn't the word that immediately comes to mind, no." He blew out a frustrated breath. Every bit of curiosity he owned screamed at him to keep pushing, to dig through another layer of this surprisingly complex woman. The rest of him, which still had hopes for self-preservation, quickly retreated to firmer ground. "So your sisters are okay?"

She sighed. "I don't know. I got a letter from them. They *sound* fine, but . . . who knows? I haven't been able to send as much money to them as I expected, and while Kate insists they're managing splendidly, and that she's become quite adept at economizing, finding it an interesting challenge, well, let's just say that's never been her strong point before."

"Why wouldn't she tell you the truth?"

"Why *would* she?"

"Oh, I don't know. Respect, honesty, all that other familial stuff?" He swallowed a gulp of coffee. "Don't you tell her the truth?"

"Good heavens, no!" she said, appalled. "If I wrote to them about what Kansas is really like, they'd do nothing but worry about me. For that matter, if Kate knew how much time I was spending with *you*, she'd be on the first train out here!"

"So instead you bend the truth to protect them, and then worry yourself sick because you're afraid they're doing the same thing to you?"

She opened her mouth to protest, then shut it just as quickly. "You really don't know much about families, do you?" she said with a rueful smile.

Pain scraped across a wound he thought thoroughly scarred over years ago. "No, I guess I don't."

"Oh, I'm so sorry!" Sympathy drew her mouth down, her brows together. "That was thoughtless of me."

"It's not worth worrying over."

"I'm certain you'll learn quickly. Now that you have Lily living with you all the time, I'm sure you'll be an excellent father."

"You think so?"

"Of course you will," she reassured him. "She's a lovely child."

"She is, isn't she?" He'd brought Lily here out of guilt and duty. It surprised him to discover he enjoyed having her around. He'd fought that for a while, until he figured, why not? Lily had no one else; why shouldn't he give her that much? What would it cost him to allow himself to care, just a little?

"She certainly inherited your eyes."

"You think so?" Damn it, didn't she know him better than that by now? "That's an interesting observation."

"I . . ." Uncertain of what she'd done to put that fierce expression on his face, she leaned back in her chair, away from him and the intimacy created between them. "What did I say?"

"You really think I'm the kind of man who'd run off and abandon my child? Leave her to the care of a woman like Clarinda?"

"But . . ." She pushed her coffee cup a bit away and folded her hands carefully before her on the table. "It's none of my business."

"Since when has that ever mattered to you?"

She stiffened, half rose from her chair. "Stop scowling at me, Gabriel Jackson. And stop talking in circles. If you've something to say to me, please say it."

"Lily's not my daughter."

"What?" She sank back down, her shoulders falling. "What do you mean, she's not your daughter? Everyone said that . . ." One look at his face showed her her mistake, and she trailed off.

"Everyone says lots of things about me. Haven't you learned that by now?"

"You didn't exactly deny it," she pointed out in her own defense.

"What good would that have done? They were bound to believe what they wanted to believe no matter what I said about it. No one in that town has ever been much interested in whether I'd really done something or not."

She stared deep into her coffee cup. "You could have told me," she said in a small voice.

"I just did," he said softly.

She looked up at him and her expression cleared. Then, surprising him once again, she got up and dragged her chair around the table, only a foot from his side, and sat down again, settling back and settling in. "Go ahead," she said. "Tell me all about it."

She was near enough that he could smell her, some sweet kind of floral soap and shampoo beneath the warm smells of the dinner she'd cooked. Her skin was flushed and very fine, her hair a tumble of pale brown silk. Compassion; he wondered if it had ever before seemed so very close to passion itself.

"If you've got a brain in that pretty head," he said, "you won't sit that close to me."

Her eyes flew to his face, wide and searching, while pink washed over the soft curve of her cheek. She wet her mouth so it gleamed like it had just after he'd kissed her, and desire slammed hard into his belly.

"I'm not worried," she whispered.

"You should be."

"I . . ." Finally she lifted up and scooted her chair around the table, a little at a time—as if he wouldn't notice that way—until the corner was wedged between them.

"Yellow-bellied," he accused her, but amusement warmed his tone.

Her smile remained, flirtatious, relieved, disappointed. "And I doubt you'd have given me fair warning, if you'd really meant to—" She stopped, unable to form the words out loud.

"If I'd really meant to what?"

"Oh, no, I'm not fool enough to fall for that one." Ah, but he wanted to kiss her. To just kiss her, sweet and gentle, almost as much as he wanted to do things that weren't sweet and gentle at all. Odd how the two could coexist, to draw from each other and grow stronger because of it. He'd never felt the like before.

"And speaking of yellow . . ." she said leadingly.

"*Me?*"

"You've managed to change the topic pretty effectively, haven't you? One would think you don't want to tell me about Lily and you and her mother."

He recognized her manipulation and still gave in with surprising ease. Were all men so simply led by the women they wanted? "What do you want to know?"

"Are you . . ." She blushed deeper, her gaze sliding away from his. "Are you certain you're not her father?"

"Oh, I'm certain."

"Her eyes *are* very like yours."

He'd noticed that himself. "Yeah, that's an interesting similarity, isn't it? I can't account for it, but I do know she didn't get them from me."

"But how do you know that—"

"Anthea." He leaned forward and tipped up her chin, forcing her to look at him, amused at how uncomfortable it made her. He'd spent far more time with women who were at ease with earthy matters than he had with women discomfited by them; he'd had no idea how entertaining the latter could be. When it was Anthea, that was. He suspected he wouldn't be nearly so interested if it were another woman. "I *do* know where babies come from. And contrary to popular opinion, I *do* tend to know where I've stuck my—"

"Gabriel!" she exclaimed, and he chuckled, as amused as she was shocked.

"You don't know who her father is?" she prodded, determined to dig through to the heart of the story, rather than keep getting distracting by his banter.

He considered his answer for a moment. He could make a fair guess, but what would it matter? And having others assume the worst of him made him unwilling to do the same to another man without proof. "What I said before was the truth. Her mother was a—" he heard her quick intake of breath, and this time amended his words for her sake "—a friendly sort. It could be almost anyone, for all I know. I haven't been here in a while, in any case." He shrugged. "If you give somebody like Letty Matheson an opening, she's bound to have some speculation. I figure whoever pinned it on me probably did so to deflect suspicion from himself. Not too observant of anyone who believed it, though; I hadn't been back here for over a year when Lily was born."

"I don't suppose it really matters who it is." The bits of himself Gabriel might reveal interested her far more than any idle speculation on Lily's sire. "How'd she end up living with you, then?"

He drummed his thumbs on the tabletop, a quick and uneven beat. "Who else would take her?" Then he hunched forward, his eyes intent, voice low and urgent. "I know what it's like, Anthea, to have no one give you a chance because of something your mother's done. I know what it's like to be the town bastard, to be marked with bad blood before you're even born. I survived it. They were talking about orphanages, talking about all kinds of terrible things . . . What chance would she have had? Better with me than any of the others, I figured. *Somebody* had to do it."

Oh, no. She'd been amused by him, irritated by him, fascinated by him, aroused by him. But this was something new entirely, a softening in the region of her heart, leaving her far more vulnerable to him than she'd been before. If she had any sense at all, she'd stop this right now, hurry back to her dreary little home and stay there until her heart was properly armored again. Nothing good could come of it.

Except he swallowed hard, and his eyes were dark and warm and close, and she didn't want to feel *nothing* when she could feel *this*. "And how did you come to understand so well? How did you become the town bastard?" she asked softly, nudging the conversation away from Lily and him to just *him*, knowing the territory she entered now was far more perilous. For she couldn't, even to herself, cloak it in the drapings of her job, or anything else other than that this man interested her, and she wanted to know him.

"Some of this she told me; some is just a guess on my part. My mother was a young farm girl from Ohio who fell head over heels for a sophisticated older man who'd come to town on business. After he left, she found herself with child, and when her letters went unanswered and her father turned her out, she followed him here, only to find him already married."

"Oh," she said, sympathy a dull ache for both Gabriel and the frightened girl his mother must have been. She shivered, wondering if there was a woman on earth who couldn't imagine herself in that story. It certainly cut closer than Anthea preferred to dwell on.

Gabriel's gaze focused over her shoulder, his rigid expression giving no hint of the emotion beneath. She wondered what it cost him to maintain that detachment, and was sorry that he felt he had to preserve it with her. "He tried to pay her off, of course. But she didn't like the thought of him escaping so easily, and she used the money to buy this place. So we stayed right here, where he had to look at her, and me, and know what he had done."

"In sight, in mind?"

He smiled, an automatic gesture absent of warmth or amusement. "Something like that."

Anthea appreciated Helen Jackson's need to punish her faithless lover. He'd still gotten off too lightly for her taste. But at the same time she also understood only too well what Helen's decision to stay in Haven had cost her son.

"Do you know who he is? What happened to him?"

"By the time I was old enough to make an educated guess, he was already dead. I could have asked her, I suppose, before she died, but what would have been the point? Makes no difference now, does it?"

Anthea tried to imagine not knowing, not even caring, who fathered her. Her own father had been so important to her, both in life and death, that she couldn't fathom it. "Didn't you want to leave?"

"I did leave, soon as I was old enough to shave." His frown deepened. "I know what you're asking, Anthea. But she was a good mother; she gave up everything to have me, to raise me, and she loved me. I always knew that."

Oh yes, she might have loved him, Anthea thought. But not enough to give up her revenge and take her son someplace where he wouldn't be "that bad Jackson boy." Anthea understood him well enough to let it lie, though; he needed to remember his mother that way, and it was not Anthea's place to meddle in his memories. It didn't stop the anger, though, deep and regretful, for what the small child he'd been then had suffered. And she realized suddenly why he'd have to take Lily away, and before much longer.

Oh, God! She was going to lose them both, far sooner than she'd ever realized. And she was only now understanding just how much it was going to hurt.

She told herself it was simple compassion that made her lay her hand over his. But as soon as the hard, rough ridge of his knuckles bumped against her palm, she knew that compassion had little to do with it.

He looked at her, breathing slowly and heavily of the air between them, thick with tension and spiraling want. His eyes were dark, as intensely focused as she had ever seen them, his jaw set at a hard angle, and she saw the effort control cost him. How near it came to shattering.

"You do know, don't you," he told her, "that the only thing that's keeping me from laying you across this table and taking you here and now is that Lily could walk back through that door at any moment."

Oh, it should have scared her to death! The fact that it didn't only proved once again what a fool she was. For she wanted him to do that, wanted to bring him deep and thick and urgent inside her. Could almost taste him in her mouth, feel his body press her down hard against the rough table, and she wanted it so much she could scarcely breathe.

"I know," she whispered, and knew it was too late for her to escape whole.

Lily hunched beneath the window, her back against the house, Broom curled in her lap. Above her she could hear the murmur of voices, of Miss Bright and Mr. Jackson talking, though she no longer paid any attention to what they said. They weren't talking about her anymore, and she'd already heard all she needed to know.

It was wrong to listen when adults were talking. Twice her mother had whacked her across her head when she'd found her listening outside their door, which she'd pushed open just a crack. Lily did it anyway. She'd rather get caught listening sometimes than walk in where she shouldn't. She'd learned that lesson well.

In fact, Lily had figured out she was good at learning lessons, period. She could sit still and listen and watch and remember, lots better than most of the other kids in school. She liked learning things; it made her feel smart, and so she liked going to school even when the other kids were mean to her, because she could listen to all those things that Miss Bright told them. Words and numbers and places all over the world that

Lily hadn't ever heard of before, and that she didn't think her mother had ever heard of, either. And Lily was determined she wasn't going to grow up to be just like her mother, even though that nasty Theron Matheson kept saying that she would.

She ran her hands over Broom; his fur had gotten lots thicker and softer since they'd come to live at Mr. Jackson's house, his belly round and solid. He purred, and she felt his body shake a little every time he made the sound.

Mr. Jackson was not her father.

That's what he'd told Teacher.

It didn't matter. Even if, for just a minute at supper, as she'd sat down between them and eaten with them and seen how they looked at each other, she'd thought that maybe, just maybe, they'd be a family.

But she should have known better. That just wasn't the kind of thing that happened to her. It'd be okay anyway. She could take care of herself.

She was good at that, too. She'd been taking care of herself, and her mother, for a long time. She'd been alone completely for a while after her mother didn't wake up that morning, until Mr. Fred came for his regular Thursday afternoon visit and wouldn't leave without coming in, even though she *told* him not to.

And now she was learning to cook, too, and learning lots of other things from both Miss Bright and Gabriel. It wouldn't matter that he wasn't her father; he didn't seem to mind having her around, and she knew she was good at being quiet and staying out of his way. And since she could cook now, she could do that for him, help him even after they moved away, and maybe he'd let her stay.

Or maybe not. It didn't matter. "We can take care of

each other, can't we, Broom?" she whispered to him, and buried her nose in his fur. He smelled good, like the barn and milk and cat. He was all she really needed.

Chapter 13

Anthea sat behind her desk, stretched the stiffness out of her shoulders, and yawned broadly, enjoying a rare, delicious break. The warm weather had held all week, and she'd shooed the children outside after lunch, figuring they'd best take advantage of it, as it could not last much longer.

For the first time, Anthea remained inside for a moment instead of closely supervising recess, but she was too worried about Lily to leave the children for too long. In fact, she'd already peeked out twice to check on her. Lily was perched on a bench beneath the oak tree, legs crossed at the ankles and tucked properly beneath her, while, with an intently serious look on her face, she watched the other girls play London Bridge. Anthea had been torn between wanting to run out and force the girls to include Lily and rushing over to comfort her herself. The strict admonishment at the institute against favoring one student be damned.

Yes, damned, she thought proudly. She'd yet to swear out loud, but her mental vocabulary was expanding. Miss Addington would be thoroughly appalled. But something about Kansas just seemed to require stronger language.

Still, while Lily's isolation worried her, being lonely was better than being tormented. And Anthea hoped that the students, while not welcoming Lily's presence, might at least become accustomed to it.

Her teaching was going . . . better. It seemed tempting fate to say *well*, but definitely better. It still took all her energy and creativity to make it through a day without bloodshed or natural disaster, and to feel satisfied at the end of it that she'd managed to engage her students enough to impart some small, new bit of knowledge.

Oh yes, she most certainly did have hopes, Anthea reflected. And because she'd had very few for a long time, since her father's death, these hopes seemed all the more precious and fragile in their cautious appearance. She treasured them, guarded them jealously.

If there was one thing above all else she wished to instill in her students, it was hopes.

One hope, however, she desperately endeavored *not* to have. It was a hope, *any* hope, centering on Gabriel Jackson.

The effort exhausted her every bit as much as teaching. She'd simply no armor against a man like him. He was so unlike her customary male acquaintances, polished, handsome, genteel men, comfortable to have around, easy to forget.

Gabriel was none of those things. Except handsome, and even that seemed a rather bland way of describing him. He was vital and harsh and unexpectedly tender, and she felt brilliantly alive in his presence, her senses sharpened, her emotions close to the surface, raw and wonderful.

It was intoxicating and joyous. And undoubtedly treacherous. Because she could not, in her most honest moments, envision a way she would get out of this situation without being irrevocably hurt.

She sighed and slumped wearily, a lapse in posture she allowed herself only in private and probably shouldn't indulge in even then. But the very worst symptom of her foolish fascination—she would not call it infatuation—with Gabriel was that she was getting very little sleep. For she no more than lay down in her bed each night before her imagination insisted on conjuring vivid fantasies of what it would be like if he came to her.

That was why, she supposed, society diligently sheltered young girls before marriage, carefully guarding their innocence. Because it would be somewhat easier to resist such yearnings if one did not have an inkling of what one missed. In fact—

A shriek froze her blood in her veins and cut off her inappropriate musings. *Lily*. She bolted from her chair and flew across the room, her heart knocking hard against her breastbone. The screaming continued, full tilt, the sound of terror. She grabbed the door and yanked it open, ready to fly to the rescue. Half out the door, one foot raised, she spotted what lay on the top landing of the stairway. She grabbed the doorframe with both hands to stop short her left foot six inches above the stairs.

And above the biggest snake she'd ever laid eyes on.

Without thinking, she slammed the door shut, whirled around as if to hold it closed, and gulped in air.

Faint impressions made their way through the fear. The screaming must be Olivia Cox; no one else could maintain that volume for so long. What if she'd been bitten?

Have to protect them. They were her children, her responsibility. There was no one else.

She eased away from the wall and only wobbled a little. "Good," she murmured to herself. Staying on one's feet in a crisis was an excellent first step. "You can do this." Unfortunately, her heart didn't seem nearly convinced; it raced as if it would burst at any moment.

She stood as far away from the door as she could manage and still reach the knob, bracing her free hand against the wall to keep from toppling over. Slowly she eased the door open, peeking through the widening crack, ready to spring away if an ugly serpentine head bent on biting her slithered through the opening.

Fat, sleek, and huge, the creature's black and tan coils, thick as her arm, wound upon themselves so that she couldn't tell which end was tail and which head. It didn't move, just lay there completely still, taking up nearly all of the step so one would have to hop *over* the thing to exit the schoolhouse.

She shuddered. *Over* it? God only knew what it might bite while she was attempting to get past it.

All her students clustered in a half circle around the base of the stairs. The girls, white-faced and shrieking, huddled behind the bigger boys, whose expressions ranged from pale but determined to, in Anthea's opinion, foolishly excited. And Olivia's screams still echoed in the air, which meant that either snakes didn't have ears or it had to be dead.

Too bad she didn't know which.

"Did it bite anyone?" she yelled at them, trying frantically to remember the procedure for drawing poison from a snakebite.

Olivia's wailing made it impossible to hear their answers, but she saw Jon Krotochvill shake his head and mouth a "no."

"Thank God," she whispered, her panic easing a slight fraction.

"Olivia," she said sternly. And then again, *"Olivia!"* at a pitch that rivaled the girl's own.

The sound abruptly ceased, like a train whistle cut off halfway through its blow. Her mouth remained open—ready to let fly at the slightest provocation, Anthea thought—her eyes just as wide.

"Thank you," Anthea told her. "Obviously noise won't frighten it off, despite your valiant attempt." Anthea debated, decided she could risk standing up fully, but kept her hand on the door just in case. "Is it dead?" she asked hopefully.

"Naw, it ain't dead." Theron, who sounded far too cheerful given the situation, piped up from his safe location behind Jon Krotochvill. Well, Anthea would be a fair site happier huddled behind Jon as well; the boy was as large as a barn. "Lifted up its head a while ago."

"His tongue came out!" Mina volunteered. "Tasting for us. My daddy said that's how they do it."

"Okay." She said it as much to herself as to them. "I want you all to back off. Get as far away as you can. All the way back to my soddy, at least."

"Awww." There were a few protests from the boys—and from Jennie Bickersdyke, who remained as calm as ever—but most of the class scrambled to obey. Anthea tore her gaze from the snake long enough to fix the laggards with a severe look.

"Now!" she snapped, and they shuffled reluctantly after the others.

With her students' safety assured, Anthea ordered her brain to formulate a foolproof plan. However, it didn't appear prone to obey her any better than Theron.

The first solution that occurred to her was sending one of the children sprinting for Gabriel to rescue her. She'd ponder the implications of instinctively turning to Gabriel later, but someone else, someone who lived closer, just might work. Anyone with a gun.

She liked that idea. She wouldn't have to do a thing except stand here shaking. She imagined she could manage that just fine.

Except the more she deliberated, the more flaws she saw in the plan. Standing in the open doorway for endless moments, knowing the snake could decide to wake up and attack her at any second, lacked a certain appeal. But she couldn't close the door; what if it decided to move while she wasn't watching? Take off after one of the children, or slither its way below the school and lurk there for days or weeks, awaiting its opportunity to strike?

No, she was going to have to deal with it herself.

"Get farther back!" she yelled when she saw Theron, with Billy and Charlie a few feet behind him, creeping closer to the school. "Tacy, run for your father. Tell him what's going on." Tacy Stoddard drew herself up, shouldering her important responsibility, and raced toward the store like a sprint champion. The store was the nearest place Anthea could be certain of finding help, and she wanted someone here as quickly as possible in case her own attempt to rid them of the serpent failed.

The terrible possibilities of what might happen if she didn't succeed made her sway, and she closed her eyes briefly. *For the children*, she reminded herself. *For Lily*.

Her stomach lodging somewhere around the base of her throat, she edged out the door, mumbling a fervent prayer beneath her breath that the thing remained still. Asleep, maybe. *Please, Lord, asleep!*

She inched sideways, keeping as much distance between her and it as possible, her rump pressed against the iron handrail.

There was no way to inch by it without her skirts nudging one of those lethal-looking coils. And she certainly wasn't going to jump over it.

So she hopped up and balanced on the shaky rail, grabbing desperately, hanging on tight while she wobbled on the skinny perch. Then she took a deep breath, whipped both legs over, and dropped to the ground, landing in a flurry of skirts and petticoats and *thank you, Gods*.

She grabbed her skirts in both hands and took off, pelting across the yard in a most unladylike manner. She heard shouts from the children, but they didn't register. "Keep an eye on it!" she shouted to them over her shoulder as she raced for her soddy, "but don't any of you dare get any closer!"

The rifle Gabriel had given her remained where she'd put it that first night, propped up in an inconspicuous corner, a chair placed in front of it to shield it from her sight. She'd endeavored to ignore its presence in her home. Gabriel had brought up the subject a few times, reminding her that he was willing to teach her how to use it, and she'd promptly changed the subject. Why, oh *why* hadn't she listened to him?

She yanked the chair out of the way and grabbed the gun in both hands, trying to remember what he'd told her. *Point, pull the trigger, and pray* seemed pretty much to sum it up.

She held the gun away from her and ran back out of her home and toward the schoolhouse, wondering if she was taking her life in her hands more with the gun than with the snake.

"Stay back," she shouted again at the children, who'd drawn together in a tight knot beneath the oak tree.

"Miss Bright!" She heard a voice yell at her, but didn't stop to identify its source.

The snake gleamed black and tan, shiny as leather, and revulsion curled in her stomach. Thank God it hadn't hurt anyone yet! She'd do her best to ensure it never did.

Raising the gun to her shoulder, she ignored the hubbub of noise from her students. She'd comfort them after the danger was eliminated.

The gun blast exploded, the force kicking her shoulder as hard as a temperamental mule, throwing her back three feet. The sudden silence buzzed in her ears, and the blackness confused her until she realized she must have squeezed her eyes shut when she'd pulled the trigger. Cautiously she cracked them open, unsure of what she'd see.

She hadn't missed after all. She'd shot the snake clean in half, the two pieces thrown a good three feet apart, the staircase shattered into a million splinters. Some of them had fallen only inches from her feet. She took a quick step back, whirling around so she didn't have to look at what she'd done, feeling vaguely sick. She didn't think she'd ever killed anything bigger than a bug before. Not even a chicken, for Mrs. Hargreaves had always done the butchering.

Theron Matheson stood right behind her, his face white as chalk. When had he come so near? She'd *told* them all to remain safely back.

"You killed it," he said in a low, shocked voice.

"Yes." And then, despite the part of her that recoiled at what she'd done, she also felt a distinct pride. She'd faced her first real crisis, protected her students from danger. She felt like a real westerner now.

"But . . . but . . ." His breathing hitched. "You *killed* it."

"I had to. I couldn't let it hurt one of you."

Some of the other students had arrived by then, stepping gingerly across the yard, some keeping their gazes carefully averted from the gruesome mess behind her, others staring in morbid fascination.

"Miss Bright," Jon said slowly, "you didn't take it for a rattler, did you?"

"That was a possibility." The edge of urgency was backing off now. "I couldn't take the chance it was dangerous."

"Rattlers are brown, got diamond markings. That's just a big ol' bull snake. Wouldn't hurt anythin' bigger 'n a rabbit."

"Oh." Anthea could scarcely tell a bull snake from an actual *bull*, much less from some other variety of serpent.

"Can't imagine what it's doin' out this time of year, though. Should be hibernatin' by now."

"You murdered my snake!" Theron's eyes were dry, flaming with virulent animosity.

"Your snake?" She'd never heard of such a thing.

"My snake."

Nausea coiled into a potent ache. She tried to explain, even as she knew it would be of little use. "Theron, I'm sorry, I had no idea, I—"

His gaze slid over her shoulder, to the remains behind her, and he swallowed heavily. Though she was likely the last person in the world he wanted comfort from, she had to try, and stretched a hand toward him. "Theron," she began again.

"It was *mine*." He whirled and ran away, head down, fists pumping hard, as if he could escape the hurt if he just ran enough. Anthea wondered if the mischievous antagonism he'd displayed toward her thus far had just hardened into true hatred.

Lily had made her way to Anthea's side, and leaned lightly, comfortingly, against her. Anthea looped her arm around her narrow shoulders and hung on.

"Come on," she told what remained of her class. "I think we'll move the rest of the day's lessons into my soddy."

Gabriel stood in a wash of cold moonlight just outside the schoolhouse. It seemed later than it truly was; heading into December, the dark came early and deep, as relentless as the cold that had finally settled in to stay more than a week ago.

The schoolhouse was jumping. The windows glowed with warm, friendly light, bright squares of glass forming an irregular checkerboard with the boarded-up panes. He could hear singing—he supposed that was what you'd call it—not much melody, but a steady one-two-three beat, and the rhythmic, considerably less steady stamping of dozens of feet.

Anthea was obviously having one of those damn dancing lessons again.

He'd sought her out to inform her she shouldn't bother walking Lily home tomorrow, for he planned to pick her up right after school with the wagon and head to Centervale to go shopping. And the anticipation he'd felt at the prospect of catching her alone convinced him that he was doing absolutely the right thing in getting out of town and putting Anthea out of his reach, if only for a few days.

The humming that substituted for music halted, followed by a smattering of applause before the infernal stomping began again. They sounded less like a group of dancers than a cattle stampede.

He blew on his cold fingers. A thin layer of snow coated the ground, and an inconsistent wind caught it now and then, blowing nearly transparent sheets into small drifts against walls and trees.

He had a sudden, sharp longing for Colorado. He wondered idly, and perhaps not so idly, whether Anthea would take to such a place.

He'd no idea what he was going to do about the woman. Lily needed her far more than he did. For Lily's sake, he had to keep their relationship simple and clean. And yet . . . and yet he spent each day, each moment in her presence, balanced on a sharp edge between control and wildfire. Every day he thought it couldn't get any worse. That he couldn't want her any more, that he couldn't see her smile at him or fuss at him without either giving in and taking her then and there or burning up. But then she'd skip in the door hand in hand with Lily, laughing and bright-eyed, her cheeks cold-stung and red, both of them glowing, and he'd not only discover that yes, he could want her more, but also remember why he couldn't have more of her than he already did.

The front door opened, a thin sliver of light that vanished in an instant, revealing a glimpse of a tall, bulky figure.

Gabriel stayed in the shadows, ignoring the man making his way down the stairs, fully expecting the man would do the same.

But he stopped halfway across the yard. "Jackson? That you?"

Shoot. So much for staying in the shadows. "Yeah, it's me."

The man ambled over to him until Gabriel could make out his face. That brief exchange had been more words than had passed between them in a dozen years.

The man took up a stance mimicking Gabriel's, studying the old schoolhouse. He tugged a flask from his hip pocket, screwed off the top, and took a deep swig. "Aaahh." He swiped the back of his hand across his mouth, then tilted the flask in Gabriel's direction. *What the hell?*

"Go on," the man urged. "Made it myself."

What the hell indeed. Figuring it couldn't be poison since he'd drunk it down first, Gabriel accepted the flask, poured a hefty draft down his throat. The harsh liquid burned its way straight to his stomach where it banked into a nice glow.

"Good?"

"Yeah. Thanks."

The man nodded. "Man's gotta have a hobby."

Gabriel couldn't think of a comment worthy of that statement, so he kept his mouth shut.

"You remember me?" the fellow asked at last.

"Sure. Davey Conroy." His open, easy features closely resembled those of his sister, Thisba Stoddard, but were genuinely rather than calculatedly genial. "Haven't changed that much."

"Oh, a little." He thumped his sturdy belly. "Stopped growing hair, started growing a stomach."

"It happens."

"To some of us." He tipped the flask in Gabe's direction. "More?"

"No, thanks."

Davey took another swig while Gabriel waited, figuring he'd get to his point sooner or later.

Davey sighed in satisfaction. "Gets a little steamy in there, all that shuffling around. Man's gotta fortify himself now and then."

"I can imagine."

Davey pointed toward the schoolhouse with his chin. "You comin'?"

"Not unless you pour about three gallons of that stuff down my throat first." Everyone in Haven staring at him as he stamped around was pretty much Gabriel's idea of hell. He'd spent too much of his life with every eye in Haven fixed suspiciously upon him to put himself voluntarily in a situation that would encourage it.

Davey chuckled. "Never can tell. Thought maybe that little schoolteacher might be incentive enough."

Gabriel assessed him warily. Is *that* why Davey'd suddenly taken it into his head to chat? Was Davey, too, concerned that he'd contaminate Anthea and the children by association? "Nope," he said in a neutral tone. "What about you? Not that I've been keeping track, but I didn't think you had kids."

"Nope. Not yet, anyway." Davey shrugged. "Got a wife, though. And she gets right friendly after an evenin' of dancing."

Gabriel didn't know how to respond to that, so he reserved comment. But he'd just about run out of patience with small talk. He turned to face Davey, crossing his arms over his chest. "We haven't as much as said hello since we were kids. Why so friendly suddenly?"

Davey met his gaze evenly. "Maybe I'm just feeling bad about the way I treated you back then. We were almost friends, least for a while. I'm sorry about the rest."

"Why'd you do it?" *Well hell*, Gabe thought. Why'd he even bother to ask? He would have sworn it had never bothered him. Not then, certainly not now.

Davey had hardly been the worst of his tormentors. But he'd been the one who'd been the closest to being a friend first.

"Hell, man, I was just a kid." He smiled ruefully. "You think I was going to stand against Cox, an' everybody else, too, for your sake? I'm not that good."

When it came right down to it, who was, when they were ten? Still, after all this time Gabe couldn't quite trust him. "Why should I believe you now?"

"No particular reason, I guess. Except why hold what the kid did against the man? Hope we've all grown up some since then." He shrugged massive, farm-built shoulders. "I ain't plannin' on holdin' the things you did then against you now."

Fair enough, Gabriel decided. "You still got that pretty bay?"

Davey's placid face lit up. "Sure do. Give me a dozen good foals before I figured she'd earned a rest."

"I might be interested in lookin' at some, if you've still got a couple around."

"That I do. You know where I am? Took over my father's place. Come by whenever. I'm always there." He rubbed his hand thoughtfully over his broad chin. "Speaking of which, if you're ever thinkin' of selling your mother's place, now that she's gone, I'd be grateful if you'd give me a shot at it. I'm plannin' to expand."

"What makes you think I'd be willing to sell?"

"No reason for you to be hanging around, now that your mother's gone. Don't figure the place holds a whole lot of fond memories for ya."

Gabriel's eyes narrowed. "You the buyer Cox told me about?"

"Huh?" Davey's look of surprise would have required more acting talent than Gabe gave him credit for.

"Never mind," Gabe said. "Is that what this sudden friendliness is about?"

"Gave me a nudge in this direction," he admitted placidly. "Doesn't make it any less true." He drained his flask and swiped the back of his hand across his mouth. "Did I just lose my chance?"

"I can respect a man who takes care of business." *What the hell*, Gabe thought again, and extended his hand. "I'll give you first shot. But it won't come cheap."

"Didn't expect it to." He pumped Gabe's hand, then

sighed in resignation. "S'pose I should go back in there and spin Fannie around for a while."

"That's right. You married Fannie Millard, didn't you?"

Davey's amiable expression darkened abruptly. "You know her?"

"Not well," Gabe lied readily, not willing to stir up old waters. Not to mention that he already had personal knowledge that Davey had a fist like a meat hook. "I remember her vaguely, that's all. She always had such a shine on you."

His face cleared. "Yeah, she did. Maybe I'll go around the floor with her a few more times, if she wants to."

"Think you missed your chance." Gabe hooked his thumb in the direction of the schoolhouse door, which had popped open and was spilling out couples in a hubbub of laughter and snatches of wordless songs. "Looks like they're done."

Davey swore under his breath. "Now she's gonna be mad that I missed the last dance."

"So dance with her when you get home."

"You mean just the two of us? Private-like?" He shook his head. "Got no music, though."

"They didn't have any in there, either," Gabriel pointed out.

"You think she'd like that?"

"I can almost guarantee it."

Chapter 14

Gabriel allowed the festive group of dancers to clear out before he approached the schoolhouse. Anthea hadn't left with the rest. Cleaning up the place for the next day, no doubt. The light inside dimmed bit by bit, until only a faint glow remained. Yes, she'd be careful not to waste the kerosene the school board was so stingy with.

His heart pounding unaccountably hard, he mounted the steps, noting absently they no longer protested beneath his weight. The last person to leave hadn't shut the door completely, and wan light spilled onto the stairs; he quietly eased through the opening.

It was considerably warmer inside, smelling of chalk dust and coffee and, faintly, the people who'd danced there—a little healthy sweat, an echo of powder and perfume.

Anthea slumped in the chair by her desk, her feet stretched out in front of her, her head drooping, an informal posture he rarely caught her in. A single lantern sat squarely in the center of her desk, limning her in shifting gold and shadow.

Most of her hair had fallen down around her shoulders—yes, she'd dance with considerable energy, he thought, enough to send her hair tumbling free of its pins. And joy, laughing, smiling, encouraging.

He watched her yawn, linking her hands and stretching them over her head, her breasts curving high against her neat white blouse, and his mouth went dry.

Odd, how he seemed to have fixed on this woman. Was it as simple as that she was the one he shouldn't have, for her sake, for Lily's sake? Passions were ever a perverse master, the world full of examples proving that point.

And yet . . . somehow it seemed like it might be as much for his own sake as theirs he resisted her. She poked and prodded places deep inside him that he didn't really want awakened. He'd lived quite comfortably for years with them safely walled off.

Even from where he stood, he could detect her deep sigh, the rise and fall of a chest with which he was becoming inordinately obsessed. She planted her hands on the desk and pushed herself to her feet, a weary set to her shoulders.

Once, he would have thought that it served her right. Would have considered it only fair justice that a woman like her, pampered and indulged her whole life, must now experience real work and the exhaustion it bred. Now he was tempted to tell her to sit down, that he'd deal with the mess left by her silly dancing lessons.

Not that he wouldn't like her thoroughly drained. But he'd rather be the one who'd caused it, to see her limp and flushed with satisfaction, sprawled across his bed.

She moved toward a small table beneath a window and began clearing off the clutter of used coffee cups and plates holding half-eaten pieces of cake.

"I'll help you," he said.

"Oh!" She started, looked up with her eyes wide and mouth open. "Oh," she said again. "Gabriel." And then she smiled, bedazzled and bedazzling, and he knew that no one, not *ever*, had looked that happy to see him. Warmth bloomed in his chest, very different from the heat she always sparked in him, no less difficult to ignore. "Did you come for a dancing lesson? I'm afraid you're too late," she teased.

"If you'll give me a private one, I might be persuaded."

Anthea opened her mouth to respond in a comfortably teasing manner, found she couldn't manage it. His voice had dropped on those words, low and unmistakably seductive, and much as she longed to, much as she *burned* to, she knew she couldn't go over and let him put his arms around her now. She'd assured a few nervous matrons that there was nothing improper whatsoever about the kind of dances she intended to teach them, but she suspected any dance in which she touched him, even so much as one finger to one finger, would become something far more than improper before she knew what happened.

"If I begin giving every person in Haven private

lessons," she said lightly, "I'll never have time to get anything done."

He grinned, a smile that said he knew very well why she avoided the subject, a grin that promised *not now, but someday soon,* and Anthea found she had to concentrate to keep her breathing normal. He was so *there,* dark as the night outside, every bit as threatening to proper schoolteachers who thought they could venture into the unfamiliar night without danger.

Except part of her wasn't a proper schoolteacher at all. And as much as she battled to keep it inside, one look from him threatened to release it, wild and perilous, and oh, so wonderful.

"Come," he said, letting her off the hook . . . this time. "I'll help you clean up."

"You don't have to do that."

"I know."

They worked easily together, side by side in the warm, intimate light. Too easily; it betrayed how much time they'd spent together recently.

"Someone finally got around to fixing those steps, huh?" he commented as he swept the floor clean of the mud the dancers had tracked in with the snow, now dried to clumps.

"There wasn't much choice."

"Hmm?"

Anthea had been stacking all the dirty plates in a dishpan to lug back to her place to wash. She straightened, blew out a breath that lifted the light hair along her temple. "The snake, remember? The steps were in a lot more pieces than it was."

"Oh." He tried not to laugh, felt the tug of a smile at the corners of his mouth. "Lily told me about that. Didn't realize you'd murdered the steps, too."

"Don't remind me." She frowned, still disturbed by the memory. "Jon Krotochvill built them for me that night while I was over trying to explain to Mrs. Matheson what had happened. Thank goodness; I wasn't up to dealing with that mess."

"Jon's taken a bit of a shine to the teacher, has he?"

"Maybe just a little one."

Gabriel didn't blame him a bit. He walked over and joined her, leaning comfortably on the handle of the broom.

"Are you ready to run home yet, city girl?"

"Not quite yet." But she would. He just knew that she would. This place was not for the likes of her. He only hoped that he and Lily would be ready to let her go when the time came.

"I'm never going to hear the end of it, am I?"

"Probably not," he admitted. "What did the Mathesons say?"

Anthea sighed, her distress evident. "*Mrs.* Matheson took me aside and *thanked* me. Seems she was terrified of the snake herself. Said she didn't sleep for a week when the thing got out once; they found it curled up under her *bed,* can you imagine? But she couldn't bring herself to force Theron to get rid of it."

"That explains a few things right there, doesn't it?"

"He wasn't fond of me to begin with."

He was close enough to smell her now, a scent that drifted through his dreams every night so he'd wake up, hot, deeply aroused. He took in her scent now, storing it up, warm hair and skin and soap.

"I can't imagine what he'll do now. He sits in the back of the room staring at me, and I can tell he's just trying to think of the best way to get back at me. There've been a few things, nothing serious yet. I keep losing my pens, and my chair broke out from under me when I sat down." She winced. "I'm still bruised."

Gabriel nobly refrained from offering to inspect her injury for her.

"I'm sorry for what happened," she went on, "but—"

"Anthea."

She looked down at her hands, gripping the edges of the enameled dishpan. She couldn't look at him. He was so near she could feel his heat; if she dared raise her head, she knew her mouth would be only inches from his. Knew, too, if she did that, she couldn't be trusted.

"I know I'm supposed to be listening right now." The words came low, his voice tight with strain, so she had to listen carefully to catch each one. "I know that this is important to you. But the truth of it is, I just can't talk to you anymore."

Anthea swallowed hard, her fingers curling tight around the smooth, cold edge of the washtub. *Move*, she told her feet. *Move!* But they were no more obedient than the rest of her. No longer under the control of her logical mind, but instead totally in thrall to raw emotion and craving and purely physical need.

"Look at me, Anthea."

"I can't." She squeezed her eyes shut. "I *shouldn't*."

"Look at me."

Oh, why had she even tried to resist? She'd known since the first that if he truly wanted her, she was his. Slowly, without conscious choice—when had she ever had a choice where he was concerned?—she did as he commanded.

The lamplight caught in his dark pupils, reflected like firelight. Or perhaps that flame came from within him, growing, burning, waiting impatiently to consume them both.

He put his big strong hands on her waist and lifted her easily, his fingers pressing firmly, and walked her backward until her back met the rough wood wall. Slow, deliberate, unstoppable, his gaze holding hers all the time, his face harsh with need.

He laid his body against hers, pinning her between himself and the wall, her feet dangling inches off the floor, her mouth level with his. She could feel every breath he took, his chest pushing against hers, and each of her own inhalations pressed her breasts against him, a sweet-hard pain. Their hearts thumped against each other's chests, so fast and wild she couldn't tell which was hers and which was his.

And then he kissed her. Hard, soft, shallow, deep, a hundred ways, a hundred moments, a hundred new things she'd never felt before. Her heart stopped and started again, a brand-new rhythm. The world whirled around her, in her, the feel and smell of him dark and rich and intoxicating. He tasted as if he'd been drinking something with bite—nothing bland or simple here, not with Gabriel.

But sweet, still. Sweet as daybreak, stunning and piercing and gentle all at the same time. His mouth was wicked, skilled, all-consuming. His tongue tasted hers, skated along the line of her teeth, tickled the roof of her mouth, claiming everything, missing nothing that might yield pleasure to them both. Her hands were on his shoulders, and her fingers clenched but found no purchase because he was all muscle and bone and hardness.

She squirmed, trying to get closer even though it was impossible. They could not be any closer without their bodies melding. Her toes drummed against his shins, and he groaned, leaned in deeper, taking her down into a place formed only of sensation and desire.

He tore his mouth away and she whimpered at the loss. "Shh," he whispered against her cheek, and her whimper changed into a moan as his mouth roamed over her cheek. He sucked her earlobe into the hot, damp hollow of his mouth, bit down gently, and she jolted against the wall. "God, I love your ears," he said, his breath flowing hot and ticklish and arousing.

His mouth was at her neck, and her head rolled against the wall. Thank heavens his body still held hers in place; if he moved away, she thought dimly, there was no way her legs would hold her up. She would sink to the floor, melted into a quivering mass.

He flexed his hips, driving her against the wall and the breath completely from her lungs. His hands edged up until his thumbs brushed against the lower curves of her breasts, and she waited, afraid to hope, afraid to want, utterly afraid to move or breathe in case he might stop.

There. Oh, there. Heaven and hell in one, too much and not enough. She felt his thumbs scrape over the tips of her breasts, pressing hard so she could feel him through the fabric of her clothing. If only her garments could disappear by her wishing them gone! She craved those hands on her, hot and rough and demanding on naked flesh.

She moved her own hands up, pushed her fingers deep into the thick, healthy luxury of his hair. All her senses were well pleased with him, and she tried to force open eyes grown heavy, so that she could look her fill as well.

He was so close she could make out the texture of his skin in the dim light, the rough stubble of a day's growth of beard, the lines that fanned around his eyes from years spent in the sun.

His big hands molded to her breasts, long fingers spanning nearly to her collarbone, where his mouth came to tantalize. Her head lolled back on her neck, her lids half-open. Through a haze of shadows and passion she saw the rough wall of the schoolhouse, the partially broken window flanked by portraits, the disapproving stares of former presidents. A tiny, unwelcome seedling of sanity sprouted.

"Wait," she said with effort, "we can't . . ." His fingers did something wickedly wonderful then, plucking at the very tips of her breasts and sending spears of pleasure down her center, and her thoughts scattered. She regathered them with effort, trying to hold on to logic when all she really wanted to do was surrender completely to the magic of his touch and never, ever think again.

"Someone . . . someone could come in. We're in the *school*, Gabriel, we can't . . ."

He went still against her, hands firmly on her breasts, mouth open against the curve of her neck. He was breathing as hard as if he'd just sprinted miles, his chest pushing against her and away with each breath. And she felt it all keenly, the texture of his jaw against the tender skin of her neck, the bluntly sexual press of his hips against hers, the precise fit of his hands cupping her breasts.

And then he moved his hands down, gripped her hips to hold her firm, and pushed himself away from her. She felt . . . abandoned, the wonder and incitement of his body against hers stolen away. Once he'd lowered her safely to the floor, he dropped his hands and stepped back.

The lines of his face were brutal, his mouth hard, eyes blazing with fire and fury.

"You're right, we can't," he said tightly.

She wanted to protest—*no, that's not what I meant, I meant not here, not now. I didn't mean not ever!* But then she bit down to hold her tongue; decisions should not be made when she was in the grip of this passion, should not be driven by something that wasn't thought or even emotion but purely a carnal urge.

He jammed his arms across his chest, his movements jerky, angry; and yet, when those arms had been around her, had held her to that hard plane, they'd felt strong, comforting, protective, each motion fluid and smoothly controlled.

"You can't come to the farm anymore. You have to stay away."

And the loss of the pleasure he'd brought her with his body became the possibility of the loss of something much more precious. "Gabriel," she said, her throat aching.

"We can't be alone."

It was sensible, it was reasonable, it was safe. It was absolutely the right thing to do. And everything in her protested. She wanted it, wanted *him*, the near violent, turbulent, treacherous rush of feeling he gave her with each look, each touch. "But Lily . . ."

"She can stay, work with you here after school." His already fierce expression hardened further. "That is, if you want her to."

"Of course I want her to," she said, hurt that he would even ask.

He gave a quick, hard nod. "I'll come in to pick her up. Right before supper."

"You don't have to do that." It all was happening so quickly, spinning away from her when she still felt dulled and slow-witted from his kisses. She couldn't get her brain to work right, couldn't come up with other solutions. She didn't like *this* one, she knew that.

Later, she thought. They'd done nothing irrevocable. She would figure out what to do later, when her head was cool and clear again. Away from him.

"I can bring her out. *After* supper," she couldn't help but add. Eating alone again seemed immeasurably lonely. "You don't have to come and fetch her."

"Yes," he said, so intense he looked cruel. "I do."

"Are you sure you want to go home?" George Bickersdyke asked from high on his buggy seat. White wisps curled from his mouth with each breath, his collar snugged up high beneath his ears. Christmas had dawned bitterly cold this year, holding nothing of soft comfort in the air. "Hate to think of you alone on Christmas. Wouldn't mind you stayin' with us at all. The girls'd think it grand fun to bunk with you."

"No." Anthea forced a smile that she fervently hoped looked a lot more cheerful than it felt. "Everyone's been so very kind, intent on making sure I wasn't lonesome, I'm ready for a little peace and quiet."

"S'pose I can't blame you, considering your days don't usually hold a whole lot of peace and quiet."

Anthea's smile widened, more genuine now. "I wouldn't have it any other way."

"All right, then. If you need anything, don't be shy about asking."

"I won't."

He lifted his hand to the brim of his felt hat, tugged it down slightly. "Be seeing you around, then. And that sure was a right fine Christmas program."

"Thank you." It had taken two weeks of nerve-wracking rehearsal, not to mention a fair amount of bribery with her best gingersnap cookies, to achieve the desired result, but she'd been quite proudly delighted with the success of the program as well. She'd had to prompt lines only four times, and there'd scarcely been a dry eye in the house during the final chorus of "Silent Night." "And please thank Mrs. Bickersdyke for me as well. It was a lovely evening."

"Will do. You scurry on in before your toes freeze off, now. I'll not be leaving until I see you safely behind that door, or my wife'd have my hide when I got home."

Despite the robes that Mr. Bickersdyke kept in his buggy, she'd stopped feeling her toes five minutes ago, so she needed no further encouragement to hurry inside, for once grateful to return home. For dreary as her abode was in most ways, it lived up to its promises in one regard: it really was quite snug.

Though the sun had set hours ago, she could see surprisingly well. New snow crunched beneath her boots and magnified the cold silver moonlight.

Hand on the door latch, she glanced over her shoulder, waved one last time to Mr. Bickersdyke, and shoved open the door. Behind her she could hear his command to his horse, and the creak of leather tack before the clopping of hooves on hard-packed snow.

Pitch darkness greeted her inside the soddy, an abrupt contrast to the brightly reflected moonlight, and so despite the cold wind at her back, she left the door open for a moment to help her locate the lantern she kept on a small, upturned crate to the left of the door. Kate had knit her thick new mittens for Christmas—she didn't figure Anthea's pretty leather gloves were of much use in Kansas, she'd written—and Anthea tugged them off, her fingers cold in spite of the hefty wool. She shuddered to think what they'd have been like in those gloves, which were utterly useless.

She groped along the splintering wood surface, found the matches, and fumbled to light the lantern. As soon as the soft light chased the worst of the shadows, Anthea quickly tugged the door closed behind her, shutting out the air that had dropped the inside temperature of the room a good ten degrees in the brief time it had been open, and leaned wearily against it. She'd spent the entire day, and Christmas eve as well, traipsing from home to home, for it seemed that every one of her students' families deemed it their responsibility to make sure the poor schoolteacher, so far from home, would not have to spend the holiday alone.

They'd all been so conscious of her presence, carefully on their best behavior, the students displaying the manners she'd taken such pains to teach them, their parents stiff with pride. It had been perfectly obvious to Anthea that, while they certainly welcomed her, they also couldn't wait until it was someone else's turn to entertain her so they could return to their family celebrations undisturbed. And so, though she was completely surrounded by people and good intentions, she'd never felt so very alone.

She started to heave a sigh but stopped on the uptake. What was that smell? She didn't believe she'd left anything out to spoil; it would be quite unlike her.

Anthea shot the bolt Gabriel had insisted upon installing for her only a few weeks after they'd met, and had made her promise that she'd use every time she was home. She made her way over to the stove, and the smell dissipated slightly. The metal door was cold to the touch as she cranked it open, even though she'd banked the coals carefully before she left that morning. Odd. They were dead ashes now, so she sighed and resigned herself to the task of building a fire.

She fed the first tiny flickers slivers of dried grass; one couldn't gorge a fire, she'd learned early on, though the patience required came hard to her.

She'd gone to the home of every one of her students over this holiday but one. And she would have traded every single visit, all the pretty little cakes they'd fed her, for ten seconds with Gabriel and Lily.

How could she miss them so much? She'd known them barely two short months. And yet their absence on this holiday left two hollow aches in her chest, twins to the ones where her sisters resided.

She'd seen him only briefly since that night in the schoolhouse. He'd come to the Christmas program late, slipping in the back door without a sound—she knew his entrance had been utterly silent, for not one head in the room had lifted but hers. But somehow she'd known he was there, and looked up from straightening Mina's Virgin Mary costume to find him standing in the shadows at the back of the room. His head was bare—foolish man, after all the trouble they'd had over his hat when it was *warm*, and now that it was approaching zero, he wandered around uncovered—his hair rumpled from the wind, his face dusky with cold, his heavy jacket unbuttoned, and she couldn't look away. She took in every detail through eyes that were hungry for the sight of him, stored them away in a mind that seemed to have a space reserved just for images of Gabriel.

Lily had been a beautiful angel, a part that Anthea took great pleasure in assigning her. And her eyes had met Gabriel's again, this time with fierce pride for this child they both claimed in some small way, and Anthea's heart lifted for the first time in weeks. *Maybe,* she thought. Maybe there was a way to make this work after all.

She wasn't entirely sure what she meant by *this*. Not friendship, which was too innocuous and bland a term for it; even she was not fool enough to believe that what was between them could be contained in such narrow boundaries. Not *lover*, surely; she was not that foolhardy, and she knew full well it risked her job and her future, and would be a terrible example for Lily and all the other children. Not to mention the disaster that would occur if she . . . if *they* . . . Her mind skirted around the possibility of a child. It was too big a thing even to wrap her thoughts around.

And not marriage, either, although that idea never failed to cause a curious little quiver in her midsection, and insisted upon popping up no matter how diligently she tried to evict it. But there were a hundred reasons to reject it—first and foremost of which was that he wasn't going to *ask* her—and only one in favor of it. The fact that she wanted, longed, *craved* to sleep with him hardly weighed equally against the fact that she must secure her sisters' futures before she could concern herself with her own. Not to mention that he was clearly not the marrying kind, and should some madness seize him to change that, the wife he'd take would be someone who would be of far more assistance to him than she could be, someone who possessed fortitude, strength, and experience. Someone who could break a colt and cook supper over a campfire.

Someone who could tell the difference between a bull snake and a rattler.

So what *did* she want, exactly? Frowning, she prodded at the small flames, fed in a few sticks as thick as her thumb.

All of them. She wanted all of those things, and wasn't going to get any of them. So what? She hadn't wanted her parents to die, hadn't wanted her father to grieve so desperately for his wife he let his business run to ruin, hadn't wanted Gerald to break their engagement, hadn't wanted to leave her sisters. She'd gotten all of them anyway, and survived them, too. And even managed to discover something new and precious, something she hadn't expected, in the process. Who knew what might come of *this*? Perhaps not what she *wanted*, but maybe something she would cherish all the same.

The fire well established, she judged it safe enough for her to risk adding a few good-sized branches. After poking them in, she straightened and turned toward her bed. While the mattress stuffed with wild grasses and laid over a simple rope frame couldn't compare with the fine four-poster she'd slept in for years, tonight she definitely looked forward to it.

"What in the world?" she murmured. Between the lantern and the firelight, she could just discern the rough outlines of the bed. It shone white, the quilt thrown back to the foot, although she was sure that she'd made it that morning, as she always did. The center of the bed lay in shadow, but as she approached it, she realized it wasn't shadows at all but something dark marring the bleached surface of the sheets.

She approached warily, the rank smell mounting with each step.

She shrieked in equal parts frustration and rage. Someone—and she'd be willing to take bets on who—had raided a barn and dumped what looked to be at least two bucketfuls of manure right in the middle of her beautiful clean sheets. The sheets she'd packed carefully in Philadelphia and brought all the way out here on the train, sacrificing her brocaded gray wool suit to free up the space in her trunk.

"Anthea!" Gabriel's fist pounding on the door followed his shout. "Anthea! Are you all right? Open up and let us in!"

Chapter 15

Anthea flew across the room, shot open the door bolt, seized the latch in both hands, and yanked.

"Look!" she cried. "Look what they did!"

Gabriel grabbed her by the shoulders so hard her head bobbed. "Are you all right?"

"Of course I'm all right," she told him. "Look!"

She clutched his hands and leaned forward as if battling a stiff wind. She dragged him across the room to the side of her bed and flung her hand wide, encompassing the entire scene. "My beautiful sheets! Kate embroidered them. She has such a fine way with a needle."

"Oh. Your sheets." Gabriel clapped a hand to his chest, pleased to discover that his heart continued to beat. When Anthea had screamed, he'd just about up and died on the spot. He sniffed the ripe air. "Pig, I'd wager."

"Pig!" She sniffed herself, but from an entirely different cause. "Katie should have sold those sheets, I just knew it. We certainly could have used the money. But when I had to come out here she thought I should have something of home, and they were . . . M-mother's once, and then—"

"Aww, sweetheart." He looped an arm around her shoulders and hauled her up against his chest. She burrowed in immediately, curling up like she meant to stay, her shoulders shaking with each sniffle. "I didn't mean to make light of it." Now that the raw terror was fading, he was getting pretty darn pissed. In fact, he rather anticipated the idea of getting his hands on whoever'd done it. He didn't care if they were too young to beat; clearly there'd been a deficiency of beating in their lives so far. "I just . . . I was so scared, when you screamed. I was afraid that you . . ."

She lifted her head, looked up at him through eyes that were watery and beautiful. "You—you were worried about me?"

He cupped her face, used his thumb to wipe away a tear. *They made Anthea cry*, he thought. *I'll have them cleaning out pigsties for a decade.* "Yeah, I was worried about you," he admitted gruffly.

"Oh." Her smile wobbled. She dropped her head back to his chest. Her arms clutched his waist, her body warm and small against his, and when he rubbed his chin lightly over the top of her head, her hair was the softest thing he'd ever felt.

Gabriel was beginning to get an inkling of why men comforted crying women instead of running the other way, which up until now he'd always considered the logical course of action.

"Mr. Jackson?" Lily hovered uncertainly in the doorway.

"It's gonna be okay, Lily." Gabriel reluctantly peeled Anthea, who appeared to be in no hurry to let go, off him. "Why don't you take Anthea over by the table. Do you think you could make her a cup of tea?"

"Of course I could," Lily said eagerly. She scurried over, took Anthea firmly by the hand, and led her away. Anthea glanced questioningly over her shoulder.

"Go ahead," he told her. "I'll take care of this."

Figuring cold was the lesser of two evils, Gabriel left the door open so the place would air out, stripped the sheets from the bed, and dragged them outside. He broke a branch off the tree and bent to work scraping off as much of the manure as he could manage, reflecting that this was certainly the strangest task he'd ever undertaken to please a woman.

Once the sheets were soaking with a hefty dose of wash soap in a big old tub in the farthest corner of the soddy, beneath a window cracked open a fraction, he went to join Lily and Anthea at the table.

Lily was talking quietly about the new dress Gabriel gave her for Christmas, her face intent, as if this spill of words was difficult for her but she'd determined to do her part to distract Anthea.

He spun around a straight-backed chair and straddled it, draping his wrists over the back. Anthea's hands wrapped around a half-empty cup of tea. Dark circles of fatigue bruised the fragile skin beneath her eyes, her hair and mouth and skin glowing soft and golden in the lamplight.

"Thank you," she said quietly. "I could have done it, but thank you anyway."

"I know you could." He shrugged. "I've cleaned up worse, more 'n once."

"I'll bet you have." She smiled, sad and sweet. "Why'd you come?"

Because I couldn't stay away. Because I thought of you more every day I didn't see you than all those days I did, and I was going to go crazy if I didn't lay eyes on you soon. "Lily insisted," he said instead. "It's Christmas."

Her shoulders drooped. "Oh."

"And *I* wanted to see you on Christmas."

And then she beamed, like a holiday angel, prettier than any tree he'd ever seen, glowing from the inside out. *I did that*, he thought. *Just by being here, just by saying something nice to her.*

It was a dangerous feeling, this warmth that bloomed up inside him when he was with her, both addictive and seductive.

Something of his thoughts must have shown in his face, for her lashes lowered demurely, the color on her cheeks deepening.

"Oh! I almost forgot. I've got something for you, Lily." She jumped up and rummaged around in the cardboard trunk set beneath the row of hooks that held her wardrobe. Crisp, tailored blouses hung next to dark, practical skirts and that long gray cape she'd often worn as she accompanied Lily home. There was nothing at all blatant or provocative about any of her clothes. And yet they interested him, tempted him, far more than any satiny bit of underthings he could recall.

"Here." She hurried back to them, as if she couldn't wait to see Lily's response, and thrust a package at her. Even Gabe could tell she'd put some time into the wrapping of it. Simple brown paper, creased as if it had been used before, bent crisply around the box. A dozen thin, curling ribbons in bright shades spilled over the edges.

Lily made no move to take the gift, only gaped at it with wide eyes.

"Open it," Anthea urged.

"But you already gave us the oranges at school."

"I know." Anthea was fairly jumping in her seat, as excited as if she were the one receiving a present. "So this has to be our secret. We wouldn't want them to know you're my favorite, would we?"

"Oooh." Lily's hands hovered over it as if she were afraid it might disappear if she dared to touch it.

"Go ahead," Sometimes in all her stiff formality, Anthea seemed older than her years, but tonight, as she glowed with anticipation, he glimpsed the vibrant, enchanting young girl she must once have been.

Lily giggled. And then she looked around, as if wondering where that sound had burst from.

She tugged carefully on the ribbons, smoothed them out and laid them aside, lining them up precisely on the table. "Pretty," she murmured, stroking them.

"They're for you, too." Anthea fingered one lightly. "I picked the colors because I thought they might look nice in your hair. Do you like them?"

"Yes," she said in a hushed voice.

"Uh-oh," Gabriel said. How could Lily's father not have claimed her the moment her mother died? Fought like a madman for her even before? What an idiot. *Thank God for fools*, he thought fervently. "Does this mean I'm going to have to learn to tie hair ribbons now? I'm afraid that's beyond my skills."

"We have faith in you. Don't we, Lily?"

Lily nodded solemnly.

"I'm flattered." He nudged the package with his knuckle. "So open it. I don't want to have to sit here and look at it anymore and remember what a mess mine was. I just couldn't figure out how to bend the paper around the box corners."

"It was pretty, too," Lily said loyally. She peeled back the paper with the same deliberate slowness she'd used with his, drawing out the anticipation and pleasure as long as possible.

"Oooh." With care unusual in one so young, she lifted a doll out of its crumpled paper nest. It was inexpertly made. Even Gabe, hardly an authority on dolls, spotted it right off. Her right arm drooped longer than her left, her feet looked like melons fastened to the ends of straws, and the stitching on her smile wandered up and down before ending somewhere around her right ear.

And Gabriel knew that a doll crafted by the most skilled artisan in the world would not have brought Lily any more joy than this one.

Gabriel had spent last Christmas on his ranch, with Sam, his family, and their hands. There'd been plenty of filling if not fancy food, a few games of cards, hearty laughter encouraged by a few bottles of pretty good whiskey. He'd thought at the time that holidays didn't come much better than that. He'd his own land, and friends, and a man couldn't ask for much more.

If someone had told him then that in less than a year he'd treasure sitting with a little girl and a school-teacher, watching them coo over a homemade doll, and count it an even better Christmas than the last, he would have thought them plumb crazy.

And maybe he was the crazy one. But he couldn't deny how he felt.

"I don't have Kate's way with a needle." Anthea adjusted a braid fashioned of bright orange yarn. "She's the first one I ever tried to make, besides the one I sent back home to my sister Emily. I guess it shows."

"No." Lily hugged the doll to her chest. "She's per-fect. Thank you."

"Thank you." The shift and skirt she'd cut up to make the dolls were certainly a worthy sacrifice, Anthea thought. "For making me miss Emily a little bit less. It's my first Christmas away from them, and I was feeling sorry for myself."

Lily nodded, and her eyes reflected a sheen of tears.

"Well, enough of that." Gabe clapped his hands to-gether. "Time for more presents."

"I think he's afraid we're going to get all sloppy on him, Lily."

"Sure I am. Man's gotta know when to head a stam-pede off at the pass."

"Not to worry. We're not going to tax you beyond your abilities. I figure once a month is over your limit, and you put in December's allotment about half an hour ago."

"That eases my mind considerably."

"Well, thank goodness. We wouldn't want your mind to be uneasy, would we?"

She grinned at him, full of mischief and spark, and something went *thump* in his chest, just like that, and he thought, *What* is *that?* He'd certainly never felt its like before.

He wasn't at all sure he wanted to experience it again. "We certainly wouldn't," he murmured. "Now, about those presents—"

"Presents?" She sat up straight, peered pointedly at his empty hands. "I thought you were just attempting to distract me."

"Worked, didn't it? But we've got a present for you, too. Don't we, Lily?"

Lily bobbed her head but didn't take her eyes off her doll.

"For me?" Anthea wiggled back in her chair and placed her hands in her lap in front of her. "There, I'm ready."

"Oh, no. You think you just get to sit there and presents drop in your lap?" He shook his head in a show of great regret. "It's not quite that simple."

"You mean"—she peered up at him through her lashes—"I have to earn it?" Anthea was flirting shamelessly, and she knew it. But, well, it was Christmas, and she was far from home, and if a girl couldn't cheer herself up with a little harmless flirting in a situation like that, when could she?

Except then he smiled, slow, full of sexual promise, and she remembered that nothing about Gabriel Jackson was harmless.

But she'd played it safe most of her life, and where

had it gotten her? Alone and lonely in the middle of Kansas. She was in a mood to forget all about safe.

"Yes," he said, his voice rough and low. "You have to go for a walk."

"A walk?" Her interest, already pretty high, piqued further. "Where are we going?"

"Ah, I'm not going to tell you that. Wouldn't want to ruin the surprise." He rose and held out his hand to her. "Lily, are you coming?"

Shooting him a look that clearly said she didn't know why he'd even bothered to ask, Lily shook her head emphatically and propped her doll up at the edge of the table, placing a cup and saucer in front of her.

"I think we've been relegated to second place."

"But of course." His hand remained in the air, still, patient, as he waited for her to come to him. Excitement edged with apprehension shivered within her; it seemed that if she gave her hand to him, she'd have done something irrevocable.

"Lily?" she asked, hoping perhaps to have the decision taken from her. "Are you sure you don't want to come with us?"

"I'm sure." Lily lifted a cup to the doll's chain-stitched mouth.

"All right, then." Taking a deep breath, she placed her hand in his. Heavens, but she loved his hands, big and hard, broad-palmed, rough-skinned. You could never be touched by those hands, she reflected, without knowing that it was a *man* who touched you.

He pulled her toward him, and closer still, until she stood beside him with their arms touching, and he linked his fingers with hers, one by one, so their hands were completely entwined.

"Do you want your cloak?"

"Are we going far?"

"No."

"Then I'll be warm enough."

"I hope so." With his free hand he scooped up a lantern.

The air and the night hit her the moment she stepped out the door. "Wh-what are you doing?" she asked, as Gabriel moved behind her, released her hand, and placed his palm over her eyes.

"Gifts are supposed to be a surprise, aren't they?"

She was enveloped in him, his chest hard and hot against her back, one arm around her, his hand over her eyes, blotting out anything but the feel of him. The cold air drenched her, incited nerves already alert, the contrast in temperatures so acute it neared pain, and she shivered.

"Trust me?" he asked.

Trust him. It had to be foolishness. She couldn't do anything else. "Yes."

They began to walk together, without hesitation. Without the assistance of sight, she was totally guided by him, forced to concentrate on every cue of his body, the flex of his muscles, the slight increase of pressure as he moved, her body responding to each movement of his. Her breathing deepened, slowed.

The air smelled of snow and wood fires. And him, leather and soap and skin. She heard the wind through bare branches, the metallic creak of the swinging lantern, the sound of his breath only inches from her ear. She'd never felt so *alive*, acutely sensitive to each second, each tiny sensation.

"All right, here we are."

"Here we are where?"

"Patience."

Something brushed against the top of her head briefly, gone so quickly she was unsure whether it had happened at all. "Gabriel?"

"Hmm?"

"Did you just kiss me?"

"Yup," he said, as if admitting to something as innocuous as opening a door.

"Gabriel . . ." His name trailed off on a sigh. Was he . . . ? Yes, he was definitely *nuzzling* her, mouth warm and sweet against the nape of her neck.

"Stay right here," he murmured against her skin. "And don't open your eyes."

And then he was gone, so abruptly she swayed, disoriented. She'd forgotten for a moment where she was, where she was going, lost in the spell of his mouth on her.

"Anthea?" She judged him to be perhaps five feet away. She heard some rustling, the scrape of something that might be a door. "You're not peeking, are you?"

She slammed her lids shut. "No, of course not." Darn it! She'd seen nothing but a sliver of tree branches against a night-dark sky.

"Good." And then he was behind her again, one arm around her waist, the other back over her eyes. "Here we go." She let out a whoop as he lifted her and spun her around so fast her legs swung wide. He took perhaps two steps before setting her down again. "Ready?"

"Yes," she said, and wondered exactly what she was saying yes to.

He removed his hand. But he didn't step away, kept his arm around her, her body up against his. She blinked, a bit unused to sight, unsure of what she was seeing.

The lamp he'd taken from her soddy was on the floor beside him, a weak light that barely illuminated the small, windowless room.

"You . . . you brought me *coal* for Christmas?"

Yes, coal, great heaping black piles of it, filling three quarters of the room nearly to the ceiling. Shiny flecks in the dense black reflected the light here and there, like small sparkling stars in a dark sky. She turned in his arms and leaned back against the sure support he offered.

"Coal?" she asked again.

"Yes," he said, looking suddenly uncertain, a shade anxious. She'd never seen him other than completely sure. *Because of me*, she thought. *Because of me*. "I thought that . . ."

He never stood a chance. She launched herself at him, throwing her arms around his neck, planting her mouth full on his. He froze, shocked into stillness.

But it didn't take him long to recover. He slanted his mouth on hers, acceptance transforming to demand in an instant, warmth exploding into potent heat. His arms vised her back, lifting her off her toes. He turned with her, her world spinning from the motion and from him, and she knew as she spun that when it settled back again it wouldn't be the same world as it had been.

Her back met the wall of the storehouse, and he

withdrew to look at her, hair, eyes, skin, mouth. And lower, the slope of her neck, the enticing curve of cotton over the swell of her breasts.

Had he really once thought her plain? he wondered now. What a shallow-brain he'd been. Perhaps still was. Her mouth was plump and lush, and he'd never again see it without remembering how sweetly she kissed. Perhaps the shape of her eyes was ordinary, but what they revealed was extraordinary: compassion, intelligence, humor, so much that it hardly seemed that one small body could contain them all.

Fine skin, golden in the lamplight, flushed with desire. He lifted one lock of her hair, rubbed it between his thumb and forefinger as if he'd never felt anything like it before. Maybe he never had. He ran his fingers down her cheek, memorizing each texture in case he never got the opportunity again. He traced her lips, dipped the tip of one finger inside her mouth while she stared, wide-eyed and breathless.

Her blouse was crisply white, starched stiff and high beneath her chin, a dozen tiny buttons in military precision down the front. His hand hovered over the first button while he let it build, anticipation, impatience, inescapable longing.

He pushed the pearly disk through its hole, the stitching so tight he had to force it through with his thumb. It abruptly popped open, and Anthea let out an "Oh" of surprise and pleasure.

The tiny opening exposed the hollow of her throat, a small, tempting triangle of skin, lamplight and shadows flickering there. He bent and pressed his mouth to it for a long moment, unmoving.

Her hair had escaped from its pins; he could feel it

lying soft and loose against his cheek. Her pulse, uneven, full of life, fluttered against his lips. His mouth
fit precisely in the deep hollow between the tendons, a
lovely curve.

He pulled back only so he could watch while he
thumbed open the next button. She trembled against
the wall, against him, and looked down, too, at his
hand, dark, male, alien against her perfectly white
blouse.

He revealed lace this time, the edge of her chemise
just peeking out. He traced it with his forefinger, feeling the delicate line of her collarbone. She was finely
made, with graceful bones and pale, elegant skin. She
looked as if Kansas should have overcome her in a
week. But she'd bloomed here, her stiffness bowing to
practicality, allowing her natural warmth to glow
through. His finger found the V where her collarbones
met, rested there. He kissed her here, too, clinging
fiercely to control. He would not hurry this, for he
didn't know when it would end, or if it would ever
come again, and he would savor each second while
she gifted it to him.

The next button exposed only more fabric, interesting only because of what it covered. And when his
mouth fell there, the flesh beneath the cloth was softer
than before, the swell of her breast rising against his
mouth.

The rest of the buttons gave way easily, no barrier at
all. His breath dampened her skin through the fabric,
and when he drew back, air as cold as well water
skimmed over her, raising chill bumps, and something
more.

He should have brought another lamp, Gabriel

thought. To view her clearly, savoring each flush of color to her skin, every line of her face and body. Instead, dark gold burnished the skin above the edge of her shift, and he could almost—almost—see the dark circle of her nipple beneath the dampened cloth. It tightened abruptly, and he groaned. So unfair, the many weapons women had to bring a man to his knees.

Carefully he traced the lace with his forefinger, her chest rising and falling heavily as she dragged in air. And then he hooked the edge and tugged the fabric down, and down, the cloth catching for a tantalizing moment on the tip before her nipple popped free, dark in the dimness, tiny and tight and sweet.

He bent his head and drew it into his mouth. She went still, then arched, her arms coming round his head to hold him tight. *"Gabriel."*

Patience evaporated; control vanished as if it had never existed. Hands, mouth, body; they sought each other, devoured each other, as if they knew there could never be enough, never enough time, never enough of *this.*

You can't do this now. You can't do this here. The protests whispered from the back of his brain, quickly ignored when her hands slid through the opening of his coat, burrowed into the warmth and around him, clutching at his lower back, her fingers resting right at his waist; if they wandered farther down, he was going to start ripping things. Her clothes or his, he wasn't sure which first; either one sounded like a right fine idea.

He slid his hands down farther, swore at froths of skirts and petticoats that barred her from his touch. He couldn't reach the hem, not without lifting his mouth from her breast, and that seemed like too much to give up. But then he suckled deep, pressed that tight bud against the roof of his mouth with his tongue, and she gave a little shriek and lifted one leg, wrapping it around his hips.

"Yes." He reached around and grasped her hem, sliding the bulk of fabric up her leg until he had to tilt his hips away for a moment to shove it the rest of the way, and it bunched around her middle.

He grasped her thighs, finally, mercifully, covered only in the thin material of her drawers, the flesh surprisingly firm and strong. He lifted her leg a little higher, and she pressed closer. He moved into space she'd made for him, for *him*, and he knew damn well he couldn't really feel a thing, but it didn't matter because he knew he was *there*.

His hips pulsed against her, and they both shuddered and groaned, strained to get closer even though it was impossible.

You can't do this to her. "Oh, God, why do you have to be a virgin?"

"Who said I'm a virgin?"

"What?" He froze, his hips in midthrust, hand cupping one bare breast, mouth against the curve of her neck.

She went still as well, barely breathing. "I didn't say anything. You didn't hear anything."

"Oh, I don't think I imagined *that*."

He placed one hand on the wall beside her head and reared back. She wouldn't look at him; he could see only the fine lines of her profile, cast in lamplight and shadow, gold kissing the luscious curve of her lips, plump and swollen from his mouth. Her hair brushed loose against her cheek, hiding her eye, curling low around her neck.

"Now," he said, "why don't you tell me what you meant by that."

"I didn't mean anything. You can't trust anything said in the heat of the moment. I'm sure *you* know that."

As she took a breath, her breast quivered in his palm. He brushed his thumb over the hard peak, just once, and her lips parted, her body arching into his touch.

"Tell me, Anthea."

"I . . ."

Another brush of his thumb, another delicious shudder.

"Tell me."

"Oh . . ." The syllable slid off into a sigh. "I was to be married. It didn't seem such a terrible thing to anticipate our vows a bit."

"You're not a virgin," he stated flatly.

"You're not going to let this go, are you?"

"There is not one chance in the entire world you're getting out that door without telling me."

"Oh, all right," Anthea said, a shade disgruntled at his insistence . . . but not disgruntled enough to ask him to move his hand, which was doing such lovely things to her breast she didn't see how she could be expected to speak. "No, I'm really not."

He let out a whoop, scooped her up, and whirled her around in glee before setting her back on her feet. She put a hand to her head, sent spinning by the motion and him.

"Of all the responses I ever expected to get when I

confessed my indiscretion," she said, "*that* one never occurred to me."

He grinned wickedly, gave her a quick, hard kiss that promised long, slow ones to come. "You have no idea how much trouble your virtue was causing me. Now I can dispense with being inconveniently honorable for your sake."

She frowned. "I didn't notice you particularly struggling with your honor, much less being constrained by it."

"I sure as hell was," he said fervently, "or we would have stopped dancing around this and I would have had you on your back weeks ago."

"Hmph." She would have crossed her arms in front of her for emphasis . . . except that might push him farther away, and she wasn't annoyed enough at him for *that*. "Seems to me you're taking a lot for granted."

"Really?" And then he kissed her again, mouth and tongue and breath, heated and slow until she practically wrapped herself around him, shuddering and gasping and more than ready for him to take her right up against the wall, freezing temperatures be damned. "I'm not taking anything for granted, Anthea," he told her, his voice rough with sex.

"Oh."

"So." He nipped at the line of her jaw, the corner of her mouth. "What happened to the fiancé?"

"Aren't you supposed to be jealous?"

"I'll be jealous tomorrow," he promised her. "In fact, if I ever lay eyes on the man, I'll beat the crap out of him, I swear. But right now I'm too damn grateful that I don't have to do the noble thing anymore."

How did he expect her to hold a conversation when he was doing *that* to her?

"Anthea?" he murmured, the movement of his lips and tongue as he spoke against her skin vibrating deep inside her.

Interesting, how she could now think of Gerald without the slightest bit of regret. "After my father died, when we discovered that our fortune wasn't there anymore, well, I didn't have a fiancé anymore, either."

"Bastard." He jerked back, his eyes hot. "Now I *will* have to beat the crap out of him."

"It's a lovely offer," she told him. "But really, I'm not particularly interested in this now."

His touch gentled. "Did you love him, Anthea?"

"I . . ." Had she? The answer seemed a far sight less simple than it once had. "I don't know. He was handsome, charming, everything I *expected* him to be. My father approved. I felt . . . happy when I was with him. I *thought* I loved him. But now, that girl who loved him, she doesn't even seem like the same person as me."

"Just one more thing." His gaze raked her. "Did you like it?"

"Gabriel!" she cried, truly shocked.

"Tell me," he demanded.

Her face flooded with heat. "Oh, all right," she admitted. "I liked it."

He leaned into her and she gasped. "You'll more than like it, Anthea. I promise."

She couldn't doubt his word. Not when he kissed her again, and caressed her breast, and drove her near crazy. When they broke apart finally, they were both panting and wild, edging close to bliss.

"I'll take Lily home," he ground out. "And then I'll be back. An hour at most. Don't plan on getting any sleep tonight."

She nodded, wondering how she was going to manage to wobble back to the soddy. She dropped her head to his shoulder, grateful that his arms held her up. "You do have a way with walls."

Chapter 16

The cold hit them like a hard-packed snowball the instant they stepped out the door, quickly followed by an equally frigid blast of reality. Gabriel tugged off his jacket and laid it around her shoulders. "Thank you," she murmured. She grabbed the front panels in each hand and tugged it around her, the skins warm from his body; it smelled of him, and Anthea huddled deeper.

On the brief walk back from the storehouse, Gabriel didn't even hold her hand. She couldn't bring herself to look at him, feeling awkward and exposed after everything that had passed between them. What did one do now, once the decision had been made? It was so much easier in the heat of the moment; much harder to quiet her conscience when

244

there was time to think, to remember all the reasons why she *shouldn't* do this. To allow doubts and what-ifs to creep in.

They paused outside the door. "Ready?" he asked her.

She smoothed her skirts. "Do I look . . . Does it show?"

His finger brushed along her cheek. "Only to me."

She blew out a shaky breath. "All right, then. Let's go."

Lily was having a tea party. Plates and forks and Anthea's two chipped cups covered the table, the plate holding a handful of crackers in its very center. Lily sat very straight, knees primly together, a napkin spread over her lap, and another over her new doll's.

Guilt washed over Anthea. "I'm sorry it took so long, Lily. There was . . ." She gestured lamely. "It took a while to get everything settled."

"You weren't gone that long." Lily looked at her curiously. "Did you like your present?"

"I *loved* my pre—" Beside her, Gabriel cleared his throat, and Anthea shot him a warning glance. He looked far too pleased with himself, his eyes glittering. "I truly do appreciate the *coal*," she finished.

"Really?" Lily tilted her head, studying Anthea for a moment, then shrugged as if to say, *Grown-ups!* "I told him it was a weird present."

"Anthea and I understand each other."

"We made a special trip for it," Lily went on conversationally. "Went all the way to Centervale to get it when Mr. Stoddard wouldn't sell us enough."

"Lily," Gabriel said warningly.

"Oh, really?" Anthea pursed her lips consideringly. "A special trip, hmm?"

"We'll be going home now, Lily." Gabriel met

Anthea's gaze evenly. "Do you have more sheets?"

"*Sheets?*" Anthea shot a horrified glance at Lily, who happily passed a plate to her doll, completely unconcerned.

"Yes, of course. We wouldn't want you to have to do without, would we, Lily?"

Sheets. She'd forgotten all about the earlier episode. Truth be told, Gabriel had driven every thought out of her mind but one. "I—"

"I'll take Lily home, get her tucked in for the night, and then I'll bring some back to you." Heat glimmered in his eyes, his jaw angled sharp and tense. Everything inside her softened, warmed, the promise in his gaze as powerful as his touch.

He waited, and she knew that he was not going to make this easy for her. He would not take the responsibility from her hands. She'd have to say yes, blatant, obvious, and the prospect of saying it out loud, laying it out bare and blunt, was surprisingly sexual.

She tried to force her lips to form a refusal. But this thing between them burned out of her control, and she'd never been able to say no to him anyway. "I'll see you then."

My dearest sister,

Oh, we shall manage Christmas without you quite nicely, never fear for us. I must confess that I am positively giddy at the thought of having the turkey neck all to my greedy self without having to battle you for it. And Emily is delighted that she won't have to break the wishbone with you. She is convinced that all her wishes must come true if she hangs on to both ends.

The sheet of thin paper in her hand quivered, and Anthea quickly placed it flat on the table, smoothing it out. Kate's neat, precise, and very darkly penned handwriting should not be difficult to read, even in the quiet lantern light, but Anthea was having a hard time making it through the letter.

For at least the dozenth time, she glanced quickly at the door, which remained stubbornly closed. Perhaps, she thought, he had changed his mind and would not come.

If she were being wise, that was what she'd hope for. But clearly it was not her brain that was in charge, for the thought that he might not come to her was immeasurably . . . disappointing.

She had dithered for a good ten minutes after he'd left. How did one prepare for an . . . assignation? It was not amongst the many useful social graces she'd learned at Miss Addington's. Should she remain in her clothes? Put on a nightgown? Wait in a chair? *In bed?*

She had a strong suspicion she knew what Gabriel would pick—the bed, and naked. But that was certainly beyond the capabilities of a former student of Miss Addington's, even one with a slightly shady past and more carnal urges than were good for her.

Anthea had pondered making coffee. Wasn't that what a proper hostess would do? But proper hardly entered into it, did it? And no matter what happened tonight, she didn't envision them sitting at her kitchen table sipping coffee.

Finally her pride had gotten the better of her. She would be embarrassed to have Gabriel return and discover her flitting around *waiting* for him. So, still fully dressed, she'd plopped herself down at the table and pulled out the letter from Kate, which she hadn't had time to read as thoroughly as she'd have liked.

And perhaps Kate's bracing good sense would bring Anthea to her own. It wouldn't hurt, before she did something irrevocable, to be reminded why she'd come to Kansas in the first place, and where her first and best loyalty resided.

But she was having a difficult time concentrating on Kate's words. Every creak of a tree limb, every squawk of a night bird, sent her flying out of her chair to the window.

Enough, she scolded herself. This would simply not do. She turned her attention back to her letter, determined to give it her full concentration.

> *I do hope you liked your scarf. I tried a new stitch on the daisies; I think it turned out exceptionally well. I've begun teaching Emily, and I'm sure that you'll be relieved to hear that she appears to favor me rather than you in this regard.*
>
> *You make no mention of new beaus in your last letter, and I am thoroughly disappointed. Are all those tales of handsome young cowboys and farmers just tales? Or are you simply being discreet to spoil my fun? I expect full details, my dear. We old maids must have our entertainments.*

Anthea laughed aloud. If Kate could be called an old maid—and at twenty-two, she supposed some might term her that—it was entirely her own choice. She was the loveliest of women, so stunning that it sometimes surprised even Anthea to look at her and realize that yes, she really *was* that beautiful. But Kate's heart had proved resistant in her youth, and now she was concerned only with Emily's well-being. But Anthea had no doubts that, should Kate change her mind, she'd need only snap her fingers and she would have more entertainment than any woman in the entire state.

Though I have to say—see, I shall give you details, and I am quite certain you'll be entertained—I rather seem to have acquired a beau, without even trying. Though I don't know that beau is precisely the right term. Instead, he offered me marriage, right out of the blue. Are you ready? It is Doctor Goodale, can you imagine? While I admit it probably does not speak well of the depth of my character, I simply could not take my eyes off that nose the entire time. Could he even kiss a bride, do you suppose? Though I imagine he could; he does have two children, after all.

Anthea's smile faded. Despite Kate's light tone and easy dismissal, a trickle of unease still settled in her belly. Dr. Goodale had been an acquaintance of their father, prone to hieing off to far corners of the world, where he'd managed to amass a great fortune in ways that had never been clear to Anthea. Five years ago, after the passing of his wife, who had always seemed delighted to be left behind in civilization, he'd returned to Philadelphia permanently and taken up the practice he'd mostly abandoned. He might be a good doctor, but he was also brusque—all right, rude—and insensitive to anything but his own greatness.

Anthea supposed she shouldn't be too surprised that his eye had settled on Kate; he would consider her beauty merely his due. Unfortunately, Goodale had never struck Anthea as the type to take rejection well.

The knock on her door startled her out of her reverie. Well, Kate's letter had effectively distracted her after all, hadn't it?

Panic exploded in her chest. *Don't let him in*, she told herself. The last thing her life, and her family, needed was another complication, and Gabriel was certain to be complicated.

But he was also a hundred other things, things she knew and things she only suspected. The knock came again, insistent, demanding, accusing her of cowardice.

Well, she could hardly just ignore it, could she? He knew she was in here. If she didn't answer it, didn't do him the courtesy of telling him her decision to his face, he would know her fear had gotten the better of her. And it'd be just plain rude, wouldn't it?

Her conscience mocked her all the way across the floor. For this had nothing to do with manners or courage, and everything to do with how she felt when he looked at her.

She took a deep breath and tugged the door open. Tall and unsmiling, he stood in a shaft of moonlight that fell across his head and shoulders as if it had been designed just for him, and every doubt, every protest that had been on the tip of her tongue, disappeared as if they'd never existed. There'd be time enough for regrets later—and she knew damn well there'd be plenty of those. But the truth, elemental and bone-deep, was she simply didn't have it in her to deny either one of them this night.

His gaze slid over her, and heat sparked along the way, igniting everywhere he looked—her cheeks, her breasts, her belly, her limbs. And when his gaze returned to meet her own, she grew dizzy with just the look of him, thought she might fall right into him and never find her way out again. Wasn't even sure she cared.

"I thought for a while you weren't going to answer the door."

"I considered it," she admitted.

Moonlight carved harsh shadows below his cheekbones, glittered in his eyes. "You have one chance. One choice." He took a step closer, filling the doorway. "If you tell me to go right now, I will. But once I step into that room, there's no going back. Not for either of us."

"I don't know what's going to happen tonight. I don't know what's going to happen tomorrow." She took a hesitant step toward him. "All I know is that if you don't touch me in the next five minutes, I think I'm going to die."

He smiled slowly, a smile rich with amusement, dark with promise. "Couldn't have that, could we?"

"I should hope not," she said, wondering when he was going to stop talking and start *doing*. Each second seemed drawn out as fine as her nerves, ready to snap.

And then he left. Just turned around and walked away.

She smothered a yelp of protest. "Where are you going?"

"I'll be right back, I promise." His voice held a hint of laughter. She tried to muster up the appropriate outrage that he'd find amusement in her . . . situation . . . but couldn't manage it. From what she knew of his life, there'd been too little amusement in it. If she could give him some, she'd be pleased to make the gift. "I brought a few things."

Things? "What kind of things?"

"Oh, you'll see."

"Things," she murmured, trying valiantly to guess what kind of *things* Gabriel would consider necessary for a night like this. Her limited experience certainly didn't include *things*.

He moved in and out of the shadows in the yard and she rose to her tiptoes, trying to see where he was going. But he must have tethered his horse around back. She tried to be grateful that he'd thought to put his horse out of sight, but her anxiety wouldn't let her. *Things*, she kept repeating. *Things*.

Finally she saw him come round the corner, a large sack in one hand, bent over beneath the weight of something very heavy, and her imagination reeled. *Things*.

He stopped right in front of where she stood clutching the door latch.

"If you're going to let me in," he said, "you're going to have to step aside."

"Oh." She managed to get her feet to move far enough to clear the doorway. "It's a mattress."

"Yup." He dropped it next to the bed with a thud, seized the one from the frame, and hefted it to his shoulder.

"You brought me a mattress?"

"Sure thing." He strode across the floor and pitched her old mattress right out. "You didn't think I was going to take any chances with tonight, did you?"

"Where'd you get it?"

"It's mine, of course. I'll get a new one."

"Coal and a mattress. Such a romantic soul you are."

"Aren't I, though? Can't imagine how you resisted me this long."

His banter relaxed her, made her almost forget why

he'd come. But once the door shut behind the old mattress, he turned to her, took her face in both hands, and simply stared at her, with eyes so dark she thought she might see heaven in them. Her heart threatened to beat its way right out of her chest, the sensation painful but making her feel oh, so wonderfully alive in a way she had doubted it would ever be again.

"I know this is the last thing you need," he said quietly, "to lie with another man and have him leave you again. But I don't have it in me not to do this."

Leave me. She ignored the cry that sprang from her heart, the *Why would you have to leave me?* She knew why. Even understood it.

"It's different, when you know going in how it'll be at the end," she told him, even as she wondered if it was the truth. "I didn't know then. I thought that Gerald . . . that he . . ."

"That he loved you?" he asked, and she nodded, feeling the unexpected burn of tears in her eyes, wondering exactly what they were for, suspecting they weren't for Gerald at all.

"It never occurred to me that he mostly wanted my father's fortune. Oh, he wanted me too, I don't doubt that. But not enough." Her smile trembled. "At least I know that it's not my fortune that attracts you."

"Ah, I've fooled you completely, have I? Little did you know I've always had a secret yen to live in my very own soddy." His thumbs stroked her cheekbones, gentle as dawn, sweet as spring. "I want *you*, Anthea, though I confess I don't understand why you draw me so. But you do." His voice went deeper, rougher. "Oh, but you do."

"I know." She didn't doubt it, and that knowledge

filled her with pleasure and pride. *He wants me*, she thought. *Me.* "How is Lily?"

"Went to sleep the moment her head hit the pillow, hanging on to that doll you gave her for dear life. Thank you for doing that for her. I don't know that she trusts it all yet, and the fact that you would do so much for her means a lot."

"It's my pleasure."

"I know that. I just don't think she does. Not yet, at any rate." His hands slid down, and she felt the pressure of his fingers against the side of her neck, his thumbs ringing it, stroking in the hollow of her throat. She knew his hands were strong; she'd seen him snap a good-sized branch as if it were a thin twig. Who would have thought he had such gentleness in him? And who would have thought such a light touch would send sensation spiraling through her? "I can't stay, Anthea, after . . . I can't stay. Because of Lily. It wouldn't be right to leave her alone all night."

"I understand." Because she couldn't stand not to touch him anymore, she put her hands on his waist, beneath the panels of his open jacket, and through the thin fabric of his old woolen shirt, she felt his muscles jump. It helped to know that she was not the only one who was so acutely aroused that the slightest touch sparked a response.

"Are you scared?" he asked her. "Nervous?"

"No, I—" She swallowed her automatic denial and returned to the truth. There could be honesty between them, at least. "I suppose so. A little of both."

"About what?" His thumbs made little circles against her throat, the pads rough with callus, and she knew that if she were blindfolded and deaf and he touched her, she would know him immediately. "What are you worried about?"

A hundred things. About whether she would please him, and whether she would regret this, and whether she would come out of this affair whole.

And then she looked at him directly. "After Gerald called off our engagement, the worst thing . . ." She'd thought she could say this without embarrassment. She was fully prepared to open her body to him, to lie naked beneath him while he put himself inside her. She should be able to say this. "Waiting to find out if I was with child. My . . . It was late, and I was terrified."

His hands went still. "I'll be careful. You know there are ways, lots of other things we can do." He smiled then, as if anticipating those things. "But I can't absolutely promise you. You know that, too."

It was a risk. She appreciated his telling her flat out, instead of simply trying to seduce her out of her concerns. Maybe she'd hoped his answer would be something different. Maybe a part of her wished he'd lie to her, give her the pretty illusions most women clung to.

But he was Gabriel, and he wouldn't try to pretty it up for her, and it was one of the reasons she wanted him so much.

"Until a few months ago, I can't recall ever taking a risk in my life," she told him. "Even Gerald didn't seem like a risk at the time, for we were to be married soon. And where did all that being careful get me? All the things I tried to keep from happening, all the ways I tried to be *safe*, it all went wrong anyway. I lost everything I didn't want to lose." She stepped closer, sliding her arms farther around his waist. His nostrils flared, his eyelids dropped, and she felt the wonderful, heady power of being the one to cause it. "And then I took a chance and came to Haven, and while it certainly didn't turn out exactly as I anticipated—" she smiled at the understatement "—not for anything would I have *not* done this. And not for anything would I miss this night with you."

He inhaled sharply, his fingers flexing against her skin. "Are you making that bed, or am I?"

"We both are."

Chapter 17

As they worked together on the mundane task of making a bed, their hands smoothing sheets and tucking in edges, nothing in their manner or actions betrayed what they prepared it for.

But then it was done, and Anthea had patted out every stray wrinkle and carefully plumped the pillows. She straightened, her fingers twisting together as if she didn't know what else to do with them.

Gabriel counted himself remarkably patient. Twice, as she'd bent over the bed to adjust a blanket, he'd almost grabbed her, tossed her across it, and laid his body over hers. What was the point of fixing it so perfectly, anyway? He had every intention of messing it up but good.

But as much as his passions rode him hard, as easy

257

as it would be to simply throw up her skirts and plunge in, releasing him from the sharp edge of desire he'd balanced on for so long, he refused to do it. They'd mentioned nothing of what might happen after tonight; in fact, they'd carefully avoided the topic. He'd make no assumptions about whether they'd be lovers, or whether this was all there would ever be.

And so he would savor each moment, difficult as it would be not to rush ahead and sate himself in her. It was a lesson hard learned, now well used: life did not tender any guarantees, and so a wise man enjoyed each second as it came and let the future be.

"Anthea," he said, and waited for her to look at him.

Seconds stretched into a long moment. The wind had come up outside, screeching around the corner of the soddy like a night owl, rattling the shutters over the windows. But inside the fire warmed the room, the light was soft and golden, and *she* was here, with him, alone.

Finally she sighed and lifted her head, her fingers still worrying each other at her waist. "Why do you suppose," she asked him, "that something one anticipates so much, *wants* so much, can still *worry* one so much?"

"It seems to me that most things that matter, good or bad, cause some worry along the way."

Lamplight glistened her eyes, gleamed on the fine curve of her cheekbones. "Does this matter?"

"It matters now."

Now. Anthea clung to the word, tried not to be hurt by it. She'd had promises before, and they'd failed her miserably. Wasn't it better not to depend on them? In the end, wasn't *now* all one could be absolutely certain of?

"Then kiss me now," she said, "so I don't have to think anymore. Kiss me and make the world go away."

His mouth inched closer, tantalizingly slow, and stopped a hairsbreadth from hers. When he spoke, she felt each word, tiny explosions of air on her lips. "Is that what happens when I kiss you? The world goes away?"

"Yes," she told him, and lifted her chin, bringing her mouth fractionally closer to his, hoping he'd take the hint. "What about you? Doesn't the world go away?"

"No." When she started to frown, he grinned at her. "The world doesn't go away, but it gets one whole helluva lot better, I can tell you that."

Oh, why was he still talking? "You are the most frustrating man." She grabbed his shirtfront with both fists and tried to yank him closer, but he was unmovable. "If five more seconds pass and you don't kiss me, I think I just might kill you."

"Really? And here I thought, if I don't kiss you, *that's* what's going to kill me." He sobered. "After this is all over, you might want to kill me anyway."

She lifted a brow at him. "Then I suppose it's up to you to decide whether it's worth the risk."

Aaahh. His mouth swallowed up her moan. There was nothing slow this time, nothing gentle or sweet. He kissed her hard, lips and tongue and breath and teeth. Not a kiss of courtship, this, but the kiss of two people becoming lovers at last, who'd fought their passion and now surrendered completely, allowing it to flood them, as turbulent as a burst dam. And once released, as impossible to contain again.

His mouth never left hers as he bent and scooped

her right off her feet. He spun toward the bed with her, and her head spun too. "Is that your answer?" she murmured against his mouth, loving the way the contact changed as she spoke, the different ways their lips fit together.

"It's the start of my answer," he growled.

He opened his arms and just dropped her right on the bed, an unexpected move that made her squeak in surprise. "Nice mattress," she commented.

"You think I'd bring you anything less than the best?"

"I certainly hope not."

He stood at the side of the bed, hands on hips, and studied her. There were still a few pins in her hair, half-up, half-down, and her clothes were the same she'd worn for visiting all day, though she'd taken off the little jacket. It shouldn't have been the least bit seductive, and yet the sight of her made the blood roar in his ears.

"Are you just going to stand there all night looking at me?" she asked him, mostly teasing, with just a hint of nerves.

"I hadn't planned on it. But I like looking at you." She lay stiffly, arms at her sides as if she didn't know quite what to do with them, her cheeks flagged with color. "Truth is, I more than *like* looking at you." He never tired of it. "I had all kinds of good intentions, Anthea. I planned to take this easy for you, make it slow and pretty and tender. You make it damn hard to remember anything about good intentions."

He saw her swallow, saw her hands fist at her sides. "So make it hard and sweaty and even rough. Make it damn hard, Gabriel."

Her blunt words sent a jolt of heat spearing to his

groin, nearly driving the breath completely from him. "Is that what you want?"

"I don't want to wait anymore." One hand fluttered toward him. "Please, Gabriel."

Sound rumbled low in the back of his throat, the sound of triumph, the sound of surrender.

He knelt on the bed, in the V between her legs. He grabbed her knees and pulled her closer, lifting her skirts as he did so until she was tight against him, her back arched, the insides of her thighs against his hips.

"I want you naked. I want to see you."

"So make me naked." She flipped her hands over her head, palms up, a position of forceful submission.

And so he did. Two buttons were sacrificed to the cause, and a shift strap. His hands moved so quickly she could hardly keep up, as gentle with her as they were rough with her clothes. Fastenings flew open; her corset string parted with one quick tug. And then she lay completely naked in front of him, gasping in shock that should have been embarrassment and instead felt more like excitement, spread wide on the bed while he still knelt between her legs fully clothed, as wanton a situation as she could possibly conceive. He'd moved the lamp closer, to an upended crate he'd dragged next to the bed, and so she knew that no softening shadows shielded her body. He made no pretense of anything, but stared at her through eyes as hot as flames; she doubted he missed an inch, and her skin heated as strongly as if he'd touched her.

"This hardly seems fair," she murmured.

"I never promised you fair, Anthea."

She was a woman made for lamplight and loving. He couldn't believe he hadn't recognized it from the first. Her small, strong, supple body glowed golden in the flickering light. He reached out and cupped one slight breast in his hand, and she arched immediately, her head bowing back, her neck a beckoning curve.

She had so much passion in her. For her job, for her students, for him. For *life*. Another woman might be bitter for what she'd lost, for the changes life forced on her. Anthea met them and looked for the best.

She'd even looked for the best in him. When everyone had been so certain there *was* no best in him, when even he had wondered, she welcomed him into her bed and her life. And not out of curiosity or rebellion or revenge, but simply because she wanted him there.

His throat tightened. "Anthea, I . . ." *I what?* How could he identify something he'd never felt before? He didn't have the words. Didn't even know if there were any.

Her smile was soft, full of promise. "If you don't come closer," she said, "I'm going to have to come to you."

He bent down and kissed her, laying his body full across hers, and forgot all about words. Who needed words when there was this?

Anthea had a dim notion that perhaps she should be doing . . . something. She didn't exactly know what, but she really didn't think lying there, accepting the pleasure he spun effortlessly over her skin, should be her only part in the proceedings. But he didn't give her time, didn't allow her air, or even thought. His mouth at her breast left her gasping. His hands on her skin left her reeling, and his kisses—on her mouth, her neck, her belly—left her helplessly in thrall, unable to do anything but rush along the path he'd drawn, heedless and entranced.

There was nothing of softness here. His chin, hours past a shave, scraped her neck and moved on, leaving her tingling, knowing she'd be marked tomorrow. *Wanting* his mark, needing some tangible proof of this night. She felt the imprint of his button against her breast, the bite of its edge as he bent to nip at her shoulder.

His knee rose between her thighs, coarse denim against delicate skin. He lifted it higher, pressing hard against her, and pleasure stabbed, sharp and strong as a duelist's blade.

Sensation blasted her from all sides. Pleasure hurtled through her, frightening in its intensity, impossible to resist.

She grabbed fistfuls of his shirt and yanked it up, uncovering skin that was hot and smooth over flesh hard as iron. She spread her fingers wide, touching as much as she could, greedy for the feel of him.

And oh, the feel of him! She ran her fingers over the corrugated ridge of his ribs, the flat, hard plane of his stomach, and the muscles jumped beneath her touch.

Thank God, she thought, that she could do that to him as well. Feeling powerful and daring, she swept her hands up and scraped the pad of her thumb over his nipple. She savored his groan, gloried in it every bit as much as the feel of his hands cupping her breasts, squeezing convulsively, wonderfully, when she did it again.

She ducked her head to kiss him as he had her, nearly swore when she found cloth in the way. She fumbled a bit and finally found the top button on his shirt.

Gabriel propped himself on his hands and reared back.

"Take it off," she commanded him. "Now. Off."

He started on the top button, made it to the third. "God. I can't stand not touching you." He reached down, took her by the upper arms, and pulled her up to him, kissing her hard, his tongue sinking deep. Then he set her gently back. "Okay," he said. "That'll hold me for a few seconds."

He grabbed her hands and put them to the next button, then leaned over her again. "You do it. I have better things to do with my hands than fiddle with my own buttons."

Who would have believed, Gabe thought, that the innocent, mannerly Miss Bright could look like this? Her mouth plump and wet, her color high, her hair a rich, wanton tumble around bare, firm shoulders? The schoolteacher facade hid a woman who could have rivaled the grandest courtesan, a woman made to pleasure a man. How could they all have missed it? How could *he*?

She smiled up at him, flirty and tempting while she toyed with the button. "May I?"

"You don't have to ask."

"Ah, but I wouldn't want you to accuse me of destruction of property after the fact." Her smile broadened and she got a good grip on his shirtfront, grabbing great fistfuls of flannel, and yanked. Buttons flew, plunked on the bed. One landed on her chest, a tiny round pearl between her breasts. "Besides which, I am abysmal at sewing those back on, so you mustn't expect it."

"That's all right," he told her, when he managed to speak again. He'd had a fair number of fantasies in his lifetime about ripping a woman's buttons off, but it had never occurred to him that the reverse could be so . . . interesting. "I can manage it."

Her hands roamed his chest, their warmth clearly discernible through the thin knit of his undershirt, found a spot on his side that made him suck in his breath.

He just had to nip at her lower lip, with it pouting out so delectably like that.

"Oh," she said, disappointed, "you've more layers on under that shirt."

"The hell with patience." He sprang up and ripped off clothes with desperate speed. Items flew through the air like flushed grouse. His shirt hit the wall and landed with a splat on top of a crate. His pants ended up somewhere deep beneath the bed. The white flag of his long drawers decorated the back of the nearest chair. And his shoes . . . well, who gave a damn what happened to his shoes?

"There," he said, panting, hands on hips, standing tall and completely magnificent to Anthea's eyes. "Satisfied?"

"Oh, not nearly," she returned, lifting a hand in invitation. "But soon, I hope. Depending upon how quickly you come back down here."

Fast. So fast he left her breathless, his body heavy and unfamiliar on hers. She felt the thrill of it all, the wiry hair on his legs ticklish against her thighs, the hard planes of his chest, the rough glide of his hands over her hips, her waist . . . everywhere. Oh, everywhere! She tried to do her share, but her head was spinning and her heart pounding and finally she gave up, throwing her arms over her head, her hands fisted, and let him do as he would.

And she felt the prod of his . . . it . . . *him?*

Despite her recently expanded vocabulary, she still did not have a proper term for *that*. But it was hard and hot and smooth against her thigh, her belly, and she squirmed, dying to get closer even though she knew it was impossible, for there wasn't room for so much as a thin sheet of paper between them.

Something bloomed deep inside her stomach, a hollow ache, making a space for him. It was wonderful and painful at the same time, a deep craving to be filled. "Please," she murmured, and only realized she said it aloud when he answered her.

"Soon," he promised, and his hand skimmed down over her breasts, her ribs, her belly.

"Aaaahh." At last. His fingers, long, blunt-tipped, impossibly clever, found her, tangling in the hair that shielded her sex, sliding easily over flesh plumped and slick with desire.

He played her with deliberate care, driving her up and stopping just short of the edge, higher each time, closer, until she whimpered in her throat and would have done anything, said anything, except she couldn't manage to mumble a word.

Finally he slid a finger deep inside her, assuaging and intensifying her need at the same time.

"Gabriel," she said, over and over. "Gabriel."

Her sighs and his; soft murmurings of pleasure and exhortation; the creak of bed ropes. The sounds hovered in the air, blended into cries of sharpening desire. Lamplight flickered over skin glistening damp with perspiration and trailing kisses.

Anthea. It was the only thought that pounded in his head, pumped through his heart. Resounded every time she called his name. *Anthea*. No other thought mattered a damn.

He should have taken her weeks ago. Now he'd waited too long, wanted too much. Then, it would have been easy and fun, entertaining. Pleasantly mild. But this . . . this held power, something strong, unnameable, entirely out of his experience.

She quivered each time he touched her. Arched, seeking more, her skin like gold-dusted silk. He could look at her, smell her, listen to her for nights on end and not get enough.

Taste her. He eased the finger inside her deeper, and she jerked, balanced on the keen edge where need nearly catapulted into ecstasy. He slipped his other arm beneath her hips and lifted her to his mouth.

"Gabriel!" Her hands struck the mattress hard beside her hips, her fingers spread wide. Then she grabbed fistfuls of his old muslin sheet, twisting hard.

There could not be a softer place on the entire earth, he thought hazily. He licked slow and deep, felt her hips rise and fall with the rhythm he set, his fingers matching the pace. And then faster, more insistent, a quick, hard push to her peak. She shuddered and cried out, buffeted from within and without by the hard lash of pleasure.

He took a stronger grip, the flesh of her butt firm and yielding, and held on, absorbing each shock even as it drove him higher. Each time her tremors faded, he stroked her with his tongue and she shuddered again, until she lay limp and trembling beneath him.

He levered up and took in the view. Her hair lay tumbled across the mattress, and so did she. Her limbs were relaxed, her arms forming a pretty curve, her legs wide, giving him glimpses of her intimate flesh, and his own jerked in response. Her head had rolled to the side, eyes closed, and he saw the lush semicircle of her lashes, the lovely curve where her jaw met her ear, and he wondered if she had any more to give. But then she slowly rolled her head his way and her eyes opened.

"Gabriel," she said, a flicker of challenge in her eyes, "why'd you stop?"

"Just letting you catch your breath," he told her. "You don't look like you could move a muscle right now."

To prove him wrong, she lifted her hips, brushing her slick softness against his shaft, and all the air hissed out of him. He grabbed her hips, pulled her closer so that she pressed fully against him. The move was blatant and raw, and he froze for a moment, until she smiled and wrapped her legs around him, intensifying the contact.

His fingers dug deep, pressing into soft flesh, but she welcomed it. Welcomed *him* as he slid against her, miming the rhythm he'd have used were he deeply inside her in truth. And she, who only seconds before had been drained and limp and thoroughly pleasured, felt it start to spike again, higher and higher with each thrust of his hips.

She kept her eyes open this time, her gaze level on his, unwilling to deny herself the delight of watching him above her in the night, his face honed to a hard edge, all sharp bones and shadows, teeth bared, ferally intense.

Mine, she thought. *At least for tonight, mine.*

And that was enough to send her up again, spiraling over the cliff into that place where there was no room for thought or intent or even emotion but only pure and brutal pleasure.

He growled immediately, coming down to lie full against her, his hips convulsing against her belly, and she felt the warm flood of his own release. She shook in his arms, wondering if her heart would ever beat normally again or if it was irreversibly altered. Suspecting the latter, but too sated to ponder that disaster yet.

Soon enough. But not yet.

He lay still on her a long time, heavy, welcome, cheek pressed against hers while she tried to memorize the feel, how her breasts flattened against his chest and how his hands found hers and linked.

"I'll get something to clean up," he mumbled against her, but made no move.

"Not yet," she said, and tightened her grip.

With supreme effort he lifted his head. "We should have done that weeks ago."

"Oh well," she said philosophically, her mouth angling for his and closing in, "I guess we'll just have to make up for lost time."

Later, much later, Gabriel lay in a tangle of bedsheets and Anthea. One of her legs looped across his thighs, an arm was thrown across his waist, and her head rested on his chest, her hair a soft wash of silk across his shoulder.

He'd no idea what time it was. Wished to God he didn't have to care.

But he needed to get home to Lily. She wouldn't be disturbed by his absence; she was safe at home, probably fast asleep, and had likely been left alone for far longer periods in her young life. What he'd told Anthea in one of their first discussions was true: children in Kansas had to shoulder their share of the responsibilities early, and Lily had learned that lesson better than most. But still . . . still, he wanted her to believe that, for once in her life, someone was there for her.

Too, it was only smart to leave before the town started stirring. The path behind the schoolhouse was seldom used and it was unlikely that anyone would stumble upon where he'd stashed Old Bill. Still . . . there was no point in taking any chances. He didn't want Anthea to suffer for what they'd just done.

Though he suspected there was no avoiding a fair amount of suffering before this was done. She was too complex a woman to keep this simple, no matter what she claimed. And he wasn't sure but that they'd already passed simple a while ago anyway.

He buried his nose in her hair and took a deep breath, breathing in the smell of her. Breathing in Anthea.

Better not to wake her up, he decided. She slept so peacefully. Had to be plumb tuckered out, he mused with a fair shot of male pride. Not to mention that, if he woke her, it'd likely be another half an hour or so before he could drag himself away.

She shifted in her sleep, her thigh sliding over his. Make that an hour, he mentally amended.

With reluctant resignation, he eased her head gently off his shoulder, himself from her hold.

And she'd likely be more comfortable if she woke up and found him already gone. Give her time to deal with self-recrimination and embarrassment in private, if she was prone to them, and decide without him smack-dab in front of her what she wanted to do from here.

And the fact that he didn't want to see either of those things on her face had not one thing to do with it. Damn it.

He dressed quickly and quietly, then paused for one last look.

Jesus, but she made a picture, all curled up in sleep. Not quite the same kind of picture she'd made beneath him an hour ago, but a picture just the same. He found a clear spot for it in his memory, made sure he tucked it carefully away.

"Merry Christmas," he murmured.

Long after he left, after he closed the door gently behind him, after the distant sound of his horse's hooves on the hard-frozen earth faded, after the deep black of the night softened into gray, Anthea whispered into the dim, empty room.

"Merry Christmas, Gabriel."

Chapter 18

Gabriel Jackson was her lover.

Over the next days, that shivering, delicious thought snuck in, catching her unawares at stray moments. She'd be correcting essays or heating water and she'd have a sudden, clear memory of him bending over her in the dark, all hot eyes and hot hands, and everything in her would go soft and shivery.

He'd come to her twice in the nearly two weeks since Christmas, in the depths of the night, kissing her awake so that by the time she swam up through her dreams to full consciousness she'd be already dizzy with him, fully aroused, completely in his thrall.

She should be guilty. She should be shamed. She *was* worried, a little. But mostly she simply couldn't get over the fact that she, plain, ordinary Anthea

Bright, had the right to put her hands on him, and welcome his on her, and cherish that cresting, consuming, golden pleasure he gave her so easily.

Realizing that she hadn't read a single word of the page in front of her, she put aside the stack of handwriting exercises and glanced up. Her students were bent industriously over their work. Oh, Billy wiggled in his spot on the floor, and Tacy Stoddard rummaged beneath the bench for her pen, but mostly the room was quiet and focused, and there was learning going on. It still surprised her just how much pride she took in it.

It seemed more than a little inappropriate how often Gabriel crept into her thoughts during the day. But she'd failed miserably at trying to evict him from her mind; it seemed the image of him was every bit as persistent as the man himself.

And deep down she really didn't want to. She knew full well this was a temporary interlude in her life and how much it was likely to hurt when it ended. She fully intended to squeeze every ounce of enjoyment out of it while she could.

"Miss Bright?" Olivia Cox stuck her finger in Anthea's copy of *Little Women* to hold her place. "It's getting a little hard to read in here. May I light the lamps?"

Shadows shrouded the room in a deep and gloomy gray. Anthea had barely noticed; sunset came early this time of year anyway, and evening was often glooming before the students left for the day. But this . . . this was far darker than usual.

"Of course, Olivia." The temperature must have dropped as well, she noticed with a sudden shiver. She rose and went to feed a few more lumps to the fire in the big old stove, resolving as she did so that she'd have to make sure she'd adequately demonstrated her gratitude to Gabriel.

The fire leapt greedily at the new fuel. The lamps, one on the corner of her desk and four more on hooks high on the walls, threw ovals of light that danced merrily over the shiny hair on the bent heads of her students. She filled a pot with the dipper and set the water on to warm; she'd fortify the children with a good shot of hot, heavily sugared tea before sending them out today.

The room seemed almost cozy, she thought with fond nostalgia. Though not so much so that she wouldn't be absolutely delighted when they moved into the bright new schoolhouse she planned to help raise enough money to build.

Except it was almost unheard-of, she reminded herself sadly, for a teacher to remain at a school longer than a single term. Some other teacher would be there when they opened the new school. And she . . . she couldn't imagine where she might be. Alone again, in another new town?

She walked slowly through the classroom, bending over to assist Jennie in forming her *R*s, letting her hand linger on the smooth bumps of Lily's braids. A new skill for Gabriel, one she'd bet he'd never expected to acquire.

A few weeks ago she'd given in and tacked brown paper over the few remaining panes of the windows that were whole, for even the unbroken ones allowed in far too much cold air. She peeled one back now and peered outside.

The sky, gunmetal gray and heavy, pressed down upon the land. It lay so low it seemed as if she might be able to reach up and touch it. Even as she watched, the clouds began to spit a few stray snowflakes.

"Children, let's finish up this lesson. You've all worked so hard, I think you've earned going home a bit early today." There were those among their parents who were sure to complain; they wanted every minute of education they'd paid for. Still, it seemed a prudent move. She was not familiar enough with Kansas's weather to read it, but it looked like a storm to her.

The children buzzed around the room, chattering happily at their unexpected reprieve. Suddenly the thin walls shuddered in a fierce blast of wind. It shrieked through the cracks in the walls, scattering the handful of papers on Anthea's desk.

"Hurry!" Anthea urged them, even as she tried to re-member which of the children had the farthest to walk home. If it appeared a storm had settled in, she'd keep them here, she decided, until the worst had passed.

She grabbed her own scarf and wound it securely around Jon's bare neck, ignoring his protest. "Men," she scolded him. "What is it that makes you believe that freezing to death proves how tough you are?"

She tugged a knit cap lower on Olivia's brow, in-spected each of her charges to make certain they were buttoned up to their chins, and reached for the door.

A fierce mix of wind and snow blasted through, stinging her eyes so that she had to blink and finally swipe at them with her hands before she could see what faced them.

Big snowflakes came at them in waves, so thickly it was impossible to discern one flake from another. The snow swirled and darted in the wind, their tracks hor-izontal as frequently as vertical.

Anthea tried to slam the door shut, struggling against the mean punch of the wind.

She faked a bright smile, hoped it was good enough. "So much for going home early."

There'd been snowstorms in Philadelphia. She'd always enjoyed them, curled up safely by the big hearth in her father's study, a thick blanket wrapped snugly around her. Mrs. Hargreaves would bring them hot chocolate and a plateful of cookies, and Anthea and her sisters would laugh and play games until Emily fell asleep in her chair. Kate would carry her upstairs, head on her shoulder, her body small and limp, and they'd all cuddle together in Kate's big bed. She loved snow.

But this—the wicked slap of the wind, the hard grains that seemed as much ice as snow—was entirely beyond her experience.

The children all clustered around, faces turned expectantly toward her. Billy Pruitt, for all his simmering energy, seemed unconcerned; he shouldered much of the work of his mother's farm, and no doubt this was no more worrisome than any one of a dozen things he'd faced in his life. Theron lurked at the back of the group, mouth drooping in a bored and sullen line. Certainly spending another hour or two in the schoolhouse was the last thing he hoped to do this afternoon.

Mina looked as if she might burst into tears at any moment. Anthea smiled reassuringly at her, and her mouth curved up in response, although the corners trembled. All the rest looked at her with varying degrees of trust, expectation, and concern.

"How about some of that tea?" she asked brightly. "It can't keep coming down at this rate very long."

The students all kept their own cups in their lunch

buckets. They scurried off to rummage for them while Anthea linked her numb fingers together in front of her waist to keep them from shaking and told herself not to worry. They were safe enough here for now.

"Miss Bright?"

Olivia stood at her elbow, her blond hair bright as new gold above her plum-colored dress, a deep square of lace at its yolk. Olivia slipped her hand, small and soft, into Anthea's and squeezed. "It'll be all right, Miss Bright."

Anthea's nerves and stomach settled abruptly. "Which of us is the teacher here, Miss Cox? Shouldn't I be the one reassuring you?"

Olivia's smile was dazzling and sweet at the same time, and Anthea felt a wash of pity for all the young men who'd undoubtedly be struck dumb at the sight of it in a few years. She wondered how many of them would never recover.

"I'm just practicing," she told her. "It's an excellent skill to acquire, don't you think?"

"You're very good at it, Olivia."

"Thank you. I usually am—good at things, you know," she said with such calm acceptance it was impossible to be anything but charmed.

"That you are," Anthea said with a laugh, and found that she was, indeed, comforted.

That comfort grew seriously strained over the next two hours. Snow found its way through cracks in the walls and snaked across the floor in cruel icicles. The structure creaked and shuddered in the wind, protesting its rough treatment, and grew colder despite the coal Anthea stuffed in the stove.

It didn't take long before she decided they must ration what they had. The coal, all that lovely coal

Gabriel had brought her, was in the storehouse, only twenty yards beyond the front door. It might as well have been twenty miles; there was not the slightest hint of its dark outline through the snowfall. Anthea had read far too many newspaper accounts of people being lost in the fierce blizzards of the West only to be found frozen a few feet from their houses to risk anyone setting one foot outside the school.

So they all wore their full complement of outerwear, gloves and all. Anthea gathered them in a tight knot at the front of the room, poured hot tea down them, and wracked her brain for every amusing tale and song and game she could dredge up to distract herself, as much as the children.

For the doubts snuck in as relentlessly as the cold. Would another teacher, one who'd been raised on the plains, have recognized the signs sooner? Would she have bundled them off and gotten them safely home before the storm hit?

Time crawled by, as slowly as if the seconds, too, had been frozen in place. The hour was impossible to judge; the world outside was one thick mass of spinning snow, where trivialities of day or night were submerged beneath the greater force of the blizzard.

Anthea peeked out at regular intervals, receiving an eyeful of snow for her trouble. It stung as she wiped it away and turned to her students.

"It can't last much longer," she said brightly, wondering if it sounded as false to them as it did to her own ears.

The elder students exchanged long looks.

"Sure thing, Miss Bright," Jon said consolingly.

"Come on," Olivia suggested, "who knows how to sing 'The Flying Trapeze'?"

While they were occupied, Jon climbed to his feet and shuffled over to Anthea.

"Jon?" she asked when he reached her. "What's the longest it's ever snowed?"

He turned away, heavy jaw bristling with the beginnings of a beard, a boy in a man's body, too often, she suspected, forced to shoulder a man's responsibility.

"Jon? It's better if I know from the start what to expect."

He sighed heavily, swung troubled eyes back to her face. "Four or five days, maybe. If what my grandma says can be trusted."

"Days?" Dear God, she thought. *Four or five days?*

"But Grandma can't much be trusted," he assured her hurriedly. "She swears that President Lincoln was sweet on her when she was young, and everybody knows he did nothin' more than wave at her from the back of a train."

Anthea studied the room while possibilities whirled in the back of her brain. The benches would keep them through one night at least. But the stove consumed wood greedily, and after that—

She jumped when Jon touched her shoulder.

His cheeks turned the color of beets and he shuffled his feet. "Sorry about that, Miss Bright."

"It's fine. I was just deep in thought, that's all."

"I'm gonna go out and fetch some coal from the shed," he said quietly.

"It's lovely and brave of you to offer, but I can't allow you to go out there. You could wander around in circles for hours and never find your way back."

"It's not as bad as it seems, Miss Bright. You just tie a rope to the door and to my waist. Once I find the storehouse the first time, I'll tie it there an' then we can go back and forth as much as we want to." He shrugged. "Do it all the time at home to get to the barn."

This, too, was something that a teacher who'd grown up in Kansas would know how to do. She didn't even have any rope in the schoolhouse. And what had she taught them? How to dance? If she—no, she would not think *if*, only *when*—saw Gabriel again, she would beg his pardon for the things she'd said. He'd been right about more than she'd given him credit for.

"Lucky that someone gave us all that coal," Jon continued. "There'll be plenty to keep us warm."

"That there will," she said with a rush of warmth for Gabriel. "Still, it can wait awhile. We've enough fuel for the moment."

"You're not thinking of going yourself, are you, Miss Bright?"

Caught, Anthea fixed a stern and, she hoped, convincing eye on him. "I would insist that it is a teacher's responsibility. I could hardly let one of my students go out there, could I?"

"Beggin' your pardon, ma'am, and God knows the last thing I'd want is to be disrespectful to you." He set his formidable jaw. "But you'd blow halfway to Missouri if you set foot outside. You're half as big as me, for all you're the teacher, and it'd be right ungentlemanly of me to allow you to try it."

"We'll discuss it when the time comes."

"No, we won't," he said stubbornly. "I'll get Clav to help me, if I gotta, but I won't be lettin' you go out there, ma'am."

"You really are a fine young man, Jon."

If anything, the color on his broad face deepened. "Flattery'll get you nowhere, ma'am."

"I—"

The door flew open, slamming into the interior wall so hard Anthea feared the knob would punch straight through the wall. Snow flew through as if propelled by a cannon. As Anthea hurried over to close it again, a dark figure materialized out of the storm, shedding clumps of snow from the deep-piled drifts on his great shoulders and hat.

He shoved the door shut behind him and gave himself a giant shake, scattering snow in all directions. He pulled the fur-lined leather mittens from his hands, then unwound the blue knit scarf that exposed nothing but his eyes, breaking the crust of ice his breath had formed over the lower half of his face. He had his hat half-off when a whirlwind hurtled itself at his legs.

"Gabriel."

He caught Lily in midlaunch. "You're going to get as wet and cold as me." But he didn't push her away. Instead, as she latched on, he laid his hand on her head as if touching a sacred object, eyes closing briefly in deep relief.

Anthea caught herself just before she copied Lily and wrapped herself as well around the most welcome sight she could ever remember. "You came."

"Just out for a quick ride." He disengaged Lily, but kept her small hand in his huge one. "Thought I might as well stop by."

Gabriel stayed right where he was planted. His knees were weak with relief, and he thought there might be an awkward bobble in his step if he tried to go to her. He hadn't let himself think about the possibilities on the way here, but they'd nibbled at the edges of his brain. What if Lily and Anthea had already begun the trek home before the storm hit? He'd strained to see through the lash of the snow all the way, searched out every shadow to assure himself it was not two small figures curled up against the storm.

So now he simply stood and drank in the sight of Anthea, and savored the feel of Lily's small, warm hand in his. Anthea looked disheveled by the day, a brush of purple beneath her eyes, her sleeves uncharacteristically unbuttoned and rolled up to the elbow, her arms round and white and firm beneath them.

Her step was sure and steady as she crossed to him, her smile lit from within. When she reached him she stopped, tilted her head up, and he remembered that first day when she'd stood just like that to challenge him and he'd thought her no more than a cute little puppy, snarling merrily at his heels because she didn't know what she'd challenged.

How little he'd understood her, the fierce strength hidden beneath a polite and polished veneer. He gripped Lily's hand tighter, to remind himself the children were here and he really couldn't grab her and kiss her hard.

"So kind of you to stop by."

He leaned toward her, lowered his voice so there was no chance of anyone but Lily overhearing. "Couldn't stay away before. Why would you think I'd start now?"

Pink bloomed across her cheekbones. "Lily, would you go over with the other children for a moment? I'd like to speak to Mr. Jackson alone."

Anthea waited until Lily had found a spot near the edge of the circle of children, all of whom watched her and Gabriel with intense interest, before she turned her attention back to him. "I can't believe you came," she said again.

"Like I said, it would take more than that—" he hooked his thumb over his shoulder "—to keep me away."

He was big and gorgeous, wrapped in his great shearling coat, his hair slicked to his head with melted snow. Conscious of their audience, she nevertheless whispered to him, "I never wanted to kiss anybody so much in my life."

He grinned. "Hold that thought. I'll be calling it in later; you can count on it."

She just smiled at him, let herself sink into the relief and delight of his presence and enjoy it for a moment before she worried about what to do next.

"Is it as bad out there as it looks from the window?"

"Worse," he said. "We get nasty ones in Colorado, but here—" he shook his head "—there's nothing to slow it down on the way, so it just keeps whipping up speed all the way across the state."

"How did you—" The thought of the danger he'd put himself in left her breathless, and she had to press her hand to her heart to calm it before she could continue. "How'd you ever make it here?"

He shrugged, making light of the trip. No use making Anthea worry over something that was done, he reasoned. "Like I said, nothing was going to keep me away."

"How long do you think it's going to last?"

"I couldn't even guess."

"Should we try to get some of the children home? The Sontesbys are close. They must be worried sick."

"I'm sure they'll all figure you kept them here safe and sound."

"All right, then. We'll settle in, hope for the best." She started to plan. Surely some of the students hadn't eaten all their lunches. They'd pool what was left, portion it out. Maybe even make soup; she thought that the Pietzkes had some beef in their sandwiches, and she herself had—

"Have you considered taking them over to your place?"

"I hadn't intended to set one foot outside unless we absolutely had to."

"You've got more food there, right? And it'd be a lot warmer, and take a lot less coal to keep it that way. It'd be a cozy fit, sure, but I don't imagine anyone'll mind that right now."

"We don't have rope to follow," she said. "I never thought to keep any here." She frowned at her oversight. "But I've been pondering it. I thought maybe we could tie together some of our shirts and scarves, good firm knots, and that would suffice."

"Figured out that little trick, did you?"

She grimaced. "Jon told me."

Gabriel dug deep in his pocket and pulled out a thick coil of rope.

"I take it back. *Now* I want to kiss you more than anyone in my whole life."

"I aim to please." He began unwinding the rope. "Always prepared, that's me."

Gabriel plunged out into the storm first and alone, the rope tied securely around his waist—Anthea had checked it herself, twice, before she'd let him open the door. And even so, she'd hovered, her heart racing painfully, until he charged back through the door.

And then he went back and forth with each student. Emily Bickersdyke first, as she was the oldest girl and deemed capable of looking over the younger ones while Anthea stayed at the schoolhouse with the rest. Then they started with the youngest and worked their way up.

That worked fine until only Jon and Anthea remained. "Go ahead," she told him. "I'll see you over there."

"Nope."

"Excuse me?"

"I said I ain't goin'. Not till after you."

Anthea crossed her arms and frowned at him. "Up until today, Jon, you have been the most cooperative of students. Whyever you have chosen now of all times to alter that pattern, I can't imagine. Your gentlemanly offer is duly noted and appreciated, but now is not the time to argue."

"Mr. Jackson? Would you please tell Miss Bright that there's no kind of man who'd escape to safety before a lady? And that, with all due respect, there ain't no way she's gonna be able to make me."

Gabriel stood beside the stove, dripping a rapidly forming puddle at his feet, stiff fingers spread toward a warmth that was dying but still far better than the bitter temperatures outside. "I'd trust the man, Anthea, when he tells you he'll be fine."

"See there, Miss Bright? He agrees with me."

"I should have known men always stick together," Anthea groused. "I don't suppose I can convince either one of you."

"Don't imagine so, ma'am."

It went against Anthea's grain to give in without a fight. But she measured the size of them, the mulish look on Jon's face and the faintly amused one on

Gabriel's, and knew she wasn't going to win this one. It would only delay getting them all safely inside the soddy.

She turned and marched toward the door. Gabriel still beat her there.

"Where're your things?" he asked.

"This is it." She indicated the cloak she'd donned hours ago. "It never seemed worth it to bundle up more just to cross to the school." Her mouth twisted as his opened. "And don't lecture me; I've learned my lesson. I won't set foot out of my house again to so much as go to the necessary without making certain I'm fully prepared."

"That's good."

He unbuttoned the front of his thick coat and spread it wide, making a place for her near his warmth. It was dark here near the door, the floor shiny wet. Gabriel's cheeks were scoured raw and red, bits of melting snow stuck in his eyebrows. A tiny cut near the corner of his eye oozed red. And he was the best thing she'd ever laid eyes on in her life.

She stepped forward, slid into the cocoon his body and coat made, and wrapped her arms around his waist. She closed her eyes, resting her cheek against his chest for a moment, and let herself savor it. Just for a second.

She felt his arms come around her, squeeze tight. And then he rubbed his hands briskly up and down her back.

"Jon?" he called over her head. "I'll give the rope a yank when we reach the soddy. Think you can follow us back alone?"

"Me?"

Anthea popped her head up to protest, but Gabriel

pressed it back to his chest with one hand. She peeked out underneath his arm.

Jon stood taller, puffing his chest out with considerable pride.

"Don't see anyone else here," Gabriel said.

"No, sir. I mean, *yes*, sir!"

"Good."

"Take good care of her, sir."

"I plan to."

Anthea thought she understood the brutality of the storm. She'd watched it all day, poked her nose out a couple of times, felt it batter the old schoolhouse all afternoon. But she'd had no idea. It hit like a blow the moment they stepped out the door. She felt Gabriel brace against it, leaning into the force. He sheltered her with his body, and yet it sliced through her, stung every bare inch of skin. She could only imagine how it pummeled Gabriel and wonder how he'd withstood it so many times.

The storm shrieked in her ears, tore at her hair, whipped at her skirts. But Gabriel's arms were steady around her, holding her secure, his body blasting heat, and she was no longer afraid. Hadn't been afraid since the moment he'd walked through the door.

"Here we are," he shouted as they reached the door of her soddy and he shouldered it open. "You okay?"

"I'm fine," she murmured, "just fine," and they burst into a hubbub of shouting children, hissing water on the stove, and steaming outerwear.

Within two hours, the hubbub had turned to peace. Completely ignoring Anthea's protests—she didn't know why she had even bothered, except it was the principle of the thing—Gabriel and Jon had made three more trips outside, lugging in a week's worth of coal. Now the soddy warmed up enough that Anthea found herself perspiring as she worked over the stove. The children shed layers, piling them all in a chair in the far corner until they mounded so high they toppled over onto the floor. She stuffed everyone with hot chocolate and big bowlfuls from a quick pot of oatmeal, bolstered with crackers and chunks of the big yellow wheel of cheese she'd bought earlier in the week at Stoddard's.

Six of the girls had taken her bed, packed in like tinned fish, feet to head to feet, and had only giggled for fifteen minutes before they'd fallen fast asleep. The boys conked out faster, lying side by side like soldiers on quilts on the floor. Lily dragged the lone upholstered chair over by the stove, curled up, and dropped off in moments.

Anthea sat at the table, a mug of hot, sweet coffee in her hand, and let her gaze rest on the still, small forms packed together. A snore rumbled from the bed. Olivia Cox, she thought, and smiled, amused that such a delicate, feminine child could produce such a decidedly unladylike sound.

Weariness seeped into her bones with the warmth. But there was peace, too, in the knowledge that her students were safe and warm and fed, and there was every reason to believe they'd stay that way.

Gabriel leaned back in his chair, long legs stretched out and crossed at the ankles, hands linked over his belly. His lids were low, slumberous, an expression that she knew was exhaustion but looked so much like the one he wore when he came to her in the night that she felt warmth bloom.

She reached across the table and seized his hand. "I really should scold you for taking the chance, for going out in the storm to come to us when we probably would have been fine."

"No scolding. Not today, anyway. Save it."

"No, no scolding." Her grip tightened. "I don't know how to thank you. As dangerous as it was, as risky as it was . . . thank you."

He stood up suddenly and dragged his chair around the table to rest next to hers before plopping back down. Exhaustion dimmed his smile, but he still managed to promise all the things he'd do to her if they weren't surrounded by sleeping children. "I'm sure you'll think of some way to thank me. I've got a few suggestions, even, if you have trouble settling on an appropriate gesture."

"That won't be necessary."

He leaned closer, his mouth near and tempting. "Aw, come on. Let me suggest . . . something."

She couldn't help it. She kissed him. Just leaned over and did it. Full and hard, his nose against her cheek still cold as ice, his mouth hot and all the more delicious for being familiar. The passion in the kiss was carefully banked, stored away for another time; this was something else entirely, warmth and friendship and an emotion she was terrified to name but that seemed to have taken up permanent lodging in her heart whether she wanted it or not.

A giggle pierced the silence. They jumped apart, guilty as schoolchildren caught putting burrs in the teacher's chair. Anthea's stomach sank to her toes as she turned and looked straight into Theron Matheson's gleeful eyes.

It snowed for nearly a week, until the drifts piled up against the roof of the house. Gabriel stabled Old Bill in the school, something that he figured Phillip Cox would have plenty to say about. The students grew snappish with the enforced inactivity, but Anthea would bet there wasn't a single one of them who didn't know his or her multiplication tables cold by the time it ended. And all the while Gabriel and Anthea stayed so circumspectly far from each other, she thought it had to be perfectly obvious they were guilty.

The first parents, the Sontesbys, arrived less than two hours after the snow stopped. Johanna burst into noisy tears and clutched Henry to her sturdy chest, much to her son's obvious dismay. The Stoddards appeared before she stopped dripping.

To Anthea's guilty eyes, Gabriel seemed to take up half of the space in the small room, so obviously *there* that the parents couldn't help but notice him the instant they stepped inside. It occurred to her, just once and briefly, that she should have asked him to leave before people started to arrive. But she didn't dare tell him that. And, scowling at every arrival, he planted himself in the center of the room, clearly daring them to comment. His presence caused plenty of raised eyebrows but no remarks. But she had no doubt they would come soon enough, when Gabriel's dampening glower wasn't there to stop them.

And it was far too late anyway, she thought glumly, the damage done. She could do nothing to keep Theron from spreading the news throughout the whole town, and there was nothing she could say to mitigate what was, in fact, the truth. Their gratitude for the children's safety wouldn't stand long against their concern for their moral development.

She would never secure another position if she was turned off from her first without references. What could she do? She'd failed her sisters; she'd have to find her way home somehow, and this time send Kate out to work while she cared for Emily.

Her eyes burned as the last student to leave, Billy Pruitt, turned and waved before clambering into his mother's sleigh. She blinked hard so that Gabriel wouldn't see. It was not his fault, and she would not allow him to think it.

"Well." She made a helpless gesture. "Thank you, again. We'll—"

"I figure we got twenty-four hours," he interrupted. "Maybe thirty-six; there's bound to be a lot of dead stock to deal with."

"Thirty-six?"

He hadn't moved, claiming his space in the center of the room, Lily by his side. Behind him was the jumble of the bed, the pile of quilts the students had left.

"Thirty-six hours to what?"

"Thirty-six hours to get married, of course."

Chapter 19

"**M**-" She tried to form the word, but it lodged in her throat. Beside Gabriel, Lily squeaked like a little mouse and gave a bounce. "*Married?*"

"Yup."

Anthea narrowed her eyes at him. He didn't *look* like he was joking. But he didn't exactly look bowled over by undying love, either, his face impassive, his body stiff and tall.

"I'm not sure I completely understand," Anthea said carefully, picking her way through the idea.

He shrugged. "What's to understand? They're going to fire you for moral misbehavior. You know that as well as I do. If we're married, they won't be able to say anything."

"Don't you—" She swallowed hard, tried to find

clear thoughts in the jumble that crowded her brain. "Don't you think getting married is a rather extreme way to keep me employed?"

"Doesn't have to be such a big thing."

" *'Doesn't have to be such a thing'?*" She gasped out the words, found they were no more comprehensible when she said them than when he did.

"It'd only have to be until the end of the term." Gabriel clamped down hard on the panic trying to spike in his chest. No reason to make too much of it, he told himself. Oh, maybe he hadn't exactly *planned* the suggestion that popped out of his mouth on its own accord. But it made perfect sense, nothing to be overly concerned about.

"Somehow I don't think it's quite that simple." All the color fled Anthea's face except two circles of bright, hectic red high on her cheeks.

"No need to make it complicated." No need to *think* about it more than he had to. "After the term's over, you'll head on to someplace else anyway. I'm going back to Colorado. All you need is to keep your job for now and a decent reference when you leave. Seems to me this is the simplest way to ensure that."

"Will I . . ." She swallowed hard. "Will I go with you to Colorado?"

That was a lot further ahead than Gabe planned on thinking. "That's pretty much up to you. I don't mind if you come."

He didn't mind if she came, Anthea thought. Well, wasn't that just lovely of him? "Aren't you forgetting about the fact that we'll be *married*?"

"Look, Anthea, marriage isn't quite the same institution out here that it is in Philly. The state government's pretty damn generous with divorce decrees, if you feel the need. Otherwise, well . . . do you know how many 'widows' out here still got husbands floating around somewhere? Won't bother anybody else if it doesn't bother you."

She swayed a bit, her eyes glassy. He hoped she wouldn't up and keel over in a dead faint. He was just trying to be helpful. It seemed an immensely practical solution to him. She'd keep teaching, there'd be the added bonus of him having her in his bed every night, and when it was all over they could go their separate ways with fond memories. Perfect.

"But—but—" Okay, maybe, once or twice, Anthea had imagined Gabriel proposing to her. Before she'd managed to get her ungovernable imagination firmly under control. But this wasn't exactly how she'd envisioned it. "But what if you want to marry again?"

"I don't expect that's going to happen."

He talked of marriage as if it were no more important than a simple business transaction. A small one at that. Selling a horse, maybe, and not a particularly prized one.

She rubbed at the ache forming behind her right temple. The frightening thing was that the more he talked, the more it started to sound eminently logical to her. She knew it shouldn't, but she couldn't come up with why. And what else was she going to do?

"What about . . ." Her gaze dropped to Lily, who stood quietly by Gabriel's side, her eyes wide and alert, very interested.

"We'll work that out later," Gabriel said with a shake of his head. Well, they could hardly negotiate the details of their marriage bed in front of the child, could they? Still, it seemed to be a rather important detail to leave undiscussed, Anthea reflected.

She was going to agree, she realized with a dawning, uncomfortable mix of excitement and panic. But first she had to ask. "Why, Gabriel?"

"Why not?" When she scowled at Gabe he decided to expand on it a bit. "I know where your responsibilities lie. You've done a lot for Lily." He cleared his throat. "For me. I can't let you lose everything that matters to you because of us. I won't."

Anthea wavered on the brink of the cliff, toes peeping over the edge. The problem, the *big* problem, was that she couldn't see, had no idea at all, what lay at the bottom of the abyss.

And you thought you took an impulsive leap of faith when you came to Kansas. "Why not indeed?"

They came to her door at three o'clock on the dot, five men wearing somber clothes and sober faces. His minions, the two other members of the school board, flanked Phillip Cox. Behind him hovered Adonijah Matheson—and, surprisingly, Davey Conroy, who had no children in the school but with whose wife, Fannie, Anthea had formed a tentative friendship over dance lessons.

She knew Davey wasn't exactly fond of dancing, but she hadn't realized he wanted to escape it so badly he was willing to help run her out of town.

"Miss Bright." For all his serious mien, anticipation lit Phillip Cox's eyes. Did he take so much joy in another's downfall? He must be positively gleeful when foreclosing on a mortgage. "We would like to speak to you about events during the storm."

"Of course." She moved aside to allow them admittance. "Please, come in."

They moved past her in a group but paused when

they discovered Gabriel standing in the middle of the room awaiting them.

Adonijah snarled. Phillip cut him off with a jerk of his hand. "Jackson. I didn't expect to see you here." Phillip clasped his hands behind his back. "Perhaps I should have."

"Yes, you should."

Though Anthea considered she'd brought only the necessities to Kansas, there'd been more to pack than she realized. Now her books were stacked on the table, awaiting a box. Already filled with clothes, her trunk sat just inside the door. Her bed linens were folded neatly at the foot of the bed, but she'd yet to find a box for them.

The men's eyes rested on her hasty packing, then shifted back to her. Unwilling to give them any satisfaction, she stiffened.

"Going somewhere?" Cox asked.

"Yes, I—"

From behind Cox, Mr. Sontesby snorted like an old bull. "Convenient, that, you being all ready."

"Now, men, let's not be hasty." Of all the people in that room, only Cox seemed entirely comfortable with the situation. Anthea half expected Gabriel to haul off and start swinging at any moment, and Adonijah appeared more than happy to accommodate him. "First, Miss Bright, I am sure that everyone here, and everyone in town for that matter, would like to extend our gratitude for your clear thinking and brave action during the terrible storm. To tell the truth, Olivia thought it quite the adventure. I don't believe she was frightened for a moment."

"Well, I don't mind admitting *I* was frightened a moment or two." Beyond that initial start of surprise, the men had apparently decided the appropriate way to deal with Gabriel's presence was to ignore him completely.

Anger burst in Anthea suddenly, unexpected, as hot as fire. "The true hero here was Mr. Jackson. He fought through the storm to reach us, and I honestly do not know what would have happened to us without his presence."

Calvin Stoddard leered over Cox's shoulder. How *did* his wife put up with him? Anthea wondered. How he'd ever sired a child as delightful as Tacy would ever be a mystery.

"Yes, I heard that, too," Cox said smoothly. He was a difficult man to read, Anthea thought. He looked as likely to continue to thank her as fire her in the next moment, his smile genial, his brow smooth. "Which leads us to another area of concern. Now, I understand that in moments of difficulty and danger, we are all susceptible to actions we might never undertake in other circumstances. Still, I—"

Gabriel's hands came down hard on her shoulders, unmistakably possessive. "I hardly think a small kiss between an engaged couple is any concern of yours."

"Engaged?" Knute Sontesby gaped. Davey blinked. And then Cox grinned in broad delight. "Why, that is wonderful news!" He thrust out his hand. "Please accept my genuine congratulations. When's the happy day?"

Gabriel glared pointedly at Phillip's extended hand. When Phillip didn't waver a bit but merely continued to smile at him, Gabriel slowly reached out and gave his hand a perfunctory shake. "Thank you. The happy day was four hours ago. In Centervale."

Cox's jaw dropped to his chest. Calvin stepped out

from behind him, his upper lip curling in a most unattractive way. "In Centervale. How convenient that you went all the way there so nobody saw you. Don't suppose you happen to have proof handy?"

Anthea flinched as Gabriel's hands tightened on her shoulders. She braced herself, ready to step in, for it would do no one any good to have a brawl break out in the middle of the soddy.

"Oh, heavens, we don't need proof." Cox positively glowed, as if his own cherished proposal had just been accept by his ladylove. Anthea exchanged a confused glance with Gabriel. "I doubt either Gabriel or Anthea is silly enough to fake something so easily checked. And besides, look at them!" He reached out and grabbed both of Anthea's hands and tugged them to his mouth for a quick kiss. "If they aren't the picture of newly wedded bliss, I don't know what is. Oh, I am so delighted for both of you!"

"But—" Adonijah's mouth worked, but all he could manage to dredge up was a few more *but*'s.

"We shall leave you alone," Cox said, winking broadly. And Anthea found herself gaping as obviously as the women in Stoddard's store when Gabe had walked in. "I'm sure we are far more company than you desire on your wedding night."

"Of course," Anthea murmured by rote. "I mean, thank you. For your good wishes."

"Oh, you have those indeed!" His expansive gesture encompassed the room. "You do not have to move out, you know. As the circumstances are somewhat unusual, I can assure you that the board would not object to your husband living here with you."

Stoddard nearly choked. "We wouldn't?"

"No, we wouldn't."

"Ahh . . . thank you," Gabriel said. "But we really do not wish to upset Lily again, and she is only now getting settled. I'm sure we'll be more comfortable at my home. And the distance is really not so great."

"No, it isn't. Well!" Cox spun, shooed the other men out the door. "Congratulations again!" he called as he hustled after them, in an obvious hurry to allow them their newlywed privacy.

But Davey hovered just inside the doorway, his bulk blocking the thin winter light, his brows drawn together.

"Please don't let us keep you," Gabriel said flatly.

"I did not come along to help run you out of town." His regard encompassed them both. "Either of you. I came . . ." He fumbled a bit, found his tongue again. "I came to see if I could help."

Gabriel considered briefly, then gave a quick nod, accepting his statement at its face. "Fair enough."

Davey crushed his hat in his big hands.

"Is there something else?" Gabriel asked him finally.

"Where's the girl? Lily?"

"She's at home. Wanted to make a special dinner to welcome Anthea, she said. She was flour from head to toe when we left."

"Do you think . . . I know it has to be hard for her, all the upsets in her life, but maybe she'd consent to come spend the night with me and Fannie." He reddened. "So the two of you could have a proper night alone."

Through the fabric of her blouse, Anthea thought she felt Gabriel's hands heat. Her own heartbeat sped up.

A whole night. Alone, with no need to rush, no reason to worry about interruptions, nothing to do but sink into each other and the pleasure their bodies spun together. She could hardly imagine it.

"We wouldn't want to impose," Gabriel said.

"It'd be no imposition. Fannie'd be happy to practice a bit." He ducked his head. "We'll be having our own, come May."

"Congratulations!" Gabriel said in genuine pleasure. "A lucky child, to have the two of you for parents."

"You think?" Pride and fear and joy radiated from his round face. "Heck of a day, huh?"

"Heck of a day," Gabriel echoed. "Does Fannie still make that dried-peach pie?"

"Sure. Better than ever." He patted his sturdy belly. "Plenty of practice."

"Then I imagine that Lily could be persuaded to visit for one evening."

"Good. I'll follow you to your place then, bring her home with me. If you're ready to go, I mean."

Gabriel's reply was fervent and heartfelt. "Oh, we're ready, all right. We surely are ready."

Whistling an old, romantic tune he'd almost forgotten, Phillip bounded up the front steps of his house. The steps were formed of sharply hewn stone, bordered by pots that held freshly cut cedar boughs, the deep green an attractive complement to the dark red brick. They'd built a lovely house, he and Cleo, and made an even more lovely daughter. Who knew what else they could build together, given an honest opportunity?

He found his wife in the front parlor, nestled in her favorite chair, feet on a tiny footstool pulled near the warm hearth. Her head bent over the needle she poked in and out of some frilly bit of fabric.

"Cleo!"

She jumped and looked up, frowning. It was only an instant, a brief flicker of dismay, before her face smoothed, revealing no hint of the emotions beneath.

She wove her needle into the fabric, rolled it carefully, and set it aside on a small mahogany table kept for just that purpose. Then she folded her hands in her lap and gave him her full attention—or every appearance of it; he'd never been quite sure which.

"You're home early. I hadn't expected you for hours yet."

"Yes, well, it's been rather an unexpected day." He started to rub his hands together, caught himself just in time.

She waited patiently for him to continue.

"We went to see Miss Bright. The school board and I. I considered it advisable to discuss the incidents of the storm."

"I should hope you did more than discuss." Animation flared in her eyes. "I am so thoroughly disappointed in that woman. What a terrible example for Olivia! You know how she admired her teacher. Is she halfway back to Philadelphia by now?"

"Oh, she's not going anywhere. At least not yet."

She frowned. "I don't understand."

"They got married, she and Jackson. Under the circumstances, their subsequent marriage and the difficult and dangerous situation they found themselves in, which surely contributed to their slight indiscretion, I believe we can overlook her minor lapse."

"Married." She said the word as if it were entirely alien to her.

"Yes." And then, because he couldn't resist, "They seem quite the happy couple. I congratulated them for both of us."

She rose shakily to her feet. Her lovely features twisted, disfigured by rage. *"You did this."*

"Did what? Fought through the snow and forced him to kiss her? I hardly think so."

"You—" Her lips were stiff, bloodless, so that she could barely make the words come out. "I don't know how you arranged this, but you did. You forced him to marry her."

"I did not." He would have, given the opportunity. He'd had every intention, when he knocked on Miss Bright's door, of encouraging the union. But they'd saved him the trouble. "You greatly overestimate me, Cleo, if you believe I can go around causing marriages. And among people I am scarcely connected to at that."

Tears brimmed in her fine eyes. "I'll never forgive you for this," she choked.

Her own anger fueled his. For once, he allowed it free rein, felt the acid burn wash over him, flood his veins. At least he felt alive, at least he felt something. "He's a married man, Cleo. And as you are a married woman, I can't imagine why it should matter to you either way. Can you?"

She struggled visibly for control and finally found it. She blinked, and her eyes were clear again, her respiration steady. "I simply object to meddling in others' affairs, that's all. I do not believe a hasty, ill-considered wedding, to Gabriel Jackson of all people, is reason to believe that Anthea Bright is after all an appropriate influence on our daughter. Far from it."

"Nevertheless, it's decided." *And you'll come to accept it,* he thought. Hoped. With Jackson irrevocably linked to another woman, Cleo would finally have to put aside her childish infatuation.

She had the bearing of a queen, the beauty of a goddess. She sailed out of the room, head held high, her shiny gold hair twisted and wrapped around it like a crown, and despite everything, he couldn't help but feel pride.

Pride. And a despair to which he refused to surrender.

He'd thought Gabriel's marriage might save his own.

Instead, it might have been the final blow that destroyed it.

Chapter 20

Once assured that Broom, who'd weathered the storm just fine with the supplies Gabriel left for her, could indeed accompany her, and promised that their cow gave the richest cream in the township, Lily agreed to visit the Conroys. When she tucked her small hand in Davey's ham-bone-sized fist, he grinned so wide it exposed his molars.

Anthea stood in the doorway, waving madly until Davey's old wagon rumbled out of sight.

Gabriel slipped his arms around her. "Come in. It's getting cold."

"Do you think we did the right thing?"

He chose to believe she was asking about Lily, not the marriage. It had been an impulsive move, proposing they wed, though when he pondered it he still believed his logic sound. But he vastly preferred not to think about it, for every time he did, vaguely unsettling and disconcerting ideas kept nipping around the corners of his brain. He'd just as soon keep them safely locked away and ignored.

"She'll be all right. Davey's a good man, and Fannie's likely to spoil her rotten."

"Lily's overdue for a little spoiling." Anthea slanted him a skeptical glance. "I've never heard you speak that well about a single person or thing in Haven before."

"Times change."

"That they do." She gazed down the road. "I feel guilty, sending her away so we can . . ."

He grinned, spun her around in his arms. "Say it."

Her mouth firmed into a mutinous line.

"So I can lick every single inch of your naked body?" he suggested.

"That's not precisely how I would have put it," she said primly.

"So I can make you peak so hard you scream?"

She crossed her arms in front of her chest, putting some space between them. "I don't scream."

"You will." He pulled her closer, so her arms were locked tight between them, and bent down to trail kisses along her jaw, down her neck. "So we can love each other until neither of us can move."

She'd completely lost the train of the conversation, Anthea thought. Oh, just exactly how did he manage to make her feel it throughout her entire body when he just suckled on her earlobe?

He drew back and waited until he knew her mind had cleared. "You underestimate Lily sometimes, Anthea. She'll be fine."

"I know. It's just . . . she's had so little coddling in her life. Is it so wrong for me to want to give her some?"

"Only if she comes to depend upon it." And then he grinned. "Besides, I told Davey to bring her home if she so much as squeaks."

"You did?" All those people in Haven who called him hard and cold and bad—how little they knew him, Anthea thought. How privileged she felt to be one of the few who did.

"Yeah. Told him to knock real loud, though, and under no circumstances come barging in."

"Oh?" She arched a brow. "What makes you so certain there'll be something to interrupt?"

In answer he kissed her, hard and tender at once, the taste of him rich, the feel of him beguiling and demanding.

"Oh," she said again when he finally lifted his head. "Maybe there will be at that."

She sighed in disappointment when he released her.

"You turn down the sheets, I'll get the lamps."

Swimming up through the haze of passion his kiss had spun, she finally grasped his words. "Lamps? Now?"

He shot her a glance full of simmering impatience. "Now."

"It's the middle of the afternoon."

"Good. I figure we've got a solid sixteen, seventeen hours until Davey shows up here again. Maybe we'll even be done, if we get started right now."

"Seventeen *hours*?" All the air left her lungs. They were going to do . . . *that* . . . for hours on end. "We'll expire."

"No. We'll be more alive than we have ever been in our entire lives."

"I'll never walk again."

"It'll be worth it."

Her stomach fluttered, nerves and anticipation and hollow want. She was not . . . well, she was experienced, but she was not *experienced*. She suddenly worried that she might disappoint him. "Don't you want supper first?"

"No," he said in a tone that left no doubt about the matter.

"But . . . seventeen hours. Won't we need sustenance?"

"If you start feeling faint, let me know. I'll feed you."

I am going to faint, she thought. *I'm going to faint for sure.*

She opened her mouth to discuss the topic further, only to discover that Gabriel had apparently finished with talking. He disappeared into the small lean-to that tilted drunkenly against the side of the house by the kitchen, reappeared moments later with a brace of candles in one fist and two lanterns in the other.

"What? Still standing there? You're falling behind on your assignments, Anthea. You were supposed to turn down the bed."

He was so male. Blunt and kind and hard. *Her husband.* All day long, even as they'd exchanged their vows in front of the old judge in Centervale, who'd taken one look at Lily and apparently decided to right an obvious wrong and performed the entire ceremony with such haste that Anthea couldn't remember a single word of it, she'd not thought of him as that. *Husband*.

It hit her like a cyclone, whirled her brutally around and set her back unsteady and stunned.

It didn't mean a thing, she told herself. It was a practical arrangement. But try as she might, the depths of her, down deep where emotion resided, refused to be as easily convinced as her head.

"All right, we can stay on top." His bed was in the far corner, behind a limp blanket tacked to the ceiling for privacy. He yanked back the blanket and hooked it around a nail, leaving the bed open to the room, starkly exposed. "But the blankets are a tad scratchy." He shot her a cocky grin. "Course, maybe you like that. Don't know all your secrets yet. Maybe by morning."

He was too much for her. She'd known it the first morning she met him. Oh, she should have left well enough alone! But she'd been unable to resist him, and look where it had gotten her. When this was all over, he was going to walk away, whistling, and she'd have given him everything inside her so there'd be nothing left. Nothing but the memories.

But they'd be some kind of memories, wouldn't they? A smile flickered through her unease, threatened to break out when he ripped off the top blanket on the bed and tossed it aside. "Decided I wouldn't want you to get scratched after all. Don't want any distractions."

He dragged a couple of chairs to the bed, one by the head and one by the foot, and set a lantern on each. Then, on the small, battered table that held a half-empty glass of water, he set out the candles in their mismatched sticks and set them aflame.

"It seems perfectly light to me."

"It'll get dark soon enough. Don't want to have to stop and light them at an inconvenient moment."

Before, he'd come to her in the depths of the night, in secret, separate darkness. Out of place, out of time, when one could ignore the realities of conscience and awkwardness and daytime, the night blotting out the real world.

But in full daylight—she could not hide from him in daylight. Any more than she'd be able to hide from herself.

When the last flame caught, he stood and stared at her across the expanse of the room. All the lightness fled his face; the angles grew harder, sharper, his mouth set, his eyes burning hot. He came to her, prowling across the floor like a cougar stalking his prey, she as helplessly captivated, knowing it was too late to escape her fate. Unsure whether she would flee even if she could. "Besides which," he said, in a low rumble, "I intend to see every single bare inch of you."

He hadn't touched her yet and she was already gasping. Her stomach jittered; her skin heated. He was less than a footstep from her, and her gaze fastened on the second button on his shirt. It was coming loose, she thought irrelevantly, latching desperately on to the mundane. She could fix it for him.

"Anthea." His forefinger beneath her chin—oh, how much warmth was contained in one fingertip!—he lifted her head to meet his gaze. "Are you nervous?"

"I—" She stopped, made a helpless gesture. "I don't imagine it would do much good to deny it, would it?"

"Why?" He studied her face as if he'd never seen it before, might never again, and meant to memorize each line. "While I'd love to surprise you, I've grown nothing new between the last night I came to you and now. Truly."

She managed a light laugh, weaker than his comment deserved. "It feels different now."

"It shouldn't. It's the same as it was before. Just you and me, and what we want as long as we want it." He smiled. "Except tomorrow morning I'll get to wake up with you in my arms, and I want that. Very much." The finger beneath her chin drifted lower, drew a shivery line down her throat. "Assuming I allow you any sleep at all, that is. Which is unlikely."

But it wasn't the same. He was her husband now, but in a marriage they hadn't undertaken for better or for worse, but for as long as convenient. Though this was sanctioned now by church and state, somehow it felt more a sin than before.

His mouth found the spot in her neck where her pulse beat, and her knees softened. "You know what I think?" he murmured against her skin.

"What?" she managed.

"That it's time for you to stop thinking."

And then his mouth closed over hers, and her thoughts scattered like windblown leaves, whirling away into the sky. His tongue thrust deep, stole her breath and gave it back again. His hands gripped her hips hard, holding her close against him, and it wasn't nearly close enough.

He drew back just far enough to talk, and his breath washed over her, moist and hot, flavored with coffee and sin. "Clothes off. You want it the fun way or the fast way?"

She had to think for only a moment. "Fast. Then it'll be even more fun."

"Good choice." He let her go reluctantly and started in on his shirt buttons. She stood there, arms at her sides, bereft because he wasn't touching her, but fascinated by the wedge of chest being revealed as he worked his way down the line of buttons.

"Well?" He paused only long enough to point at her own buttons. "Hurry up. This isn't going to be the fast way if you don't get started."

She tucked her tongue in her cheek. "Maybe I think it's more fun to watch you. After all, you had me at just this disadvantage the first time. Maybe it's your turn to be bare while I'm fully dressed."

He tugged his shirt from his waistband, ripped it off, and balled it up before hurling it away. "I can get those off you pretty fast if I rip them to shreds." His gaze raked her, hot with speculative promise. "I bet I'd find that pretty fun, too, but you'd have a helluva time putting that skirt back together again."

"Since I'm not that good with a needle, I guess I'd best get them off then, hmm?"

"I guess you'd better."

Gabriel stripped off the rest of his clothes while he watched her work at her own fastenings with industrious speed. But when, after she'd removed her corset, she shimmied the straps of her shift off her shoulders and her breasts sprang free, small and round and high, his hands fell still at his waistband.

Jesus. How was a man supposed to look at that and move? How was a man supposed to think? How was a man supposed to touch that, put his mouth on her and slide his tongue over the tight nipple, and ever give her up?

In the midst of pushing her shift down her torso, she stopped and looked pointedly at his motionless hands. "What happened to fast?"

The thin fabric of her shift sagged low, barely hanging on. He saw the indent of her navel, the slight upper curve of her belly, and his mouth went dry.

"Forget fast," he said, and closed the distance between them in an instant. "I changed my mind, I vote for fun." His hands closed over her hips, stopping her shift in its descent.

"Don't I get a vote?"

"No."

"Now, whyever did I think I would?" But she smiled in a way that said she didn't mind, not one bit.

Through the thin fabric that swirled around her legs, she could feel the heat of his hands, scalding her. They stood there like that for a moment, gazes locked, breath coming hard, while they savored the anticipation, let it build and grow, knowing what followed would be all the sweeter for the wait.

He bent, pressed his mouth to the hollow of her throat, and her head fell back on a moan. It was only a mouth, she thought vaguely, teeth and tongue and lips, nothing that every person on earth didn't own. And yet it was *his* that burned her, shattered her nerves with each touch, made her head swim and her heart pound.

His mouth roamed down, over the swell of her breast, and found her nipple. She dragged her head up and looked down at him, seeing the gleam of his dark hair against her paleness, feeling it brush softly over her skin when he angled his head to take her breast deeper. He drew back, moved to the other breast, and she saw the wet shine he'd left on her nipple, the mark of his mouth, and she shivered.

He dropped to one knee and kissed her navel, which made her jerk, and slid his open mouth, hot and damp, over the top of her stomach. She couldn't move, couldn't look away, completely caught by the sight of him doing such wicked things to her body.

And then he kissed her through the fabric, mouth wide and full, right on the very center of her, and the whisper of a moan escaped her throat. There was a small spasm of pleasure, a piercing dart through her, a foretaste of the feast she knew awaited.

He wrapped his arms around the backs of her thighs and straightened, lifting her right off the floor until her head almost touched the low plastered ceiling of the small cottage. Her head went dizzy with the height, and she put her hands on his shoulders to hold herself steady.

His head, his mouth, nudged her with each step, and she felt a shiver of purely physical joy each time. And then they were beside the bed—she'd no idea how he found it, but his step had been unerring—and he let her slide slowly down him all the way, her shift rising up, gathering above her hips. She stood with her bare breasts against his chest, her nakedness pressed to the hard ridge in his pants.

They didn't move, didn't say a word. Just memorized the feel of each other while the need spiked higher with each passing second. How could that happen, Anthea wondered, when all they did was stand tightly together? And yet it did, his nearness enough to send her spiraling up.

Husband, she thought again. For now, for tonight. It

was her right to be here with him. Her right to put her hands on him, to revel in his every touch. *Mine.* Maybe not forever, but now. And maybe now would be enough. She hadn't thought ever to be able to call him hers, and it intoxicated her, sent excitement frothing through her veins.

Wife, he thought, and for once didn't shy from it. She'd vowed to give herself to him fully. What a tempting offer that was; he would revel in the opportunity completely while he could.

She'd been lovely in the dark, dreamy-eyed, soft-edged. But he liked her even better in the light; he could see the narrow curve of her waist, the rosy color of her nipples, the lively snap of blue in her eyes.

She smiled, slow and sensual, and he felt the power of it clean down inside him. Deliberately she reached out and hooked a forefinger in his waistband, and he felt his muscles leap at the brush of her fingertips.

"May I?" she asked coyly, perfectly sure of the answer but enjoying asking all the same.

He spread his arms wide. "Whatever you want."

She lifted a brow. "Whatever I want?" she purred in tones that would have shocked that snooty old Miss Ad-whatever she talked about so much clear down to her bones.

"Sure," he agreed, and grinned at the calculating glint in her eye. Let Anthea have her fun, wondering and plotting. He rather liked the idea of her wearing herself out thinking of ways to shock him.

She began unfastening his pants, her thumbs outside, her fingers brushing down inside, her knuckles pressing against him as she worked. When she'd reached the last button, she turned her hand and palmed him through his drawers and he sucked in a breath. She had clever hands, testing, wrapping firmly around him, and he fought to keep himself still and allow her to explore as she would.

Finally, biting back an oath, he bent, shucked off his pants and drawers in one quick motion, and kicked them aside. He grabbed her hand, put it back on him, and pressed her palm against him with his own. "Ahhh," he said through gritted teeth.

So, she thought, fascinated, that's what it feels like. She hadn't touched him, those other times—he'd been so busy touching her, melting her down into one pliant puddle, she hadn't gathered her scattered wits enough to touch him back.

She'd been curious. But she hadn't expected to *like* it so much. So hard—how could that be just flesh? But the skin was soft, unlike anything else on his body, fever-hot. She ran her thumb over the thick tip, heard the air hiss out of him.

He wrapped his hands around her wrists and gave a tug, pulling her flat against him. He fell back on the bed, bringing her with him so she landed fully on top of him. His hands were quick at her waist, ridding her of her shift and drawers so that she was as naked as he. And then she was lying on him, kissing him, his sex trapped hard between them, and she thought, *Well, why didn't we try it this way before, me on top?* and then she wasn't thinking at all.

Pleasure shimmered with every touch. Burst with every kiss. It was as if every structure in their bodies, every tissue, every inch of skin, was specifically designed for the other's delight. Need crested higher with each caress, punched more insistently with every kiss.

Too much, Anthea thought. It beat too strongly

within her. Pulsed too deeply in her belly, her heart. She was going to shatter, and when the pieces fell back together again, they'd be different. *She'd* be different.

He kissed her deeply, mouth fusing to hers, tongues tangling and meeting until her head swam. Finally, arms around her, leg hooked behind hers, he rolled, sweeping her beneath him.

He filled her. Her nose with his deep male scent, her eyes with the glorious look of him, her mouth with the taste of him. Filled her heart, with the joy of being with him, of having this man to call, however briefly, her own. Filled her in every way that mattered except the one she was growing to crave the way her lungs craved air.

He braced himself on his hands, lifting above her, his sex positioned at the entrance to her body. He circled there, taunting them both, sliding over her wet softness, forcing her to the brink of ecstasy and stealing away until a sob caught in her throat and threatened to burst into full-fledged tears.

He clenched his teeth in a brutal line. His forehead gleamed. There was a hollow ache in her belly, painfully empty, making a space for him to fill. Except he wouldn't. He slid forward a bare inch, pressing himself just inside her, and retreated, back and forth, never entering her fully, just giving them each a taste of heaven before taking it away. She could no longer remember why they denied themselves. He was her husband. And if she didn't feel him deep inside her, filling that echoing space, she was going to die.

He went a bit farther this time, and she felt the burn of it, the thick tip stretching her tender flesh, a glorious sensation. And then, with a harsh groan, he pulled out completely.

"No!" She clutched at his rear, trying to pull him back. "Don't stop. Don't leave me."

"I have to." He glared down at her, angry, gorgeous. "I can't promise you . . . If I don't leave now, I never will."

Her grip tightened. "I want you inside me, Gabriel. As far as you can get, so far you'll never be out completely again."

"God!" He looked to the sky for help and found none. "You're only making it worse."

"No. I want you to make it better."

"You don't know what you're asking." His arms shuddered with the strain.

She lifted herself against him, trying to force him in a fraction deeper. "Yes I do."

His lips drew back from his teeth, a feral snarl of strain and need. "I want you to know one thing, *understand* one thing. If you conceive, you'd better leave before I ever suspect. Because I will never, *never*, willingly let my child go from me. If I know, you will never be able to take it from me. Not ever."

Why would I go? she thought vaguely, then pushed the thought from her mind. Indistinct possibilities seemed so far in the future, and all she knew was that right here and now she didn't think she could exist another second without feeling him deep inside her. "I understand," she whispered.

Those words released him. He drove inside her and gave a harsh shout, so deep she thought he must touch her womb, and the image ignited a spark in her that rippled through her belly, her chest, all the way out to her extremities.

He plunged forward once and she gasped, felt herself spiral toward completion. And again, and again, him deep and full within her, their breaths staggered, bodies moving together, faster, harder. *More. Higher.* A driving beat, primal, carnal, still almost holy.

And then they burst together, shouting, clinging to each other, shuddering violently in each other's arms. Hanging on as if to shelter each other from the storm.

Mine, Gabe thought. *At last, mine.*

Chapter 21

The letter from Philadelphia came two weeks after her wedding. She and Lily fetched the mail at Stoddard's after school, along with a lovely ham and a cupful of raisins. They'd gathered fresh eggs that morning, and she made an excellent spice cake, a recipe she'd not yet taught Lily.

It was much more fun cooking for three than one. And Lily showed both a talent and interest in cooking, which Anthea intended to encourage at every opportunity.

Anthea couldn't escape the truth: everything was more fun since she'd married Gabriel. It was so pleasant to walk home with Lily, to prepare dinner with her, to wait with shivery anticipation for Gabriel to walk in the door and see him smile when he saw them. He'd sniff the air and start snitching from pots, and then he'd turn to her and his eyes would be full of promise for the night to come.

On the surface, they appeared a normal family, one that was luckier than most and whose members loved each other well. And the fact that the appearance was not the truth didn't keep it from *feeling* like the truth, and its temporary nature only made her cherish it all the more while she had it. A pretty good way to live, she'd discovered, cherishing the moment, for whoever was promised more?

And so she tucked the letter—thinner than Kate's norm; she must have been too shocked at Anthea's telegram to take the time to write more—into her pocket to savor later and took Lily's hand.

"I believe Mr. Stoddard would be quite disappointed with us if we don't purchase at least one or two maple candies before we go, don't you think?"

Lily nodded solemnly; her smiles were still rare, but they were all the sweeter for that. Anthea could be patient and wait for them, because life itself was sweeter than she'd believed it would ever be again, a mere three months ago.

Their activities that evening followed the pattern of many. After supper Gabriel went out to attend to the animals while Lily and Anthea cleaned the kitchen together. And then she tucked Lily into bed, often staying beside her until Lily drifted off to sleep. Gabriel would have told her she spoiled the girl. But Anthea thought that because Lily hadn't had someone watching over her while she slept, keeping the night's monsters at bay, for so much of her life, she'd earned a little making up. And besides, Anthea loved to see her sleep, curled on her side with her fist by her cheek, so relaxed and young and perfect.

Tonight she settled at the kitchen table with one last cup of coffee and waited for Gabriel to return. She pulled out the letter from her sisters and fingered it for a moment. Not so long ago, Kate had held this, maybe Emily too, and sent a few good thoughts her way before they folded the letter and tucked it into the envelope. Suddenly she missed them, more deeply and immediately than she had in weeks, a piercing wave of melancholy and loneliness. How long would it be until she saw them again? Her life had taken so many unexpected turns of late, she could no longer plan it with any surety.

The letter was the worse for its journey. Kate's dark, strong handwriting smeared across the front. The lower right corner was missing, as if some small creature had taken a hefty bite out of it.

She turned it over and over again, wondering why she was delaying. Usually she ripped into a letter from home the moment she received it, reading it down in one great gulp before reading it several times more, lingering over every word.

But this time the address read *Anthea Jackson.* She brushed her fingers over the strange name; her students called her Mrs. Jackson when they remembered, but she hadn't seen it written out before. Hard to believe that it was meant for her.

She picked up a knife and worked it under the flap, slitting it cleanly. The envelope held only a single sheet of paper.

Anthea! Anthea, Anthea, Anthea,

My dearest sisters. Stop. I got married to Gabriel Jackson. Stop. Good man. Stop. Don't worry. Stop. All will be fine. Stop.

You don't really think that this is an adequate way to inform us of such a momentous development, do you? We are simply bubbling over with curiosity. Who is he? Why haven't we heard of this? How dare you get married without us? I suppose he swept you off your feet. You always did have a romantic soul. I expect that this letter will cross yours in the mail, with all the delicious details. If not, be assured you shall hear from me again.

However, you are required to pass on this message to your new husband: if he is not good to you, very, very good, he will have to deal with your big sister. I shall depend upon you to impress on him the true seriousness of this threat.

You have our dearest love and best wishes. But you know that. However, I have a surprise for you as well! And it is much the same as yours. Yes, I got married too! Only two days before your own ceremony, I believe, given the date of your telegraph's arrival. And so you did not after all usurp my privilege as the older sister to wed first. Apparently this is simply the time for the Bright sisters to wed. Though I am resolved to keep an eagle eye on Emily for a while. She is a charming child, and young Master Norman, Cordelia Teaddle's grandson, seems quite taken with her.

Who, do you ask? Why, Dr. Goodale, of course. I find I can overlook the nose after all. And so you no longer have to worry about us, or Emily's future. Dr. Goodale has promised to take care of that, as you know he can well afford to.

He appears quite taken with her. Even he, it seems, cannot resist her sunshiny nature, and has even allowed her to visit with his patients on occasion. He says they dwell on their pain less with her present.

I have had the very best time shopping since we wed, I can tell you that! Dr. Goodale is most generous.

So we are settled, all of us. You need worry about nothing except enjoying your new husband.

Oh! And Emily says to tell you that her embroidery skills already far exceed yours. She cannot wait to show you.

> *With boatloads of love and*
> *my deepest congratulations,*
> *Kate Goodale*

The letter slipped from Anthea's numb fingers and drifted down to the floor.

Married. Kate had married that awful Dr. Goodale.

"Anthea?" Gabriel's evening duties had taken longer than usual; Old Bill looked a little peaked, and he'd worried over his friend before leaving him with a pat and a promise to check on him later.

He'd hurried back to the house, a lift to his step that had become more and more usual in the last few weeks. A wife, he'd mused, was a far better thing to have than he'd ever suspected. His day sped by ever so much more easily when he knew she'd be at the end of it.

And so he'd bounded through the door, anticipating the night to come, and found her sitting at the table, eyes glazed, face drained of all color. "Anthea? Is everything all right?"

She blinked, focusing on him slowly, and shook her head.

He closed the space between them in an instant. "What is it? Is it Lily—"

"No!" She shook her head again, vigorously this time. "I didn't mean to frighten you. Lily's fine, she's already asleep. It's my sister."

He crouched down on the floor beside her and took her hand in his, his heart clenching at the fear he saw on her face. "Which one? Is she . . ." He stopped and swallowed hard.

"She got married." She looked dazed, as if the sound of the words coming out of her mouth shocked her again. "Kate got married."

He knew how close Anthea was to her sisters. She must feel terrible that they missed each other's weddings. Still, she'd look on the bright side soon enough. "But that's great," he said heartily. "Must be going around." But then he caught the fierce frown she aimed at him. "It's . . . not great?"

"Here." She glanced wildly around, then snatched a crumpled sheet of paper off the floor and thrust it at him. "Read it."

He scanned the page quickly. "That's what you telegraphed about us? About me?"

"What else was I supposed to say? It's a little complicated to explain in a wire. Not to mention I didn't want the clerk reading much of anything else."

Good man. Talk about damned with faint praise. "Heck, Anthea, don't you think you could have at least pretended to be wildly in love with me, all things considered?"

She glared at him. "If that's your bruised pride showing, Gabriel, you can just put it away and get over it. Read the rest of it!"

"I did."

"And?"

She looked like she was tempted to whack him, but for the life of him he couldn't figure out what he'd done to annoy her so much.

"And she married that horrid man!"

"Is he horrid?" Gabriel shrugged, then drew back a fraction, taking it as fair warning when her eyes narrowed sharply on him. "He's a doctor. Seems comfortably set, like he should be able to take care of her."

"Oh, he's comfortably set, all right." If the good Dr. Goodale had been there right now, Gabriel reflected, and he had a brain in his head, he'd be running the other way as fast as he could. "He's downright rich, that's what he is."

"So what's the problem?"

"He's self-centered and rigid and cold, that's what's the matter with him. And generous? Calling him a miser would be too kind, and it's all my fault that she married him!"

"All your fault? How do you figure that?" Anthea was usually the most reasonable of women. Okay, not when they'd first met, but he'd allowed her a little latitude there; he'd not been exactly calm, either. But she was not given to illogical conclusions.

"She married him so I wouldn't have to fret about her or Emily anymore. So I could lead my life with you

without being burdened with worrying over them."
She sniffed. "And there wasn't any reason for her to
make such a sacrifice!"

Well. So much for thinking there might be something to this marriage after all.

He waved the letter in the air to remind her. "But
she said they married days before we did."

The look she shot him simmered with disdain. "Oh,
for heaven's sake, Gabriel. You don't really believe
that, do you? She only said that for my benefit."

"Oh. How silly of me, to forget that you all have this
penchant for lying to protect each other."

Her shoulders drooped, her mouth trembled, making Gabriel instantly sorry for what he'd said.
"Anthea." He stood, lifted her into his arms, and sat
down in her chair. Tucking her safely up against him,
he smoothed his hand over her hair. "I don't know
your sister, and I don't know the man she married. But
if she's anything like you, I'd have to say that she
knows her own mind, isn't likely to make a decision
thoughtlessly, and wouldn't be one to be talked out of
it by her younger sister in any case. Hmm?"

Anthea made a muffled sound against his chest—
not agreement, but not vehement denial either. He
took it as encouragement. "And if it is, as you say, a
marriage of pure convenience, she's hardly the first to
do that, either." His voice warmed. "Sometimes they
work out surprisingly well."

It was such a comfortable place to be, Gabriel's lap.
For a moment Anthea let herself be soothed by the
even strokes of his warm hand on her head, by the
solid reassurance of his body near hers.

He didn't understand. Why should he? As he said,

he knew little of her sisters, little of her life, and nothing of Dr. Goodale.

It was still her fault. Her fault because she'd wanted Gabriel and had given in to the powerful physical need he sparked in her. It had been an entirely selfish move on her part.

If she were stronger, she'd pull away this instant instead of accepting the consolation he offered. But denying herself now wouldn't change anything, and she'd need all the strength she could get.

She couldn't do anything about Kate's marriage right now. She had to finish out the term, saving every penny she could and getting the best darn recommendation any first-year teacher had ever received. And then she'd go back to Philadelphia and drag Kate out by her hair if she had to. She'd get a position where her sisters could live with her, and she'd get Kate away from Dr. Goodale.

She'd have to give up Gabriel to do it. The pain of that eventuality tried to gain admittance, needling at the edges of her consciousness, but she pushed it away. It would come soon enough, and it wasn't as if she hadn't expected it all along. Not like this, certainly; she'd assumed it would be because Gabriel tired of playing house and went on to greater adventures than she offered.

She lifted her head, took his in both hands, and pulled his mouth down to hers with a greed that bordered on desperation.

"Kiss me," she said. "Kiss me and don't stop until you have to."

"Who says I have to stop?" he murmured, and complied.

* * *

On a lovely Tuesday afternoon, sun dazzled off the fresh coating of snow that had fallen the night before. Anthea hadn't the heart to make her students sit through yet another recitation of the division tables, and so she'd released them a half hour early. They'd shrieked and tossed handfuls of snow at each other, frolicking like puppies.

She stayed to finish a bit of work. A few compositions needed correction, and if she brought them home to read at night, Gabriel tended to tempt her away from them, and she'd promised the children she'd have them done by tomorrow. So she remained at her desk, the room almost warm from the sun bursting through the few whole windowpanes. Lily volunteered to wash the slates, but as soon as she finished she asked if she could go out to build a snowman. Anthea couldn't see the harm in it and promised to join her for the finishing touches in a few minutes.

Anthea dashed through the rest of the duties. She'd grown selfish, carefully guarding her time with Lily and Gabriel because she now knew its limits, regretful even of the time she must waste in sleep.

The compositions were excellent, by and large, though a messy, halfhearted paper from Theron made her frown. He did not have to like her, but he *did* have to bend some effort to his schoolwork. She'd saved Olivia's for last, a delightful, perfectly penned treatise comparing three of Emerson's poems.

Realizing Lily must be nearly done with her snowman, Anthea threw on her cape but took a moment longer to select two small lumps of coal from the bucket, wrap them in a handkerchief, and tuck them in her pocket for the snowman's eyes. The sunshine outside made her squint, and she shaded her eyes with her fuzzy-mittened hand, scanning the school yard, etched with the trails left by a lunchtime game of fox and goose.

Suddenly her eyes adjusted, and she saw the entire scene in an instant. Lily's Christmas doll, torn in four pieces and scattered over the snow, its red dress like a splash of blood. Lily, flat on her back in a drift, her legs and arms sticking up and thrashing madly. And Theron Matheson sitting on her belly, pressing her deeper into the snow, one gloved hand over her mouth to keep her from screaming.

The sparkling white landscape hazed with red.

"Theron! You let her up right now!" she shouted.

He swung his head toward her, cheeks ruddy with cold and excitement, eyes fever-bright. And then he smiled, smugly challenging, cold as the snow. Still holding Anthea's horrified gaze, he reached down with his free hand, scooped a huge handful of icy crystals, and deliberately ground it into Lily's face.

Anthea never knew how she got across the school yard. It seemed as if she blinked and was there. She launched herself at Theron, tumbling him off Lily and into a drift, planting herself on top of him very much the way he had sat on Lily. His eyes were wide, his breath harsh, and she hoped—oh, how she hoped!—that she'd just scared the hell out of him.

"Not much fun, is it?" She twisted her hands in his collar and lifted his head up until his face was only inches from hers. "Of course, at least I'm picking on someone my own size. Not quite so cowardly."

He struggled to look unconcerned but couldn't quite manage it.

"You don't have to like me. In fact, you can keep

trying to hurt me all you want. Because you won't. But don't you ever, *ever*," she snarled at him, "EVER again think you can hurt me through Lily. If you do, I will make you very, very sorry. I promise you that. Do you understand me?"

When she got no response, she shook him, his head imprinting a spherical hollow into the snow. *"Do you understand me?"*

For a moment she thought he might spit in her face. She glared at him, daring him to try it. She'd almost welcome the excuse.

Finally he nodded.

She climbed to her feet, dragging him up with her. And heard the sound of applause.

Gabriel held Lily, cuddling her close as a newborn in its mother's arms, clapping against her back. His horse stood beside him, reins trailing as if Gabriel had just ridden up and vaulted off.

"I was going to jump in," he said, "but you seemed like you had things well under control. Didn't want to interrupt your fun."

Anthea tried to be embarrassed at having her totally unladylike display witnessed, but couldn't dredge it up. "Lily? Are you all right?"

Lily twisted in Gabriel's arms, her face peeping out from the scarf wrapped around her head. She nodded, and the coil in Anthea's belly released one kink. "Will you stay with her?"

"Of course."

"Good." She released Theron only long enough to take a firm grip on his ear.

"Ow!"

"Theron and I are overdue a discussion with his parents." And she towed him off by the ear, Theron bent over at the waist by the force of her grip, arms flailing wildly in his attempt to keep up with her determined march.

Who would have thought it? Gabriel marveled. Who would have thought that a fierce warrior princess lurked in the small, proper body of Anthea Bright? He knew more of her depths than most. Had seen her worried, and sad, and vibrating with passion. And still he hadn't expected it. Her color had been high, her expression ferocious, hair streaming wantonly around her shoulders, and he'd been struck. Dazzled, bewitched, and all those other words the poets liked to spout but that had never, until right then, had anything to do with him.

He hugged Lily until she squealed with it. "Come on," he said, "let's get you inside and warmed up."

He gathered up the pieces of the broken doll and stuffed them in his pocket for the Anthea to fix later. Once inside, he set her down beside the stove and peeled off her soaked coat, unwound a blue scarf as wet as if it had been dunked in a tub. The heat from the stove radiated weakly, so he shoved in an uneconomical pile of coal until it glowed like the sun. It'd be uncomfortably hot in twenty minutes, but he didn't give a damn.

Lily hadn't said a word since he'd arrived. If the Matheson boy had done worse than it appeared, God save him. Come to think of it, even God couldn't save him from Gabriel.

"I had to go to the store and buy some lumber," he said conversationally. "Thought I'd come by and see you both home. Wasn't expecting such excitement."

If they hadn't moved nearly everything out of Anthea's old soddy, he would have taken Lily there to warm and dry her. But the place was nearly empty, and he didn't want to take Lily out in the cold without protection for no good reason. He glanced quickly around the room—ah, there. Anthea's shawl lay on the back of her chair. He snatched it up and draped it over Lily, bending down to snug it tightly beneath her chin.

"There. You'll be warmer soon." Lily's eyes were big and blue and steady on his. "Lily, what did he do to you? What did he say?"

Lily didn't answer. For the first time in a long while Gabe felt his inexperience. Did he push for answers, get the worst of it out of her? Or allow her to pretend nothing terrible had happened?

She didn't seem overly upset. That disturbed him almost more than anything; had she learned to pretend so well? Or had she become so accustomed to poor treatment over the years that she didn't expect better?

"Lily?"

"She jumped him," she said wonderingly.

"She sure did." He couldn't help but grin at the memory. He'd ridden up just as Anthea had attacked in a burst of wild, furious female energy. He'd been too stunned to move for a moment, and by then there'd been no need.

"She did it for *me*." Awe spiked her voice. "For me," she repeated again, as if she still couldn't believe it.

"Of course she did." He pushed back the wet strands of hair clinging to her cheek. "I'm a little disappointed she got to it before me, to tell you the truth."

Lily swallowed hard, those big blue eyes widening even farther. *"Why?"*

There was a world of questions held in that simple syllable. Why was my mother what she was? Why'd she have to die? Why aren't the other kids nice to me? Why can't I have a family like the rest of them?

He'd asked himself those questions a million times, and never found an answer for them. Still didn't have any.

But there was one answer he did have.

"Because she likes you, goose." He tapped the tip of her nose. "And so do I."

"But . . ." She gulped in a deep breath. "But you're not even my father."

Well, hell. "Who told you that?"

"I heard you." She lifted her chin, a gesture that reminded him of Anthea. "I heard you talking to her. You said you weren't my father."

"Oh." There might as well have been quicksand in front of him, dozens of places he didn't dare step, and no path that seemed assured of being safe. "Been doing a little listening in, have you?"

"Y-yes," she said, bracing herself as if for a blow.

"You know that Anthea would say that's not good manners."

She nodded bravely, prepared to accept the consequences.

"But I guess sometimes you just have to find out how things stand any way you can, huh?" He figured the punishment she used to receive for eavesdropping was probably a far sight less than the one she'd have gotten for barging in when she wasn't supposed to. "I've been pressed into it a time or two in my life, too."

"Really?"

"Yeah. So maybe we won't tell Anthea about it this time."

Lily, face pinking up in the glowing heat, nodded.

"Long as you promise not to do it again," he added sternly.

"I promise," she said gravely.

"Now then, about what you heard." The quicksand got a far sight more precarious. "As far as the rest of the world is concerned, I guess that yeah, technically speaking, you're not my daughter."

"Oh." Her face fell, as if until right then she'd clung to a shred of hope.

"But I'd like you to be."

She brightened a fraction. "You would?"

"I would. A lot." Until that precise moment he hadn't known how much. But when he said the words he *felt* them, settling into his heart like they'd always belonged there. What a surprise life was turning out to be. "A *whole* lot."

She waited, her thin body tense.

"Would you like to be mine?"

It took her a full, long minute to work up the courage to take the chance. The "yes" burst out of her as if she'd been unable to hold it in anymore, and it had to come fast in case she might take it back otherwise.

"That's good, then." He straightened and his knees creaked. *Become a father and immediately your body starts aging*, he thought, and didn't mind a bit.

"But—" She clamped her mouth shut, as though reluctant, if he didn't see the flaws in that plan, to point them out to him.

"I want you to be my daughter. You want to be my daughter. What difference does it make what anybody says?" Just let someone dare to try and say anything else, he thought. The guy wouldn't talk again for a month. "Aren't we the only ones that matter?"

Joy burst onto her face, eyes shining, a smile so blindingly bright he blinked. For he certainly wasn't blinking because his eyes were stinging.

She slipped her small hand into his huge one and it fit just perfectly.

Chapter 22

Gabriel left Anthea fussing over the refreshment tables, arranging and rearranging plates of cookies. When she'd asked his opinion for the third time, rather than admit the display looked exactly the same to him, he'd mumbled something about needing fresh air and made a beeline for the front door.

Gabriel ambled down toward the creek, scuffing his boots through the thin layer of snow that drifted across the path the children had made, glad to leave the growing chaos of the schoolhouse behind. Somehow Anthea had persuaded him to overcome his instinctive aversion to doing anything for the benefit of Haven and gotten him there. Although she hadn't convinced him to dress up for the occasion, she had lured him into spending the last two days hanging strings of lopsided paper hearts her students had fashioned and dangling silhouetted cupids from the ceiling. Mostly because she rewarded him so sweetly for his help, he thought with delight.

But he still wasn't thrilled with the idea of standing around making nice during the Saint Valentine's Day Ball, ignoring the looks of suspicion, curiosity, and barely concealed hostility directed his way, depending upon who was doing the looking.

The weather had obeyed her command, too, and they'd gotten an unusually pleasant evening. For February, anyway. He enjoyed the brisk air against his face and the bright, thin sliver of the moon shining through the tracery of black, bare branches.

He tucked his hands deep in the pockets of his jacket and let the night soothe him. Behind him he heard the bright tinkle of the piano he and Davey had nearly killed themselves moving in, mixed with an occasional spray of happy laughter. For Anthea's sake he hoped the evening went well. She'd been so tense the last few weeks, her expression pinched, her brilliant smiles shadowed, her laughter more rare. Once or twice she'd mentioned leaving Haven and how much she wanted to be able to give the children a good start on the school they needed before she left.

He hoped it was only worrying over the success of the party that disturbed her. She'd certainly worked herself too hard planning it. Some mornings he would rise with the sun to find her already dressed, obviously up for hours, poring over her lists or plotting the decoration scheme. He and Lily had certainly eaten well, for she was forever testing potential recipes for the menu.

But he suspected it wasn't only the party that concerned her. Once when he came in from the evening chores he found her again reading that letter from her sister. She'd hastily wiped her eyes and greeted him with a smile noticeably dimmer than usual, at least to one as familiar with her smile as he.

He tried to convince himself he imagined it. There was not one single change in her behavior he could point to. At night she more than welcomed him; she turned to him with keen and deep passion, an intense need edged with desperation, as if she must fill herself up on experiences, on *him*, now, unsure there would be any more. It was exciting and physically glorious. But not playful, not easy, nothing that could be taken for granted.

He figured she was getting ready to leave him.

And he wasn't at all prepared to let her go.

A night owl, mournfully lonely, hooted across the creek. The breeze picked up, tossing the branches back and forth, the trees creaking.

Okay, enough solitude, he decided. Perhaps he could tolerate the partygoers if he could look his fill at Anthea all night.

Footsteps crunched over the snow behind him. Before Anthea, people used to respect his privacy. He didn't mind a bit when she and Lily kept barreling up to him, but he really could have done without all the rest, and he turned toward the sound reluctantly.

Cleo drifted toward him, the hem of her cloak sweeping over the snow. *What now?* He considered making some excuse and heading in before she got near him.

Except now he owed her.

"Evening," he said when she reached him.

She bent her head back to look up at him, and

moonlight clung to her face, her skin picking up the pearly sheen. Her rich fur collar brushed softly beneath her chin.

"How're things going in there?" he asked.

"I suppose they're going well." Her gaze settled on his face, direct and full. "You left."

"Not fond of crowds. Less fond of dancing."

"Yes." Her laugh was intimate, full of memory. "I do recall that."

He shifted, uncomfortable that the topic of their past had come up so quickly. "Look, Cleo, I want to—"

"I always liked how you said my name. A little rough around the edges, strong. I never thought of myself that way except with you."

Okay, that was it. He'd say his piece and get out of there. "I need to thank you. For allowing Lily to stay over with Olivia tonight. She was thrilled to be invited."

"Oh." Her face brightened, blooming under that slight praise. "It's no problem. Mrs. Rankin will take good care of them. I must confess I was a bit surprised when Olivia asked. I hadn't realized the girls were friendly."

"I figured you'd object. Considering Lily's background and all." Truthfully, he'd been shocked that she'd agreed. He'd half figured she'd ship Olivia off to boarding school rather than have her consort with the likes of Lily. Clearly he'd underestimated her.

"I must admit that Phillip required a healthy bit of convincing."

"Gee, what a surprise," he said wryly.

Her smile flickered. She pulled one hand from her muff and fingered the fur lightly. "I know how to convince Phillip, never fear. And why would I reject the girl? She's yours, isn't she?"

"Yes." Surprising how easy it came. How right it felt. He'd barely had to think about it, and guessed it wouldn't be much longer before he wouldn't hesitate a second. "Yes, she is."

She nodded, as if her reasons for accepting Lily were then obvious.

"Well, thank you in any case. It meant a lot to her. To me." There was a sudden shout from inside the school-house, followed by a hearty round of applause. "Sounds like they're having fun in there."

"If you like that sort of thing. I've always pre-ferred—" her voice dropped to a low purr "—more private entertainments."

Enough, Gabriel decided. So much for polite grati-tude. "I'd best be getting back inside. To my *wife*," he added with emphasis.

Her smooth, polished expression twisted. "How can you call her that?" she spat out. "Your *wife*?"

"Because she is." His heart thumped. "She is my wife."

"Don't say it." And suddenly it showed through the polish, the willful, spoiled child she'd been all those years ago; amazing that so much of that young girl re-mained. "Don't think it. You only married her because you had to."

"No, that's pretty much the reason *she* married *me*. Do you really think they could *make* me do something? That your husband could?" He chuckled. "I married her because I wanted to."

Amazing, how the truth kept popping out of his mouth without him realizing it. He rolled the thought around in his head for a while and found it didn't bother him at all. Quite the opposite, in fact. Well, well. Who knew what else he'd figure out if he kept talking?

"No, you didn't." The muff dropped to the ground as she reached out and clutched his forearm. "You don't mean it. You can't. Not after everything we've meant to each other."

"Meant to each other?" He shook off her hand, less gently than he'd intended to. He wasn't in the mood to waste any more time out here with Cleo when Anthea was inside. Waiting for him. "Cleo, we never meant anything to each other but an easy—" He bit off the word just in time. It was no less than the truth, but she didn't deserve it.

"That's not true!" Her voice carried a strong note of panic. "I've always known it. Even after I married Phillip—oh, Gabriel, how that must have hurt you, I'm so sorry! When you knew we couldn't be together, and you stayed away all those years rather than be tempted, I've always known that our love was strong and pure. Forever. A love like we shared just doesn't go away."

"Love?" Jesus, where had *that* come from? "It was never love, Cleo. For God's sake, *remember* what it was like. I do."

Tears welled and spilled over. Her nose reddened, eyelids immediately puffing. Cleo Cox, the prettiest girl in Haven, was not a pretty crier. "I remember. I remember the passion, I remember the joy—"

His patience snapped. "Damn it, Cleo!" Anthea would have been proud of him for holding on to his manners this long. "I was fifteen years old! If it took more than thirty seconds, I'd be surprised. Not that it does me any credit, but there sure as hell wasn't any joy in it for you."

"There was," she insisted, her delicate sniffle turning into a snort.

The hell with guarding her feelings. If her poor husband was ever to have a chance, she was going to have to face the truth.

And just when the hell had he started feeling sorry for Phillip Cox?

"It wasn't about the physical," she said, "it was—"

"You were young and wild and sick of being told what not to do by your mother," he said, speaking each word clearly so she'd catch it, *hear* it. "The only thing you knew about me was that I was as far from the fellow your mother picked out as possible."

She jerked as if to escape the words. He kept relentlessly on.

"The only thing I knew about you was that you were pretty, you were Phillip's, and that you were willing to spread your legs for me. That was enough."

"No," she whispered.

"Yes," he said brutally. "It was nothing. It *is* nothing."

"You loved me," she repeated by rote but without conviction.

"For God's sake, Cleo, grow up!"

She pressed her fist to her mouth, but a sob escaped. Whirling, she dashed off through the trees. For a brief moment he considered going after her. She shouldn't be running around town alone in that mood. But heck, the only dangerous, disreputable person in Haven was *him*. And the last thing either of them needed was him charging after her to save her.

Sighing, he headed for the schoolhouse. A dark figure separated itself from the big oak, stepping right into Gabriel's path.

Phillip Cox was bareheaded and without a coat. The wind whipped his hair and blew his shirt against him, but he didn't seem to notice.

Blast it! Gabriel thought. He tugged his hands from his pockets and curled them by his sides, just in case Phillip took it in his head to jump him. He was no match for Gabriel, as they'd both discovered years ago, which was why Phillip had always tended to run with a couple of followers. Still, no telling what the man might be pushed into, depending upon how much of Gabriel's conversation with his wife he'd overheard.

"If you'll excuse me," Gabriel said, "I'm sort of in a hurry to get back to my wife."

His face impassive, Cox didn't move. "That's a malady I've been known to suffer from myself upon occasion."

As it seemed Cox had no intention of moving out of the way, Gabriel stepped off the path, plunging shin-deep into snow. Cox grabbed his upper arm to halt him. Gabriel pointedly looked at the hand on his jacket, then met Phillip's gaze.

"Forgive me," Phillip murmured, and removed the offending hand. "I meant no insult."

"There's a first."

"Yes, I suppose it is." He heaved a sigh and ran his hands through his hair, leaving it standing up, far from its usual careful arrangement. "There's a first time for a lot of things, isn't there?"

"Was there something you wanted? Besides my land, of course. And I might as well tell you right now, I'll be selling it to Davey when I leave town."

Cox made a dismissive gesture. "No, that's not it." He shivered suddenly. "When I realized Cleo had left the dance, and that you were absent too, I thought . . . well, you can imagine what I thought."

Figuring it was the safest route, Gabriel kept his mouth shut and waited.

"I just wanted to thank you."

"Thank me?" Gabe couldn't have been more surprised if Phillip suddenly handed over the mortgage deed, marked "paid in full." "For what? For sleeping with your wife all those years ago, or *not* sleeping with her now?"

"Neither, actually, though now that you mention it, I suppose I owe you for the latter, too." He had to be freezing in his fancy black leather shoes; he kept shifting back and forth from foot to foot.

"Wouldn't you rather go in, do this someplace warmer?"

"No, it won't take long."

"Suit yourself."

"I certainly intend to," Phillip said. "Thank you for telling her what you did. She's been clinging to that pure, flawless memory for years. Maybe, if she realizes her version never existed . . ." He trailed off, his face drawn, the utter exhaustion of a man who'd been trying for years and had just now accepted his efforts might never pay off.

"It was the truth." Gabriel shrugged. "Guess she felt guilty, doing what she wasn't supposed to, and so she tried to make it some vast, perfect thing in order to justify it."

Phillip's shoulders sagged. "I've lived with her for nearly half her life. How can you know her better?"

"Sometimes it's hard to see what's too close to you."

"That's true." Phillip swallowed visibly. "You didn't have to tell her, though. Even if it was the truth, you could have allowed her to continue believing her fantasy, knowing it would hurt me."

"I didn't do it for you." Trying to do the right thing sure brought a heck of a lot of complications with it. Life had been simper when all he had to worry about was his horse.

"Still, I owe you one." Phillip studied him for a moment longer, then apparently came to a decision. "Was my father also yours?" he asked suddenly.

"Well. I didn't expect that question." Gabe stuck his hands back in his pockets, considering his response. "And I don't know the answer. Not for certain, anyway. I always figured he probably was, though."

"Yes. So did I." Phillip nodded. "Well. I won't keep you any longer."

"Oh, what the hell. Long as we're digging all this up. Is Lily your daughter?"

His head jerked in surprise, then a small, sad smile lifted his mouth before he echoed Gabriel's words. "I don't know. Not for sure, anyway, though I always suspected she was."

"Life's strange sometimes."

"That it is," Phillip agreed. "You'll take care of her, won't you?"

"As if she were my own," he affirmed. "She *is* my own, in every way that matters to either of us."

"Good." Cox nodded in the direction of the schoolhouse. "I won't keep you from your bride any longer. Lovely girl, by the way. I never would have suspected that *she'd* be the one for you, but you fit somehow."

"Yes. We do." Cautiously Gabe probed his emotions, all the places he generally left alone. He figured this conversation with Cox probably got them good and roiled up.

And found nothing but peace.

And so he decided he owed Phillip one, too. "Your wife"—he thumbed toward the main section of town—"went that way. She's going to be in need of a little comfort, I'm guessing. And maybe a new memory or two."

"Yes." He turned and stared thoughtfully off in the direction Cleo had fled. "Perhaps she will at that."

"It's cold." Gabe began shrugging out of his jacket. "Might take a while to track her down. Take my coat, I'm going back inside anyway."

"No." In no hurry, he started strolling away. "I'll manage just fine."

Chapter 23

Phillip had little trouble finding his wife. He first checked his home to make sure she hadn't returned, even though he suspected that the house he'd built for her was the last place she'd go right now. He was right, so he peeked in on Olivia and Lily, bent over a game of checkers in Olivia's room, and felt such a wash of love and pain and hope, he had to grab the doorjamb to keep his knees from buckling under him.

He wandered the silent streets of Haven for perhaps a quarter of an hour, enjoying the quiet emptiness of deep winter, the shops dark. The wind and cold tore through his insufficient clothing, bit into his flesh until it was tingling and raw. It only made him feel alive. Here and there a light glowed cheerfully in the window of a home where children resided, who'd been left home while their parents frolicked at the school, a neat twist of the usual way of things. But the popular evening haunts of Hound's Saloon and the restaurant in the Best Hotel were fully dark. All of Main Street was dark, in fact, except for a tiny flicker of light in the window of Phifer's Livery.

Everything inside him seemed unusually quiet. He wasn't aware of his own breathing, the beat of his heart. Every part of him, heart, soul, and body, had stilled, waiting for the next moments when his life would change irrevocably. Whether for the good or bad, he didn't know, but at least he'd be done with the waiting he'd endured for so many years. For he finally understood he could not go on like that.

A foot-wide space gaped between the great double doors of the stables. He squeezed through and the smell of the place, hay and leather under the pungent scent of horses, enveloped him. The steed in the nearest stall stamped and snorted in welcome. Phillip passed a soothing hand over its velvety nose before following the pale beacon of light down the central passage between the dozen stalls and into one at the far end.

This stall was not used for boarding. Hooks high on the walls held tack, great loops of reins drooping almost to the ground. A stack of blankets filled one corner, and piles of straw filled the rest. Beside the biggest heap, a lantern cast an intimate circle of golden light over his wife.

Dressed in the fur and velvet he'd bought her, she huddled in the humble mound of straw, weeping quietly into her hands. He wondered why she'd chosen this place. To his knowledge, she'd not entered a stable in years, preferring to send the houseman to saddle her horse.

Perhaps she'd met Gabriel in a stable all those years ago. The thought sliced through him, leaving him raw and bleeding to the core, determined to drive the memory from her.

"Cleo."

"Oh." She started and lifted her head. Her damp cheeks gleamed like moonlight on water. Her hair had fallen from its queenly corona and tumbled down around her shoulders, a shiny robe. "Phillip." Her eyes widened, and she shrank back into the straw.

Was she afraid of him, of what he might do? Surprisingly, he found he welcomed the thought. Better fear than the mild tolerance she usually awarded him.

"How did you find me?"

I'll always find you. "Except where there were children, this was the only place with a light."

"I'm sorry that I left without telling you. I felt suddenly ill, and I thought perhaps a bit of fresh air—"

"Did you?" he asked mildly. "How odd that you thought to find fresh air in a livery."

She shifted uneasily at his unprecedented interruption. "No, of course not. I intended a brief walk, but when I felt a bit worse and needed to sit down, this was the nearest place."

"Really." Unhurriedly he paced across the small stall and stood looking down at her. She could even make a pile of straw look like a throne, he marveled. Was it any wonder that she could have transformed a memory so completely and clung to it all these years?

But that would stop now. By God, it would stop now.

When he continued simply to stare at her, she began to gather her skirts. "We can go, then. I—"

He threw himself on top of her, pressing her back

into the rough nest, and caught her hands above her head.

"Phillip!" she exclaimed, shock and a tremor of uncertainty in her voice. "This is hardly the place—"

"I find," he said, "that I do not appreciate my *wife* throwing herself at another man." He wondered at the calm of his voice. It was as if, with the decision made, his emotions had settled and smoothed.

Her eyes flew wide. "Phillip, I . . ." Then she took a breath, visibly drawing herself together. "I have no idea where you came up with such an idea. And I am more than slightly insulted that you would accuse me of such a thing. I have been nothing but a faithful and obedient wife to you," she said, so imperious and reproachful he couldn't help but admire her control. But her gaze darted away from his, and her chest rose quick and shallow.

"You have never been faithful to me," he said, surprised at the savagery that underlaid the words, and she caught her breath.

"I—" She abandoned denial, attempted the truth. "You knew?"

"I've always known." He brought her wrists together, and they were so small and fragile he could manacle them easily with one hand, allowing him to free the other.

"I am sorry for that, Phillip, you have no idea how sorry. But that was before we were married, and I was so *young*." She bit her lip, tiny white teeth catching the plump lower curve. "And foolish. Surely you can forgive me that."

"I don't care about what you did before we were married. Not anymore." He flipped open her cape and deliberately laid his hand across her breast. "But you've never, *never* been faithful in your heart. And that I do care about, Cleo. I care about that very much."

"I . . ." For the first time in their marriage, she didn't know what to do. Didn't know what to say to him. Finally, Phillip thought. *Finally.*

"Not to mention," he went on, "that the only reason you were not unfaithful to me in truth is because Jackson wasn't interested in you. Not one bit."

Even in the dimness, he could see the color that burned in her cheeks, the anger that snapped in her eyes. But she couldn't deny it, and they both knew it.

"Now, there's no accounting for tastes. It's only to my advantage the man is obviously a fool about such matters." His gaze raked her hair, eyes, mouth, neck, and where his hand still rested possessively on her bodice. "But you are my wife, Cleo, by law and God and your own vows, and I've been patient with you long enough. You won't deny me any longer. I won't allow it."

"I've never denied you," she forced out.

"You've always denied me!"

She flinched at his vehemence.

"You've denied me your thoughts. You've denied me your heart. You've denied me your pleasure. Well, no more!"

His mouth came down, a brutal possession. She made a sound of protest, but it couldn't escape his mouth. She bucked once, hard, and his flesh swelled at the feel of her pushing against him. She squirmed beneath him, tried to pull her hands from his grip, and her struggle unleashed a demon inside him, dark and powerful, one that neither of them had ever suspected existed.

He tore his mouth away. "You are my wife," he panted. *"My wife."*

She rolled her head to the side, away from his gaze. "Stop," she whispered weakly. "Stop."

"Say it." With his free hands, he tore at the buttons of her pretty lace blouse, ripping the trim until it gave way and exposed the full, luscious curve of her bosom above shift and corset. He pushed the garments down, revealing fully her breasts, the nipples large and dark in the dim light, the edge of her underclothes cutting into the soft lower curves. "My wife."

"Please," she whispered, weak and conciliatory. "Not here. We're in the livery. Take me home and I'll do anything you ask."

"You'll do anything I ask now. You are my wife." Years of denial roared in him, demanding to be released.

He kissed her again, hard stamps of possession on her mouth, her neck, her breasts. His left hand retained his iron grip, allowing his free hand to claim what he owned. Her eyes were wide now, with disbelief and wild shock. Perhaps she hadn't known he had this in him. Perhaps she hadn't believed he was strong enough to hold her if she struggled. Well, she'd been wrong on both counts.

"My wife," he said, over and over, a litany that accompanied each word, each touch. Louder each time she tried to pull from his grasp, each time she turned her mouth away from his seeking kiss.

Her skirts were up now, her legs pale and shapely against the satin lining of her robe. His hand hovered over her and he held his breath. If he touched her and she was dry, completely unaroused, he knew he wouldn't be able to go any further. He'd have lost his gamble and be left destroyed.

He touched her gently, probing deep. He lifted his hand and his fingers gleamed in the lamplight, and joy and passion slammed through him. He unfastened his trousers in an instant and she went still when he drove himself deeply inside her. He started slowly, one thrust, two, whispering his talisman with each stroke. *My wife. My wife.*

It happened so gradually he nearly couldn't believe it at first. Her hips lifted a fraction, then a shade more until she met him fully, their bodies slamming together with each thrust, her head thrown back, a whimper escaping each time.

And then he felt her stillness, the calm before the maelstrom, the first small spasms of her body gripping his. He froze, braced on his arms above her—when had he released her? when had she stopped fighting and embraced him?—and commanded her, "Say it. My wife."

For a brief, terrible instant, he thought she would resist, clinging to her pride and her delusions even to the end. He'd never seen her more beautiful, her hair tangled and wild, her eyes glazed, her cheeks suffused with dusky color, her mouth tight with strain.

And then it happened. He'd dreamed of it for years, clung to hope beyond all reason. For this moment, he realized. For this moment that was worth it all.

"Your wife," she said. "I am your wife."

He plunged deeply, and she cried out, shattering in his arms. Giving him everything she'd withheld from him.

And so he gave, too, poured himself within her, for

the first time holding nothing back because he finally dared to give it all to her.

In the aftermath, he lay upon her, his cheek pressed to her wet one, their exhalations sighing in each other's ears.

His heart pounded, the residue of passion, the beginning of the future.

Leave it alone, he told himself. *Don't risk it, just accept that you've gotten this much without being greedy for more.*

But he had to ask. "Do we have a chance, Cleo?"

He felt her swallow, felt as well as heard the long and potent silence before she spoke. "I don't know. Maybe."

It wasn't yes. But it wasn't no, and his heart swelled.

Maybe was a possibility. And right at that moment, a possibility was enough.

Gabriel stood in the darkened doorway of the schoolhouse. Couples whirled across the floor to the uneven, enthusiastic beat of three musicians who claimed the corner where Anthea's desk usually resided. The dancers laughed gaily, bouncing up and down with dubious skill but certain zest. The women were dressed in their best, a few extra curls in their hair, a few more frills on their blouses. The men were buttoned up to their chins, the sheen of oil on their carefully combed hair.

They looked happy, comfortable in their relationships, secure in their place in this town. As hard as Gabriel had worked to form his own life, as much as he valued his relationship with Sam, as much blood as he'd poured into his lands, he'd never felt the bone-deep certainty that he belonged that he saw on the faces around him.

He shifted, for the first time vaguely aware of being underdressed in his old denims and even older boots. He'd worn them because he'd no interest in impressing the denizens of Haven, because he vastly preferred comfort over fashion, and because, for all the decorating Anthea had coerced him into, he'd attended under protest. And because he was a bit annoyed at her for withholding what was bothering her. He figured it had something to do with her sisters, but still, she could have confided in him. He was her husband.

But then he saw her. George Bickersdyke moved away from the punch bowl, and there was Anthea behind it, filling another cup. She handed it to Ella with a smile, turned, and saw him. He knew she'd found him because the sweet, friendly smile she'd bestowed on the Bickersdykes transformed, becoming blindingly brilliant, joyous, intimate. And his heart thumped, just like that, *bang* against his rib cage, as if making damn sure he knew it was there and what it wanted.

She put her ladle aside, murmured what he assumed were her excuses, and unerringly wound her way through the crowd to him. She'd dressed for the occasion in the same thing she'd worn to marry him, creamy lace frothing over fabric as bright a blue as her eyes.

When she reached him, she extended her hands for him to take. He linked his hands with hers, and it felt so natural that, still, he couldn't believe it. How'd they gotten here? he wondered, not for the first time. How had this—*she*—happened to him?

And suddenly he wished his mother had had the

opportunity to meet Anthea. Her dying had been long—years, really—and expected. He'd done most of his mourning long ago, had felt only relief and residual sadness when she was finally released from her pain. And a fair shot of guilt, because he'd figured she'd held on as long as she had only because she hadn't wanted him to be alone.

"Looks like the evening is a success." It was the safest thing he could think of to say, a substitute for the words that he was terrified were going to spill out of his mouth without asking his permission first.

"Yes, it does, doesn't it?" She whirled around, arms spread wide, taking in the entire scene. "The school looks wonderful, don't you think? Thank you so much for helping."

"Maybe it looks too good. People'll be wondering why you need a new schoolhouse, when this one's so nice."

She laughed happily, with her whole self, the first time there'd been nothing guarded in her mood in weeks. And then she sobered.

"Where were you?" she asked. "I didn't see you leave, and when I realized Mr. and Mrs. Cox had left as well, I worried. A little."

"Did you miss me?"

Oh, he looked so handsome, Anthea thought. The bubbling, happy room had taken on so much more color the moment he entered it. Her *life* had taken on so much more color the moment he'd entered it.

Did she dare, knowing what had come before, what had to come in the future? She took a deep breath and plunged in. "Yes," she confessed.

"I didn't mean to worry you." Gabriel mulled over the possibilities, knowing he was way out of his usual territory here. A gentleman wasn't supposed to kiss and tell, even after all these years. But if someone besides Phillip had seen him and Cleo by the stream . . . wouldn't it worry her less if it came from him?

"Cleo Cox wished to speak to me," he said carefully. "We knew each other, years ago—well, I guess you figured that—and—" He broke off as the Pietzkes wheeled by, Marshall's elbow accidentally spearing his back.

"Sorry," Marshall called, puffing and red-faced, already spinning halfway across the room.

"Anthea, could we go somewhere more private? I'd like to speak to you."

Her eyes searched his face. "Of course. But if you're going to confess you had a . . . relationship with Cleo Cox years ago, really, there's no confession necessary."

"You knew?"

He looked so horribly shocked that Anthea bit back a smile. "Really, do you think there's one single misstep you took in your misspent youth that I haven't been told of a dozen times, with grand embellishment?"

"Oh."

She could have kissed him, right then and there, for worrying what she thought of him.

"Well, about tonight, then, really, nothing happened, I—"

"Gabriel." She squeezed his hands. "You don't have to go any further. I am not one bit worried about what happened between you and Cleo Cox."

"You're not?" Shouldn't his wife be jealous? Just a little bit?

"No. For one thing, it's cold out there." And then

she couldn't help it; she did smile, at his bemusement and concern. "Gabriel, don't worry. I trust you."

I trust you. The whirling couples around him spun faster, joined by the walls of the room as his mind swirled as well. Never. Never once, in all his life, had someone uttered those words to him and meant them.

"Anthea, I—"

"Fire!" Jon Krotochvill burst through the front door of the schoolhouse. "Fire!" The room went silent, save for the trailing twang of a fiddle.

The couples stopped bouncing. Knute Sontesby went still with a slice of lemon cake halfway to his mouth; Arozina Culbertson shut up with a juicy piece of gossip halfway out of hers.

"Didn't you hear me?" Jon panted. "Fire!"

Gabriel dropped his hand on Jon's shoulder. "Where?"

"Mr. Cox's stables! I was coming by, going over to—" Flushing, he cleared his throat. "Guess it don't matter where I was goin'. Saw the flames through the window, peeked in. Went and roused the house, but nobody was there but Mrs. Rankin and the girls."

Anthea gasped. Color abandoned her face, and she swayed until Gabe slipped his arm around her waist to support her.

"Don't worry, Miss Bright—Mrs. Jackson," Jon assured her. "I got them out first thing. Took 'em over to the neighbors before I even came here."

"Good work, Jon."

The room buzzed, punctuated with an occasional, clear, "Where's Cox?" The men tossed glances at each other, shrugging, as if they were so used to looking to Phillip for direction, they now had no idea who to turn to without him.

Gabriel had a fair idea what Phillip was doing at the moment and figured he wasn't going to come strolling into the schoolhouse anytime soon.

"All right, guess we better go put it out." He scanned the crowd and picked out a couple of men he vaguely remembered as sturdy, dependable sorts. "Fred, you take two or three fellows and start digging up all the buckets you can find. George, you take the west side, and Davey, the east—start getting the buckets going." He returned his attention to Jon. "When you looked— you see, or hear, any animals in the stables?"

"I—" He gasped before catching enough air to continue. "I think so, yes."

"Okay, I'll see to getting them out." Gabriel's commanding gaze scanned the room, marking each man who stood unmoving and uncertain. "Well? What do you say we go see about saving Cox his stables?"

Gabriel spun for the door, but Anthea clutched at his forearm with a strength few would have suspected she had. "Gabriel."

"Don't worry." He patted her hand. "If it looks like there's any chance of it spreading, I'll get Lily and Olivia well out of harm's way first thing. I promise you I won't let anything happen to them."

"I know that," she snapped. "I wish I was as sure about *you*."

He was what had put that tremor in her voice, the sheen of fear in her eyes? It lumped unexpectedly in his throat, and hope sprang up, showed every intention of taking firm root.

In full view of everyone, he bent down and stamped a kiss full on her mouth. "You're not getting rid of me that easily," he told her. "I'll be back in no time. I promise."

And with that he was gone, sprinting toward where he'd tied Old Bill, a dozen men trailing in his wake.

Anthea hovered in the doorway, completely abandoning the decorum of a lifetime, and screamed after him like a fishwife, "You had damn well better!"

Chapter 24

Seconds ground by like minutes, minutes ticked as agonizingly slowly as endless hours. And hours . . . well, it hadn't yet *been* an hour, as Fannie repeatedly told Anthea, every three minutes when Anthea asked her, and with a little less tolerance each time.

Anthea paced. She wrung her hands. She peered out the front window a dozen times. Twice, when she was absolutely *sure* she'd heard hoofbeats approaching, she'd lunged for the door and flung it open, only to discover nothing but an empty yard, cool moonlight, and the rush of the wind.

She'd been bereft and confused when her mother died. Unbearably sad when her father had. Deeply worried when she'd discovered the depth of their financial ruin, hurt and furious when Gerald abandoned her. Not to mention so anxious her stomach hadn't settled for weeks when she'd taken this position in Kansas.

But she'd never before experienced this raw terror. It hurt to breathe. Her heart galloped along, out of control, painfully uneven. Her stomach knotted upon itself, threatening at any moment to eject the refreshments she'd ingested during the party.

The other women appeared so calm. They milled around, murmuring in low voices to themselves. Even nibbling the corner of a cookie now and then. She couldn't stand it. Maybe they were used to their husbands being in danger now and then. Had come to terms with the prospect of losing them. But *she* . . . she was not about to let it happen.

"I'm going over there," she announced, and strode for the door. "Maybe I can help." And she could sure as heck make sure that Gabriel didn't do anything stupidly heroic, if she had to restrain him herself.

"Oh no, you don't." Fannie shot across the floor and put herself between Anthea and the door. "You're staying right here."

Anthea narrowed her eyes. "Get out of my way."

"No." Fannie, who outweighed Anthea by a good fifty pounds, jammed her fists on her well-padded hips. "Gabriel ordered me before he left to make well and sure that you don't go running off into trouble. And I don't want to be dealing with that man if I let him down."

So, he thought he had her all figured out, did he? The fact that he'd predicted her behavior so accurately didn't make her any happier. Quite the opposite, in fact. And the anger was a far sight better than the fear, so Anthea let it grow, welcoming the heat.

She measured her opponent. Okay, so Fannie was a tad bigger than she was. Anthea was pretty sure that in her present mood, Fannie posed no match for her at all.

"And besides," Fannie went on, her voice softening, "you don't really want him making mistakes because he's worryin' about you instead of payin' attention to that fire, do you?"

Her anger deflated abruptly, pricked by the inescapable truth. "Oh. Is that why none of you went?"

"Yes." Now that the prospect of battle seemed to have dissipated, Fannie relaxed her posture and strolled over to take Anthea's hand. "I know it's hard to wait. There's an awful lot of waitin' to bein' a wife. Nobody warns you about that part. But you gotta trust 'em. That they're smart and careful and strong, and that they'll come back to you."

Anthea felt the burn behind her lids and blinked rapidly to stop it. "I do trust him." But it was much harder to trust the vagaries of a fate that seemed unconcerned with such trivialities as the hearts of mortals.

"It'll be all right," Fannie said, and for the first time Anthea detected the flicker of worry almost hidden beneath Fannie's confident tone. She patted Anthea's hand and led her over to a chair. "Here, sit. You're making the rest of us twitchy, popping around like that."

Anthea tucked her hands between her knees, rocked back and forth, and prayed. *Please,* she thought, *oh, please!* As if politeness would help. She didn't dare pray for Gabriel to come back to her.

She just prayed for him to come *back*.

"I'll get us some tea," Fannie murmured, and jumped up before Anthea could tell her she couldn't swallow a drop. For all she'd commanded Anthea to sit, Fannie couldn't seem to settle either.

Letty Matheson slid into the seat Fannie left. She angled her body away, as if unwilling to get too close to Anthea, and darted uncertain glances her way.

Theron had not attended school since Anthea had hauled him home by his ear. Anthea had visited twice. The first time she'd received no answer to her knock, although she'd been certain she'd seen the yellow calico curtains at the front window flutter. The second time Adonijah had opened the door a crack, told Anthea that they'd not yet made a decision about Theron's continued education, and slammed it in her face.

Anthea regretted not making a stronger effort. She really should have gone and hauled Theron *back* to school by his ear as well. But she could hardly do so over his parents' objections, and the classroom had been so much more serene without him that she hadn't been able to bring herself to address the issue more permanently as of yet.

She'd been shocked to see the Mathesons attending that evening. Been even more surprised to see the two of them cutting quite a figure on the dance floor.

Anthea sighed. What a time for Letty to choose to approach her. She could hardly think, much less argue her position coherently.

"May I help you, Mrs. Matheson?"

Letty pleated her fingers together in her lap. "I just thought you should know. Theron will not be returning to school."

"I'm sorry to hear that," Anthea said, surprised at her own sincerity. But at the center of the matter, Theron Matheson truly did have too good a brain to waste.

Letty blinked, startled. "He'll be attending the Wentworth Military Academy."

"That's a very fine school."

"Yes." Letty dabbed at her eyes with the handkerchief clutched in her hand. "My husband's uncle, the colonel, insisted upon it. He . . ." That was as much as she could manage. She sniffled into the kerchief.

"I'm sure that Theron will do very well there, Mrs. Matheson. When military discipline is applied to his intelligence and energy, I'm certain he shall be an exceptional young man." And pity the poor army that might oppose him.

Letty lifted her face from the limp square of snowy linen. "Do you think so?" she asked hopefully. "Adonijah insisted, but I—"

The door flew open, and Knute Sontesby burst through it.

"They're back!" Thisba cried, and a cheer went up from women who'd evidently been far more worried than they'd let on.

The dapper black felt hat that began the evening on Knute's head was gone. His hair stood out stiffly, the lines on his face were dark with ash, and the front of his formerly crisp shirt was soaked beneath his open jacket. Still, Johanna shrieked in joy and flew across the room to hurl herself into his arms as if he were the handsomest creature she'd ever laid eyes on.

"Is it out?" Arozina called to him.

He wrapped his arms around his wife and hung on,

closing his eyes while he rested his darkened chin on the top of her hair, unconcerned for Johanna's careful coiffure. "Yeah, it's out."

One by one the men of Haven, grimy and tired and triumphant, stumbled through the door. One by one, relieved women dashed for their returning husbands and ruined their pretty party dresses by throwing themselves at their chests.

Every time the door opened, Anthea rose to her feet and pressed her hand to her heart, hope lifting inside her. And every time another man came through the door, she dropped back down into her chair, a little more worried, a little more disappointed, until she was good and frantic.

"Davey?" She grabbed him away from Fannie to ask him. "Did you see Gabriel?"

He reluctantly released his wife and turned to face Anthea with his arm still draped over her shoulders, Fannie leaning against him. "Well, yeah, I saw him leading that big red stallion of Cox's out of the blaze, way back at the beginnin', and then . . ." He stopped, did a double take. "You mean he ain't back yet?" Frowning, he released Fannie to address the crowd. "Now, listen here. When's the last time any of you saw Gabriel? He—"

This time, when the door slammed open, it hit the wall so hard the handle finally punched a good-sized hole in it, where the door caught and stayed.

"Gabriel," Anthea whispered as he stepped in, tall and dark, filling the doorway every bit as much as he had that first day. And her heart beat just as hard, but from a different emotion entirely.

" 'Bout two seconds ago, Davey," Fred Skinner called, and chuckles swept the room.

Gabriel took another step forward. "Sorry about the wall."

"We're getting a new one anyway," Anthea said.

Ash and soot coated his face, turning the skin so dark it nearly matched his hair, and when he smiled his teeth flashed, a brilliant white slash against the darkness. His shirt, too, no longer made any claim to whiteness.

And as he crossed the room to her, his stride steady, unhurried, unmistakably purposeful, she realized he must have stopped somewhere before coming back. For around his neck he'd tied a bright red batswing necktie, the one clean article of clothing on his entire body.

He halted a foot from her. She tried to speak, couldn't find the right words because she was too busy drinking in the sight of him. He just smiled again and swept low in a formal bow. "May I have this dance?"

"I . . ." She looked around, at the interested people crowding near them and the abandoned instruments. "I thought you couldn't dance."

"Said I *didn't* dance," he corrected her. "Didn't say I *couldn't*." He held out his arms and waited.

"Oh."

And then and there, in front of God and everyone, Gabriel Jackson danced with his wife.

She went into his arms as if they'd danced together a hundred times before. He tightened his hold, pulling her far too close for proper dancing, and it never occurred to her to protest. He swept her into the rhythms, moving easily, expertly, and she floated along without thought, without music, the two of them dancing as beautifully together as any couple at a formal Philadelphia ball ever had.

She touched the necktie, a bright slash of color between his sooty collar and his equally sooty neck. "You changed."

"Man can hardly take his best girl to a dance without gussyin' up a little, can he?"

He'd done it for her. No expensive gift, no extravagant gesture could have pleased her more.

"Where'd you get it?"

"Borrowed it from Phillip. Though he doesn't know it yet." He whirled her into a spin, and she thought her head would never stop twirling again. Not as long as she was near Gabriel. "Figure he owes me one."

"You saved the stables?"

"Most of it. And all the horses."

"That's good," she murmured. "That's very good."

Someone had picked up the fiddle, Anthea realized vaguely. The tones floated, clear and sweet, over her head, sang in her blood.

Never once breaking step, Gabriel bent to her ear. "You remember what I said on our wedding night, Anthea? About how, if you found yourself carrying my child, you'd better leave before I found out, because I'd never let it go if I did? And all that nonsense I spewed about easy western divorces?"

"Hmm?" She was the one who missed a step, who would have stumbled if he hadn't held her so securely. "I'm not expecting." Did he know something she didn't? He couldn't, she thought, confused. But then, "At least, I don't think—"

"Well, you can forget it." His expression hardened reminding her of the determined, unwavering manner he'd worn the day she met him. "Because you're not getting away from me. Baby or no baby. Want to or don't want to. You've lost your chance. I've decided. I'm not letting you go."

"But . . ." Just how many times *had* he spun her around? She was dizzy, unable to get a firm grasp on his words. "I've nothing to say about it at all?"

"Not one damn thing." His embrace tightened. "You had your chance, Anthea. Now it's too late. You're mine."

The fiddle fell silent. The room, too, as if everyone there held their breath. Gabriel stepped back, took both of her hands in his, and spoke in a clear, strong voice.

"Anthea Jackson, will you marry me?"

Her knees dipped. "Forgive my failing memory, but, ah, didn't we do that already?" As if from a distance, she heard the shocked murmurs around her, one fizzy bright giggle. Her own ears roared. But Gabriel . . . Gabriel, she heard with perfect clarity.

"Not the right way. Not the way that matters. Not for forever."

Her mouth opened, closed again. How could she talk when she could scarcely believe what she was hearing? And then he said the one thing she'd never dared hope to hear.

"I love you, Anthea."

"Oh, Gabriel, I—" She had to stop to breathe before she could continue. "I love you, too."

"And?"

"And?" she repeated. She'd just told him she loved him, and his only response was *and?*

"Yeah, *and.*" He grinned at her, cocky and wonderful, and she thought, *Well, of course. What woman wouldn't love him?* "Not to be disrespectful, sweetheart, but you've never been one to be subtle about how you're feeling." And then he sobered, his eyes warm, his face full of an intensity that said this mattered, more than anything. "But that doesn't answer my question, does it? Will you marry me, for real this time? For forever and Lily and kids, and everything else until death do us part, Amen?"

And then her heart, which had been soaring up with the clouds and angels, plummeted down to six feet beneath her toes. "Gabriel, my sisters, I have to—"

"So we'll go get 'em."

"Gabriel?"

"Never seen the East myself. Rather fancy a wedding trip that way. We'll pick them up—let that highfalutin doctor you dislike so much try and stop me—and bring them back to the ranch with us. It's a going concern, plenty good enough to take care of all of us. I think you'll like it. I think you'll all like it."

"Oh, Gabriel!" She threw herself at him. He caught her by the upper arms, holding her away from him.

"I couldn't wait to clean up," he warned her. "I'm a mess. You'll ruin your pretty dress."

"Do you think that I care?" And then she was against him, clinging, laughing, dropping kisses across his soot-streaked face. He smelled of smoke, tasted of ashes, and she couldn't get enough of him.

"Guess we'll just have to get you a new dress for this wedding."

Grinning, he scooped her into his arms like a groom carrying a bride over the threshold. He whirled with her in his arms, her skirts floating wide, their laughter twirling up to the old, cracked, stained ceiling. And when he stopped, the world kept spinning, and Anthea knew it would never stop.

She laid her head right down on his chest, on his

ash-coated shirt, and his heart thumped beneath her ear, strong and steady and much beloved.

"Gabriel?"

"Hmm?"

"I knew that coming to Kansas was the best idea I ever had."

Author's Note

The Haven in this story is a fictional place, and any resemblance to the real town is purely accidental. Here's an inside publishing story: The book, as originally conceived, was set in another state where there is no Haven. When I was asked to change the setting, I was already too settled on the town name to come up with a new one I liked as well. However, this change turned out to be fortuitous, for, conveniently for me, a deadly blizzard hit the central plains in January 1886, trapping my characters together.